PENGUIN

WEDNESDAY'S CHILD

Peter Robinson grew up in Leeds, Yorkshire. He emigrated to Canada in 1974 and attended York University and the University of Windsor, where he was later Writer in Residence. He received the Arthur Ellis Award in 1992 for *Past Reason Hated* and in 1997 for *Innocent Graves*, and was shortlisted for the John Creasey Award in Britain for his first Inspector Banks mystery, *Gallows View*. *Past Reason Hated* also won the 1994 TORGI Talking Book of the Year Award, and *Wednesday's Child* was nominated for an Edgar Award. Six additional Inspector Banks novels have all been published to critical acclaim. Peter Robinson is also the author of the psychological thriller *Caedmon's Song* and the LAPD procedural *No Cure for Love*. He lives in Toronto.

Other Inspector Banks mysteries published by Penguin:

Gallows View
A Dedicated Man
A Necessary End
The Hanging Valley
Past Reason Hated
Final Account
Innocent Graves
Dead Right
In a Dry Season

Also by Peter Robinson:

Caedmon's Song
No Cure for Love

WEDNESDAY'S CHILD

An Inspector Banks Mystery

Peter Robinson

Penguin Books

PENGUIN BOOKS
Published by the Penguin Group
Penguin Books Canada Ltd, 10 Alcorn Avenue, Toronto, Ontario,
Canada M4V 3B2
Penguin Books Ltd, 27 Wrights Lane, London W8 5TZ, England
Penguin Putnam Inc., 375 Hudson Street, New York, New York 10014, U.S.A.
Penguin Books Australia Ltd, Ringwood, Victoria, Australia
Penguin Books (NZ) Ltd, cnr Rosedale and Airborne Roads, Albany,
Auckland 1310, New Zealand

Penguin Books Ltd, Registered Offices: Harmondsworth, Middlesex, England

First published in Viking by Penguin Books Canada Limited, 1992
Published in Penguin Books, 1993

10 9 8 7 6 5 4 3

*Publisher's note: This book is a work of fiction. Names, characters, places and
incidents either are the product of the author's imagination or are used fictitiously,
and any resemblance to actual persons living or dead, events, or locales is entirely
coincidental.*

Manufactured in Canada

Canadian Cataloguing in Publication Data

Robinson, Peter, 1950-
  Wednesday's child

ISBN 0-14-017474-5

I. Title.

PS8585.O25W42 1993   C813'.54   C92-094125-7
PR9199.3.R62W42 1993

Visit Penguin Canada's web site at **www.penguin.ca**

For Sheila

WEDNESDAY'S CHILD

"Lost in the desart wild
Is your little child.
How can Lyca sleep
If her mother weep?"

.   .   .

Sleeping Lyca lay
While the beasts of prey,
Come from caverns deep,
View'd the maid asleep.

William Blake
"The Little Girl Lost"

1

I

The room was a tip, the woman a slattern. On the floor, near the door to the kitchen, a child's doll with one eye missing lay naked on its back, right arm raised above its head. The carpet around it was so stained with ground-in mud and food, it was hard to tell what shade of brown it had been originally. High in one corner, by the front window, pale flowered wallpaper had peeled away from a damp patch. The windows were streaked with grime, and the flimsy orange curtains needed washing.

When Detective Chief Inspector Alan Banks perched at the edge of the scuffed olive-green armchair, he felt a spring dig into the back of his left thigh. He noticed Detective Constable Susan Gay turn up her nose as she looked at a garish oil-painting of Elvis Presley above the mantelpiece. "The King" was wearing a jewelled white cape with a high collar and held a microphone in his ringed hand.

In contrast to the shabby decor, a compact music centre in mint condition stood against one wall, a green-and-yellow budgie in a cage nonchalantly sharpened its bill on a cuttlefish, and an enormous matte black colour television blared out from one corner. "Blockbusters" was on, and Banks heard Bob Holness ask, "What 'B' is the name of an African country bordering on South Africa?"

"Could you turn the sound down, please, Mrs Scupham?" Banks asked the woman.

She looked at him blankly at first, as if she didn't understand his request, then she walked over and turned off the TV altogether. "You can call me Brenda," she said when she sat down again.

Banks took a closer look at her. In her late twenties, with long dirty-blonde hair showing dark roots, she possessed a kind of blowzy sexuality that hinted at concupiscent pleasure in bed. It was evident in the languor of her movements, the way she walked as if she were in a hot and humid climate.

She was a few pounds overweight, and her pink polo-neck sweater and black mini-skirt looked a size too small. Her full, pouty lips were liberally coated in scarlet lipstick, which matched her long, painted fingernails, and her vacuous, pale blue eyes, surrounded by matching eye-shadow, made Banks feel he had to repeat every question he asked.

Seeing the ashtray on the scratched coffee-table in front of him, Banks took out his cigarettes and offered the woman one. She accepted, leaning forward and holding back her hair with one hand as he lit it for her. She blew the smoke out through her nose, emulating some star she had seen in a film. He lit a cigarette himself, mostly to mask the peculiar smell, redolent of boiled cabbage and nail-polish remover, that permeated the room.

"When did you first get the feeling something was wrong?" he asked her.

She paused and frowned, then answered in a low voice, husky from too many cigarettes. "Just this afternoon. I phoned them, and they said they'd never heard of

Mr Brown and Miss Peterson."

"And you got worried?"

"Yes."

"Why did you wait so long before checking up?"

Brenda paused to draw on her cigarette. "I don't know," she said. "I thought she'd be all right, you know. . . ."

"But you could have called this morning. That's when they said they'd bring her back, isn't it?"

"Yes. I don't know. I suppose so. I just . . . besides, I'd got things to do."

"Did the visitors show you any identification?"

"They had cards, like, all official."

"What did the cards say?"

Mrs Scupham turned her head to one side, showing only her profile. "I didn't really get a good look. It all happened so fast."

"Did the cards have photographs on them?"

"No, I don't think so. I'm sure I would have noticed."

"What exactly did they say to you?" Banks asked.

"They told me their names and said they was from the social, like, and then they showed their cards . . ."

"This was at the door, before you let them in?"

"Yes. And then they said they'd come to see me about my Gemma. Well, I had to let them in, didn't I? They were from the authorities."

Her voice cracked a little when she mentioned her daughter's name, and she sucked her lower lip. Banks nodded. "What happened next?"

"When I let them in, they said they'd had reports of Gemma being . . . well, being abused . . ."

"Did they say where they'd heard this?"

She shook her head.

"Didn't you ask them?"

"I didn't think to. They seemed so . . . I mean, he was

wearing a nice suit and his hair was all short and neatly brushed down, and she was dressed proper smart, too. They just seemed so sure of themselves. I didn't think to ask anything."

"Was there any truth in what they said?"

Mrs Scupham flushed. "Of course not. I love my Gemma. I wouldn't harm her."

"Go on," Banks said. "What did they say next?"

"That's about it really. They said they had to take her in, just overnight, for some tests and examinations, and if everything was all right they'd bring her back this morning, just like I told you on the phone. When they didn't come, I got so worried . . . I . . . How could anyone do something like that, steal someone else's child?"

Banks could see the tears forming in her eyes. He knew there was nothing he could say to console her. In fact, the best thing he could do was keep quiet about how bloody stupid she'd been, and not ask her if she hadn't heard about the cases, just a few years ago, when bogus social workers had visited homes all around England with stories just like the one they'd given her. No, best keep quiet.

She had a fear of authority, probably bred into her, that meant she would believe just about anything that someone in a suit with a card, a nice haircut and an educated accent told her. She wasn't unique in that. Most often, the phoney social workers had simply asked to examine the children in the home, not to remove them. For all the mothers who had sent them packing, Banks wondered how many had allowed the examination and had then been too afraid or ashamed to admit it.

"How old is Gemma?" Banks asked.

"Seven. Just seven."

"Where's your husband?"

Mrs Scupham crossed her legs and folded her hands

on her lap. "I'm not married," she said. "You might as well know. Well, there's no shame in it these days, is there, what with so much divorce about."

"What about Gemma's father?"

"Terry?" She curled her upper lip in disgust. "He's long gone."

"Do you know where he is?"

Mrs Scupham shook her head. "He left when Gemma was three. I haven't seen or heard from him since. And good riddance."

"We need to contact him," Banks pressed. "Can you give us any information at all that might help?"

"Why? You don't . . . surely you don't think Terry could have had anything to do with it?"

"We don't think anything yet. At the very least he deserves to know what's happened to his daughter."

"I don't see why. He never cared when he was around. Why should he care now?"

"Where is he, Brenda?"

"I've told you, I don't know."

"What's his full name?"

"Garswood. Terry Garswood. Terence, I suppose, but everyone called him Terry."

"What was his job?"

"He was in the army. Hardly ever around."

"Is there anyone else? A man, I mean."

"There's Les. We've been together nearly a year now."

"Where is he?"

She jerked her head. "Where he always is, The Barleycorn round the corner."

"Does he know what's happened?"

"Oh, aye, he knows. We had a row."

Banks saw Susan Gay look up from her notebook and shake her head slowly in disbelief.

"Can I have another fag?" Brenda Scupham asked. "I

meant to get some more, but it just slipped my mind."

"Of course." Banks gave her a Silk Cut. "Where do you work, Brenda?"

"I don't . . . I . . . I stay home." He lit the cigarette for her, and she coughed when she took her first drag. Patting her chest, she said, "Must stop."

Banks nodded. "Me, too. Look, Brenda, do you think you could give us a description of this Mr Brown and Miss Peterson?"

She frowned. "I'll try. I'm not very good with faces, though. Like I said, he had a nice suit on, Mr Brown, navy blue it was, with narrow white stripes. And he had a white shirt and a plain tie. I'm not sure what colour that was, dark anyways."

"How tall was he?"

"About average."

"What's that?" Banks stood up. "Taller or shorter than me?" At around five foot nine, Banks was small for a policeman, hardly above regulation height.

"About the same."

"Hair?"

"Black, sort of like yours, but longer, and combed straight back. And he was going a bit thin at the sides."

"How old would you say he was?"

"I don't know. He had a boyish look about him, but he was probably around thirty, I'd say."

"Is there anything else you can tell us about him? His voice, mannerisms?"

"Not really." Brenda flicked some ash at the ashtray and missed. "Like I said, he had a posh accent. Oh, there was one thing, though I don't suppose it'd be any help."

"What's that?"

"He had a nice smile."

And so it went. When they had finished, Banks had a description of Mr Brown that would match at least half the young businessmen in Eastvale, or in the entire country, for that matter, and one of Miss Peterson—brunette, hair coiled up at the back, well-spoken, nice figure, expensive clothes—that would fit a good number of young professional women.

"Did you recognize either of them?" he asked. "Had you seen them around before?" Banks didn't expect much to come from this—Eastvale was a fair-sized town—but it was worth a try.

She shook her head.

"Did they touch anything while they were here?"

"I don't think so."

"Did you offer them tea or anything?"

"No. Of course I didn't."

Banks was thinking of fingerprints. There was a slight chance that if they had drunk tea or coffee, Mrs Scupham might not have washed the cups yet. Certainly any prints on the door handles, if they hadn't been too blurred in the first place, would have been obscured by now.

Banks asked for, and got, a fairly recent school photograph of Gemma Scupham. She was a pretty child, with the same long hair as her mother—her blonde colouring was natural, though—and a sad, pensive expression on her face that belied her seven years.

"Where could she be?" Brenda Scupham asked. "What have they done to her?"

"Don't worry. We'll find her." Banks knew how empty the words sounded as soon as he had spoken them. "Is there anything else you can tell us?"

"No, I don't think so."

"What was Gemma wearing?"

"Wearing? Oh, those yellow overall things, what do you call them?"

"Dungarees?"

"Yes, that's right. Yellow dungarees over a white T-shirt. It had some cartoon animal on the front. Donald Duck, I think. She loved cartoons."

"Did the visitors mention any name other than Brown or Peterson?"

"No."

"Did you see their car?"

"No, I didn't look. You don't, do you? I just let them in and we talked, then they went off with Gemma. They were so nice, I . . . I just can't believe it." Her lower lip trembled and she started to cry, but it turned into another coughing fit.

Banks stood up and gestured for Susan to follow him out into the hall. "You'd better stay with her," he whispered.

"But, sir—"

Banks held his hand up. "It's procedure, Susan. And she might remember something else, something important. I'd also like you to get something with Gemma's fingerprints on it. But first I want you to radio in and tell Sergeant Rowe to phone Superintendent Gristhorpe and let him know what's going on. You'd better get someone to contact all the Yorkshire social services, too. You never know, someone might have made a cock-up of the paperwork and we'd look right wallies if we didn't check. Ask Phil to organize a house-to-house of the neighbourhood." He handed her the photograph. "And arrange to get some copies of this made."

Susan went out to the unmarked police Rover, and Banks turned back into the living-room, where Brenda Scupham seemed lost in her own world of grief. He touched her lightly on the shoulder. "I have to go," he said. "DC Gay will be back in a moment. She'll stay with you. And don't worry. We're doing all we can."

He walked down the short path to the patrol car and tapped on the window. "You told me you searched the place, right?" he said to the constable behind the wheel, pointing back up the path with his thumb.

"Yes, sir, first thing."

"Well, do it again, just to be certain. And send someone to get Mrs Scupham a packet of fags, too. Silk Cut'll do. I'm off to the pub." He headed down the street leaving a puzzled young PC behind him.

II

Detective Superintendent Gristhorpe squatted by his drystone wall in the back garden of his house above the village of Lyndgarth and contemplated retirement. He would be sixty in November, and while retirement was not mandatory, surely after more than forty years on the job it was time to move aside and devote himself to his books and his garden, as the wise old Roman, Virgil, had recommended.

He placed a stone, then stood up, acutely aware of the creak in his knees and the ache in his lower back as he did so. He had been working at the wall for too long. Why he bothered, the Lord only knew. After all, it went nowhere and closed in nothing. His grandfather had been a master waller in the dale, but the skill had not been passed down the generations. He supposed he liked it for the same reason he liked fishing: mindless relaxation. In an age of technocratic utilitarianism, Gristhorpe thought, a man needs as much purposeless activity as he can find.

The sun had set a short while ago, and the sharp line of Aldington Edge cut high on the horizon to the north, underlining a dark mauve and purple sky. As Gristhorpe walked towards the back door, he felt the chill in the light breeze that ruffled his thatch of unruly grey hair. Mid-September, and autumn was coming to the dale.

Inside the house, he brewed a pot of strong black tea, threw together a Wensleydale cheese-and-pickle sandwich, then went into his living-room. The eighteenth-century farmhouse was sturdily built, with walls thick enough to withstand the worst a Yorkshire winter could throw at them, and since his wife's death Gristhorpe had transformed the living-room into a library. He had placed his favourite armchair close to the stone hearth and spent so many an off-duty hour reading there that the heat from the fire had cracked the leather upholstery on one side.

Gristhorpe had given the television his wife had enjoyed so much to Mrs Hawkins, the lady who "did" for him, but he kept the old walnut-cabinet wireless so he could listen to the news, "My Word," cricket and the plays that sometimes came on in the evenings. Two walls were lined with floor-to-ceiling bookshelves, and a series of framed prints from Hogarth's "The Rake's Progress" hung over the fireplace.

Gristhorpe set his tea and sandwich beside the books on the small round table, within easy reach, and settled back with a sigh into his chair. The only sounds that broke the silence were the wind soughing through the elms and the ticking of the grandfather clock in the hall.

To retire or not to retire, that was the question that kept him from immediately picking up *The Way of All Flesh*. Over the past few years he had delegated most of the investigative work to his team and spent his time on administrative and co-ordinating duties. He had absolute trust in Alan Banks, his protégé, and both DS Richmond and the recently appointed DC Gay were coming along well. Should he move aside and clear the space for Banks's promotion? Certainly Alan showed an enthusiasm for work and learning that reminded Gristhorpe of himself as a young lad. Both lacked formal education beyond the local grammar school, but neither let it hold him back. Banks was a good detective, despite his anti-authoritarian tendencies, occasional rashness and a loathing for the politics that were now becoming so much a part of the job. But Gristhorpe admired him for that. He, himself, hated police politics. Banks, though twenty years younger, was a real copper, a man who had come from the street. He also had imagination and curiosity, two qualities that Gristhorpe thought essential.

And what would he do with his time if he did retire? There was the dry-stone wall, of course, but that was hardly a full-time occupation. Nor was reading, especially with the way his eyesight had been declining of late. He was at an age when every odd ache or pain brought a little more fear than it had before, when colds lingered and settled on the chest. But he was no hypochondriac. The Gristhorpes were robust, always had been.

He would like to travel, he decided, to revisit Venice, Florence, Paris, Madrid, and go somewhere he had never been before—the Far East, perhaps, or Russia. But travel cost money, and a policeman's pension wouldn't stretch that far. Gristhorpe sighed and picked up Samuel Butler. He didn't have to make his decision tonight; best wait for a while.

He had hardly got through the first paragraph when the phone rang. Marking the page with a leather strip and putting the book aside, he got up and walked into the hall. It was Sergeant Rowe from the station. He had received a message from Susan Gay about a child gone missing from the East Side Estate. Could the superintendent come in as soon as possible? Gristhorpe could get few more details over the phone, except that the child had been taken by a man and a woman pretending to be social workers and that she had been gone over a day. As he listened to Sergeant Rowe deliver the message in his flat, emotionless voice, Gristhorpe felt a shiver go up his spine.

Grimly, he put on his tweed jacket and went outside to the car. It was completely dark now, and the lights of Lyndgarth twinkled below on the daleside. Gristhorpe drove through the village, past the squat St Mary's, and onto the main Eastvale road. It was a journey he had made hundreds of times, and he drove automatically, without even having to think about the dips and turns. Normally, even in the dark, he would glance at certain landmarks—the lights of the old Lister house way up on the opposite slopes of the valley; the six trees bent over by the wind on the drumlin to the west—but this time he was too distracted to notice the landscape.

As he drove towards the lights of Eastvale, he remembered that long Saturday in October, 1965, when he and dozens of other young policemen had stood in the drizzle and the biting wind 1,600 feet up the Pennines listening to their orders. There they all stood, in anoraks and wellington boots, shivering in the late autumn cold on the top of Saddleworth Moor, complaining about the Saturday afternoon football they were missing. It was eerie enough just being up there in the banshee wind, the rain and inky light, with those outcrops of rocks like decayed teeth on the skyline. All day they had searched, dragging their feet through the mud and peat, from 9:30 A.M. until well after three o'clock. The rain had stopped by then, and the weather was a little warmer, the moor shrouded in a slight mist.

Suddenly Gristhorpe had heard the shout from a searcher in the distance: a young lad, he remembered, just out of training college, who had taken a break to answer a call of nature. Those nearby, Gristhorpe included, hurried towards him, and watched in horror as Detective Sergeant Eckersley came and scraped away the clinging peat from a child's arm bone. A little more digging revealed a head. Eckersley stopped at that. He sent for the scene-of-crime officers, and soon they all arrived, out of nowhere, the Assistant Chief Constable, police surgeons, photographers, Joe Mounsey, the lot.

They put up canvas screens and everyone but the brass and the SOCOs had to stand back. As the doctor scraped off the dirt and the flash camera popped, the whole gruesome discovery finally lay revealed. Gristhorpe caught only a glimpse of the body through a gap in the canvas, but it was enough.

They had been looking for a boy called John Kilbride, but what they had found was the near-skeletal body of a girl lying on her side with her right arm raised above her head. Close to her feet, her clothes lay bundled—a blue coat, a pink cardigan, a red-and-green tartan skirt. Instead of John Kilbride, they had found the body of Lesley Ann Downey, aged ten, another victim of the couple who came to be called the "Moors Murderers," Ian Brady and Myra Hindley.

Somehow, that day stood engraved in Gristhorpe's memory more than any other day in his life. Months, even years, might go by and he wouldn't even think of that October day in 1965, but when something like this happened, there it was, every bit as real and as horrifying as if he were back there on the moor seeing that arm sticking up through the quagmire as if it were waving or pointing.

He had thought of it only once in the past few years, and that was when a sixteen-year-old girl had gone missing from one of the Swainsdale villages. And now two people, a man and a woman—just as Brady and Hindley had been—had walked bold as brass into a house on the East Side Estate and abducted a seven-year-old girl.

As Gristhorpe drove down narrow North Market

Street past the Town Hall, the lit window displays of the tourist shops and the community centre, he gripped the wheel so hard his knuckles turned white as he once again heard the girl's voice in his head from the tape Brady and Hindley recorded before they murdered her: Lesley Ann whimpering and begging for her mummy and daddy to help her; Brady telling her to put something in her mouth and saying he wants to photograph her. And that damn music, that damn music, "The Little Drummer Boy." Gristhorpe had never been able to listen comfortably to any music since then without hearing the girl screaming and begging for mercy in his head, and he let everyone believe he was tone deaf to avoid awkward explanations.

He turned his car into the parking area at the back of the station, an old Tudor-fronted building, the front of which faced Eastvale's market square, and sat for a few moments to calm himself down and rid himself of the memory. And before he went inside, he delivered a silent prayer—not without some embarrassment, for he wasn't a religious man—that there should be nothing, *nothing* to compare between this affair and the Moors Murders. No time for thoughts of retirement now.

III

As Banks walked down the street towards The Barleycorn, he glanced at the rows of identical red brick houses. There was no doubt about it, the East Side Estate was a disaster. True, some tenants had bought the houses when the Thatcher government sold them off, and many had added a white fence here, a lick of paint there, or even a dormer window. But it was a shabby area, with junk-littered lawns, children's tricycles left in the street, and mangy dogs running free, fouling the pavements, barking and snapping at passers-by.

And The Barleycorn was a typical estate pub, right from its unimaginative name and its squat flat-roofed exterior to its jukebox, video games and poorly kept keg beer.

Banks pushed open the door and glanced around. Little Richard's "Good Golly Miss Molly" was playing too loudly on the jukebox. The cash register rang up another sale. Most of the tables were empty, and only a few diehard drinkers stood at the bar.

As the door shut behind him, Banks noticed the people look in his direction, and suddenly one man took off towards the back. Banks dashed after him, bumping his knee on a chair and knocking it over as he went. He caught the man by the shoulder just before he had reached the exit. The man tried to pull free, but Banks kept his grip, spun him around and hit him hard, just once, in the solar plexus. The man groaned and doubled up. Banks took him by the elbow and helped him to a table the way one escorts an elderly relative.

As soon as they had sat down, the barman rushed over.

"Look, mister, I don't want no trouble," he said.

"Good," Banks answered. "Neither do I. But I'd like a small brandy for my friend here, just to settle his stomach."

"What do you think I am, a bloody waitress?"

Banks looked at the man. He was about six feet tall and gone to fat. His nose looked as if it had been broken a few times, and old scar tissue hooded his left eye.

"Just bring the drink," Banks said. "I won't have anything myself. Not while I'm on duty."

The barman stared at Banks, then his jaw dropped. He shrugged and turned back to the bar. In a few seconds he came back with the brandy. "It's on the house," he mumbled.

Banks thanked him and passed the glass over to his companion, who sat rubbing his stomach and gasping for breath. "Here's to your health, Les."

The man glared at him through teary eyes, knocked back the brandy in one and banged the glass down hard on the table. "You didn't need to have done that," he said. "I was only off for a piss."

"Bollocks, Les," said Banks. "The only time I've seen anyone run as fast as that to the bog they had dysentery. Why were you running?"

"I told you."

"I know, but I want you to tell me the truth."

Les Poole was well known to the Eastvale police and had been a frequent guest at the station. He had congenitally sticky fingers and couldn't stand the idea of anything belonging to anyone else but him. Consequently, he had been in and out of jail since Borstal, mostly for burglary. No doubt, Banks thought, had he the intelligence, he might also have risen to the dizzy heights of fraud and blackmail. Les had never held a job, though rumour had it that he had, in fact, once worked as a dustbin man for six weeks but got the sack for wasting too much time rummaging through people's rubbish looking for things he could keep or sell. In short, Banks thought, Les Poole was little more than a doodle in the margin of life. At least until now.

Les was an odd-looking character, too, like someone who had fallen through a time warp from the 1950s. He had greased-back hair, complete with quiff, sideboards and duck's arse, a triangular face with a Kirk Douglas dimple on his chin, a long, thin nose, and eyes as flat and grey as slate. About Banks's height, he was wearing a black leather jacket, red T-shirt and jeans. His beer-belly bulged over the belt. He looked as if he should be playing stand-up bass in a rockabilly band. Why he had al-

ways been so attractive to women, Banks couldn't
fathom. Maybe it was his long dark eyelashes.

"Well?" prompted Banks.

"Well what?"

Banks sighed. "Let's start this again, Les. What we'll
do is we'll back up and lead nice and slowly to the question. Maybe that way you'll be able to understand it, all
right?"

Les Poole just glared at him.

Banks lit a cigarette and went on. "I came down here
to ask if you know anything about young Gemma's disappearance. Do you?"

"She was taken away, that's all I know. Brenda told
me."

"Where were you when it happened?"

"Eh?"

"Where were you yesterday afternoon?"

"Out and about."

"Doing what?"

"Oh, this and that."

"Right. So while you were out and about doing this
and that, a man and a woman, both well-dressed and offi-
cial-looking, called at your house, said they were child-
care workers, talked their way inside and persuaded
Brenda to hand over her daughter for tests and further
examination. Now what I want to know, Les, is do you
know anything about that?"

Les shrugged. "It's not my kid, is it? I can't help it if
she's so fucking daft she'll give her kid away."

The barman appeared at Banks's shoulder and asked if
they wanted anything else.

"I'll have a pint, Sid," Les said.

"Bring me one too, this time," Banks added. "I feel
like I bloody well need it."

After the barman had brought the beer, which tasted

more like cold dishwater than real ale, Banks carried on.

"Right," he said, "so we've established you don't give a damn about the child one way or another. That still doesn't answer my questions. Where were you, and do you know anything about it?"

"Now come on, Mr Banks. I know I've been in a bit of bother now and then, but surely even you can't suspect me of doing a thing like that? This is what they call persecution, this is. Just because I've got a record you think you can pin everything on me."

"Don't be a silly bugger, Les. I'm not trying to pin anything on you yet. For a start, I couldn't picture you in a suit, and even if you'd managed to nick one from somewhere, I think Brenda might still have recognized you, don't you?"

"You don't have to take the piss, you know."

"Let's make it simple, then. Do you know *anything* about what happened?"

"No."

"Right. Another one: what were you doing?"

"What's that got to do with anything? I don't see what that's got to do with anything. I mean, if you don't suspect me, why does it matter where I was?"

"Got a job, Les?"

"Me? Nah."

"I don't suppose you'd want me to know if you did have, would you? I might tell the social and they'd cut off your benefits, wouldn't they?"

"I don't have a job, Mr Banks. You know what it's like these days, all that unemployment and all."

"Join the rest of us in the nineties, Les. Maggie's gone. The three million unemployed are a thing of the past."

"Still . . ."

"Okay. So you don't have a job. What were you do-ing?"

"Just helping a mate move some junk, that's all."

"That's better. His name?"

"John."

"And where does he live, this John?"

"He's got a shop, second-hand stuff, down Rampart Street, over by The Oak . . ."

"I know it. So you spent the afternoon with this bloke John, helping him in his shop?"

"Yeah."

"I suppose he'd confirm that?"

"Come again?"

"If I asked him, he'd tell me you were with him."

"Course he would."

"Where'd you get the nice new television and stereo, Les?"

"What do you mean? They're Brenda's. She had them before she met me. Ask her."

"Oh, I'm sure she'll back you up. The thing is, they don't look that old. And Fletcher's electronics warehouse got broken into last Friday night. Someone took off with a van full of stereos and televisions. Did you know that?"

"Can't say as I did. Anyway, what's all this in aid of? I thought you were after the kid?"

"I cast a wide net, Les. A wide net. Why did Brenda wait so long before calling us?"

"How should I know? Because she's a stupid cow, I suppose."

"Sure it was nothing to do with you?"

"What do you mean?"

"She said you had a row. Maybe you didn't want the police coming to the house and seeing that television, or the new music centre."

"Look, I told you—"

"I know what you told me, Les. Why don't you answer the question? Was it you persuaded Brenda to wait so long before calling us?"

Poole looked away and said nothing.

"Do you know Gemma could be dead?"

Poole shrugged.

"For Christ's sake, don't you care?"

"I told you, she's not my kid. Bloody nuisance, if you ask me."

"You ever hit her, Les?"

"Me? Course I didn't. That's not my style."

"Ever see Brenda do it?"

Poole shook his head. Banks stood up, glanced at the beer in his glass and decided to leave it.

"I'm off now, Les," he said, "but I'll be around. You'll be seeing so much of the police in the next few days you'll think you've died and gone to hell. And I want you to stick around, too. Know what I mean? Be seeing you."

Banks left The Barleycorn for the dark autumn evening. He was wearing only his sports jacket over his shirt, and he felt the chill in the air as he walked back to Brenda Scupham's with a terrier yapping at his heels. Television screens flickered behind curtains, some pulled back just an inch or two so the neighbours could watch all the excitement at number twenty-four.

As he turned up the path, he thought of Brenda and the enormity of what she had allowed. He could have told her about the recent Children's Act, designed to protect parents from over-zealous social workers, but he knew he would only get a blank stare in return. Besides, telling her that was as clear an example as you can get of bolting the stable door after the horse has gone.

He thought again about Les Poole and wondered what he was hiding. Maybe it had just been the criminal's typical nervousness at an encounter with the police. Whatever it was, it had been evident in his clipped answers, his evasions, his nervous body language, and most of all in the guilty thoughts Banks could see skittering about like tiny insects behind the slate eyes.

IV

Gristhorpe tried to recall whether he had left anything undone. He had informed the ACC, made sure the press had all the information they needed, set up a mobile unit on a patch of waste ground at the end of Brenda Scupham's street, drawn up a search plan, arranged to draft in extra personnel, and got someone working on a list of all known local child-molesters. Also, he had faxed the bare details and a copy of Gemma's photograph to the paedophile squad, which operated out of Vine Street police station, in London. Soon, every policeman in the county would be on the alert. In the morning, the searchers would begin. For now, though, there was nothing more he could do until he had discussed developments with Banks.

His stomach rumbled, and he remembered the cheese-and-pickle sandwich left uneaten on the table at home, the tea going cold. Leaving a message for Banks, he went across the street to the Queen's Arms and persuaded Cyril, the landlord, to make him a ham sandwich, which he washed down with a half-pint of bitter.

He had been sitting hunched over his beer at a dimpled, copper-topped table for about ten minutes, oblivious to the buzz of conversation around him, when a voice startled him out of his dark thoughts.

"Sir?"

Gristhorpe looked up and saw Banks standing over him. "Everything all right, Alan?" Gristhorpe asked. "You look knackered."

"I am," said Banks, sitting down and reaching for his cigarettes. "This Gemma Scupham business . . ."

"Aye," said Gristhorpe. "Get yourself a drink and we'll see what we can come up with."

Banks bought a packet of cheese-and-onion crisps and a pint, then told Gristhorpe about his suspicions of Les Poole.

Gristhorpe rubbed his chin and frowned. "We'll keep an eye on him, then," he said. "Give him a bit of slack. If we bring him in over that Fletcher's warehouse job it'll do us no good. Besides, we can hardly cart off the poor woman's telly when someone's just abducted her child, can we?"

"Agreed," said Banks. "OK. So far we've got six men working on the house-to-house, questioning the neighbours. Phil and Susan are with them. At least there's a chance someone might have seen the car."

"What about the mother? Who's with her?"

"Susan stayed for a while, then she offered to get a WPC to come in, but Mrs Scupham didn't want one. I don't think either she or Les feel comfortable with the police around. Anyway, she's got a friend in."

"I suppose we'd better start with the obvious, hadn't we?" Gristhorpe said. "Do you believe the mother's story?"

Banks took a sip of beer. "I think so. She seemed genuinely shocked, and I don't think she's bright enough to make up a story like that."

"Oh, come on, Alan. It doesn't take much imagination. She could have hurt the child, gone too far and killed her—or Poole could have—then they dumped the body and made up this cock-and-bull story."

"Yes, she could have. All I'm saying is the story seems a bit over-elaborate. It would have been a hell of a lot easier just to say that Gemma had been snatched while she was out playing, wouldn't it, rather than having to make up descriptions of two people and risk us finding it odd that no one in the street saw them. They're a nosy lot down on the East Side Estate. Anyway, I had the officers on the scene search the house thoroughly twice and they didn't come up with anything. We've got a SOCO team there now doing their bit. If there's any chance Gemma was harmed in the house then taken somewhere else, they'll find it."

Gristhorpe sighed. "I suppose we can rule out kidnapping?"

"Brenda Scupham's got no money. She might be fiddling the social, making a bit on the side, but that hardly makes her Mrs Rothschild."

"What about the father? Custody battle? Maybe he hired someone to snatch Gemma for him?"

Banks shook his head. "According to Brenda, he's not interested, hasn't been for years. We're tracking him down anyway."

Gristhorpe waved a plume of smoke aside. "I don't like the alternatives," he said.

"Me neither, but we've got to face them. Remember those stories a while back? Paedophiles posing as social workers and asking to examine people's kids for evidence of abuse?"

Gristhorpe nodded.

"Luckily, most parents sent them away," Banks went on. "But suppose this time they succeeded?"

"I've checked on the descriptions with the divisions involved," Gristhorpe said, "and they don't match. But you're right. It's something we have to consider. Someone else could have got the idea from reading the papers. Then there's the ritual stuff to consider, too."

Not long ago, the press had been rife with stories of children used for ritual abuse, often with satanic overtones. In Cleveland, Nottingham, Rochdale and the Orkneys, children were taken into care after allegations of just such abuse involving torture, starvation, humiliation and sexual molestation. Nobody had come up with any hard evidence—in fact, most people thought it was more likely that the children needed to be protected from the social workers—but the rumours were disturbing enough. And Gristhorpe didn't fool himself that such a thing couldn't happen in Eastvale. It could.

That Satanists now existed out in the dale was beyond doubt. There had been trouble with them recently, when local farmers had complained of finding sheep ritually slaughtered in copses and hollows. There was a big difference between sheep and children, of course, as there was between Satanism and witchcraft. Gristhorpe had been aware of local witch covens for years. They consisted mostly of meek husbands and bored housewives in search of an evening's naughtiness dancing naked in the woods. But the Satanists were a different breed. If they could go as far as killing sheep and draining their blood, what would they stop at?

"But you know what I'm thinking about most of all, don't you, Alan?" Banks was one of the few people Gristhorpe had talked to about his small role in the Moors Murders and the lasting effect it had on him.

Banks nodded.

"Different way of operating, of course. Brady and Hindley snatched their victims. But there could be reasons for that. It's the couple aspect that bothers me. A man *and* a woman. I know there's been a lot of argument about Myra Hindley's degree of involvement, but there's no doubt they acted together. Call it what you will— maybe some kind of psychotic symbiosis—but without the other, it's a good bet neither would have committed those crimes. Alone, they were nothing, nobodies living in fantasy worlds, but together they progressed from Hitler-worship and pornography to murder. Hindley acted as a catalyst to turn Brady's fantasies into reality, and he acted them out to impress her and exercise his power over her. Christ, Alan, if a couple like that's got hold of little Gemma Scupham, God have mercy on her soul." Again, Gristhorpe remembered the tape, Lesley Ann begging, "Please don't undress me!" Brady telling her, "If you don't keep that hand down I'll slit your neck." And that other gruesome touch, the children's choir singing carols in the background.

"We don't know," said Banks. "We know bugger-all so far."

Gristhorpe rubbed his brow. "Aye, you're right. No sense jumping to conclusions. On the bright side, let's hope it was some poor young childless couple who just went too far to get themselves a kiddie." He shook his head. "It doesn't make sense, though, does it? If they took the child out of love, how could they reconcile themselves to the mother's pain? There'd be too much guilt to allow them any happiness. And I doubt they'd be able to keep a secret like that for very long."

"I've asked Phil if he can tie in with HOLMES on this," Banks said. "Remember that course he went on?"

Gristhorpe nodded. HOLMES stood for Home Office Large Major Enquiry System. Developed during the hunt for the Yorkshire Ripper, HOLMES basically allows all reports coming out of an investigation to be entered and organized into a relational database. That way, a key word or phrase can be tracked more accurately through previously unrelated data than before.

And that was as far as Gristhorpe could follow. The rest, like most computer talk, was gobbledegook to him. In fact, the mere mention of megabytes and DOS brought out the latent Luddite in him. Still, he didn't underestimate their value. An enquiry like this would generate a lot of paperwork, and every statement, every report, no matter how minor or negative, would be entered, and cross-checks would be made. He wanted no cock-ups along the lines of the Yorkshire Ripper investigation, where the left hand hadn't seemed to know what the right hand was doing.

"Phil says he'd like computers in the mobile unit," Banks added. "That way the officers can put everything on disk and pass it on to him without any retyping."

"I'll see what I can do. Any more ideas?"

"Just a couple. I'd like a chat with the girl's teacher, see what I can find out about her. I'm damn sure there's been some abuse involved. Both Poole and Brenda Scupham deny it, but not convincingly enough."

Gristhorpe nodded. "Go on."

"And I think we should consider bringing Jenny Fuller in. She might at least be able to give us some idea of what kind of people we're looking for."

"I couldn't agree more," Gristhorpe said. He liked Jenny Fuller. Not only was she a competent psychologist who had helped them before in unusual cases, but she was a pleasure to have around. A right bonny lass, as Gristhorpe's father would have said.

"Should we bring Jim Hatchley back from the seaside?" Banks asked.

Gristhorpe scowled. "I suppose there might come a time we'll need him. Leave it for now, though." Detective Sergeant Jim Hatchley had been transferred to a CID outpost on the Yorkshire coast, largely to make way for Philip Richmond's promotion. Gristhorpe had never much liked Hatchley, but grudgingly admitted he had his uses. As far as Gristhorpe was concerned, he was an idle, foul-mouthed, prejudiced slob, but his brain worked well enough when he took the trouble to use it, and he had a list of dirty tricks as long as your arm that often got results without compromising procedure.

Banks drained his glass. "Anything else?"

"Not tonight. We'll have a meeting first thing in the morning, see what's turned up. You'd better get home and get some sleep."

Banks grunted. "I might as well have another pint first. There never seems to be anyone in these days."

"Where's Sandra?"

"Community Centre, still organizing that local artists' exhibition. I'll swear she spends more time there than she does at home. And Tracy's out at the pictures with that boyfriend of hers."

Gristhorpe caught the anxiety in Banks's tone. "Don't worry about her, Alan," he said. "Tracy's a sensible lass. She can take care of herself."

Banks sighed. "I hope so." He gestured towards Gristhorpe's empty glass. "What about you?"

"Aye, why not? It might help me sleep."

While Banks went to the bar, Gristhorpe considered the night ahead. He knew he wouldn't be going home. For years, he had kept a camp-bed in the station store-room for emergencies like this. Tonight, and perhaps for the next two or three nights, he would stay in his office. But he doubted that he would get much sleep. Not until he found out what had happened to Gemma Scupham, one way or the other.

2

I

Early the next morning, Banks stood on his doorstep holding the milk bottles and breathed in the clear air. It was a magnificent day: not a cloud in the light blue sky, and hardly any wind. He could smell peat-smoke in the air, and it seemed to accentuate the chill autumn edge, the advancing touch of winter. More than anything, it was a day for walking out in the dale, and it would bring dozens of tourists to the Eastvale area.

He went inside and put the milk in the fridge. He could hear Tracy taking her morning shower and Sandra moving about in the bedroom, getting dressed. It had been a good night when he got back from the Queen's Arms. Sandra had got home before him, and before bed they enjoyed a nightcap and some Ella Fitzgerald on the CD player she had bought him for his fortieth birthday. Tracy came home on time, cheerful enough, and Banks couldn't detect any change for the worse in her that he could attribute to her boyfriend, Keith Harrison. Still, he thought as he poured himself a cup of coffee, domestic life had changed a lot over the summer.

For one thing, Brian had left home for Portsmouth Polytechnic, where he intended to study architecture.

Much as they had locked horns the past few years—especially over music and staying out too late—Banks missed him. He was left with Tracy, now so grown-up he hardly knew her: blonde hair chopped short and layered raggedly, mad about boys, make-up, clothes, pop music.

They never seemed to talk any more, and he missed those chats about history—her former passion—especially when he had been able to educate her on a point or two. Banks had always felt insecure about his lack of a good formal education, so Tracy's questions had often made him feel useful. But he knew nothing about the latest pop groups, fashion or cosmetics.

And Sandra had become absorbed in her work. He told himself, as he buttered his toast, not to be so damned selfish and to stop feeling sorry for himself. She was doing what she wanted—getting involved in the arts—after so many years of sacrifice for the sake of the family and for his career. And if he hadn't wanted an independent, spirited, creative woman, then he shouldn't have married her. Still, he worried. She was late so often, and some of these local artists were handsome young devils with the reputation of being ladies' men. They were more free-spirited than he was, too, with Bohemian attitudes about sex, no doubt.

Perhaps Sandra found him boring now and was looking for excitement elsewhere. At thirty-eight, she was a fine-looking woman, with an unusual mix of long blonde hair and dark eyebrows over intelligent blue eyes. The slim, shapely figure she had worked hard to maintain always turned heads. Again he told himself not to be such a fool. It was the work that was taking up her time, not another man.

Sandra and Tracy were still upstairs when he had finished his coffee and toast. He called out goodbye, put on his charcoal sports jacket, patting the side pocket for cigarettes and lighter, and set off. It was such a fine morning—and he knew how quickly the day could turn to misery—that he decided to walk the mile or so to Eastvale Regional Headquarters rather than drive. He could always sign a car out of the pool if he needed one.

He stuck the Walkman in his pocket and turned it on. Ivor Gurney's setting of "In Flanders" started: "I'm homesick for my hills again—My hills again!" Banks had come to Gurney first through some of his poems in an anthology of First World War poetry, then, learning he had been a composer too, went in search of the music. There wasn't much available, just a handful of songs—settings of other people's poems—and some piano music, but Banks found the spareness and simplicity intensely moving.

As he walked along Market Street, he said hello to the shopkeepers winding out their awnings and called in at the newsagent's for his copy of *The Independent*. Glancing at the front page as he walked, he spotted Gemma Scupham's photograph and a brief request for information. Good, they'd been quick off the mark.

When he got to the market square, the first car was disgorging its family of tourists, dad with a camera slung around his neck, and the children in orange and yellow cagoules. It was hard to believe on such a day that a seven-year-old girl probably lay dead somewhere in the dale.

Banks went straight to the conference room upstairs in the station. It was their largest room, with a well-polished oval table at its centre, around which stood ten stiff-backed chairs. It was rare that ten people actually sat there, though, and this morning, in addition to Banks, only Superintendent Gristhorpe, Susan Gay and Phil Richmond occupied chairs. Banks helped himself to a black coffee from the urn by the window and sat down.

He was a few minutes early, and the others were chatting informally, pads and pencils in front of them.

First, Gristhorpe tossed a pile of newspapers onto the table and bade everyone have a look. Gemma Scupham's disappearance had made it in all the national dailies as well as in the *Yorkshire Post*. In some of the tabloids, she even made the headline: the photo of the melancholy-looking little girl with the straggly blonde hair appeared under captions such as HAVE YOU SEEN THIS GIRL? in "Jesus type." The stories gave few details, which hardly surprised Banks as there were scant few to give. A couple of pieces implied criticism of Brenda Scupham, but nothing libellous. Most were sympathetic to the mother.

"That might help us a bit," Gristhorpe said. "But I wouldn't count on it. And remember, the press boys will be around here in droves as soon as the London trains come in this morning. Let's be careful what we say, eh, or before we know it we'll be up to our necks in tales of satanic rituals." Gristhorpe stood up, grimaced and put his hand to the small of his back. "Anyway, let's get on. We've circulated Gemma's picture, and Susan managed to lift a set of her prints from a paint-box, so we've got them on file for comparison. Nothing new came up during the night. We did about as well as can be expected on the house-to-house. Four people say they remembered seeing a car parked outside Brenda Scupham's house on Tuesday afternoon. Of these, two say it was black, one dark brown and one dark blue." Gristhorpe paused. "I think, therefore, that we can be certain it was a dark car." He refilled his coffee cup and sat down again. "As far as the make is concerned we got even less. They all agreed it was a pretty small car, but not as small as a Mini, and it looked quite new. It wasn't an estate car or a van of any kind, so we're looking at a compact. One said it reminded him of those Japanese jobbies he's seen advertised on television, so it may be an import. Needless to say, no one got the number."

"Did anyone see the couple?" Banks asked.

"Yes." Gristhorpe looked at the file in front of him. "The woman at number eleven said she was washing her windows and she saw a well-dressed couple going up the path. Said they looked official, that's all. She thought maybe Mrs Scupham or her friend had got in trouble with DHSS."

"Hmm," said Banks. "Hardly surprising. I don't suppose anybody saw them leaving with the child?"

Gristhorpe shook his head.

"Well," Banks said, "at least it helps confirm Brenda Scupham's story."

"Aye." Gristhorpe looked over at Susan Gay, who had done most of the questioning. "Who would you say was our most reliable witness?"

"Mr Carter at number sixteen, sir. It wasn't so much that he'd seen more than the others, but he seemed to be thinking very seriously about what he *had* seen, and he told me he had a strong visual memory—not quite photographic, but he could close his eyes and picture scenes. He seemed careful not to make anything up. You know, sir, how a lot of them embroider on the truth."

"What colour did he say the car was?" Banks asked.

"Dark blue, and he thought it was a Japanese design, too. But he didn't see this Peterson and Brown couple, just the car."

"Shame," said Gristhorpe. "Had he seen it around before?"

"No, sir."

"Think it would do any good talking to him again?"

"It might," said Susan. "I'll drop by sometime today. He's a pensioner and I get the impression he's lonely. He seemed pleased to have a bit of company. It took me a while to get him round to what he'd seen."

Gristhorpe smiled. "Let him ramble a while, if it helps. Indulge him. And we'd better organize a house-to-house of the entire estate. I want to know if anything like this has happened there before, people posing as social workers after children. No one's likely to admit to it, but if you get the feeling that anyone's being particularly evasive, for whatever reason, make a note and we'll get back to them. Can you handle that, Susan?"

Susan Gay nodded.

"Take as many PCs as you can find, and make sure you give them a damn good briefing first. Most of the lads are out on the search, but we've been promised extra manpower on this." He turned to Richmond. "We've got to check with all the garages in the area and see if they remember anyone matching the description stopping for petrol. And I want to see all the police traffic reports— parking or speeding tickets—for Tuesday. In fact, make it for the past week. I want to know if anyone remembers a smartly dressed couple with a little girl in a dark blue compact. Better check with the car-rental agencies, too. Phil, can you handle all that?"

Richmond nodded. "Yes, sir. I've already got a computer print-out of locals with any kind of history of child molestation. None of the descriptions match. Do you want me to start on that too?"

"How many?"

"Six, sir—that's four in the Swainsdale area and two in Sergeant Hatchley's patch. But we've no way of telling where our couple started out from."

"I know," said Gristhorpe. "I'll get onto DS Hatchley, and you just do the best you can. We'll see if we can't pay a couple of visits ourselves. But I want priority on tracking down that car. Someone must have noticed it.

By the way, those computers you wanted have been delivered to the mobile unit. Do you think you can take a trip out there and give the lads a quick lesson?"

"No problem."

"Any questions?" Gristhorpe asked.

"Did forensics find anything at the house?" Banks asked.

Gristhorpe shook his head. "Not a sausage. The SOCO team did a thorough job, and they couldn't find any traces of a struggle—no blood, nothing—or any indications that Gemma had been harmed on the premises. I think we can assume that Mrs Scupham is telling the truth and this couple really did abduct the lass."

"Anything new on Les Poole?" Banks asked.

"Nothing," Gristhorpe answered. "According to the PCs on the night shift, he got back from the pub about ten o'clock and hasn't been out since. Anything else?"

"What about Gemma's father?" Susan asked.

"As far as we know, he's serving with the army in Belfast, poor sod. We'll arrange to get the locals to interview him today, if possible, just to make sure he's got nothing to do with it." Gristhorpe clapped his hands. "Right. If there's nothing else, we'd better get cracking." As they left, he touched Banks on the shoulder. "Alan, a moment?"

"Of course."

Gristhorpe poured more coffee for himself and Banks. He didn't look too bad for someone who hadn't had much sleep, Banks thought. Perhaps the bags under his eyes were heavier than usual, but he seemed alert and full of drive.

"I'm getting involved in this one, Alan," he said. "At every level. I'll not be content just to sit in my office and co-ordinate, though I'll be doing that, of course. I'll be spending a fair amount of time at the mobile unit and I'll be conducting some interviews myself. I want you to know that, and I want you to know so you don't let it interfere with your usual way of working. I've always given you a pretty free hand, and it's usually got results. I don't want to change that. What I *do* want is to be present when we get the breaks. Know what I mean?"

Banks nodded.

"And there's something else," Gristhorpe said. "Something the ACC made very clear as a priority concern."

Banks thought he could guess what was coming, but kept silent while Gristhorpe went on.

"Gemma Scupham might be the first," he said, "but she might not be the last. Let's bear that in mind."

Banks carried his coffee through to his office, where he lit a cigarette, then stood by the venetian blind and looked down on the market square. The façade of the Norman church and the cobbles of the market square shone pale gold in the pure light. Two more cars had arrived, and yet another was just pulling in. Banks watched the young couple get out and stand hand in hand gazing around them at the ancient square with its weathered stone cross. Honeymooners, by the look of them. The church clock rang nine.

He thought about Brenda Scupham, with her aura of sexuality, and of the sly, weasly Les Poole, and he tried to imagine what kind of parents they must have made. They can't have had much time for Gemma, with Les always at the pub or the bookie's and Brenda at home doing God knows what. Watching television, most likely. Did they talk to her? Play with her? And did they abuse her?

Then he thought of Gemma herself: that haunted face, those eyes that had seen much more and much worse than her young mind could comprehend, possibly lying dead out there right now in some ditch, or buried in a makeshift grave. And he thought of what Gristhorpe had just said. He stubbed out his cigarette and reached for the telephone. No time for brooding. Time to get to work.

II

A desolate, stunned air pervaded the East Side Estate that morning, Banks sensed, as he walked from the mobile unit to the school. Even the dogs seemed to be indoors, and those people he did see going on errands or pushing babies in prams had their heads bowed and seemed drawn in on themselves. He passed the maisonettes with their obscene messages scrawled on the cracked paint-work, and the two blocks of flats—each fourteen storeys high—where he knew the lifts, when they worked, smelled of urine and glue. Hardly anyone was out on the street.

The school itself was a square red brick building with only a few small windows. A high chain-link fence bordered the asphalt playground. Banks looked at his watch. Eleven o'clock. Gemma's teacher should be waiting for him in the staff-room.

He walked through the front doors, noting that one of the glass panes was cracked in a spider-web pattern, and asked the first adult he saw the way to the staff-room. As he walked along the corridor, he was struck by the brightness of the place, so much in contrast with its ugly exterior. Most of it, he thought, was due to the children's paintings tacked along the walls. These weren't skilled, professional efforts, but the gaudy outbursts of untrained minds—yellow sunbursts with rays shooting in all directions, bright golden angels, red and green stick figures of mummy and daddy and cats and dogs.

There was a funny smell about the place, too, that transported him back to his own infants' school, but it took him some moments to identify it. When he did, he smiled to himself, remembering for the first time in ages those blissful, carefree days before school became a matter of learning facts and studying for exams. It was Plasticine, that coloured putty-like stuff he had tried in vain to mould into the shapes of hippos and crocodiles.

He walked straight into the staff-room, and a woman, who looked hardly older than a schoolgirl herself, came forward to greet him. "Chief Inspector Banks?" she asked, holding out her hand. "I'm Peggy Graham."

It was a big room with well-spaced tables and chairs, a notice-board full of mimeographed memos, handwritten notes and printed flyers for concerts, courses and package holidays. A couple of other teachers, sitting over newspapers, glanced up at his entry, then looked down again. One corner of the room had been converted into a mini-kitchen, complete with a fridge, microwave and coffee-maker. Here and there on the rough, orange-painted walls hung more examples of untrammelled art.

"A bit overwhelming, isn't it?" Peggy Graham asked, noticing him looking around. "I could do without the orange walls myself, but it was a playroom before we got it, so. . . . Sit down. Can I get you some coffee or something?"

"If it's no trouble," Banks said.

She went to get it. Peggy Graham, Banks noticed, was a small, bird-like woman, perhaps fresh out of teachers' training school. Her grey pleated skirt covered her knees, and a dark blue cardigan hung over her white cotton blouse. She wore her mousy hair in a pony tail, and large glasses made her nose look tiny. Her eyes, behind them, were big, pale and milky blue, and they seemed charged with worry and sincerity. Her lips were thin and curved slightly downwards at the corners. She wore no make-up.

"Well," she said, sitting down beside him with the coffee. It came in a mug with a picture of Big Bird on it. "This is just dreadful about Gemma, isn't it? Just dreadful."

She spoke, he thought, as if she were talking to a class of five-year-olds, and her mouth was so mobile she looked as if she were miming. Banks nodded.

"What could have happened?" she asked. "Have you got *any* idea?"

"I'm afraid not," Banks said.

"I don't suppose you could say anything even if you did have, could you?"

"We have to be very careful."

"Of course." She sat back in her chair, crossed her legs and rested her hands on her lap. Banks noticed the thin gold wedding band. "How can I help you?" she asked.

"I'm not really sure. In cases like this it helps to find out as much as you can about the child. What was Gemma like?"

Peggy Graham pursed her lips. "Well, that's a hard one. Gemma's a very quiet child. She always seems a bit withdrawn."

"In what way?"

"Just . . . quiet. Oh, she's bright, very bright. She's an excellent reader, and I think, given the opportunity, she could be very creative. That's one of hers on the wall."

Banks walked over to the crayon sketch Peggy had pointed at. It showed a girl with pigtails standing beside a tree on a carpet of grass under a bright sun. The leaves were individually defined in bright green, and the grass was dotted with yellow flowers—buttercups, perhaps, or dandelions. The girl, a stick-figure, just stood there with her arms stretched out. Banks found something disturbing about it, and he realized that the girl's round face had no features. He went back to his chair.

"Very good," he said. "Did you ever get the feeling that there was something bothering her?"

"She always seems . . . well, preoccupied." Peggy gave a nervous laugh. "I call her Wednesday's child. You know, 'Wednesday's child is full of woe.' She seemed woeful. Of course, I tried to talk to her, but she never said much. Mostly she was attentive in class. Once or twice I noticed she was weeping, just quietly, to herself."

"What did you do?"

"I didn't want to embarrass her in front of the others. I asked her afterwards what was wrong, but she wouldn't say. Gemma's always been a very secretive child. What goes on in that imagination of hers I've no idea. Half the time she seems to be in another world."

"A better one?"

Peggy Graham twisted her ring. "I don't know. I like to think so."

"What was your impression?"

"I think she was lonely and she felt unloved."

Her first use of the past tense in reference to Gemma wasn't lost on Banks. "Lonely? Didn't she have any friends?"

"Oh yes. She was quite popular here, even though she was quiet. Don't get the wrong impression. She liked playing games with the other girls. Sometimes she seemed quite gay—oops, I shouldn't have said that, should I, now they've censored it from all the Noddy books—cheerful, I suppose. It's just that she was moody. She had these woeful, silent moods when you just couldn't reach her. Sometimes they'd last for days."

"And you don't know why?"

"I can only guess. And you mustn't tell anyone I said this. I think it was her home life."

"What about it?"

"I think she was neglected. I don't mean she wasn't well fed or clothed, or abused in any way. Though she did look a bit . . . well, shabby . . . sometimes. You know, she was wearing the same dress and socks day after day. And sometimes I just felt like picking her up and dumping her in a bath. It wasn't that she smelled or anything. She was just a bit grubby. I don't think her parents spent enough time with her, encouraging her, that sort of thing. I think that was the root of her loneliness. It happens a lot, and there isn't much you can do about it. A supportive home environment is perhaps even more important than school for a child's development, but we can't be parents as well as teachers, can we? And we can't tell parents how to bring up their children."

"You mentioned abuse," Banks said. "Did you ever notice any signs of physical abuse?"

"Oh, no. I couldn't . . . I mean, if I had I would certainly have reported it. We did have a case here a year or so ago. It was dreadful, just dreadful what some parents can sink to."

"But you saw no signs with Gemma? No bruises, cuts, anything like that?"

"No. Well, there was one time. About a week or so ago, I think it was. It was quite warm, like now. Gemma was wearing a short-sleeved dress and I noticed a bruise on her upper arm, the left one, I think. Naturally, I asked her about it, but she said she'd got it playing games."

"Did you believe her?"

"Yes. I had no reason to doubt her word."

"So you didn't report it?"

"No. I mean, one wouldn't want to be alarmist. Not after that business with the Cleveland social workers and everything. Look, maybe I should have done something. Lord knows, if I'm in any way responsible. . . . But if you brought in the authorities every time a child had a bruise there'd be no time for anything else, would there?"

"It's all right," Banks said. "Nobody's blaming you. Everybody's a bit sensitive about things like that these days. I picked up plenty of bruises when I was a lad, believe me, and my mum and dad wouldn't have appreciated being accused of abusing me. And I got a good hiding when I deserved it, too."

Peggy smiled at him over her glasses. "As I said," she went on, "Gemma's explanation seemed perfectly reasonable to me. Children can play pretty rough sometimes. They're a lot more resilient than we give them credit for."

"Was that the only mark you ever saw on her?"

"Oh, yes. I mean, if it had been a regular occurrence I'd have said something for certain. We do have to keep an eye open for these things."

"And she never seemed in pain of any kind?"

"Not physical pain, no. She just sometimes seemed withdrawn, lost in her own world. But children often create their own imaginary worlds. They can be very complex beings, Chief Inspector. They're not all the same. Just because a child is quiet, it doesn't mean there's anything wrong with her."

"I understand. Please believe me, I'm not criticizing. I'm just trying to find out something about her."

"How could it help?"

"I honestly don't know."

"You think she's dead, don't you?"

"I wouldn't say that."

"She's been gone nearly two days now. That's what the papers say. Not in so many words, perhaps, but . . ."

"She could still be alive."

"Then she might be better off dead," Peggy Graham whispered. She felt up the sleeve of her cardigan for a tissue, lifted her glasses and wiped her moist eyes. They looked small and shy without the lenses to magnify them. "I'm sorry. It's just . . . we're all so upset."

"Did you, or anyone else on staff, notice any strangers hanging around the school recently?"

"No. And I'm sure anything like that would have been reported. We have very strict guidelines to follow."

"Nobody saw a dark blue car? Are you sure?"

She shook her head. "I'm sure."

"Did you ever see Gemma talking to any strangers nearby? Male or female?"

"No. She always came and left with her friends, the ones from the same street. She didn't live far away."

Banks stood up. "Thank you very much," he said. "If you do remember anything, here's my card. Please call."

Peggy Graham took the card. "Of course. But I don't see how there could be anything else."

"Just in case."

"All right." She got to her feet. "I'll walk to the door with you."

As they walked, a host of children came out of one of the classrooms. Some were laughing and scrapping, but many of them seemed subdued. Perhaps they were too young to understand the enormity of what had happened, Banks thought, but they were old enough to sense the mood of tension and fear. One little girl with glossy dark curls and brown spaniel eyes tugged at Banks's sleeve.

"Are you the policeman?" she asked.

"Yes," he answered, wondering how on earth she knew.

"Are you looking for Gemma?"

"Yes, I am."

"Please find her," the little girl said, clutching his sleeve tighter. "Bring her back. She's my friend."

"I'll do my best," said Banks. He turned to Peggy

Graham. She blushed.

"I'm afraid I told them a policeman was coming," she said. "Sorry."

"It's all right. Look, can I talk to this girl?"

"Elizabeth? Well . . . I suppose so. Though I don't know what. . . . Come this way." And she led both Banks and Elizabeth into the empty classroom.

"Now, Elizabeth," she said. "The nice policeman wants to talk to you about Gemma, to help him to find her. Just answer his questions. I'll stay here with you." She glanced at Banks to ask if he minded, and he nodded his agreement. Elizabeth took hold of Peggy Graham's hand and stood beside her.

Banks crouched, hearing his knees crack as he did so, and rested his elbows on his thighs. "You know we're trying to find Gemma," he said. "Did she ever say anything to you about going away?"

Elizabeth shook her head.

"Or about anyone wanting to take her away?"

Another shake.

"Did she have any older friends, big girls or big boys?"

"No."

"Did she ever talk about her mummy and daddy?"

"It wasn't her daddy."

"Mr Poole?"

Elizabeth nodded. "She wouldn't call him Daddy."

"What did she say about him?"

"I don't know."

"Did she like him?"

"No."

"Did he ever hurt Gemma?"

"She cried."

"Why did she cry?"

"Don't know."

"Did he ever hurt her, Elizabeth?"

"I don't know. She didn't like him. She said he smelled and he always told her to go away."

"When did he tell her to go away?"

"He said she was a sp . . . sp . . . a spilled cat."

"A spilled cat? Do you mean 'spoiled brat'?"

"Yes."

"When did he say this?"

"He wouldn't let her have the book."

"What book?"

"She wanted a book and he wouldn't let her have it. He threw her other books away."

"Why?"

"She spilled some paint on his newspaper. It too dirty. He was angry. He threw her books away and he wouldn't let her have any more."

"What was too dirty, Elizabeth?"

"No. It too dirty."

Banks looked at Peggy Graham. "I think she's trying to say 'at two-thirty,' " she said, frowning.

"Is that right?" Banks asked Elizabeth. "She spilled paint on his newspaper at two-thirty, so he threw her books away?"

She nodded.

"What were the books?"

"Story books. With pictures. Gemma likes reading. She reads to me. I'm not very good. Please find her." Elizabeth started crying. Peggy Graham put an arm around her. "It's all right, dear. The nice policeman will find Gemma. Don't cry."

Elizabeth sniffled a few moments longer, then wiped her nose on her sleeve and left the room. Banks sighed.

"What was all that about?" Peggy asked.

"I wish I knew. Thanks for letting me talk to her anyway. I hope she doesn't stay upset."

"Don't worry. Elizabeth's tough enough."

Banks walked through the playground full of children. They were skipping, playing hopscotch, running around as usual, but like the ones coming out of the classroom they seemed much quieter, more subdued than children usually are.

He looked at his watch. Close to noon. Time to write up his notes before lunch with Jenny. Not that he had learned much from the teacher that he hadn't known or suspected already. Gemma kept herself to herself, perhaps suffered neglect at home, but was probably not physically abused. Still, there was the business of the bruise. How had she got it? And what had Elizabeth meant about "at two-thirty" and Gemma's books? Banks walked past the tower block with JESUS SAVES written in red on the wall and back to the unmarked car he had parked by the mobile unit.

III

Damn it, cursed Jenny Fuller. She had pulled up at the lights just in time and all the essays on the back seat had slid off onto the floor. So few of the students bothered with paper-clips or staples; it would a hell of a job reshuffling them. If she hadn't been in such a hurry to meet Banks it would never have happened. She was on the south-eastern edge of Eastvale, coming up to the roundabout by the Red Lion, and she only had five minutes to park and get to Le Bistro. Still, Alan would wait.

The lights changed and the car lurched off again. To hell with the papers. She shouldn't be teaching until October anyway, and if it hadn't been for those American students—those American students with odd ideas of academic timetables and thousands of dollars to spend on an English education—then she could have been relaxing on a beach somewhere.

She smiled to herself, imagining Alan Banks sitting at one of Le Bistro's wobbly little tables, no doubt feeling out of place among the yuppie lunch crowd with their Perriers and portable telephones. He would be far more comfortable in the Queen's Arms with a pie and a pint in front of him, not at a table covered in a coral cloth with a long-stemmed rose in a vase at its centre. But Jenny had been lecturing to the Americans all morning, and she was damned if she was going to be done out of the shrimp *provençale* and the glass of white wine she had promised to treat herself.

Jenny remembered her surprise the first time the Eastvale CID had brought her into a case, involving a peeping Tom, three years ago. She had guessed (correctly) that they wanted a visible female presence as a sop to Dorothy Wycombe and the Eastvale feminist contingent, WEEF, Women of Eastvale for Emancipation and Freedom. Still, she had done a good job, and since then her professional field of interests had broadened to include a certain amount of criminal and deviant psychology. She had even attended a series of fascinating lectures on the psychological profiling of serial killers, given by a visiting American from the FBI Behavioral Sciences section.

She had also had a brief fling with the visitor, but she didn't care to remember that too clearly. Like most of her affairs, it was best forgotten. Still, that was eighteen months ago, when she had been still hurting over her split with Dennis Osmond. Since then she had not been involved with anyone. Instead, she had done a lot of thinking about her lousy relationships, and the reasons for them. She hadn't come up with any answers yet. Most often she ended up wondering why the hell her professional insights seemed to shed no light at all on her personal life.

The tires screeched as she turned right at the market square and drove down by Castle Hill between the terraced river gardens and the formal gardens. People sat on the terraces and ate packed lunches on one side of the road, while on the other, mothers dragged bored children around the displays of fading flowers.

At last, she crossed the small bridge over the River Swain, turned right and pulled up outside the café.

Le Bistro was one of Eastvale's newest cafés. Tourism, the dale's main industry, had increased, and the many Americans drawn to do the "James Herriot" tour wanted a little more than fish and chips and warm beer, quaint as they found such things. In addition, a more sophisticated, cosmopolitan crowd had moved up from London while property in the north was still a good deal cheaper than down south. Many of them commuted from Eastvale to York, Darlington, and even as far as Tyneside, Leeds and Bradford, and they naturally demanded a little more diversity in matters of dining.

Best of all, as far as Jenny was concerned, was that Le Bistro was actually situated in a converted Georgian semi only four houses south of her own. The new owners had, somehow, received planning permission to knock down the wall between the two houses and turn them into a café. For Jenny it was a godsend, as she often couldn't be bothered to cook after a hard day. The food was good and the prices were relatively reasonable.

She dashed through the door. The place was fairly busy, but she saw Banks immediately. There he was in a dark grey sports jacket, white shirt and tie. As usual, his top button was open and the tie loose and askew. Under close-cropped black hair, his dark blue eyes sparkled as he looked over at her. He was working on a crossword and holding what looked like a glass of mineral water. Jenny couldn't suppress a giggle as she sat down in a flurry of apologies. Le Bistro didn't serve pints.

"It's all right," said Banks rather glumly, putting his newspaper away in his briefcase. "I'm supposed to be cutting down on the ale anyway."

"Since when?"

Banks patted his stomach. "Since I turned forty and noticed this beginning to swell."

"Nonsense. You're as lean as ever. You're just suffering from male menopause. Next you'll be having an affair with a twenty-one-year-old rookie policewoman."

Banks laughed. "Chance would be a fine thing. But don't joke about it. You never know. Anyway, how are you?"

Jenny shrugged and tossed back the thick mane of red hair that cascaded over her shoulders. "Okay, I suppose. I'm not sure I like teaching summer school though."

"Working in summer?" mocked Banks. "Tut-tut, what a terrible thing. What is the world coming to?"

Jenny thumped him on the arm. "It's supposed to be one of the perks of the job, remember? Teachers get summers off. Not this year, though."

"Never mind. You're looking well for it."

"Why, thank you, kind sir." Jenny inclined her head graciously. "And you haven't changed. Honestly, Alan. You still don't look a day over thirty-nine. How's Sandra?"

"Busy."

"Oh-oh. Feeling all neglected, are we?"

Banks grinned. "Something like that. But we're not here to talk about me."

"And how's Susan Gay?" Jenny had spent some time helping Susan adjust to her CID posting, on a semi-professional basis, and the two had become fairly close.

They were different personalities, but Jenny saw something in Susan—a sense of determination, a single-mindedness—that both appealed to her and disturbed her. If she could persuade Susan to relax a little, she felt, then a more balanced and attractive personality might be permitted to emerge.

Banks told her Susan was doing well, though she still seemed a little tense and prickly, and the two chatted about family and mutual friends. "Have you studied the menu yet?" Jenny asked him after a short silence.

"Mm. No sausage and chips, I noticed. How's the croque monsieur?"

"Good."

"Then I'll have that. And by the way, I like the music."

Jenny cocked an ear. Singing quietly in the background was the unmistakable voice of Edith Piaf. Typical of him to notice that, she thought. Left to herself she would have ignored it as wallpaper music.

"Wine?" she asked.

"Not for me. It makes me sleepy and I've a lot of paperwork to do this afternoon."

"So, it's about little Gemma Scupham, is it?" Jenny said, unfolding a coral napkin and spreading it over her lap. "That's why you've called me in?"

Banks nodded. "Superintendent Gristhorpe thought you might be able to help."

"At least I'm not the token feminist this time."

"No. Seriously, Jenny, can you help?"

"Maybe. What do you want from me?"

"For the moment I'd just like grounding in a few basics. I can understand a lot about things most people don't even want to think about—robbery, murder, even rape—but I can't seem to grasp the motivation for something like this."

Jenny took a deep breath and held it a moment. "All right. I'll do what I can. Shall we order first, though?" She called over the waitress and gave their orders, asking for a glass of white wine for herself right now, and a coffee for Banks, then she sat back in her chair. "First you'd better tell me the details so far," she said.

Banks told her. Before he finished, the food arrived, and they both tucked in.

Jenny pushed her plate away and set the half-full wineglass in front of her. Banks ordered another coffee.

"I don't really know where to start," she said. "I mean, it's not really my field."

"You do know something about sexual deviance, though."

"Honestly, Alan, you make me sound like a real pervert. Basically, nobody really knows what causes someone to be a paedophile or a rapist or a sadist. They don't necessarily realize they're doing anything wrong."

"Are you telling me that a man who sexually assaults little children doesn't think he's doing anything wrong?"

"Depends what you mean by wrong. He would know he's breaking the law, of course, but. . . . He's only satisfying desires he can't help feeling. He never *asked* to feel them in the first place. And many also feel tremendous guilt and remorse."

"For doing something they don't even think is wrong? You make it sound almost legitimate."

"You asked. I'm just telling you what little I know."

"I'm sorry. Go on."

"Look, you might think a person is simply born the way he or she is, but sexual behaviour isn't fixed from the start. There are theories that almost everything is biologically based, caused by chemicals, or by genes. For what it's worth, most studies indicate that sexual behaviour is mostly a matter of learning. At first, everything is diffuse, in a kind of flux—polymorphous perverse, I believe Freud called infant sexuality. It depends on a number of factors what preferences come to the fore."

"Like what?"

"Experience. Learning. Family. They're probably the most important. You try something, and if you like it, you do it again. That's experience. Many people are given no information about sex, or such wrong-headed information that they become very confused. That's learning, or lack of it. Even what we call normal sexuality is a dark, murky thing at best. Look at the extremes of sexual jealousy, of how sex and desire can so easily turn to violence. There's loss of control. Then there's the association of orgasm with death. Did you know it used to be called the 'little death'?"

"You don't make it sound like much fun."

"That's the point," Jenny said. "For a lot of people, it isn't. Desire is a ball and chain they can't get rid of, or a ringmaster they don't dare disobey. Sexuality has lots of possible outcomes other than what we label 'normal' or socially acceptable. It's *learned* behaviour. When you're prepubescent or adolescent, any object or situation *could* become stimulating. Remember the thrill you used to get looking at pictures of naked women? It's easy as an adolescent to get fixated on things like underwear, big breasts, the image rather than the real thing. Remember our peeping Tom? That was his particular fixation, a visual stimulation.

"It doesn't take long before most of us start to prefer certain stimuli to others. Pretty soon sexual excitement and satisfaction become limited to a certain, fairly narrow range. That's what we call normal. Your good old, socially approved, heterosexual sex. The problem with most sexual deviants, though, is that they can't handle what we regard as normal personal relationships. Many try, but they fail. It's a lot more complicated than that, of course. It may not be apparent on the surface that they've failed, for example. They may become very good at faking it in order to cover up their real needs and actions."

"So what kind of person are we talking about? You said it's someone who can't handle ordinary relationships."

"I'll have to do some research and see what I can come up with, but your basic deviant is probably pretty much the chap-next-door type, with some very notable exceptions, of course. By the way, you don't have to look around so nervously, you can smoke if you want. Giselle will fetch an ashtray. Remember, it's a *French* restaurant. Everyone smokes over there."

Banks lit up and Giselle duly brought the ashtray along with their bill. "Go on," he said. "You were telling me about the chap next door."

"It's just that most sex offenders become skilled at leading quite normal lives on the surface. They learn to play the game. They can hold down a job, keep a marriage going, even raise children—"

"Paedophiles?"

"Yes."

"I must admit that's a surprise," said Banks. "I've come across psychopaths and deviants of various kinds before—I mean, I'm not entirely ignorant on the subject—and it *has* often amazed me how they keep their secrets. Look at Dennis Nilsen, for Christ's sake, chopping up kids and putting their heads on the ring to boil while he takes his dog for a walk, saying hello to the neighbours. Such a nice, quiet man." Banks shook his head. "I know the Boston Strangler was married, and Sutcliffe, the Yorkshire Ripper. But how the hell can a paedophile keep a thing like that hidden from his wife and kids?"

"People can become very adept at keeping secrets if they have to, Alan. You don't spend all your life in someone else's company, under someone's scrutiny, do you? Surely you managed to find time alone to masturbate when you were a kid? And you probably thought about it a fair bit, too, anticipated the picture you'd look at or the girl you'd imagine undressing. The whole thing takes on a kind of magical intensity, a ritualistic element, if you like. A sex offender will simply spend all his free time anticipating and planning his deviant acts."

Banks loosened his tie a little more. Jenny noticed him look around the restaurant and smile at the three businessmen at the next table, who seemed to have been listening with growing fascination and horror to the conversation. "You seem to know a lot about adolescent male behaviour," he said.

Jenny laughed. "Alan, I've embarrassed you. Oh, don't look so uncomfortable. It *is* part of my field, after all. The things little boys and little girls get up to."

"What's your prognosis?" Banks asked.

Jenny sighed. "For you? I'm afraid there's no hope. No, really, I honestly haven't done enough research for anything like that yet." She frowned, the lines crinkling her smooth forehead. "You know what really puzzles me, though? Again, it's probably something you've already considered from your point of view, but psychologically it's interesting, too."

"What's that?"

"The woman."

"You mean why she was there?"

"Yes. What's her part in the whole business?"

"Well, her presence would certainly give credibility to the social worker story. I doubt that even someone as thick as Brenda Scupham would have trusted a man alone."

"No. I realize that. But think about it, Alan." Jenny leaned forward, her hands clasped on the table. "She's a woman. Surely you're not telling me she didn't know what they were doing, taking the child?"

"They acted together, yes. But he may have conned her into it somehow, for the sake of credibility. She might not have known what his motives were, especially if, as you say, paedophiles are good at keeping secrets."

"Except from themselves. But I still think it's a strange thing for a woman to do—help abduct another woman's child. It's an even stranger thing for a couple to do. What on earth would she want with Gemma?"

"Now don't tell me you're going to give me all that sisterhood crap, because I just don't accept it. Women are just as—"

Jenny held her hand up. "All right. I won't. But there's no need to start getting all shirty. It's not sisterhood I'm talking about, it's a very practical thing. As far as I know, sexual deviants can be fat or thin, big or little, young or old, rich or poor, but they almost always act *alone*. To put it technically, we're talking about people who exhibit primary characteristics of social aversion."

"Hmm. I'm not saying we haven't considered they might have simply wanted a child so badly that they took someone else's, that they're not paedophiles. We just don't know. But think of the risk involved."

Jenny ran her fingers around the stem of her wineglass. "Maybe it does seem far-fetched. But women have snatched babies from prams. It's not my job to evaluate that kind of information. All I'm saying is that the couple element is curious, in psychological terms. And the method is unusual. As you say, think of the risk involved. Maybe the risk was part of the thrill."

A short silence followed. Banks lit another cigarette. Jenny pulled a face and waved the smoke away. She no-

ticed that Edith Piaf had finished now, replaced by some
innocuous accordion music meant to evoke the Gauloise
atmosphere of Parisian cafés.

"The superintendent mentioned the Moors Murderers,
Brady and Hindley," said Banks. "I know he's got a bee
in his bonnet about that case, but you have to admit there
are parallels."

"Hmm."

"What I'm saying," Banks went on, "is it may be one
way of explaining the couple aspect. Brady thought human beings were contemptible creatures and pleasure the
only end worth pursuing. And Hindley was besotted with
him. She was witnessing it all as a demonstration of
some form of love for him. I know it sounds weird, but
. . ."

"I've heard the theory," said Jenny. "It's all to do with
dominance. And I've heard a lot weirder theories, too.
Christ, Alan, you know as well as I do that most psychology is guesswork. We don't really *know* anything. But
Superintendent Gristhorpe may be right. It *could* be
something like that. I'll look into it."

"So you'll help?"

"Of course I'll help, idiot. Did you think I'd say no?"

"Quickly, Jenny," said Banks, taking money from his
wallet and placing it on the bill. "Especially if there's
even the slightest chance that Gemma Scupham might
still be alive."

IV

"Have you found her yet?"

Nothing much had changed in Brenda Scupham's
front room by Thursday afternoon. The doll still lay in
the same position on the floor, and the peculiar smell

remained. But Brenda looked more tired. Her eyes were red-rimmed and her hair hung limp and lifeless beside her pale cheeks. She was wearing a grubby pink track-suit bottom and a loose green sweatshirt. Les Poole slouched in the armchair, feet up, smoking.

"What's wrong, Les?" Banks asked. "Is The Barleycorn not on all-day opening?"

"Very funny. I don't *live* there, you know."

Brenda Scupham shot him a mean look, then turned to Banks. "Leave him alone. He's not done anything. He might not be much, but he's all I've got. I asked you, have you found my Gemma yet?"

"No," said Banks, turning from Poole. "No, we haven't."

"Well, what do you want? More questions?"

"I'm afraid so."

Brenda Scupham sighed and sat down. "I don't know where this is going to get us."

"I need to know more about Gemma's habits, for a start."

"What do you mean, habits?"

"Her routines. How did she get to school?"

"She walked. It's not far."

"Alone?"

"No, she met up with the Ferris girl from over the street and the Bramhope kid from two houses down."

"Did she come home with them, too?"

"Yes."

Banks made a note of the names. "What about lunch-time?"

"School dinners."

"Why?"

"What do you mean, why?"

"The school's not far away. Surely it'd have saved you a penny or two if she came home for lunch?"

Brenda Scupham shrugged. "She said she liked school dinners."

"Did she ever say anything about anyone following her or stopping her in the street?"

"Never."

"And she wasn't out on her own?"

"No. She was always with her friends, whether she was off to school or playing out. Why are you asking all these questions?"

"Brenda, I'm trying to figure out why Gemma's abductors came to the house rather than snatching her in the street. Surely she must have been alone out there at some time?"

"I dare say. She'd nip to the shop now and then. You can't keep your eyes on them every minute of the day. She is seven, you know. She knows to look right before left when she's crossing the street, and not to take sweets from strangers." When she realized what she'd said, she put her hand to her mouth and her eyes filled with tears.

"I'm sorry if this is painful for you," Banks said, "but it is important."

"I know."

"Was Gemma a happy child, would you say?"

"I suppose so. They live in their own worlds, don't they?"

"Would she be given to exaggeration, to lying?"

"Not that I know of, no."

"It's just that I heard a story about Les here throwing some of Gemma's books out. Does that mean anything to you?"

Les Poole sat up and turned to Banks. "What?"

"You heard, Les. What's so important about her spilling paint on your paper at two-thirty?"

Poole looked puzzled for a few seconds, then he laughed out loud. "Who told you that?"

"Never mind. What's it all about?"

He laughed again. "It was *the* two-thirty. The two-thirty from Cheltenham. Silly little bugger spilled coloured water all over my racing form. You know, the jar she'd been dipping her bloody paintbrush in."

"And for that you threw her books out?"

"Don't be daft. They were just some old colouring books. She was painting in them on the other side of the table and she knocked her paint jar over and ruined my bloody paper. So I grabbed the books and tore them up."

"How did she react?"

"Oh, she whined and sulked for a while."

"Did you ever grab her hard by the arm?"

"No, I never touched her. Just the books. Look, what's all this—"

"Why wouldn't you get her the new book she wanted?"

Poole sat back in the chair and crossed his legs. "Couldn't afford it, could we? You can't give kids everything they ask for. You ought to know that if you've got kids of your own. Look, get to the point, Mr Banks. I might not have had much time for the little beggar but *I* didn't run off with her, did I? We're the victims, not the criminals. I think it's about time you realized that."

Banks looked at him, and Poole quickly averted his gaze. It made Banks think of his first lesson in police thinking. He had been involved in interviewing a petty thief about a burglary in Belsize Park, and he came away convinced that the man hadn't committed it. Surprised to see the charges being laid and the evidence gathered, he had mentioned his doubts to his commanding officer. The man, a twenty-year veteran called Bill Carstairs, had looked at Banks and shaken his head, then he said, "He might not have done this job, but he sure as hell has done something he ought to be put away for." Looking at

Poole made Banks feel the same way. The man was guilty of something. If he had nothing to do with Gemma's disappearance, or even with the Fletcher's warehouse job, he was still guilty of *something*.

Banks turned back to Brenda Scupham.

"You think we abused Gemma, don't you?" she said.

"I don't know."

"You've been listening to gossip. Probably gossip from kids, at that. Look, I'll admit I didn't want her. I was twenty-one, the last thing I wanted was to be lumbered with a kid, but I was brought up Catholic, and I couldn't get rid of her. I might not be the best mother on earth. I might be selfish, I might not be up to encouraging her in school and paying as much attention to her as I should. I'm not even a very good house-keeper. But all that . . . I mean, what I'm saying is I never abused her."

It was an impassioned speech, but Banks got the feeling that she was protesting too much. "What about Les?" he asked.

She glanced over at him. "If he ever touched her he knows he'd be out of here before his feet could touch the floor."

"So why did you give her up so easily?"

Brenda Scupham chewed on her lip and fought back the tears. "Do you think I haven't had it on my mind night and day since? Do you think there's a moment goes by I don't ask myself the same question?" She shook her head. "It all happened so fast."

"But if you hadn't abused Gemma in any way, why didn't you just tell Mr Brown and Miss Peterson that and send them away?"

"Because they were the authorities. I mean, they looked like they were and everything. I suppose I thought if they'd had some information then they had to look into it, you know, like the police. And then when they found there was nothing in it, they'd bring Gemma back."

"Did Gemma go willingly?"

"What?"

"When she left with them, did she cry, struggle?"

"No, she just seemed to accept it. She didn't say anything."

Banks stood up. "That's it for now," he said. "We'll keep you informed. If you remember anything, you can report it at the mobile unit at the end of the street."

Brenda folded her arms and nodded. "You make *me* feel like a criminal, Mr Banks," she said. "It's not right. I've tried to be a good mother. I'm not perfect, but who is?"

Banks paused at the door. "Mrs Scupham," he said, "I'm not trying to prove any kind of case against you. Believe it or not, all the questions I ask you are to do with trying to find Gemma. I know it seems cruel, but I need to know the answers. And if you think about it for a while, considering how many other children there are on this estate, and all over Swainsdale, and how many of them really *are* abused, there's a very important question needs answering."

Brenda Scupham's brow furrowed, and even Poole glanced over from his fireside seat.

"What's that?" she asked.

"Why Gemma?" Banks said, and left.

3

I

Marjorie Bingham lingered behind the others on the narrow track and kicked at small stones as she walked. She could hear her husband's muffled voice, carried back on the breeze, as he explained the history of Dales lead mining to Andrew and Jane.

"Most people think that lead mining here only goes back as far as Roman times. It doesn't, you know. It goes back much further than that. It might even go back as far as the Bronze Age—though there's no hard evidence for that, of course—but certainly the Brigantes . . ."

God, she thought, what a bloody bore Roger has become. Only six months up from Coventry after the company move and here he is, playing the country squire and rabbiting on about spalling hammers, knockstones, buckers and hotching tubs. And just look at him: pants tucked into the expensive hiking boots, walking-stick, orange Gore-Tex anorak. All for a quarter-mile track from the Range Rover to the old mine.

Knowing Andrew, Marjorie thought, he was probably thinking about opening time, and Jane was absorbed with her new baby, which she carried in a kind of makeshift sack on her back. Little Annette was asleep, one leg poking out each side of the central strap, her head lolling, oblivious to them all, and especially oblivious to the bloody lead mines.

"Of course, the Romans used lead in great quantities. You know how advanced their plumbing systems were for their time. I know you've been to the Roman Baths in Bath, Andrew, and I'm sure you'll agree . . ."

Young Megan capered ahead picking flowers, reciting, "He loves me, he loves me not . . ." as she pulled off the petals and tossed them in the air. Then she spread her arms out and pretended to walk a tightrope. She didn't have a care in the world, either, Marjorie thought. Why do we lose that sense of wonder in nature? she asked herself. How does it happen? Where does it go? It wasn't that she didn't appreciate the countryside—there was no denying it was beautiful, not to mention healthy, especially on a lovely autumn morning like this—but she couldn't feel ecstatic about it. To be honest, she loved the shops and the busy hum of city life much more. Even Eastvale would have been preferable. But no: Roger said they had to seize their opportunity for a newer, better lifestyle when it came along. And so they had ended up in dull, sleepy Lyndgarth.

A weekend in the country now and again suited Marjorie perfectly—that was what it was there for, after all, unless you were a farmer, a painter or a poet—but this felt more like incarceration. She hadn't been able to find a job, and the new neighbours weren't particularly friendly, either. Someone told her you have to winter out two years before you are accepted, but she didn't think she could stand it that long. And the fact that Roger was in his element didn't help much either. She was bored stiff. She didn't have children to fill her days like Jane. Still, at least their visit had brought a welcome break to the routine. She should be grateful for that. She would have been if it hadn't been for Roger seizing his chance to pontificate.

"The Pennine mines are the only ones in Yorkshire. Know why? It's because the lead ore occurs in Carboniferous rocks—the Yoredale Series and Millstone Grit. The ores aren't exactly *part* of the rocks, you understand, but . . . "

At last they reached the old smelting mill, not much more than a pile of stones, really, and not much bigger than a detached house. Most of the roof had collapsed, leaving only the weatherworn beams. Inside, sunlight shone through the roof and through the gaps between the stones onto the ruined ore hearths and furnaces, and picked out the motes of dust they kicked up. Marjorie had never liked the old mill. It was a dry, smelly, spidery sort of place. Over in one corner, the dusty ground was darkened, as if some wandering drunk had been sick there.

"In the earlier mills," Roger went on, "they used to burn off the sulphur first, changing the lead to oxide. Of course, for that you need places to roast then reduce the ore. But by the time this mill was built, they'd invented vertical furnaces that used bellows . . . "

They all obediently followed his pointing stick and oohed and aahed. He should have been a bloody tour guide, Marjorie thought.

Suddenly, Jane looked nervously around the mill. "Where's Megan?" she asked.

"Probably playing outside," Marjorie said, noting the anxiety in her voice. "Don't worry, I'll find her. I've heard this bit before, anyway." Roger glared at her as she left.

Thankful to be out of the gloomy smelting mill and away from the droning echo of Roger's voice, Marjorie shielded her eyes and looked around. Megan was clam-

bering over a pile of scree towards the opening of the
flue. Marjorie knew all about the flue, because she'd
heard Roger read her the relevant sections from the book
several times out loud. "Listen to this, darling . . ." But
the only thing she needed to know right now was that it
could be dangerous.

Built originally to extract and condense the fumes of
the smelting process and carry them far away from the
immediate area, the flue was a bricked hump about two
hundred yards long. It looked very much like a tall fac-
tory chimney that had fallen on its side and half buried
itself in the gentle slope of the hillside. Because it was
old, sections of the arched roof had collapsed here and
there, and more were liable to follow suit at any moment.
It had originally ended at a vertical chimney on the hill-
top, designed to carry the lead fumes away, but that had
long since fallen down.

Megan was happily scrambling along over the scree to
the dark entrance. Marjorie set off after her. "Megan!"
she shouted. "Come away!" Behind, she noticed that the
others had come out of the smelting mill and stood
watching a few yards away. "It's all right," Marjorie said
over her shoulder. "I'll catch up with her before she gets
inside. It's quite safe out here."

Maybe she had underestimated the six-year-old's
speed and nimbleness, she thought, as she struggled over
the rocks, trying not to trip up. But she made it. Megan
got to the verge of the flue just as Marjorie managed to
grab her shoulder.

"It's not safe, Megan," she said, sitting down to catch
her breath. "You mustn't go in there." As she looked into
the black hole, she shivered. Far up ahead, she could see
the tiny coin of light where the flue ended. Its floor was
scattered with bits of stone, most likely fallen from the
arched roof. A few yards or so in, she noticed a large,

oddly-shaped hump. It was probably a collapsed section, but something about it made her curious. It looked somehow deliberate, not quite as random as the other scatterings. She packed Megan off down the rise to join her parents and crawled into the opening.

"Where do you think you're going?" she heard Roger calling. "Marjorie! Come back!" But she ignored him. Just for a moment, the sunlight had flashed on something ahead.

It was dark inside the flue, despite the light from behind her, and she hurt her knees as she crawled over the bed of flinty stones. She tried to stand, back bent low. The place smelled dank and foisty, and she tried to keep her breathing to an absolute minimum. She remembered Roger saying that the poisonous fumes of the volatilized lead condensed on the flue walls, which boys were employed to scrape at regular intervals. What a job that would be, she thought, crawling through here day after day and scraping lead off the stone.

When she arrived about six feet away from the hump, she could still make out nothing clearly. If she edged to one side and moulded her back against the curve of the wall, some light passed her and provided a faint outline. Then Roger blocked the entrance and yelled for her to come back.

"Get out of the way," she shouted. "I can't see a bloody thing!"

Oddly enough, Roger did as she asked. A faint wash of light picked out some of the details in the heap of stones, and as soon as Marjorie saw the small hand sticking out of the pile, she screamed and started to turn. As she did so, she stumbled and kicked some small stones near the body. A cloud of flies rose out of the heap and buzzed angrily up the flue.

II

"We've had three confessions already," said Gristhorpe, as Banks took the Helmthorpe road out of Eastvale. Roger Bingham's message had been vague, and both avoided speculating whether the body of Gemma Scupham had been discovered. "One of them told us at great length exactly what he'd done with Gemma and how much he enjoyed it. I tell you, Alan, sometimes it's a bloody shame you can't lock a man up for his thoughts." He ran a hand through his unruly grey hair. "Good God, did I really say that? Shows how much this business is getting to me. Anyway, we got him for wasting police time instead. He'll do six months with any luck."

"The searchers turn up anything yet?" Banks asked.

Gristhorpe shook his head. "They're doing the area east of the estate now, past the railway tracks. We've taken on a few civilian volunteers. And we've interviewed all the known local child-molesters. Nothing there."

At Fortford, Banks turned left by the pub and passed between the Roman fort and the village green.

"Anything on the car?" Gristhorpe asked.

After his visit to Brenda Scupham the previous afternoon, Banks had caught up with his paperwork on the case, helped Susan with the house-to-house and Richmond check the garages and car-rental agencies.

"Not so far. We've got through most of the garages and agencies. Phil's still at it."

"Well, maybe it was their own car, after all," said Gristhorpe. "They've vanished into thin air, Alan. How can they do that?"

"Either very clever or very lucky, I suppose. No one on the estate was very communicative, either," he went on. "I only did a couple of streets with Susan, but she said the others were no different. And she had another chat with that Mr Carter at number sixteen. Waste of time, she said. He just wanted to talk about Dunkirk. People are scared, you know, even when we show them our warrant cards."

"I don't blame them," said Gristhorpe.

"But I reckon if it *had* happened to someone else around there, they'd speak up now."

"You never know with people, Alan. Remember the old Yorkshire saying, 'There's nowt so queer as folk.'"

Banks laughed. At the junction in Relton, he turned right. A slow-moving tractor in front pulled over to the side and gave him just enough space to squeeze by. "I've been on the phone to Belfast, too," he added. "The lads over there spent most of yesterday with Terry Garswood, Gemma's father, and they're certain he had nothing to do with it. For a start, he was on duty that day and couldn't have got away without someone noticing, and apparently he had neither the inclination nor the money to hire someone else to steal her for him."

"Well, look on the bright side," said Gristhorpe. "At least that's one less lead to follow. There it is." He pointed out of the car window. "Pull in here."

They were on Mortsett Lane, about halfway between Relton and Gratly, below the looming bulk of Tetchley Fell. Banks pulled up on the gravelled lay-by next to a Range Rover and looked at the narrow track. There was no way you could get a car up there, he thought. The stony path was only about three feet wide, and it was bordered by small boulders and chips of flint that would play havoc with tires. Ahead, he could just make out the partially collapsed roof of the smelting mill over the rise.

He had seen the place before, but from a different perspective. Looking down from the Roman road that cut diagonally across the fell, he had been impressed by the range of colour, from pale yellow to dark green, purple and grey, and by the flue hugging the hillside like a long stone tunnel. Now, as they neared the mill, all he could see was the murky opening to his left and the group of people huddled together by the mill to his right.

"Which one of you is Mr Bingham?" Gristhorpe asked, after he had introduced Banks and himself.

"I am," said a countryish type, in gear far too expensive and inappropriate for the short walk. "My wife, Marjorie, found the . . . er . . . Well, I remembered there was a phonebox back down on the road."

Gristhorpe nodded and turned to the woman. "Did you disturb anything?"

She shook her head. "No. I never touched . . . I . . . When I saw the hand I ran back. And the flies . . . Oh, my God . . . the flies . . ."

Her husband took her hand and she buried her face in his shoulder. The other couple looked on sadly, the man with a grim set to his mouth and the woman stroking her child's golden hair. Banks noticed a head over her shoulder, a sleeping baby in a backpack.

Gristhorpe turned to Banks. "Shall we?"

Banks nodded and followed him over the scree. They had to walk carefully, as many of the stones wobbled under them. Finally, they managed to scrabble to the gloomy semi-circle and peer inside. Gristhorpe brought the torch out of his pocket and shone it ahead. They could easily see the heap that Marjorie Bingham had mentioned, but couldn't pick out any details from so far away. Gristhorpe had to bend almost double to walk, which made it very difficult to negotiate a path through the rubble that littered the flue's floor. Banks, being a little shorter, found it easier. But he felt uncomfortable.

He had never liked caves; they always seemed to bring

out a latent sense of claustrophobia. Once he and Sandra had visited Ingleton and gone in the caves there. When he had to stoop and almost crawl on his belly to get under a low overhang, he had felt the weight of the mountain pressing on his back and had to struggle to keep his breathing regular. The flue wasn't as bad as that, but he could still feel the heavy darkness pushing at him from all sides.

Gristhorpe walked a few feet behind him with the torch. Its beam danced over lead-stained stones, which glistened here and there as if snails had left their slimy tracks. They went as cautiously as they could in order not to destroy any forensic evidence, but it was impossible to pick a narrow path through the rubble of the flue. Finally, they stood close enough, and Gristhorpe's torch lit on a small hand raised from a heap of rocks. They could see nothing else of the body, as it had been entirely covered by stones.

As they stood and looked at the hand, a gust of wind blew and made a low moaning sound in the flue like someone blowing over the lip of a bottle. Gristhorpe turned off the torch and they headed back for the entrance. They had probably disturbed too much already, but they had to verify that there was indeed a body on the site. So often people simply *thought* they had found a corpse, and the truth turned out to be different. Now they had to follow procedure.

First they would call the police surgeon to ascertain that the body was indeed dead. No matter how obvious it might appear, no matter even if the body is decapitated or chopped into a dozen pieces, it is not dead until a qualified doctor says it is.

Then the SOCO team would arrive and mark off the area with their white plastic tape. It might not seem necessary in such an isolated place, but the searching of a crime scene was a very serious business, and there were guidelines to follow. With Vic Manson in charge, they would take photographs and search the area around the body, looking for hairs, fibres, anything that the killer may have left behind. And then, when the photographs had been taken, the doctor would take a closer look at the body. In this case, he might move aside a few stones and look for obvious causes of death. There was nothing more that Banks and Gristhorpe could do until they at least had some information on the identity of the victim.

Banks gulped in the fresh, bright air as they emerged into daylight. He felt as if he had just made an ascent from the bottom of a deep, dark ocean with only seconds to spare before his oxygen ran out. Gristhorpe stood beside him and stretched, rubbing his lower back and grimacing.

"I'll call it in," said Banks.

Gristhorpe nodded. "Aye. And I'll have another word with this lot over here." He shook his head slowly. "Looks like we've found her."

There was nothing to do but wait after Banks had made the call over the police radio. Gristhorpe got Marjorie Bingham's story, then let the shocked group go home.

Banks leaned against the rough stone of the smelting mill and lit a cigarette as Gristhorpe walked carefully around the flue entrance looking down at the ground. It was quiet up there except for the occasional mournful call of a curlew gliding over the moorland, a cry that harmonized strangely with the deep sigh of the breeze blowing down the flue and ruffling the blades of grass on the hillside. The sky was the whitish blue of skim milk, and it set off the browns, greens and yellows of the desolate landscape. Beyond the mill, Banks could see the purple-grey cleft of a dried-up stream-bed cutting across the moorland.

Gristhorpe, kneeling to peer at the grass a few yards to the right of the flue entrance, beckoned Banks over. Banks knelt beside him and looked at the rusty smear on the grass.

"Blood?" he said.

"Looks like it. If so, maybe she was killed out here and they dragged her into the flue to hide the body."

Banks looked at the blood again. "It doesn't look like much, though, does it?" he said. "And I'd say it's smeared rather than spilled."

"Aye," said Gristhorpe, standing. "Like someone wiped off a knife or something. We'll leave it to the SOCOs."

The first to arrive was Peter Darby, the photographer. He came bounding up the track, fresh-faced, two cameras slung around his neck and a square metal case at his side. If it's Gemma Scupham in there, Banks thought, he won't look so bloody cheerful when he comes out.

Darby went to take some preliminary photographs, starting with the stained grass, on Gristhorpe's suggestion, then the flue entrance, then carefully making his way inside. Banks could see the bulbs flash in the black hole as Darby took his pictures. When he'd finished in the flue, he took more photographs in and around the smelting mill.

About half an hour after Peter Darby, Dr Glendenning came huffing and puffing up the path.

"At least I didn't need a bloody truss to get here this time," he said, referring to the occasion when they had all been winched up the side of Rawley Force to get to a body in a hanging valley. He pointed towards the flue. "In there, you said?"

Gristhorpe nodded.

"Hmphh. Why the bloody hell do you keep on finding

bodies in awkward places, eh? I'm not getting any younger, you know. It's not even my job. You could get a bloody GP to pronounce the body dead at the scene."

Banks shrugged. "Sorry." Glendenning was a Home Office pathologist, one of the best in the country, and both Banks and Gristhorpe knew he would be offended if they didn't call him to the scene first.

"Aye, well . . ." He turned towards the entrance.

They accompanied Glendenning as he picked his way over the scree, complaining all the way, and ducked to enter the flue. Banks held the torch this time. It didn't provide much light, but the SOCOs had been instructed to bring bottled-gas lamps as it would be impossible to get a van with a generator up the narrow track.

Glendenning knelt for a while, sniffing the air and glancing around the inside of the flue, then he touched the small hand and moved it, muttering to himself. Next he took out a mercury thermometer and held it close to the body, measuring the air temperature.

The entrance of the flue darkened and someone called out. It was Vic Manson, fingerprint expert and leader of the SOCO team. He came up the passage with a gas-lamp and soon the place was full of light. It cast eerie shadows on the slimy stone walls and gave an unreal sheen to the heap of the stones on the ground. Manson called back to one of his assistants and asked him to bring up some large plastic bags.

Then everyone stood silent, breath held, as the men started to lift the stones and place them in the bags for later forensic investigation. A few spiders scurried away and a couple of obstinate flies buzzed the men angrily then zigzagged off.

Banks leaned against the wall, his back bent into its curve. One stone, two, three. . . . Then a whole arm became visible.

Banks and Gristhorpe moved forward. They crouched over and looked at the small hand, then both saw the man's wristwatch and frayed sleeve of a grey bomber-jacket. "It's not her," Gristhorpe whispered. "Jesus Christ, it's not Gemma Scupham."

Banks felt the relief, too. He had always clung to a vague hope that Gemma might still be alive, but the discovery of the body had seemed to wreck all that. Nobody else in the dale had been reported missing. And now, as Manson and his men picked stone after stone away, they looked down at what was obviously the body of a young man, complete with moustache. A young man with unusually small hands. But, Banks asked himself, if it isn't Gemma Scupham, then who the hell is it?

III

Jenny darted into the Eastvale Regional Headquarters at two o'clock, just in time for her appointment with Banks. She always seemed to be rushing these days, she thought, as if she were a watch a few minutes slow always trying to catch up. She wasn't even really late this time.

"Miss Fuller?"

Jenny walked over to the front desk. "Yes?"

"Message from Detective Superintendent Gristhorpe, miss. Says he's on his way. You can wait in his office if you wish."

Jenny frowned. "But I thought I was to see Alan—Chief Inspector Banks?"

"He's at the scene."

"What scene?"

"It looks like a murder scene. I'm sorry I can't say any more, miss. We don't really know anything yet."

"That's all right," Jenny said. "I'll wait."

"Very well. The superintendent's office—"

"I know where it is, thanks."

Jenny poured herself some coffee from the machine at the bottom of the stairs then went up to Gristhorpe's office. She had been there before, but never alone. It was larger than Alan's, and much better appointed. She had heard that rank determines the level of luxury in policemen's offices, but she also knew that the department itself was hardly likely to supply such things as the large teak desk, or the matching bookcases that covered one wall. The cream and burgundy patterned carpet, perhaps—it was hardly an expensive one, Jenny noticed—but not the shaded desk lamp and the books that lined the shelves.

She glanced over the titles. They were mostly works of criminology and law—the essential *Archbold's Criminal Pleading, Evidence & Practice* and Glaister's *Medical Jurisprudence and Toxicology* in addition to several other technical and forensic texts—but there were also books on history, fishing, cricket, a few novels and Sir Arthur Quiller-Couch's edition of *The Oxford Book of English Verse*. What surprised Jenny most was the number of mystery paperbacks: about four feet of them, mostly Margery Allingham, Ngaio Marsh, Edmund Crispin and Michael Innes.

"That's just the overflow," a voice said behind her, making her jump. "The rest are at home."

"I didn't hear you come in," Jenny said, putting her hand to her chest. "You startled me."

"We coppers are a light-footed lot," Gristhorpe said, with a twinkle in his baby-blue eyes. "Have to be to catch the villains. Sit down."

Jenny sat. "This murder, I couldn't help thinking . . . It's not . . . ?"

"No, it's not, thank God. It's bad enough, though. We don't know who the victim is yet. I left Alan at the scene. I decided to stick with the Gemma Scupham case and let him handle the murder."

Jenny had never felt entirely at ease with Superintendent Gristhorpe, but she didn't know why. He seemed very much his own man—self-contained, strong, determined—and he projected a solid, comforting presence. But something made her feel awkward. Perhaps, she speculated, it was the underlying sense of isolation she sensed, the fortress he seemed to have built around his feelings. She knew about his wife's death from cancer several years ago, and guessed that perhaps a part of him had died with her. Susan Gay, she remembered, had said that she also felt uncomfortable with him, yet he had a reputation as a kind and compassionate man.

His physical presence was difficult to ignore, too. He was a big man—bulky, but not fat—with bushy eyebrows and an unruly thatch of grey hair. With his reddish, pock-marked complexion and the slightly hooked nose, he was very much the dalesman, she thought, if indeed there was such a creature, weathered and moulded by the landscape.

"I did a bit of preliminary research last night," Jenny began. "I *can* probably give you a capsule version of the paedophile types."

Gristhorpe nodded. As she spoke, Jenny somehow felt that he probably knew more than she did about the subject. After all, some of his books dealt with criminal psychology and forensic psychiatry, and he was reputed to be well read. But she didn't feel he was simply being polite when he let her speak. No, he was listening all right, listening for something he might not have come across or thought of himself. Watching her carefully with those deceptively innocent eyes.

She balanced her black-rimmed reading-glasses on her nose and took her notes out of her briefcase. "Basically, there are four types of paedophile," she began. "And so far it doesn't seem like your couple fits any. The first kind is someone who hasn't really been able to establish satisfactory relationships with his peers. It's the most common type, and he only feels sexually comfortable with children. He usually *knows* his victim, maybe a family friend, or even a relation."

Gristhorpe nodded. "What about age, roughly?"

"Average age is about forty."

"Hmm. Go on."

"The second type is someone who seems to develop normally but finds it increasingly difficult to adjust to adult life—work, marriage, et cetera. Feels inadequate, often turns to drink. Usually the marriage, if there is one, breaks down. With this type, something sets things in motion. He reaches a kind of breaking-point. Maybe his wife or girlfriend is having an affair, intensifying his feelings of inadequacy. This kind doesn't usually know his victim. It may be someone he sees passing by in a car or something. Again, not much like the situation you described at Brenda Scupham's."

"No," agreed Gristhorpe. "But we've got to keep an open mind at this point."

"And I think we can dismiss the third type, too," Jenny went on. "This is someone who generally had his formative sexual experiences with young boys in an institution of some kind."

"Ah," said Gristhorpe. "Public school?"

Jenny looked up at him and smiled. "I suppose that would qualify." She turned back to her notes. "Anyway, this type is generally a homosexual paedophile, the type that cruises the streets for victims or uses male prostitutes."

"And the last?"

"The wild card," Jenny said. "The psychopathic pae-dophile. It's hard to pin this type down. He's in search of new sexual thrills, and pain and fear are generally in-volved. He'll hurt his victims, introduce sharp objects into the sexual organs, that kind of thing. The more ag-gressive he gets, the more excited he becomes. A person like this usually has a history of anti-social behaviour."

Gristhorpe held the bridge of his nose and grunted.

"I'm sorry I can't really be of any more help yet," Jenny said, "but I'm working on it. The really odd thing, as I told Alan, is that there were two of them, a man and a woman. I want to look a bit further into that aspect."

Gristhorpe nodded. "Go ahead. And please don't un-derestimate your usefulness."

Jenny smiled at him and shuffled her notes back into the briefcase.

"This stuff the newspapers were on about," Gristhorpe went on, "organized gangs of paedophiles, what do you think of that?"

Jenny shook her head. "It doesn't figure. Paedophiles are like other sexual deviants, essentially loners, solo op-erators. And most of the allegations of ritual abuse turned out to be social workers' fantasies. Of course, when you get abuse in families, people close ranks. They might look like organized gangs, but they're not really. Paedophiles simply aren't the types to form clubs, except . . ."

"Except what?"

"I was thinking of kiddie porn, child prostitution and the like. It's around, it happens, there's no denying it, and that takes a bit of organization."

"Videos, magazines?"

"Yes. Even snuff films."

"We're doing our best," Gristhorpe said. "I've been in

touch with the paedophile squad. Those rings are hard to penetrate, but if anything concerning Gemma turns up, believe me, we'll know about it."

Jenny stood up. "I'll do a bit more research."

"Thanks." Gristhorpe walked over to open the door for her.

Jenny dashed back to her car, got in and turned her key in the ignition. Suddenly, she paused. She couldn't remember where she was supposed to go or why she was in such a hurry. She checked her appointment book and then racked her brains to see if she had forgotten anything. No. The truth was, she had nowhere to go and no reason at all to hurry.

IV

Banks breathed deeply, grateful for the fresh air outside the flue. Claustrophobia was bad enough, but what he had just seen made it even worse.

After Gristhorpe had gone to meet Jenny, the SOCOs had slowly and carefully removed all the stones from the body of a man in his mid- to late-twenties. When they had finished, Dr Glendenning bent forward to see what he could find out. First, he opened the bomber-jacket and cursed when he had to stop the tangle of greyish intestines from spilling out of the man's shirt. A couple more flies finally gave up the ghost and crawled out from under the tubing and took off indignantly. The wind moaned down the flue. Quickly, Banks had searched the dead man's pockets: all empty.

Banks lit a cigarette; fresh air wasn't enough to get the taste of the flue and of death out of his mouth. The smell was difficult to pin down. Sickly, sweet, with a slight metallic edge, it always seemed to linger around him like an aura for days after attending the scene of a murder.

Glendenning had been crouched in the flue alone for over half an hour now, and the SOCOs were still going over the ground inside the taped-off area: every blade of glass, every stone.

Banks wandered into the smelting mill and looked at the ruins of the furnace and the ore hearth while he waited, trying to put the first shocking glimpse of those spilled intestines out of his mind. He had seen the same thing once before, back in London, and it wasn't something even the most hardened policeman forgot easily. He stared at the dullish brown patch in the corner, marked off by the SOCOs as blood. The murder, they said, had probably taken place in the mill.

At last, Glendenning emerged from the flue, red in the face. He stood upright and dusted his jacket where it had come into contact with the stones. A cigarette dangled from his mouth.

"I suppose you want to know it all right away, don't you?" he said to Banks, sitting on a boulder outside the smelting mill. "Time of death, cause of death, what he had for breakfast?"

Banks grinned. "As much as you can tell me."

"Aye, well, that might be a bit more than usual in this case. Given the temperature, I'd say rigor mortis went basically according to the norm. It was just after two o'clock when I got the chance to have a really good look at him. Allowing, say, two to three hours for rigor to start, then about ten or twelve to spread, I'd say he was killed sometime after dark last night, but not much later than ten o'clock. His body temperature confirms it, too. Is that good enough for you?"

Banks said it was, thank you very much, doctor, and mentioned the blood in the smelting mill.

"You're probably right about that," Glendenning said.

"I'll check post-mortem lividity later when I get him on the table, but as far as I could tell there was no blood around the body, and there would be, given a wound like that."

"What about cause of death?"

"That's not difficult. Looks like he was gutted. You saw that for yourself." Glendenning lit a new cigarette from the stub of his old one. "It's an especially vicious crime," he went on. "In the first place, to do something like that you have to get very close."

"Would it take a lot of strength?"

"Aye, a fair bit to drag the knife up when it's stuck so deeply in. But not a superman. Given a sharp enough knife. What are you getting at? Man or woman?"

"Something like that."

"You know how I hate guesswork, laddie, but I'd go for a moderately strong man or an exceptionally strong woman."

"Thanks. First we'll check all the female bodybuilders in Yorkshire. Left-handed or right?"

"I should be able to tell you later when I get a good look at the entry point and the direction of the slit."

"What about the weapon?"

"Again, you'll have to wait. All I can say now is it looks like a typical upthrust knife wound. Have you made arrangements for the removal?"

Banks nodded.

"Good. I'll get to it as soon as I can." Glendenning stood up and headed down the track to his car. Banks looked at his watch: almost three o'clock and he hadn't had lunch yet. Maybe an hour or so more up here and he'd be able to leave the scene for a local constable to guard. He called Vic Manson over.

"Any sign of the murder weapon?"

"Not so far. I don't think it's around here. The lads

have almost finished the third grid search, and they'd
have found it by now."

Banks walked back over to the smelting mill and
leaned against the wall watching the men examine the
scree outside the flue entrance. "A particularly vicious
crime," Dr Glendenning had said. Indeed it was. It was
hard to believe, thought Banks, that in such beautiful
countryside on such a fine autumn evening, one human
being had got so close to another that he could watch,
and perhaps even savour, the look in his victim's eyes as
he thrust a sharp knife in his groin and slowly dragged it
up through the stomach to the chest.

V

Brenda Scupham lay alone in bed that night. Les was out
at the pub. Not that she really cared. These days he was
practically worse than useless. He mostly kept out of her
way, and that suited her fine. The only thing was, she
didn't really want to be alone tonight. A nice warm body
to love her and hold her would help take her mind off the
bad things she couldn't seem to stop herself from feeling.

She hadn't wanted Gemma, it was true. But things like
that happened. She had done her best. At first, there always seemed to be so much to do: changing nappies,
feeding, scraping and saving for new clothes. And the
sleepless nights she had listened to Gemma cry from her
cot, leaving her till she cried herself to sleep because her
own mother had said you shouldn't make a habit of being at a baby's beck and call. Well, she should know all
about that, Brenda thought.

Even as she got older, Gemma had got in the way, too.
Every time Brenda had a man over, she had to explain
the child. Nobody stayed with her when they found out

she had a kid. One night was the best she could expect from most, then a hasty exit, usually well before dawn, and Gemma there wailing away.

Brenda understood women who had beaten or killed their children. It happened all the time. They could drive you to that. One night, she remembered with shame, she had wrapped three-month-old Gemma in blankets and left her on the steps of the Catholic church. She hadn't been home five minutes before guilt sent her racing back to reclaim the bundle. Luckily, nobody else had got there first.

But no matter what those policemen tried to say, she had never abused Gemma. Some mothers sat their children on the elements of electric cookers, poured boiling water on them, locked them in the cellar without food or drink until they died of dehydration. Brenda would never have done anything like that. She put up with Gemma and took her pleasure when she could. True, she had left the child alone for visits to the pub. But nothing had ever happened to her. Also true, she never had much time to spend with her, what with the odd bit of waitressing she did on the sly to eke out her social. Meals had occasionally been forgotten, old clothes left unwashed too long. Gemma herself, like most kids, was not overfond of bath-time, and she had never complained about going without a bath for a couple of weeks.

What upset Brenda most as she lay there alone in the dark was accepting that she had never really *liked* her child. Oh, she had got used to her, all right, but there was something secretive and isolated about Gemma, something alien that Brenda felt she could never reach. And there was something creepy about the way she skulked around the place. Many a time Brenda had felt Gemma's accusing, woebegone eyes on her. Even now, alone in the dark, she could feel Gemma's eyes looking at her in that way. Still, you didn't *choose* your child, no more than she chose to be born. She wasn't made to order.

But now Gemma was gone, Brenda felt guilty for feeling relieved when Miss Peterson and Mr Brown took her away. Why did it have to be so complicated? Why couldn't they have been real social workers like they said they were? Then she wouldn't have to feel so guilty for being relieved. Now she couldn't even bear to think about what they might have done to Gemma. She shivered. Gemma must be dead. Brenda only hoped it had happened quickly and painlessly and that soon the police would find out everything and leave her alone to get her grieving done.

Again she replayed what she could remember of the social workers' visit. Maybe she had been a fool for believing them, but they *had* looked so real, and they *had* been so convincing. She knew she had neglected Gemma and that she was wrong to do so, however much she couldn't help herself. She knew she was guilty, especially after what happened the week before. But they surely couldn't have known about that? No, they were right. She had to let them take the child. She found herself hoping, after the door closed, that they would decide to keep her or find her a good home. It would be best for everyone that way.

And then there was Les. She remembered defending him to the police that morning, saying he wasn't much but he was better than nothing. She wasn't even sure that was true any longer. Mostly, she'd been thinking of sex. He used to do it three, four times a night, if he hadn't had a skinful of ale, and she couldn't get enough of him. He had made her laugh, too. But lately all the passion had gone. It happened, she knew, and you became nothing more than a maid, your home no more than a hotel room.

She turned on her side and put her hand between her

legs, then began gently stroking herself with her fingers.
It would help her forget, she thought, rubbing harder.
Forget her foolishness, forget her guilt, forget Gemma.
Gemma, precious stone, name stolen from an old school-
friend whose serene beauty she had always envied.

Just before the climax flooded her, an image of
Gemma going out of the door with Mr Brown and Miss
Peterson appeared in her mind's eye. As she came, it re-
ceded, like someone waving goodbye from a train window.

4

I

At ten past eleven on Saturday morning, Banks stood at his office window, coffee in hand, and looked down on the market square. It was another beautiful day—the fifth in a row—with a pale blue sky and high wispy clouds. It was also four days since Gemma Scupham's abduction.

Down in the cobbled square, the market was in full swing. Tourists and locals browsed the stalls, where vendors dealt in everything from clothes and used books to car accessories and small electrical gadgets. As Banks watched them unload new stock from the vans, he speculated how much of the goods were stolen, fallen off the back of a lorry. Most of the things for sale were legitimate, of course—over-production or sub-standard stuff rejected by a company's quality control and sold at slightly above cost—but a busy market was an ideal place for getting rid of hot property.

There would be nothing from the Fletcher's warehouse job, though; televisions and stereos attracted too much attention at outdoor markets. Mostly, they would be sold by word of mouth, through pubs and video retailers.

Banks thought again about how smooth the operation

had been. The burglars had cut through a chain-link fence, drugged a guard dog, and disabled the alarm system. They had then loaded a van up with electrical goods, taken off into the night and never been seen since. It would have taken at least three men, he speculated, and Les Poole was probably one of them. But there were far more serious things to think about now. At least Poole was under surveillance, and any step he made out of line would soon come to Banks's attention.

The traffic along Market Street slowed almost to a standstill as yet more tourists poured into town. Because it was market day, parking was a problem. Drivers would spend an extra half-hour cruising around the narrow streets looking for a parking space. It would be a busy day for the traffic police.

Banks opened the window a couple of inches. He could hear the honking horns and the babble of voices down in the square, and the smell of fresh bread drifted up from the bakery on Market Street, mingled with exhaust fumes.

At their morning conference, Gristhorpe had assigned Banks and DC Susan Gay to the lead-mine murder; Gristhorpe himself, along with DS Richmond, would pursue the Gemma Scupham investigation, with Jenny Fuller acting as consultant. With each day that went by, the pressure increased. Parents were scared; they were keeping their children home from school. Ever since Gemma had disappeared, police forces county-wide had been knocking on doors and conducting searches of wasteland and out-of-the-way areas. The surprising thing was that nothing had come to light so far. The way it seemed, Gemma had disappeared from the face of the earth. Despite his reassignment, Banks knew he would have to keep up to date on the case. He couldn't forget Gemma Scupham that easily.

For a moment, he found himself wondering if the two cases could be connected in some way. It was rare that two serious crimes should happen in Swainsdale at about the same time. Could it be more than mere coincidence? He didn't see how, but it was something worth bearing in mind.

His first task was to identify the body they had found. Certainly a photograph could be published; clothing labels sometimes helped; then there were medical features—an operation scar, birthmark—and dental charts. It would be easy enough to track down such information if the man were local, but practically impossible if he were a stranger to the area. Banks had already sent DC Gay to make enquiries in Gratly and Relton, the nearest villages to the mine, but he didn't expect much to come of that. At best, someone might have seen a car heading towards the mine.

A red van had got itself wedged into the junction of Market Street and the square, just in front of the Queen's Arms, and irate motorists started honking. The van's owner kept on unloading boxes of tights and women's underwear, oblivious to the angry tourists. One man got out and headed towards him.

Banks turned away from the window and went over the lead-mine scene in his mind. The victim had probably been murdered in the smelting mill, an out-of-the-way place. His pockets had been emptied and his body had been hidden in the flue, which few people ever entered due to the danger of falling stones. Safe to assume, Banks thought, that the killer didn't want the body found for a while. That made sense, as most leads in an investigation occur in the first twenty-four hours. But the body *had* been found much sooner than the killer expected, and that might just give Banks an edge.

Just as Banks was about to leave his office in search of

more coffee, the phone rang. It was Vic Manson from the forensic lab near Wetherby.

"You've been quick," Banks said. "What have you got?"

"Lucky. You want to know who he is?"

"You're sure?"

"Uh-huh. I'd like to claim brilliant deduction, but it was routine."

"Fingerprints?" Banks guessed. It was the first thing they would check, and while most people's prints weren't on file anywhere, a lot were. Another break.

"Got it. Seems he did a stretch in Armley Jail. Tried to con an old lady out of her life's savings, but she turned out to be smarter than him. Name's Carl Johnson. He's from Bradford, but he's been living in your neck of the woods for a year or so. Flat 6, 59 Calvin Street."

Banks knew the street. It was in the north-eastern part of Eastvale, where a few of the large old houses had been converted into cheap flats.

"You can get your man to pull his file from the computer," Manson said.

"Thanks, Vic. I'll do that. Keep at it."

"Have I any bloody choice? We're snowed under. Anyway, I'll get back to you soon as we find out any more."

Banks hurried over to Richmond's office. Richmond sat over his keyboard, tapping away, and Banks waited until he reached a point when he could pause. Then he explained what Vic Manson had said.

"No problem," said Richmond. "Just let me finish entering this report in the database and I'll get you a printout."

"Thanks, Phil."

Banks grabbed a coffee and went back to his office to wait. The market square was teeming with people now, lingering at stalls, feeling the goods, listening to the vendors' pitches, watching the man who juggled plates as if he were a circus performer.

Carl Johnson. The name didn't ring a bell. If he had been in London, Banks would have got out on the street to question informers and meet with undercover officers. Someone would have heard a whisper, a boast, a rumour. But in Eastvale no real criminal underbelly existed. And he certainly knew of no one capable of killing in the way Carl Johnson had been killed. There were low-lifes like Les Poole, of course, but Poole was a coward at heart, and whatever he was, he wasn't a murderer. Still, it might be worth mentioning Johnson's name to him, just to see the reaction.

Had the killer not known about Johnson's record, that he would be easy to identify? Certainly whoever it was had gone to great lengths to hide the body, but he hadn't tried to destroy the fingerprints, as some killers did. Perhaps he was squeamish—unlikely, given the way he'd killed Johnson—or he was careless. Careless or cocky. Whatever the reason, Banks at least had something to go on: Flat 6, 59 Calvin Street. That was the place to start.

II

If Gristhorpe had expected inverted crosses, black candles, pentagrams and ceremonial robes, he couldn't have been more mistaken. Melville Westman's Helmthorpe cottage was as ordinary as could be: teal wallpaper with white curlicue patterns, beige three-piece suite, television, music centre. Sunlight poured through the windows past the white lace curtains and gave the place a bright, airy feel. The only clues to Westman's interests were to be found in the bookcase: Eliphas Levi's *Le Dogme et le*

Rituel de la Haute Magie, Mathers's translation of *The Key of Solomon*, Crowley's *Magick in Theory and Practice, Malleus Maleficarum* and a few other books on astrology, Cabbala, the tarot, witchcraft and ritual magic. In addition, a sampler over the fireplace bore the motto, "Do what thou wilt shall be the whole of the law," in the same kind of embroidery one would expect to find such ancient saws as, "A house is built of bricks; a home is built on love."

Similarly, if Gristhorpe had expected a bedraggled, wild-eyed Charles Manson look-alike, he would have been disappointed. Westman was a dapper, middle-aged man with sparse mousy hair, dressed in a grey V-neck pullover over a white shirt, wearing equally grey pants with sharp creases. He was a short, portly man, but he had presence. It was partly in the slightly flared nostrils that gave his face a constant expression of arrogant sneering, and partly in the controlled intensity of his cold eyes.

"It took you long enough," he said to Gristhorpe, gesturing towards an armchair.

Gristhorpe sat down. "What do you mean?"

"Oh, come on, Superintendent! Let's not play games. The girl, the missing girl. I read about it in the paper."

"What's that got to do with you?"

Westman sat opposite Gristhorpe and leaned forward in his chair, linking his hands on his lap. "Nothing, of course. But you have to ask, don't you?"

"And?"

Westman smiled and shook his head slowly. "And nothing."

"Mr Westman," Gristhorpe said. "In cases like this we have to consider every possibility. If you know anything about the child's disappearance, it'd be best if you told me."

"I told you. I know nothing. Why should I?"

"We both know about your involvement in witchcraft and Satanism. Don't be naïve."

"Involvement? Witchcraft? Satanism? Superintendent, just because I practise a different religion from you, don't assume I'm some kind of monster. I'm not a Satanist, and I'm not a witch, either. Most people you would call witches are silly dabblers who appropriate the old ways and practices as an excuse for sexual excess. Ex-hippies and New Agers."

"Whatever you call yourself," Gristhorpe said, "there's a history of people like you being involved in sacrifice."

"Sacrificial virgins? Really! Again, you're confusing me with the psychopathic Satanists who use the ancient ways as an excuse. People who read too much Aleister Crowley—he *did* exaggerate, you know—and found he appealed to their sick fantasies. You find a few bloody pentagrams daubed on a wall and a bit of gibberish in Latin and you think you're dealing with the real thing. You're not."

Gristhorpe pointed towards the bookcase. "I notice you have a few Aleister Crowley books yourself. Does that make you a psychopathic Satanist?"

Westman's lips curled at the edges like an old sandwich. "Crowley has things to teach to those who understand. Do you know the purpose of magic, Superintendent?"

"Power," said Gristhorpe.

Westman sniffed. "Typical. It comes from the same root as 'magi,' wise man. The purpose of the 'Great Work' is to become God, and you dismiss it as mere human hunger for power."

Gristhorpe sighed and tried to hold onto his temper. The man's sanctimonious tone was grating on his nerves. "Mr Westman, I don't really give a damn what illusions you cling to. That's not the purpose—"

"Illusions! Superintendent, believe me, the work of the magician is far from an illusion. It's a matter of will, courage, intense study of—"

"I don't want a lecture, Mr Westman. I know enough about the subject already. I know, for example, that sacrifice is important because you regard living creatures as storehouses of energy. When you kill them, when you spill their blood, you release this energy and concentrate it. I also know it's as much a matter of blood-lust, of murderous frenzy, as it is of any practical purpose. The incense, incantations, and finally the gushing of blood. It's orgasmic, a sexual kick."

Westman waved his hand. "I can see you know nothing, Superintendent. Again, you're talking about the deviants, the charlatans."

"And," Gristhorpe went on, "a human sacrifice is the most effective of all, gives you the biggest kick. Especially the sacrifice of a pure child."

Westman pursed his lips and put his forefinger to them. He stared at Gristhorpe for a few moments, then shrugged and sat back in the chair. "Human sacrifice is rare in true magic," he said. "It's difficult enough for those who practise such arts to simply exist in such a narrow-minded world as the one we inhabit; we are hardly likely to make things worse by kidnapping children and slaughtering them."

"So you know nothing at all about Gemma Scupham?"

"Only what I read in the newspapers. And though I expected a visit, given my notoriety, as far as I can gather, I bear no resemblance to either of the suspects."

"True, but that doesn't mean you're not associated with them in some way. A lot of people don't do their own dirty work."

"Insults, is it now? Well, maybe you're right. Maybe I

prepared a couple of zombies to do the job. Do you remember the Rochdale scandal, Superintendent? Ten children were taken from their parents and put into care by child-workers who believed a few wild tales about ritualistic, satanic abuse. And what happened? They were sent home. There was no evidence. Children have overactive imaginations. If some six-year-old tells you he's eaten a cat, the odds are it was a chocolate one, or some kind of animal-shaped breakfast cereal."

"I know about the Rochdale affair," Gristhorpe said, "and about what happened in Nottingham. It didn't come out at the trial, but we found out later there *was* ritual abuse involved. These kids were tortured, starved, humiliated and used as sex objects."

"But they weren't sacrificed to the devil, or any such nonsense. All these tales about organized satanic abuse were discredited. Most such abuse takes place in extended families, between family members."

"That's not the issue." Gristhorpe leaned forward. "Gemma Scupham was abducted from her home and we can't find hide nor hair of her. If she'd been killed and dumped somewhere in the dale, we'd most likely have found her now. We haven't. What does that imply to you?"

"I don't know. You're supposed to be the detective. You tell me."

"One of two things. Either she's dead and her body has been very well hidden, perhaps somewhere other than Swainsdale, or someone is keeping her alive somewhere, maybe for a part she's due to play in some ritual. That's why I'm here talking to you. And, believe me, I'd rather be elsewhere."

"I applaud your deductive abilities, Superintendent, but you'd be making better use of your time if you *were* somewhere else. I know nothing."

Gristhorpe looked around the room. "What if I were to arrange for a search warrant?"

Westman stood up. "You don't need to do that. Be my guest."

Gristhorpe did. It was a small cottage, and it didn't take him long. Upstairs was a bedroom and an office, where a computer hummed on a messy desk and a printer pushed out sheets of paper.

"I'm a systems consultant," Westman said. "It means I get to do most of my work at home. It also means I have to work weekends sometimes, too."

Gristhorpe nodded. They went downstairs and looked at the kitchen, then into the cellar, a dark, chill place with whitewashed walls, mostly used for storing coal and the various bits and pieces of an old Vincent motorcycle.

"A hobby," Westman explained. "Are you satisfied now?"

They climbed back up to the living-room. "Do you know of anyone who might be involved?" Gristhorpe asked. "For any reason?"

Westman raised his eyebrows. "Asking for help now, are you? I'd be happy to oblige, but I told you, I've no idea. I do not, have not, and never will sacrifice children, or any other human beings for that matter. I told you, I'm not a dabbler. It would take too long to explain to you about my beliefs, and you'd probably be too prejudiced to understand anyway. It's certainly not tabloid Satanism."

"But you must know people who do know about these things. These dabblers you mentioned—these Satanists, thrill-seekers—any of them around these parts?"

"Not that I know of. There are a couple of witches' covens, but they're pretty tame, and you probably know about them, anyway. Amateurs. You'd never find them sacrificing a fly, let alone a child. Their get-togethers are a bit like a church social. No, Superintendent, I think you're on the wrong track."

Gristhorpe stood up. "Maybe, Mr Westman, but I like to keep an open mind. Don't trouble yourself, I'll see myself out."

In the street, Gristhorpe breathed in the fresh air. He didn't know why he felt such distaste for Westman and his kind. After all, he had read a fair bit about the black arts and he knew there was nothing necessarily *evil* about an interest in magic. Perhaps it was his Methodist background. He had given up going to chapel years ago, but there was still an innate sense that such desire for God-like power, whether mumbo-jumbo or not, was a sacrilege, a blasphemy against reason and common sense as much as against God.

The limestone face of Crow Scar towered over the village to the north. Today it was bright in the autumn sun, and the higher pastures were already turning pale brown. The dry-stone walls that criss-crossed the daleside shone like the ribs and vertebrae of a giant poking through the earth.

Gristhorpe walked along High Street, busy with tourists window-shopping for walking-gear and local crafts, or ramblers sitting at the wooden picnic-tables outside The Dog and Gun and The Hare and Hounds, sipping pints of Theakston's and nibbling at sandwiches. It was tempting to join them, but Gristhorpe decided to wait until he got back to Eastvale before eating a late lunch.

He turned at the fork and headed for the Helmthorpe station. It was a converted terrace house, built of local greyish limestone, and was staffed by a sergeant and two constables. Constable Weaver sat pecking away at an old manual typewriter when Gristhorpe entered. Gristhorpe remembered him from the Steadman case, the first murder they'd had in Helmthorpe in a hundred years.

Weaver looked up, blushed and walked over. "I can't seem to get used to the computer, sir," he said. "Keep giving the wrong commands."

Gristhorpe smiled. "I know what you mean. I can't help but feel like an incompetent idiot when I have to deal with the things. Still, they have their uses. Look lad, do you know Melville Westman?"

"Yes."

"Anything on him? I'm not asking for anything that might be on record, you understand, just rumours, suspicions?"

Weaver shook his head. "Not really, sir. I mean, we know he's one of those black magicians, but he's not stepped out of line in any real way. Can't say I believe in it myself, curses and whatnot."

"What about the sheep?"

"Aye, well we suspected him, all right—still do, for that matter—but there was nowt we could prove. Why, sir?"

"It might be nothing, but I'd like you to keep a discreet eye on him, if you can. And keep your ears open for gossip."

"Is this about the young lass, sir?"

"Yes. But for Christ's sake don't spread it around."

Weaver looked hurt. "Of course not, sir."

"Good. Let me know if you see or hear anything out of the ordinary, and try not to let him know you're watching. He's a canny bugger, that one is."

"Yes, sir."

Gristhorpe walked outside and headed for his car. Westman was probably telling the truth, he thought, but there had been so many revelations about the links between child abuse and satanic rituals in the past few years that he had to check out the possibility. It couldn't happen here, everyone said. But it did. His stomach rumbled. Definitely time to head back to Eastvale.

III

Banks believed you could tell a lot about people from their homes. It wasn't infallible. For example, a normally fastidious person might let things go under pressure. On the whole, though, it had always worked well for him.

When he stood in the tiny living-room of Flat 6, 59 Calvin Road and tried to figure out Carl Johnson, he found very little to go on. First, he sniffed the air: stale, dusty, with an underlying hint of rotting vegetables. It was just what one would expect of a place unoccupied for a couple of days. Then he listened. He didn't expect to hear ghosts or echoes of the dead man's thoughts, but homes had their voices, too, that sometimes whispered of past evils or remembered laughter. Nothing. His immediate impression was of a temporary resting-place, somewhere to eat and sleep. What furniture there was looked second-hand, OXFAM or jumble-sale stuff. The carpet was worn so thin he could hardly make out its pattern. There were no photos or prints on the cream painted walls; nor was there any evidence of books, not even a tattered bestseller.

The kitchen was simply a curtained-off portion of the room, with a hotplate, toaster and a little storage space. Banks found a couple of dirty pans and plates in the sink. The cupboards offered nothing more than tea-bags, instant coffee, sugar, margarine and a few cans of baked beans. There was no refrigerator, and a curdled bottle of milk stood by the sink next to some mouldy white bread and three cans of McEwan's lager.

The bedroom, painted the same drab cream as the

living-room, was furnished with a single bed, the covers in disarray, pillow greasy and stained with sweat or hair-cream. Discarded clothes lay in an untidy heap on the floor. The dresser held socks and underwear, and apart from a couple of checked shirts, sneakers, one pair of Hush Puppies, jeans and a blouson jacket, there was little else in the closet. Banks could spot no evidence of Johnson having shared his flat or bed with anyone.

Banks had never seen a place that told so little about its occupier. Of course, that in itself indicated a number of things: Johnson clearly didn't care about a neat, clean, permanent home; he wasn't sentimental about posses-sions or interested in art and literature. But these were all negatives. What *did* he care about? There was no indica-tion. He didn't even seem to own a television or a radio. What did a man do, coming home to such surroundings? What did he think about as he sat in the creaky winged armchair with the threadbare arms and guzzled his baked beans on toast? Did he spend every evening out? At the pub? With a girlfriend?

From what Banks knew of his criminal record, Carl Johnson was thirty years old and, after a bit of trouble over "Paki-bashing" and soccer hooliganism in Bradford as a lad, he had spent three years of his adult life in prison for attempted fraud. It wasn't a distinguished life, and it seemed to have left nothing of distinction to pos-terity.

Banks felt oppressed by the place. He levered open a window and let some fresh air in. He could hear a baby crying in a room across the street.

Next, he had to do a more thorough search. He had found no letters, no passport, no bills, not even a birth certificate. Surely nobody could live a life so free of bu-reaucracy in this day and age? Banks searched under the sofa cushions, under the mattress, over the tops of the doors, deep in the back of the kitchen and bedroom cupboards. Nothing. There aren't many hiding places in a flat, as he had discovered in his days on the drug squad, and most of them are well known to the police.

Carl Johnson's flat was no exception. Banks found the thick legal-sized envelope taped to the underside of the cistern lid—a fairly obvious place—and took it into the front room. He had been careful to handle only the edges. Now he placed it on the card table by the window and slit a corner with his penknife to see what was inside. Twenty-pound notes. A lot of them, by the looks of it. Using the knife, he tried to peel each one at a time back and add it up. It was too awkward, and he kept losing his place. Patience. He took an evidence bag from his pocket, dropped the money in and took one last look around the room.

The whole place had a smell of petty greed about it, but petty criminals of Johnson's kind didn't usually end up gutted like a fish in old lead mines. What was different about Johnson? What had he been up to? Blackmail? Banks could read nothing more from the flat, so he locked up and left.

Across the hallway, he noticed a head peeping out of Flat 4 and walked over. The head retreated and its owner tried to close the door, but Banks got a foot in.

"I didn't see anything, honest, mister," the woman said. She was about twenty-five, with straight red hair and a pasty, freckled complexion.

"What do you mean?"

"I didn't see you. You weren't here. I've got nothing. Please—"

Banks took out his warrant card. The woman put her hand to her heart. "Thank God," she said. "You just never know what might happen these days, the things you read in the papers."

"True," Banks agreed. "Why were you watching?"

"I heard you in there, that's all. It's been quiet for a while."

"How long?"

"I'm not sure. Two or three days, anyway."

"Do you know Carl Johnson?" Johnson's identity hadn't been revealed in the press yet, so the woman couldn't know he was dead.

"No, I wouldn't say I knew him. We chatted on the stairs now and then if we bumped into each other. He seemed a pleasant enough type, always a smile and a hello. What are you after, anyway? What were you doing up there? Has he done a moonlight flit?"

"Something like that."

"He didn't look like a criminal type to me." She hugged herself and shuddered. "You just can't tell, can you?"

"What did you talk about, when you met on the stairs?"

"Oh, this and that. How expensive things are getting, the weather . . . you know, just ordinary stuff."

"Did you ever meet any of his friends?"

"No. I don't really think he had any. He was a bit of a loner. I did hear voices a couple of times, but that's all."

"When? Recently?"

"Last couple of weeks, anyway."

"How many people do you think were talking?"

"Only two, I'd say."

"Could you describe the other voice?"

"I'm sorry, I wasn't really listening. I mean, it's muffled anyway, you couldn't actually hear what anyone was saying. And I had the telly on. I could only hear them in the quiet bits."

"Was it a man?"

"Oh, yes, it was another man. I'm certain about that.

At least, he had a sort of deep voice."

"Thank you, Mrs . . . ?"

"Gerrard. Miss."

"Thank you, Miss Gerrard. Do you know if Mr Johnson owned a car?"

"I don't think he did. I never saw him in one, anyway."

"Do you have any idea what he did for a living?"

She looked away. "Well, he . . ."

"Look, Miss Gerrard, I don't care if he was cheating on the social or the taxman. That's not what I'm interested in."

She chewed her lower lip a few seconds, then smiled. "Well, we all do it a bit don't we? I suppose even coppers cheat on their income tax, don't they?"

Bank smiled back and put a finger to the side of his nose.

"And an important detective like yourself wouldn't be interested in something as petty as that, would he?"

Banks shook his head.

"Right," she said. "I only know because he mentioned the weather once, how nice it was to have outdoor work."

"Outdoor work?"

"Yes."

"Like what? Road work, construction?"

"Oh, no, he weren't no ditch-digger. He was a gardener, Mr Johnson was, had real green fingers."

It was amazing the skills one could learn in prison these days, Banks thought. "Where did he work?"

"Like I say, I only know because we got talking about it, how some people are so filthy rich and the rest of us just manage to scrape by. He wasn't no communist, mind you, he—"

"Miss Gerrard, do you know who he worked for?"

"Oh, yes. I do go on a bit, don't I? It was Mr Harkness, lives in that nice old house out Fortford way. Paid quite well, Mr Johnson said. But then, he could afford to, couldn't he?"

The name rang a bell. There had been a feature about him in the local rag a year or two ago. Adam Harkness, Banks remembered, had come from a local family that had emigrated to South Africa and made a fortune in diamonds. Harkness had followed in his father's footsteps, and after living for a while in Amsterdam had come back to Swainsdale in semi-retirement.

"Thank you," Banks said. "You've been very helpful."

"Have I?" She shrugged. "Oh well, always a pleasure to oblige."

Banks walked out into the street and mulled over what he had learned from Miss Gerrard. Johnson had been working for Adam Harkness, probably for cash in hand, no questions asked. That might explain the thousand or so pounds in the envelope. On the other hand, surely gardening didn't pay *that* much? And why did he hide the money? To guard against thieves, perhaps? Having sticky fingers himself, Johnson would probably be all too aware of the danger of leaving large sums of money lying around the place. Maybe he didn't have a bank account, was the kind who hid his fortune in a mattress or, in this case, under the cistern lid. But it still didn't ring true. Banks looked at his watch. Almost four in the afternoon. Time to pay Adam Harkness a visit before dinner.

IV

Detective Sergeant Philip Richmond's eyes were beginning to ache. He saved his data, then stood up and stretched, rubbing the small of his back. He'd been at it for four hours, much too long to sit staring at a screen. Probably get cancer of the eyeballs from all the radiation it emitted. They were all very well, these computers, he mused, but you had to be careful not to get carried away with them. These days, though, the more courses he took, the more he learned about computers, the better his chances of promotion were.

He walked over to the window. Luckily, the new computer room faced the market square, like Banks's office, but the window was tiny, as the place was nothing but a converted storage room for cleaners' materials. Anyway, the doctor had told him to look away from the screen into the distance occasionally to exercise his eye muscles, so he did.

Already many of the tourists were walking back to their cars—no doubt jamming up many of Eastvale's sidestreets and collecting a healthy amount in tickets—and some of the market stalls were closing.

He'd knock off soon, and then get himself ready for his date with Rachel Pierce. He had met her last Christmas in Barnard Castle, at the toy shop where she worked, while checking an alibi on a murder case, and they had been going steady ever since. There was still no talk of wedding bells, but if things continued going as well as they had been for much longer, Richmond knew he would seriously consider tying the knot. He had never met anyone quite as warm and as funny as Rachel before. They even shared a taste for science fiction; they both loved Philip K. Dick and Roger Zelazny. Tonight they would go and see that new horror film at the Crown—new for Eastvale, anyway, which was usually a good few months behind the rest of the country. Rachel loved scary films, and Richmond loved the way they made her cling to him. He looked at his watch. Barring emergencies, he would be with her in a couple of hours.

The phone rang.

Richmond cursed and answered it. The switchboard operator told him it was someone calling for Superintendent Gristhorpe, who was out, so she had put the call through to Richmond.

"Hello?" a woman's voice came on the line.

Richmond introduced himself. "What can I do for you?"

"Well," she said hesitantly, "I really wanted the man in charge. I called that temporary number, you know, the one you mentioned in the paper, and the constable there told me to call this number if I wanted to talk to Superintendent Gristhorpe."

Richmond explained the situation. "I'm sure I can help you," he added. "What's it about?"

"All right," she said. "The reason I'm calling you so late is that I've only just heard it from the woman who does the cleaning. She does it once a week, you see, on Saturday mornings."

"Heard what?"

"They've gone. Lock, stock and barrel. Both of them. Oh, don't get me wrong, it's not as if they aren't fully paid up or anything, and I wouldn't say they looked exactly like the couple the papers described, but it is funny, isn't it? People don't usually just take off like that without so much as a by-your-leave, not when they've paid cash in advance."

Richmond held the receiver away from his ear for a moment and frowned. Why didn't this make any sense? Was he going insane? Had the computer radiation finally eaten its way into his frontal lobes?

"Where are you calling from?" he asked.

She sounded surprised. "Eastvale, of course. My office. I'm working late."

"Your name?"

"Patricia. Patricia Cummings. But—"

"One thing at a time. You said your office. What kind of office?"

"I'm an estate agent. Randall and Palmer's, just across the square from the police station. Now—"

"All right," Richmond said. "I know the place. What are you calling about?"

"I thought I'd made myself perfectly clear, but apparently you need it spelled out."

Richmond grinned. "Yes, please. Spell it out."

"It's about that girl who disappeared, Gemma Scupham. At least it might be. That's why I wanted to speak to the man in charge. I think I might know something about the couple you're looking for, the ones who did it."

"I'll be right over," Richmond said, and hung up. He left a message at the front desk for Gristhorpe and dashed out into the market square.

5

I

As Banks drove west towards Fortford again, the low sun silhouetted the trees ahead. Some of them, stripped bare by Dutch elm disease, looked like skeletal hands clawing their way out of the earth. An evening haze hung over Fortford and softened the edges of the hills beyond the village. It muted the vibrant greens of the ryegrass on the lower dalesides and washed out the browns and greys of the upper pastures.

Banks drove into the village and passed the green, to his left, where a group of elderly locals sat gossiping and passing the time on a bench below the partially excavated Roman fort on the round hillock opposite. Smoke from their pipes drifted slowly on the hazy evening air.

It felt like a summer evening, Banks thought, and wondered just how long the fine weather would last; not long, if you believed the forecasters. Still, at least for now he could drive with his window down and enjoy the fresh air, except when it was permeated by the overripe tang of manure. Sometimes, though, a different smell would drift in, a garden bonfire, burning vegetation acrid on the air. He listened to Gurney's "Preludes" and felt that the piano music possessed the same starkly beautiful quality as the songs, unmistakably Gurney, heart-rending in the way it snatched moments of order from chaos.

At the corner, by the whitewashed sixteenth-century pub, he turned right onto the Lyndgarth road. Way ahead, about halfway up the daleside, he could see Lyndgarth itself, limestone cottages clustered around a small green, and the stubby, square tower of St Mary's. About half a mile north of the village, he could make out Gristhorpe's old grey farmhouse. Just to the left of Lyndgarth, a little lower down the hillside, stood the dark ruin of Devraulx Abbey, partially hidden by trees, looking eerie and haunted in the smoky evening light.

Banks drove only as far as the small stone bridge over the River Swain and turned left into a gravelled drive. Sheltered on all sides but the water by poplars, "Leasholme" was an ideal, secluded spot for a reclusive millionaire to retire to. Banks had phoned Adam Harkness earlier and been invited that very evening. He doubted he would find out much from Carl Johnson's employer, but he had to try.

He parked at the end of the drive beside Harkness's Jaguar. The house itself was a mix of Elizabethan and seventeenth-century styles, built mostly of limestone, with grit-stone lintels and cornerstones and a flagged roof. It was, however, larger than most, and had clearly belonged to a wealthy, landowner. Over the door, the date read 1617, but Banks guessed the original structure had been there earlier. The large garden had little to show but roses that time of year, but it looked well designed and cared for. Carl Johnson's green fingers, no doubt.

Finally, irritated by the cloud of gnats that hung over him, Banks rang the bell.

Harkness opened the door a few moments later and beckoned him inside, then led him along a cavernous hallway into a room at the back of the house, which turned out to be the library. Bookcases, made of dark wood, covered three walls, flanking a heavy door in one and a stone hearth in another. A white wicker armchair faced the fourth wall, where french windows opened into the garden. The well-kept lawn sloped down to the river-bank, fringed with rushes, and just to the left, a large copper beech framed a view of the Leas, with Lyndgarth and Aldington Edge beyond, just obscuring Devraulx Abbey behind its thick foliage. The river possessed a magical quality in the fading light; slow-moving, mirror-like, it presented a perfect reflection of the reeds that grew by its banks.

"It is spectacular, isn't it?" Harkness said. "It's one of the reasons I bought the place. It's much too big for me, of course. I don't even use half the rooms."

Banks had noticed the dust in the hall and a certain mustiness to the atmosphere. Even the library was un-tidy, with a large desk littered with papers, pens, rubber bands and a few books placed in small piles on the floor beneath the shelves.

"How long have you been here?" Banks asked.

"Two years. I still travel a fair bit. I'm not retired yet, you know, still got a lot of life in me. But I thought it was time I deserved to take things easy, put in a bit more golf."

Harkness looked about fifty-five. He was Banks's height, with silver hair and that brick-red, lined complex-ion peculiar to the Englishmen who have spent years in warmer climates. He wore a white short-sleeved shirt and navy-blue trousers. The pot-belly and sagging breasts showed he wasn't a man who took much exercise off the golf course.

"Drink?"

"A small Scotch, please," Banks said.

"Sit down." Harkness offered Banks the wicker chair

and pulled a swivel chair for himself from behind the desk.

Banks sat. Music played softly in the background: the Radio Three Dvorak concert, by the sound of it. He glanced at the books on the shelves and, for some reason, got the impression they were more for show than use, bought by the yard. A full set of the *Encyclopaedia Britannica*, some Book Club editions of Jane Austen and Dickens, a mail-order "Great Writers" series.

Harkness passed Banks the drink in a heavy crystal glass then joined him, carefully tugging up the creases of his trousers before he sat. "You didn't tell me very much on the telephone," he said. "How can I help you?"

"I'd just like to ask you a few questions about Carl Johnson."

Harkness shook his head slowly. "I still find it hard to believe such a thing could happen. We live in dangerous times." His accent was an odd mix of South African and public-school English, his manner relaxed. A man used to being in charge, Banks guessed.

"Did you know much about Mr Johnson? About his life, his background?"

Harkness shook his head. "I rarely saw him. He would come and put in his hours whether I was here or not. That was our arrangement. I'm afraid I know nothing at all about his personal life."

"Did you know he had a criminal record?"

Harkness raised an eyebrow and looked at Banks over the top of his glass. "I know he'd been in jail, if that's what you mean."

"How did you find out?"

"He told me when he came for the interview." Harkness allowed a brief smile. "In fact, he told me that's where he learned the job."

"And that didn't bother you?"

"The man had served his time. He was obviously honest enough to let me know about his past right from the start. Besides, I believe in giving everyone another chance. Everyone's capable of change, given the right conditions. Carl was a good, hard worker. And he was always very open and honest in his dealings with me. Anyway, I'm not an easy man to defraud."

"I thought you hardly ever talked to him."

"We had to discuss his work occasionally."

"How much did you pay him?"

"Five pounds an hour. I know that's not very much for a skilled worker, but he seemed grateful enough. And it was . . . how shall I say? . . . cash in hand."

"How long had he been working for you?"

"Since March."

"How did you make contact with him?"

"My previous gardener left. I placed an advertisement in the local paper and Carl Johnson replied. He seemed to know his stuff, and I was impressed with his frankness, so I took him on. I never regretted it." He pointed towards the windows. "As you can see, he did a fine job."

Banks put his glass down. Harkness offered him another, but he refused. The light had almost gone now, and the river seemed to hoard its last rays and glow from deep within. Harkness turned on the desk lamp.

"Do you know any reason," Banks asked, "why someone might want to kill him?"

"None. But as I said, I knew nothing about his personal life."

"When did you last see him?"

"Monday."

"Did he seem worried about anything?"

"Not that I could tell. We had a brief conversation about the lawn and the roses, as far as I can remember, and that's all. As I said, he didn't confide in me."

"He didn't seem different in any way?"

"No."

"Did he ever mention any of his friends or acquaintances, a girlfriend, perhaps?"

"No. I assumed he acted like any normal young man on his own time."

"Ever heard of a bloke called Les Poole?"

"No."

Banks scratched the scar by his right eye and crossed his legs. "Mr Harkness," he said, "can you think of any reason why Johnson had over a thousand pounds hidden in his flat?"

"A thousand pounds, you say? Well . . . no. I certainly didn't pay him that much. Perhaps he saved up."

"Perhaps."

"He may have worked for others, too. We didn't have an exclusive contract."

"You never asked?"

"Why should I? He was always available when I needed him."

"Where were you on Thursday evening?"

"Really, Chief Inspector! You can't believe I had anything to do with the man's death?"

"Just a matter of elimination, sir."

"Oh, very well." Harkness rubbed his chin. "Let me see . . . Well, Thursday, I'd have been at the Golf Club. I played that afternoon with Martin Lambert, and after the game we had dinner at the club."

"What time did you leave?"

"Not until well after eleven. The others will vouch for me."

Banks nodded. He felt that Harkness was enjoying the game, one he knew he could win. There was a kind of smugness and arrogance about him that irked Banks. He had come across it before in powerful and wealthy people and had never been able accept it.

"I understand you were born around these parts?" he asked.

"Yes. Lyndgarth, as a matter of fact. We emigrated when I was four."

"South Africa?"

"Yes. Johannesburg. My father saw opportunities there. He liked to take risks, and this one paid off. Why do you ask?"

"Out of interest. You took over the business?"

"When he died. And, I might add, I succeeded him out of ability, not nepotism. I worked with him for years. He taught me all he knew."

"Is the company still in existence?"

"Very much so. And our mines are still productive. But I've had very little to do with that part of the operation of late. I moved to Amsterdam over ten years ago to handle the sales end of the business." He looked down, swirled the amber liquid in his crystal snifter, then looked Banks in the eye. "Quite frankly, I couldn't stomach the politics over there. Apartheid disgusted me, and I lacked the courage to become a revolutionary. Who wants another white liberal, anyway?"

"So you moved to Amsterdam?"

"Yes."

"But you kept your business interests in South Africa?"

"I said I couldn't stand living with the politics, Chief Inspector. I didn't say I was a fool. I also don't believe in sanctions. But that's not what you came to hear about."

"Still, it is fascinating. Are you married?"

"Divorced, back in Amsterdam." He shifted in his chair. "If you don't mind—"

"I'm sorry." Banks put down his empty glass and

stood up. "It's just a copper's instinct. Curiosity."

"It's also what killed the cat."

Harkness said it with a smile, but Banks could hardly miss the cutting edge. He ignored it and walked to the library door.

As they walked down the gloomy hall with its waist-high wainscoting, Banks turned to one of the doors. "What's in here?" he asked.

Harkness opened the door and turned on a light. "Living room."

It was a spacious, high-ceilinged room with wall-to-wall thick pile carpeting and a burgundy three-piece suite. Next to the fireplace stood a tall bookcase stacked with old *National Geographic* magazines. A couple of landscapes hung on the walls: original oils, by the look of them. Banks couldn't tell who the artists were, but Sandra would probably know. Again, Banks noticed how untidy the room was and how dusty the fixtures. Beside the sofa was a long, low table, and at its centre stood a tarnished silver goblet encrusted with dirt. Banks picked it up. "What's this?" he asked.

Harkness shrugged. "Carl found it when he was digging the garden one day and he brought it to me. It looks old. I keep meaning to get it cleaned up and valued. He thought it might be worth something. I suppose," he went on, "you could take that as another example of his honesty. He could have kept it."

Banks examined the goblet. It had some kind of design engraved on it, but he couldn't make out what it was through the grime. It looked like a coat of arms. He put it back down on the table. It was something Tracy would be interested in, he thought. Would have been, he corrected himself.

Harkness noticed him looking around. "It's a bit of a mess, I'm afraid. But as I said, the house is too big and I don't use all of it anyway."

"Don't you have a cleaning lady?"

"Can't abide maids. Ever since I was a child in South Africa we had them, and I never could stand them. Always fussing around you. And I suppose as much as anything I couldn't stand the idea of anyone having to clean up after anyone else. It seemed so undignified, somehow."

Banks, whose mother had charred at a Peterborough office block to bring in a bit of extra money, said, "Yet you employed a gardener?"

Harkness led the way to the front door. "That's different, don't you think? A gardener is a kind of artist in a way, and I've no objection to being a patron of the arts. I always thought of the grounds as very much Carl's creation."

"I suppose you're right," Banks said at the door. "Just one more question: Did he ever mention the old lead mine near Relton?"

"No. Why?"

"I just wondered if it was special to him for some reason. Can you think of any reason he might have been there?"

Harkness shook his head. "None at all. Digging for hidden treasure, perhaps?" His eyes twinkled.

"Perhaps," Banks said. "Thank you for your time."

"My pleasure."

Harkness closed the door slowly but firmly and Banks got into his car. As he drove back to Eastvale in the blue-grey twilight with the haunting piano music playing, he wondered about Harkness. Many business dealings don't bear close scrutiny, of course, and you don't get as rich as Harkness without skirting the law and stepping on a few toes here and there. Is that what Harkness was getting at with his remark about curiosity killing the cat? If that was so, where did Johnson fit in? It might be useful having a criminal for a gardener if you wanted other kinds of dirty business done. On the other hand, it might also, after a while, turn out to be very inconvenient, too. At least, Banks concluded, it might be worthwhile asking a few questions about Mr Adam Harkness.

II

"This must be it, sir," said DS Richmond as he pulled in behind Patricia Cummings outside the last cottage in a terrace of four, right on the north-western edge of Eastvale, where the road curved by the side of River Swain into the dale. It was a pleasant spot, handy for both the town life, with its cinemas, shops and pubs, and for getting out into the more rural reaches of the dale itself. The holiday cottages were small—just right for a couple—and the view of the entry into the dale proper was magnificent. Of course, the slopes there were not as dramatic as they became beyond Fortford and Helmthorpe, but looking down the valley even in the fading light one could make out the grey, looming shapes of the higher fells and peaks massed in the distance, and the nearer, gentler slopes with their dry-stone walls and grazing sheep showed a promise of what was to come.

Patricia Cummings opened the door, and Richmond entered the living-room with Gristhorpe, who had returned to the station just a few minutes after Richmond had been to see Patricia. She turned on the light, and they looked around the small room that the estate agent would probably describe as cosy, with its two little armchairs arranged by the fireplace. Gristhorpe felt he had to stoop under the low ceiling, even though a few inches remained. He felt like Alice must have done before she took the shrinking potion.

What struck Gristhorpe immediately was the absolute cleanliness of the place. It reminded him of his grand-mother's cottage, a similarly tiny place in Lyndgarth, in which he had never seen a speck of dust nor a thing out of place. The dominant smell was pine-scented furniture polish, and the gleaming dark surfaces of wood stood testament to its thorough application. They glanced in the kitchen. There, too, everything shone: the sink, the small fridge, the mini-washer and dryer unit under the counter.

"Did the cleaner do the place?" Gristhorpe asked.

Patricia Cummings shook her head. "No. It was like this when she found it. Spotless. She phoned me because she was sure they were supposed to be staying another two weeks."

"And were they?"

"Yes."

"They'd already paid the rent?"

"For a month, altogether. Cash in advance."

"I see."

Mrs Cummings shifted from one foot to the other. She was a middle-aged woman, neatly dressed in a grey suit with a pearl blouse and ruff. She had a small lipsticked mouth and pouchy rouged cheeks that wobbled as she spoke. Gristhorpe noticed a gold band with a big dia-mond cluster biting into the flesh of her plump ring fin-ger.

"They said they were responding to an advertisement we placed in *The Dalesman*," she said.

"What names did they give?"

"Manley. Mr and Mrs Manley."

"Did you see any identification?"

"Well, no . . . I mean, they paid cash."

"Is that unusual?"

"Not really. Not normal, but it happens."

"I see." Gristhorpe looked over towards Richmond, who seemed similarly constrained by the tininess of the place. "Let's have a look around, shall we, Phil?"

Richmond nodded.

"I'll show you," Patricia Cummings said.

"If you don't mind," Gristhorpe told her, "it would be best if you waited here. It would give forensics one less person to eliminate, if it comes to that."

"Very well. Is it all right if I sit down?"

"By all means."

The stone staircase was narrow and its whitewashed ceiling low. Both men had to stoop as they went up. Upstairs were two small bedrooms and a bathroom-toilet. Everywhere was just as spotless as the living-room, ceramic surfaces gleaming.

"Someone's really done a job on this, sir," Richmond said as they entered the first bedroom. "Look, they've even washed the sheets and folded them." It was true; a small pile of neatly folded sheets lay on the mattress, and the oak chest of drawers shone with recent polish. The same pine scent hung in the air. The second bedroom was a little shabbier, but it was easy to see why. From the neatly made bed and the thin patina of dust that covered the wardrobe, it was clear the room hadn't been used by the cottage's most recent occupants.

"I can't imagine why there'd even *be* two bedrooms," Richmond said. "I mean, it'd feel crowded enough in this place with two people, let alone children as well."

"Aye," said Gristhorpe. "It's old-world rustic charm all right."

Both the sink and the bathtub had been thoroughly cleaned out, and shelves and medicine cabinet emptied.

"Come on," said Gristhorpe. "There's nothing for us here."

They went back downstairs and found Patricia Cummings painting her nails. The sickly smell of the polish pervaded the small room. She raised her eyebrows when they entered.

"Are all the cottages rented out?" Gristhorpe asked.

"All four," she said.

They went outside. The row reminded Gristhorpe of Gallows View, a similar terrace not too far away, where he and Banks had investigated a case some years ago. The light of the cottage next door was on, and Gristhorpe thought he saw the curtains twitch as they walked towards it. Gristhorpe knocked, and a few moments later a skinny young man with long, greasy hair answered.

Gristhorpe introduced himself and Richmond, and the young man let them in. The place was furnished exactly the same as next door: sideboard along one wall, a small television on a stand, two armchairs, an open fireplace, wall-to-wall dark carpets and wallpaper patterned with grapevines against an off-white background. Job lot, no doubt. The young man had made his mark by arranging a row of books along the sideboard, using wine bottles as bookends. They were mostly poetry, Gristhorpe noticed, and a couple of local wildlife guides.

"This won't take long," he said to the youth, who had introduced himself as Tony Roper. "I'd just like to know if you can tell me anything about your neighbours."

"Not really," said Tony, leaning against the sideboard. "I mean, I came here mostly for the isolation, so I didn't do much mixing." He had a Scottish accent, Gristhorpe noticed, leaning more towards Glasgow than Edinburgh.

"Did you meet them?"

"Just in passing."

"Did they introduce themselves?"

"The Manleys. Chris and Connie. That's what they said. They seemed pleasant enough. Always had a smile and a hello whenever we bumped into one another. Look, what's wrong? Nothing's happened to them, has it?"

"When did you last see them?"

Tony frowned. "Let me see . . . It was a couple of days ago. Thursday, I think. Thursday morning. They were going off in the car."

"Did they say where?"

"No. I didn't ask."

"Had they packed all their stuff, as if they were leaving?"

"I'm afraid I didn't notice. Sorry. I was out walking most of the time."

"It's all right," Gristhorpe said. "Just try and remember what you can. Did you see or hear them after that time?"

"Come to think of it, I don't reckon I did. But they never made much noise anyway. Maybe a bit of telly in the evenings. That's about all."

"Did they ever have any visitors?"

"Not that I know of."

"You never heard them arguing or talking with anyone?"

"No."

"Were they out a lot?"

"A fair bit, I'd say. But so was I. I've been doing a lot of walking, meditating, writing. I'm really sorry, but I honestly didn't pay them a lot of attention. I've been pretty much lost in my own world."

"That's all right," Gristhorpe said. "You're doing fine. What did they look like?"

"Well, he . . . Chris . . . was about medium height, with light, sandy-coloured hair brushed back. Receding a bit. He looked quite fit, wiry, you know, and he had a pleasant, open kind of smile. The kind you could trust."

"Any distinctive features?"

"You mean scars, tattoos, that kind of thing?"

"Anything."

Tony shook his head. "No. He was quite ordinary looking, really. I just noticed the smile, that's all."

"How old would you say he was?"

"Hard to say. I'd guess he was in his late twenties."

"What about the woman?"

"Connie?" Tony blushed a little. "Well, Connie's a blonde. I don't know if it's real or not. Maybe a year or two younger than him. Very pretty. A real looker. She's got lovely blue eyes, a really smooth complexion, a bit pale . . ."

"How tall?"

"An inch or two shorter than him."

"What about her figure?"

Tony blushed again. "Nice. I mean, nice so's you'd notice in the street, especially in those tight jeans she wore, and the white T-shirt."

Gristhorpe smiled and nodded. "Did you notice what kind of car they drove?"

"Yes. It was parked outside often enough. It was a Fiesta."

"What colour?"

"White."

"Did they always dress casually?"

"I suppose so. I never paid much attention, except to her, of course. Now I think of it, Chris was a bit more formal. He usually wore a jacket and a tie. You don't think anything's happened to them, do you?"

"Don't worry, Tony," Gristhorpe said. "I'm sure they're fine. Just one more thing. Did you ever hear sounds of a child there at all?"

Tony frowned. "No."

"Are you sure?"

"I'd have noticed. Yes, I'm sure. They didn't have any

children."

"Fine. Thanks very much, Tony," Gristhorpe said. "We'll leave you to enjoy the rest of your holiday in peace."

Tony nodded and accompanied them to the door.

"You'll let me know, will you, if they're all right? I mean, I didn't really know them, but they *were* neighbours, in a way."

"We'll let you know," said Gristhorpe, and followed Richmond to the car.

"Will you be needing me any more?" asked Patricia Cummings.

Gristhorpe smiled at her. "No, thanks very much, Mrs Cummings. You can go home now. Just one thing, could you leave that set of keys with us?"

"Why?"

"So we can let the scene-of-crime team in."

"But—"

"This *is* important, Mrs Cummings, believe me. I wouldn't ask it otherwise. And don't rent the place out again until we give the OK."

Her cheeks quivered a bit, then she dropped the keys into Gristhorpe's outstretched hand, climbed into her car and drove off with a screech of rubber. Gristhorpe got into the police Rover beside Richmond. "Well, Phil," he said, "what do you think?"

"I'm not sure, sir. The description doesn't fit."

"But it would if they dyed their hair and got dressed up in business clothes, wouldn't it? Both descriptions were vague enough—Brenda Scupham's *and* Tony Roper's."

"That's true. But what about the car?"

"They could have stolen one for the abduction, or rented one."

"A bit risky, isn't it? And we've checked all the rental

agencies."

"But we used the descriptions Brenda Scupham gave us." Gristhorpe scratched his ear. "Better get back to the rental agencies and find out about *any* couples their general age and appearance. Mention the man's smile. That seems to be a common factor. And the woman is clearly attractive. Someone might remember them."

Richmond nodded. "You think it was this Manley couple, sir?"

"I'm not saying that, but I think we'd better treat them as serious contenders for the moment."

"It certainly seems odd the way they left the place in such a hurry."

"Yes," Gristhorpe muttered. "And that cleaning job. Why?"

"Just a fastidious couple, maybe?"

"Maybe. But *why* did they leave in a hurry?"

"Could be any number of reasons," Richmond said. "A family emergency, maybe?"

"Did you notice a phone in the cottage?"

"No. I suppose that's part of the rustic peace."

"Mm. There is one thing."

"Sir?"

"Let's say, for the sake of argument, that they did have to leave because of a family emergency. Nobody could have phoned them, but they could have used the nearest phonebox if they had to keep checking on someone who was ill."

"You mean they wouldn't have stayed behind to clean up the place, sir?"

"There's that, aye. But there's something odder. The money. They paid cash in advance. How much do these places go for?"

"I don't know, sir. I forgot to ask.."

"It doesn't matter, but it must be a fair whack. Say a

hundred and fifty a week."

"Something like that. And probably a deposit, too."

"Then why didn't they ask for some of their money back?"

"They might have had a hard time getting it."

"Perhaps. But they didn't even try. That's three hundred quid we're talking about, Phil. Plus deposit."

"Maybe they were loaded."

Gristhorpe fixed Richmond with the closest his benign features could get to a look of contempt. "Phil, if they were loaded, the *first* thing they would do is ask for their money back. That's how the rich get that way, and that's how they stay that way."

"I suppose so," Richmond mumbled. "What do we do now?"

"We get the forensic team in, that's what we do," Gristhorpe said, and reached for the radio.

III

The house was in darkness when Banks got home from the station around ten o'clock that Saturday evening. Tracy, he remembered, was at a dance in Relton with her friends. Banks had grilled her thoroughly about who was going and who was driving. He had been undecided, loath to let her go, but Sandra had tipped the balance. She was probably right, Banks admitted. Barring a punch-up between the Eastvale lads and the Relton lads, a fairly regular feature of these local dances, it ought to be a harmless enough affair. And Tracy was a big girl now.

So where was Sandra? Banks turned the lights on, then went into the kitchen thinking he might find a note. Nothing. Feeling anxious and irritated, he sat down, turned on the television and started switching channels: an American cop show, a documentary on Africa, a pirate film, a quiz show. He turned it off. The silence in the house closed in on him. This was absurd. Normally he would change into jeans and a sports shirt, pour a drink, put some music on, perhaps even smoke a cigarette if both Sandra and Tracy were out. Now all he could do was sit down and tap his fingers on the chair arm. It was no good. He couldn't stay home.

Grabbing his jacket against the evening chill, he walked along Market Street past the closed shops and the Golden Grill and the Queen's Arms. The light through the red and amber coloured windows beckoned, and he could see people at tables through the small clear panes, but instead of dropping in, he continued along North Market Street, quiet under its old-fashioned gas-lamps, window displays of gourmet teas, expensive hiking gear, imported shoes and special blends of tobacco.

The front doors of the community centre stood open. From the hall, Banks could hear a soprano struggling through Schubert's "Die Junge Nonne" to a hesitant piano accompaniment. It was Saturday, amateur recital night. He took the broad staircase to his left and walked up to the first floor. He could hear voices from some of the rooms, mostly used for the meetings of local hobby clubs or for committees of various kinds. The double glass doors of the gallery were closed, but a faint light shone from behind the partition at the far end of the room.

Banks walked softly down the carpeted gallery, its walls bare of pictures at the moment, and stopped outside the cramped office at the end. He had already heard Sandra's voice, but she was unaware of his presence.

"But you can't *do* that," she was pleading. "You've already agreed—"

"What? You don't give a . . . Now look—" She moved the receiver away from her ear and swore before slamming it down in its cradle. Then she took two deep breaths, tucked loose strands of blonde hair behind her ears, and picked up the phone again.

"Sandra," Banks said as gently as he could.

She turned round and put her hand to her chest. Banks could see the angry tears burning in her eyes. "Alan, it's you. What are you doing here? You scared me."

"Sorry."

"Look, it's not a good time. I've got so damn much to do."

"Let's go for a drink."

She started dialling. "I'd love to, but I—"

Banks broke the connection.

Sandra stood up and faced him, eyes blazing. "What the hell do you think you're doing?"

He took her arm. "Come on. Let's go."

She shook him off. "What are you playing at?"

Banks sighed and sat on the edge of the desk. "Look at you," he said. "You're frustrated as hell." He smiled. "You look pretty close to murder, too. I think it's time you took a break, that's all. God knows, you've helped take my mind off my problems often enough when you've watched me beating my head against a brick wall. I'm just trying to return the favour."

Sandra bit her lower lip. Some of the anger left her eyes, but the tears still burned there. "It's just that bloody Morton Ganning," she said. "He's only pulled out of the show, that's all."

"Well, bugger him," Banks said.

"But you don't understand."

Banks took her coat from the rack by the office door. "Come on. You can tell me over a drink."

Sandra glared at him for a moment, then smoothed her

skirt and walked over. Before she could put her coat on,
Banks put his arms around her and held her close. At
first she stood limp, then slowly, she raised her arms and
linked them behind him. She buried her head in his
shoulder, then broke free, gave him a playful thump on
the arm and that cheeky smile he loved so much. "All
right, then," she said. "But you're buying."

Ten minutes later, they managed to squeeze into a
small corner table in the Queen's Arms. The place was
busy and loud with the jokes and laughter of the
Saturday night crowd, so they had to put their heads
close together to talk. Soon, though, the noise became a
background buzz and they no longer had to strain to hear
one another.

"He's the most famous of the lot," Sandra was saying.
"He's got paintings in galleries all over the country. It
was going to be a hell of a coup to get him, but now he's
backed out. He's a real bastard."

"I thought the idea was to give locals a chance, the
lesser-known ones?"

"It is. But Ganning would have drawn a damn good
crowd. Indirectly, he'd have got them all more publicity,
given them more chance of making a sale."

"For the right reasons?"

"That doesn't matter. So what if they come to see *his*
work? They'd see the others too."

"I suppose so."

Sandra sipped her gin and tonic. "I'm sorry to go on
about it, Alan, really I am. It's just that I've been so involved. I've put in so much bloody work it makes me
boil."

"I know."

"What's that supposed to mean?"

"Nothing."

Her blue eyes hardened. "Yes it is. I can tell by your

tone. You're not complaining, are you? That I haven't been doing my little wifely duties—cooking your meals, washing your clothes?"

Banks laughed. "I didn't marry you for your 'little wifely duties' as you call them. I can look after myself. No. If I am complaining at all, it's about hardly seeing you over these past few weeks."

"Like I hardly see you when you're on a case?"

"*Touché.*"

"So what do you mean? You expect me to be there whenever you decide to come home?"

"No, it's not that."

"What is it then?"

Banks lit a cigarette, playing for time. "It's . . . well, just that the house seems so empty. You're never there, Tracy's never there. I feel like I'm living alone."

Sandra leaned back in her chair. She reached out and grabbed one of Banks's cigarettes. "Hey," he said, putting his hand over hers. "You've stopped."

She broke free. "And I'll stop again tomorrow. What's really bothering you, Alan?"

"What I said. The empty house."

"So it's not just me, what I'm doing?"

"No, I don't suppose it is."

"But you take it out on me?"

"I'm not taking anything out on you. I'm trying to ex- plain what the problem is. For Christ's sake, you asked me."

"Okay, okay. Keep your shirt on. Maybe you need an- other pint."

"Wouldn't mind."

Sandra held out her hand. "Money, then."

Banks looked gloomily into the last quarter-inch of deep gold liquid in his glass while Sandra threaded her way to the bar. She was right. It wasn't just her at all. It was the whole damn situation at home. He felt as if his children had suddenly become different people overnight, and his wife hadn't even noticed. He watched her coming back. She walked slowly, concentrating on not spilling the drinks. It was absurd, he felt, but even after all these years just seeing her made his heart speed up.

Sandra placed the glass carefully on the beer-mat in front of him and he thanked her.

"Look," she said, "I know what you mean, but you have to accept things. Brian's gone. He's got his own life to lead. When did you leave home?"

"But that's not the same."

"Yes it is."

"It was stifling in Peterborough, with Dad always on at me and Mum just taking it all. It wasn't the same at all."

"Perhaps the circumstances weren't," Sandra allowed. "But the impulse certainly is."

"He's got a perfectly good home with us. I don't see why he'd want to go as far as bloody Portsmouth. I mean, he could have gone to Leeds, or York, or Bradford and come home on weekends."

Sandra sighed. "Sometimes you can be damned obtuse, Alan Banks, do you know that?"

"What do you mean?"

"He's left the nest, flown the coop. For him it's a matter of the farther the better. It doesn't mean he doesn't love us any more. It's just of part of growing up. You did it yourself. That's what I mean."

"But I told you, that was different."

"Not all that much. Didn't you used to get on at him all the time about his music?"

"I never interfered with what he wanted. I even bought him a guitar."

"Yes. In the hope he'd start playing classical or jazz or something other than what he did."

"Don't tell me you liked that bloody racket any more than I did?"

"That doesn't matter. Oh, what's the use. What I'm trying to say is that we didn't drive him away, no more than your parents drove you away, not really. He wants to be independent like you did. He wants his own life."

"I know that, but . . ."

"But nothing. We still have Tracy. Enjoy her while you can."

"But she's never home. She's always out with that Harrison boy, getting up to God knows what."

"She's not getting up to anything. She's sensible."

"She doesn't seem interested in anything else any more. Her schoolwork's slipping."

"Not much," Sandra said. "And I'll bet yours slipped a bit when you got your first girlfriend."

Banks said nothing.

"Alan, you're jealous, that's all."

"Jealous? Of my own daughter?"

"Oh, come on. You know she was the apple of your eye. You never were as close to Brian as you were to her. Now she seems to have no time for you, you resent it."

Banks rubbed his cheek. "Do I?"

"Of course you do. If only you could bring as much perception to your own family as you do to your cases you wouldn't have these problems."

"Knowing is one thing, feeling all right about it is quite another."

"I realize that. But you have to start with knowing."

"How do you cope?" Banks asked. "You've been like a stranger to me these past few months."

"I didn't say I'd been coping very well either, only that I've been doing a lot of thinking about things."

"And?"

"It's not easy, but we've reached that time where our children are no longer children. They can no longer keep us together."

Banks felt a chill run through him. "What do you mean they can't keep us together?"

"What I say. Oh, for God's sake don't look so worried. I didn't mean it *that* way. Maybe I didn't choose the best words. The kids gave us a lot in common, shared pleasures, anxieties. They'll still do that, of course, though I'm sure more on the anxieties side, but we can't relate to them the same way. They're not just children to be seen and not heard. You can't just order them not to do things. They'll only rebel and do worse. Remember your own childhood? You were a bit of a shit-disturber even when I met you. Still are, if truth be known. See Brian and Tracy for what they are, for what they're becoming."

"But what did you mean about them keeping us together? It sounded ominous to me."

"Only that we won't have them to gather around for much longer. We'll have to find other things, discover one another in other ways."

"It could be fun."

Sandra nodded. "It could be. But we've both been avoiding it so far."

"You too?"

"Of course. How many times have we spent an evening in the house alone together these past eighteen years?"

"There's been times."

"Oh yes, but you can count them on the fingers of one hand. Besides, we knew Brian would be back from Boys' Brigade or Tracy from the Guides, or they were up in their rooms. We're not old, Alan. We married young and we've got a lot ahead of us."

Banks looked at Sandra. Not old, certainly. The earnest face, her eyes shining with emotion, black eyebrows contrasting the blonde hair that hung down over her shoulders. A lump came to his throat. If I walked into the pub right this moment, he thought, and saw her sitting there, I'd be over like a shot.

"Where do we start?" he asked.

Sandra tossed back her head and laughed. People turned to look at her but she paid them no attention. "Well, I've got this bloody show to organize still, and it's not all been a matter of staying late at the gallery to avoid facing things. I *do* have a lot of hours to put in."

"I know that," Banks said. "And so do I."

Sandra frowned. "There's still nothing on that missing child, is there?"

Banks shook his head. "No. It's been five days now since she was abducted."

"Just imagine what her poor mother must be going through. Have you given up hope?"

"We don't expect miracles." He paused. "You know something? She reminds me of Tracy when she was that age. The blonde hair, the serious expression. Tracy always did take after you."

"You're being sentimental, Alan. From the photo I saw in the paper she didn't look a bit like Tracy."

Banks smiled. "Maybe not. But I'm on another case now. That reminds me. Have you ever heard of a bloke called Adam Harkness?"

"Harkness? Of course I have. He's pretty well known locally as a patron of the arts."

"Yes, he mentioned something like that. Has he given your lot any money?"

"We weren't as needy as some. Remember that bumper grant we got?"

"The oversight?"

"They still haven't asked for it back. Anyway, he's given money to the Amateur Operatic Society and a couple of other groups." She frowned.

"What is it?"

"Well, some of the arts groups are a bit, you know, leftish. They tend to get blinkered. It's the old package deal: if you're against this, you have to be against that too. You know, you have to be pro-abortion, anti-apartheid and green to boot."

"Well?"

"Some of them wouldn't take Harkness's money because of the way he makes it."

"South Africa?"

"Yes."

"But he's anti-apartheid. He just told me. That's partly why he left. Besides, things have changed over there. Apartheid's fallen to pieces."

Sandra shrugged. "Maybe. And I wouldn't know about his personal beliefs. All I know is that Linda Fish—you know, that woman who runs the Writers' Circle—wouldn't take any money towards engaging visiting speakers and readers."

"Linda Fish, the Champagne socialist?"

"Well, yes."

"What does she know about him?"

"Oh, she's got contacts among South African writers, or so she claims. All this anti-apartheid stuff is a load of bunk, she thinks. She's got a point. I mean, after all, whatever he professes to believe he's *still* earning his fortune by exploiting the system, isn't he?"

"I'd better have a talk with her."

"Well," Sandra said, "you don't make his kind of money by being square and above-board, do you? Let's drop it anyway. I'm sure Linda will be delighted to see you. I think she's secretly fancied you ever since she found out you'd read Thomas Hardy."

Banks gave a mock shudder. "Look," he said, "I've just had an idea."

Sandra raised her eyebrows.

"Not that kind of idea. Well. . . . Anyway, when all this is over—the show, the case—let's go on holiday, just you and me. Somewhere exotic."

"Can we afford it?"

"No. But we'll manage somehow. Tracy can stay with your mum and dad. I'm sure they won't mind."

"No. They're always glad to see her. I bet she'll mind this time, though. To be separated from the first boyfriend for even a day is a pretty traumatic experience, you know."

"We'll deal with that problem when we get to it. What about the holiday?"

"You're on. I'll start thinking of suitably exotic places."

"And . . . er . . . about that other idea . . ."

"What other idea?"

"You know. *Erotic* places."

"Oh, *that* one."

"Yes. Well?"

Sandra looked at her watch. "It's ten past eleven. Tracy said she'll be home at twelve."

"When has she ever been on time?"

"Still," Sandra said, finishing her drink and grabbing Banks's arm. "I think we'd better hurry."

IV

The tea was cold. Wearily, Brenda Scupham picked up her cup and carried it to the microwave. When she had reheated it, she went back into the living-room, flopped down on the sofa and lit a cigarette.

She had been watching television. That was how she had let the tea get cold. Not even watching it really, just sitting there and letting the images and sounds tumble over her and deaden the thoughts that she couldn't keep at bay. It had been a documentary about some obscure African tribe. That much she remembered. Now the news was on and somcone had blown up a jumbo jet over a jungle somewhere. Images of the strewn wreckage taken from a helicopter washed over her.

Brenda sipped her tea. Too hot now. It wasn't tea she needed, anyway, it was a drink. The pill she had taken had some effect, but it would work better with a gin and tonic. Getting up, she went and poured herself a stiff one, then sat down again.

It was that man from the newspaper who had got her thinking such terrible thoughts. Mostly the police did a good job of keeping the press away from her, but this one she had agreed to talk to. For one thing, he was from the *Yorkshire Post*, and for another, she liked the look of him. He had been kind and gentle in his questioning, too, sensitive to her feelings, but had nevertheless probed areas Brenda hadn't even known existed. And somehow, talking about her grief over the loss of her "poor Gemma" had actually made her feel it more, just as speculating about what might have happened to the child had made her imagine awful things happening, fears she couldn't shut out even now, long after the man had gone, after she had taken the tranquillizer, and after the images of Africa had numbed her. It was like being at the dentist's when the anaesthetic numbs your gums but you can still feel a shadow of pain in the background when he probes with his drill.

Now she found herself drifting way back to when she first got pregnant. Right from the start she knew instinctively that she didn't want the child growing inside her. Some days, she hoped to fall and induce a miscarriage, and other, worse days, she wished she would get run over by a bus. The odd thing was, though, that she couldn't actually bring herself to do any of these things—throw herself down the stairs, get rid of the foetus, jump out of a window. Maybe it was because she had been brought up Catholic and believed in a sort of elemental way that both suicide and abortion were sins. She couldn't even sit in a bathtub and drink gin like that dateless June Williams had done when Billy Jackson had got her in the family way (not that it had worked anyway; all June had got out of it was wrinkled skin and a nasty hangover). No, whatever happened just had to happen; it had to be God's will, even though Brenda didn't think now that she really believed in God.

Later, still stunned by the pain of childbirth, when she saw Gemma for the first time, she remembered wondering even back then how such a strange child could possibly be hers. And she turned her back. Oh, she had done the necessaries, of course. She could no more neglect to feed the child and keep her warm than she could have thrown herself under a bus. But that was where it stopped. She had been unable to feel love for Gemma, which is why it felt so strange, after talking about her loss to the reporter, that she should actually *feel* it now. And she felt guilty, too, guilty for the way she had neglected and abandoned Gemma. She knew she might never get a chance to make it up to her.

She poured another gin. Maybe this would do the trick. The thing was, it had been guilt made her hand Gemma over in the first place. Guilt and fear. The social workers, real or not, had been right when they talked about abuse; it was their timing that seemed uncanny, for though Brenda might have neglected her daughter, she had never, *ever* hit her until a few days before they called. Even then, she hadn't really hit Gemma, but when the man and the woman with their posh accents and their well-cut clothes called at her door, she somehow felt they had arrived in answer to a call; they were her retribution or her salvation, she didn't really know which.

Gemma had angered Les. When she spilled the paint on the racing page of his paper, he retaliated, as he usually did, not by violence, but by hitting her where it hurt, tearing up and throwing out some of her colouring books. Afterwards, he had been in a terrible mood all through tea-time, needling Brenda, complaining, arguing. And to cap it all, Gemma had been sitting there giving them the evil eye. She hadn't said a word, nor shed a tear, but the accusation and the hurt in those eyes had been too much. Finally, Brenda grabbed her by the arm and shook her until she did start to cry, then let go of her and watched her run up to her room, no doubt to throw herself on her bed and cry herself to sleep. She had shaken Gemma so hard there were bruises on her arm. And when the social workers came, it was as if they knew not only how Brenda had lost her temper that day, but that if it happened again she might keep on shaking Gemma until she killed her. It was silly, she knew that— of course they couldn't *know*—but that had been how she felt.

And that was why she had given up Gemma so easily, to save her. Or was it to get rid of her? Brenda still couldn't be sure; the complexity of her feelings about the whole business knotted deep in her breast and she couldn't, try as she might, sort it all out and analyze it like she assumed most people did. She couldn't help not being smart, and most of the time it never really bothered her that other people knew more about the world than she did, or that they were able to talk about things she couldn't understand, or look at a situation and break it down into all its parts. It never really bothered her, but sometimes she thought it was bloody unfair.

She finished her gin and lit another cigarette. Now she had talked to the reporter she thought she might like to go on television. They had asked her on the second day, but she had been too scared. Maybe, though, in her best outfit, with the right make-up, she might not look too bad. She could make an appeal to the kidnapper, and if Gemma was still alive. . . . Still alive . . . no, she couldn't think about that again. But it might help.

She heard a key in the door. Les back from the pub. Her expression hardened. Over these past few days, she realized, she had come to hate him. The door opened. She went and poured herself another gin and tonic. She would have to do something about Les soon. She couldn't go on like this.

V

Later that Saturday night, after closing-time, a car weaved its way over a desolate stretch of the North York Moors some thirty miles east of Eastvale. Its occupants—Mark Hudson and Mandy Vernon—could hardly keep their hands off one another. They had been for a slap-up dinner and drinks at the White Horse Farm Hotel, in Rosedale, and were now on their way back to Helmsley.

As Mark tried to concentrate on the narrow, unfenced road, the rabbits running away from the headlights' beam, his hand kept straying to Mandy's thigh, where her short skirt exposed a long stretch of delectable nylon-encased warm flesh. Finally, he pulled into a lay-by. All around them lay darkness, not even a farmhouse light in sight.

First they kissed, but the gear-stick and steering wheel got in the way. Metros weren't built for passion. Then Mark suggested they get in the back. They did so, but when he got his hand up her skirt and started tugging at her tights, she banged her knee on the back of the seat and cursed.

"There's not enough room," she said. "I'll break my bloody leg."

"Let's get out, then," Mark suggested.

"What? Do it in the open air?"

"Yes. Why not?"

"But it's cold."

"It's not that cold. Don't worry, I'll keep you warm. I've got a blanket in the back."

Mandy considered it for a moment. His hand found her left breast inside her blouse and he started rubbing her nipple between his thumb and forefinger.

"All right," she said. "We've not got much choice, have we?"

And indeed they hadn't. They couldn't take a room at the hotel because Mark was married, supposed to be at a company do, and Mandy still lived with her mother and brother, who expected her home from her girlfriend's by midnight. He had bought her an expensive five-course dinner, and they had drunk Châteauneuf-du-Pape. Going home, he had even negotiated the winding one-in-three hill that led over the open moors because it was more isolated up there than on the valley road. This might be one of the last warm evenings of the year; he might never get another chance.

Using the torch, they made their way over the heather and found a shaded knoll surrounded by rocks and boulders about fifty yards from the road. Mark spread the blanket and Mandy lay down. Open moorland stretched for miles all around, and a half-moon frosted the heather and gave the place the eerie look of a moonscape. It *was* cold, but they soon ceased to notice as they warmed each other with caresses. Finally, Mark got Mandy's tights and knickers down around her ankles, pushed her knees apart and lay on top of her.

Mandy stretched out her arms and snatched at the heather as the waves of pleasure swept through her. Soon, Mark speeded up and began to make grunting sounds deep in his throat. Mandy knew the end was close. She could smell the port and Stilton on his breath and feel his stubble against her shoulder. The more he groaned, the more she snatched at the heather by the nearest rock, but even as he came and she encouraged him with cries of ecstasy, she was aware that what she clutched in her right hand wasn't grass or heather, but something softer, some kind of material, more like an article of clothing.

6

I

That Sunday morning in Eastvale passed as most Sundays did. The locals read the papers, washed their cars, put the roast in, went to church, messed about in the garden. Some took walks in the dale or went to visit nearby relatives. The fine weather held, and tourists came, of course, jamming the market square with their cars, posing by the ancient cross or the façade of the Norman church for photographs, perhaps enjoying a pub lunch at the Queen's Arms or tea and sandwiches at the Golden Grill, then driving on to the craft show at Helmthorpe, the sheep fair at Relton, or the big car-boot sale in Hoggett's field near Fortford. And out in the dale, around massive Witch Fell between Skield and Swainshead, the search for seven-year-old Gemma Scupham went into its fourth full day.

Back in Eastvale, at eleven-thirty that morning, a very nervous and hungover Mark Hudson walked into the police station carrying a Marks and Spencer's bag. He quickly placed it on the front desk, mumbling, "You might be interested in this," then tried to make a casual exit.

It was not to be. The desk sergeant caught a glimpse of

yellow cotton in the bag, and before he knew it Mark Hudson was whisked politely upstairs to the CID.

Gristhorpe, aware that his office was far too comfortable for the interrogation of suspects, had Hudson taken to an interview room with a metal desk and chairs bolted to the floor and a small window covered by a metal grille. It smelled of Dettol and stale cigarette smoke.

With Richmond along to take notes, Gristhorpe planted himself firmly opposite a sweating Mark Hudson and began.

"Where did you find the clothes?"

"On the moors."

"More precisely?"

"On the road between Rosedale Abbey and Hutton-le-Hole. I don't remember exactly where."

"When?"

"Last night. Look, I just—"

"What were you doing out there?"

Hudson paused and licked his lips. He looked around the room and Gristhorpe could tell he didn't like what he saw. "I . . . well, I'd been to a company do at the White Horse. I was on my way home."

"Where do you live?"

"Helmsley."

"What company do you work for?"

Hudson looked surprised at the question. "Burton's. You know, the rag trade. I'm a sales rep."

"And this do you were at, what was it in honour of?"

"Well, it wasn't really . . . I mean, it was just an informal affair, some of the lads getting together for a meal and a chat."

"I see." Gristhorpe eased back in his chair. "And what made you stop in such a godforsaken place?"

"I needed to . . . you know, call of nature."

"Were you by yourself?"

"Yes."

Gristhorpe sniffed a lie, but he left it al..1e.

"Why did you wait so long before coming here? You must have known what you'd found. It's been in all the papers."

"I know. I just thought . . . It was very late. And I didn't want to get involved." He leaned forward. "And I was right, wasn't I? I decide to help, and here I am being interrogated like a suspect."

"Mr Hudson," said Gristhorpe, "in the first place, you're not being interrogated, you're simply being questioned, and in the second place, a child is missing, perhaps dead. How would you treat someone who walks in here, drops a bundle of what looks like the child's clothes and then tries to scarper?"

"I didn't try to scarper. I just wanted you to have the clothes, in case there was a clue. As I said, I didn't want to get involved. I thought of putting them in the post, but I knew that would take too long. I know how important time is in things like this, so I finally decided to come forward."

"Well, thank you very much, Mr Hudson."

"Look, if I really had done anything to that child, I'd hardly have come in here at all, would I?"

Gristhorpe fixed Hudson with his baby-blue eyes. "Psychopaths are unpredictable, Mark," he said. "We never know what they'll do next, or why they do it."

"For God's sake!"

"Where's the girl, Mark?"

Hudson hesitated, looked away. "What girl?"

"Come on, Mark. You know who I mean. The girl who was with you. Your accomplice."

"Accomplice?"

"Miss Peterson. Where is she?"

"I've never heard of anyone called Peterson."

Gristhorpe gave that one a "maybe." "Where's Gemma Scupham?"

"Please, you've got to believe me. I don't know anything. I had nothing to do with it. I'm just trying to do my civic duty."

Gristhorpe let the staring match continue until Hudson looked down at the stained metal desk, then he asked, "Can you remember exactly where you found the bundle of clothing?"

Hudson rubbed his damp forehead. "I was thinking about that on my way here," he said. "That you might want to know."

"It could be useful. We still haven't found the girl's body."

"Yes, well . . . I could try. I mean, I think I might remember if I saw the spot again. But it was dark and it's pretty bleak up there. I must admit after I found the clothes I didn't want to hang around."

"And you were no doubt under the influence of Bacchus?"

"What?"

"You'd been drinking."

"I'd had a little wine, yes. But I wasn't over the limit, if that's what you mean."

"I don't care how much you had to drink," said Gristhorpe, standing up. "Although judging by your eyes this morning I'd say you're a bloody liar. It's your memory I'm concerned about. What I want you to do is to take me to the spot where you found the clothes. I'll go with you in your car and DS Richmond here will follow. All right?"

"I don't have much choice, do I?"

"No," said Gristhorpe. "No, you don't."

II

Gristhorpe said nothing during the journey. They crawled up Sutton Bank into the Hambleton Hills, passed through Helmsley, then turned off the main road into Hutton-le-Hole. On the broad village green, split by Hutton Beck, the sides connected by a small white bridge, tourists ate picnics. Several sheep also picnicked from the grass itself, keeping their distance from the humans. It was a marvel of work-saving, Gristhorpe thought, letting the sheep wander the village and keep the green well cropped.

Beyond Hutton, they turned north onto a narrow, unfenced road over the desolate moors.

"I'd have more chance if we were going the other way," Hudson said. "I mean, that was the way I was driving, and it was very dark."

"Don't worry," said Gristhorpe, "you'll get your chance."

They had no luck on the way to Rosedale, so Gristhorpe turned in the car park and set off back again, up the one-in-three hill, with Richmond still behind. The moorland stretched for miles on all sides, a dark sea of purple heather, just past its prime. Hudson seemed to be concentrating as they drove, screwing up his eyes and looking into the distance, trying to remember how long he had been driving before he stopped. Finally, he pointed to a small outcrop of rocks among the heather about fifty yards from the roadside. "This is it!" he shouted. "This is the place."

Gristhorpe turned into the lay-by and waited for Richmond to pull in behind. "Are you sure?" he asked.

"Well, I can't be a hundred percent, but I'd been driving about this long, and I remember those rocks over there. There aren't many spots like that around here."

Gristhorpe opened the door. "By the roadside here, then? Let's take a look."

"Well, actually," Hudson said, "it was further from the road, closer to the rocks."

Richmond had joined them, and Gristhorpe gave him a puzzled look before he said, "Phil. If you stopped for a piss on this road at half past twelve at night, would you walk fifty yards or so away from your car to do it?"

Richmond shook his head. "No way, sir."

"I thought not." He fixed Hudson with his innocent gaze again. "But you did, right?"

"Yes."

"Why?"

"I don't know. I wasn't really thinking about it. I suppose I didn't want to be seen."

Gristhorpe looked around the desolate landscape in disbelief. "Didn't want to be seen?"

"That's right."

"You had a torch, I assume?"

"Yes."

Gristhorpe raised his bushy eyebrows and shook his head. "Come on, then, show us where."

Hudson led them over the rough, springy heather towards the outcrop, a natural shelter, and pointed. Gristhorpe didn't want to ruin any more evidence there might be, so he stood at the entrance and looked. It was a small area, maybe three or four yards square, surrounded on all sides but one with rocks, some as high as Gristhorpe's chest, but most of them no more than knee-high stones. In the centre, a small area of heather looked as if it had been flattened recently. There had been some blood on the yellow dungarees, he recalled. In all likelihood, there would be more blood around here, and perhaps other valuable trace evidence.

"Where exactly did you find the bundle of clothes?"

Gristhorpe asked.

Hudson thought for a moment, then pointed towards one of the smaller rocks near a corner of the flattened heather. "There. Stuffed under there. I think."

"What made you look there?"

He shrugged. "I don't know. Maybe I saw something out the corner of my eye."

Gristhorpe stood for a few moments taking in the scene, then turned to go back to the car.

"Can I go home now?" Hudson asked when they arrived. "My wife. She'll be wondering where I am."

"You can phone her when we get back to the station."

"Station?"

"Yes. Phil?" Gristhorpe ignored Hudson's protests. "Radio in and get the SOCO team, if you can raise any of them on a Sunday afternoon."

"Will do, sir." Richmond went to his car.

"But I don't understand," Hudson went on as Gristhorpe took him by the arm and gently guided him into the passenger seat.

"Don't you? It's simple really. I don't believe you. First off, I don't believe anyone would walk this far for a piss on a dark night in a place like this, and second I don't like the fact that you didn't show up at the station till nearly noon and then tried to leave as soon as you'd dumped the bag."

"But I've explained all that."

Gristhorpe started the car. "Not to my satisfaction, you haven't. Not by a long chalk. I don't like it at all. Besides, there's another thing."

"What?"

"I don't like *you*."

III

When Jenny Fuller pulled up outside Superintendent Gristhorpe's house above Lyndgarth at about seven o'clock that evening, lights shone a welcome from the lower windows. She hadn't phoned to say she was coming, but Phil Richmond had told her at the station that the superintendent had finally abandoned his camp-bed and gone home.

She knocked at the heavy door and waited. When Gristhorpe opened it, he was clearly surprised to see her there but didn't hesitate to invite her in.

"I've just finished doing a bit of work on the wall," he said as they stood in the hall. "Until it got too dark. Fancy a cup of tea?"

"Mm, yes please," Jenny said.

"I can offer you something stronger if you'd like?"

"No. No, tea will be fine. I was just on my way to visit a colleague in Lyndgarth and I thought I'd drop by. I don't have much, I'm afraid, but I can give you a sketch of what I've dug up so far. It might be some help."

Gristhorpe directed her to the study while he went to the kitchen. Jenny stood and gazed at the books, the clearly divided sections on military and naval history, general history, Yorkshire, then the novels, philosophy, poetry. On the small table by the armchair lay a paperback copy of *The Way of All Flesh*. Jenny had always loved the title but had never read it. Her background in English was distinctly weak, she realized.

Somehow the house and this room in particular spoke of a solitary, meditative, serious man, perhaps ill at ease in company. All that was missing was a pipe lying in an ashtray on the table, and perhaps a pipe-rack over the hearth. But Gristhorpe had a gregarious side to his character, too, she knew. He enjoyed telling tales with his mates and colleagues over a pint; he wasn't at all uneasy in groups. A man's man, perhaps?

Gristhorpe came back bearing a tray with a teapot and two mugs, a little jug of milk and a bowl of sugar. Jenny moved the book from the table and he set the tray down. He bade her sit in the leather armchair that she knew instinctively was "his" and pulled up a smaller chair for himself.

"That camp-bed was beginning to make me feel like an old man," he said. "Besides, they know where I am if anything breaks."

"No progress?"

"I wouldn't say that. We've talked to the neighbours again, and to Gemma's schoolfriends, the kids she played with, and none them saw anyone hanging about or heard Gemma mention anyone they didn't know. So that's a blank. But . . ." Gristhorpe went on to tell her about the Manleys' deserted cottage and his outing to the moors with Mark Hudson.

"What's happened to him?" she asked.

"I sent him home when I finally got the truth out of him. He led us on a merry dance, but he's got nothing to do with Gemma. He was out for a bit of extramarital activity. He'd settled on the spot in advance because it was some distance from the road and the rocks offered protection. He just stumbled across the clothing. We've got the woman's name. Of course, we'll talk to her and have another chat with him, just for procedure's sake."

"So the clothing *is* Gemma Scupham's?"

"Yes. The mother identified it. And there's a bit of blood on it—at least, it looks like blood. But we won't know much more till tomorrow, when the forensic team gets its job done."

"Still. . . ." Jenny shivered.

"Cold?"

"Oh, no. I'm fine, really." Jenny was wearing jeans and a fuzzy russet jumper that matched the colour of her hair, a warm enough outfit for a mild night. "Someone walked over my grave, that's all." She sipped some soothing tea. "I've been looking at instances of pairs of sexual deviants, and quite frankly there's hardly any. Often you'll find a couple who might commit crimes for gain, like Bonnie and Clyde, I suppose, but deviants usually act solo."

"What about the ones who don't?" Gristhorpe asked.

"There are *some* case studies. Usually you get a dominant leader and an accomplice, and usually they're both male. Leopold and Loeb, for example."

Gristhorpe nodded.

"Have you read *Compulsion*?" Jenny asked.

"Yes. It was one of Ian Brady's favourite books, you know."

"There are some parallels. The way your couple seem to have coldly planned and executed the crime, for a start," Jenny said. "But there's another thing: mixed pairs are very rare. Brady and Hindley come to mind, of course."

"Aye," said Gristhorpe. "Maybe Alan's told you I've got what you might call an unhealthy preoccupation with that case. But I was involved in the search. And I heard the tape of young Lesley Ann Downey pleading for her life." He shook his head and let the silence hang.

"Is that why you're getting so actively involved in this case? I mean, you don't usually."

Gristhorpe smiled. "Partly, I suppose. And maybe I'm trying to prove there's life in the old dog yet. I'm getting near retiring age, you know. But mostly I want to stop them before they do it again. We spend most of our time making cases against people we think have broken the law. Oh, we talk about prevention—we have coppers on the beat, keeping their eyes open—but mostly we come on the scene after the fact. That's also true this time, I realize. Gemma Scupham may be lost to us, but I'm damned if I'm going to let it happen to another child on my patch. Make sense?"

Jenny nodded.

"So what do you think?" he asked.

"From what little I know so far," Jenny said, "I'd say it's certainly possible we could be dealing with a Brady-Hindley pair. And they may not be paedophiles, as such. Paedophiles have a genuine sexual attraction to children, and they don't usually go in for murder unless they panic, but children also make good victims just because they're very vulnerable, like women. Brady's last victim was a seventeen-year-old male homosexual, I gather. Hardly a child."

"You've obviously done your research," Gristhorpe said. "Owt else?"

"I'd look more closely at why they did it the way they did, and why they chose Gemma Scupham. It's also come out from a few studies lately that more women are involved in paedophilia than we'd ever thought before, so I wouldn't discount that possibility altogether. Maybe she wasn't along just for the ride."

"Could *he* have been the one along for the ride?" Gristhorpe asked.

"I doubt it. Not according to the statistics, at least."

"Any good news?"

Jenny shook her head. "What it comes down to," she said, leaning forward, "is that in my opinion—and remember it's still all basically guesswork—you're probably dealing with a psychopath, most likely the male, and a woman who's become fixated on him, who'll do anything he says. There's something odd about them, though, something odd about the whole business. The psychology doesn't quite add up." She frowned. "Anyway, I'd concentrate on him. He might not be a paedophile in particular, so I wouldn't depend on criminal records. I think it's more likely that he just likes to act out sadistic fantasies in front of an adoring audience. I—Oh, God, what am I saying? That poor damn kid." Jenny flopped back in the chair and put her hand to her forehead. "I'm sorry," she said. "I'm behaving like a silly girl."

"Nay, lass," said Gristhorpe. "When they played that tape there wasn't a dry eye in the courtroom—and they were hardened coppers all."

"Still," said Jenny, "if I'm to be any help I have to try to remain calm and objective."

"Aye," said Gristhorpe, sitting down again. "Aye, you can try. But I don't imagine it's easy for any of us with a possible psychopath on the loose, is it? Another cup of tea?"

Jenny looked at her watch. No, she didn't have to hurry; she had plenty of time. "Yes," she said. "That'd be very nice. I think I will."

7

I

"Don't tell me you've been burning the midnight oil?" Gristhorpe said, when Vic Manson phoned at nine o'clock Monday morning.

Manson laughed. "Afraid so."

"Anything?"

"Where do you want me to start?"

"Start with the search of the moorland."

"The lads haven't finished yet. They're still out there. No sign of a body so far."

"What about the clothes?"

"I've got Frank's report in front of me. He's our blood expert. It was a dry stain, so we can't tell as much as we'd like—the presence of certain drugs, for example— but it *is* blood, it's human, and it's group A, one of the most common, unfortunately, and the same as Gemma's, according to our files. We're doing more tests."

"Anything else?"

"Well, we can tell a fair bit about how it came to be there and—this is the interesting part—first, there wasn't very much, nowhere near enough to cause loss of life. It was restricted to the bib area of the T-shirt and the dungarees, which might make you think on first sight that someone cut her throat, but no way, according to Frank. At least not while she was wearing them."

"Then how did it get to be there?"

"It didn't drip. It was smeared, as if you cut your finger and wiped it on your shirt."

"But you surely wouldn't wipe it on a white T-shirt and yellow dungarees?"

"I wouldn't, no. That'd be grounds for divorce. But Gemma was only seven, remember. How careful were you about getting your clothes dirty when you were seven? Someone else washed them for you."

"Still . . . And less of your cheek, Vic. What kind of injury could have caused it?"

"We can't say for certain, but most likely a scratch, a small cut, something like that."

"Any idea how long the clothes had been out there?"

"Sorry."

"Anything else at all?"

"Yes. In addition to the items I've mentioned, we received a pair of white cotton socks and child's sneakers. There was no underwear. You might care to consider that."

"I will."

"And there was some whitish powder or dust on the dungarees. It's being analyzed."

"What about the cottage?"

"Very interesting. Whoever cleaned that place up really did a good job. They even took the vacuum bag with them and combed out all the fibres from the brushes."

"As if they had something to hide?"

"Either that or they were a right pair of oddballs. Maybe house-cleaning in the nude got them all excited."

"Aye, and maybe pigs can fly. But we've got nothing to tie them in to the missing lass?"

"No prints, no bloodstains, no bodily fluids. Just hair.

It's practically impossible to get rid of every hair from a scene."

"And it's also practically impossible to pin it down to any one person," said Gristhorpe.

"There's still the DNA typing. It takes a bloody long time, though, and it's not as reliable as people think."

"Was there anything that might have indicated the child's presence?"

"No. The hairs were definitely adult. Some sandy coloured, fairly short, probably a man's, and the others we found were long and blonde. A woman's, I'd say. A child's hairs are usually finer in pigment, with a much more rudimentary character. We found some fibres, too, mostly from clothes you can buy anywhere—lambs-wool, rayon, that kind of thing. No white or yellow cotton. There was something else, though, and I think this will interest you."

"Yes."

"Well, you know we took the drains apart?"

"Will Patricia Cummings ever let me forget?"

"There's a fair bit of dark sludge in there."

"Could it be blood?"

"Let me finish. No, it's not blood. We haven't run the final tests yet, but we think it's hair-dye, the kind you can wash out easily."

"Well, well, well," said Gristhorpe. "That *is* interesting. Just one more thing, Vic."

"Yes."

"I think you'd better get the lads digging up the cottage gardens, front and back. I know it's a long shot— most likely somebody would have seen them burying anything out there—but we can't overlook it."

"I suppose not," Manson sighed. "Your estate agent's going to love us for this."

"Can't be helped, Vic."

"Okay. I'll be in touch later."

Gristhorpe sat at his desk for a moment running his palm over his chin and frowning. This was the first positive link between Mr Brown and Miss Peterson, who had abducted Gemma Scupham on Tuesday afternoon, and Chris and Connie Manley, who had abandoned a prepaid holiday cottage in spotless condition on the Thursday of that same week. Coincidence wasn't enough; nor was the fact that Manson's men had found traces of hair-dye in the drains, but it was a bloody good start. His phone buzzed.

"Gristhorpe," he grunted.

"Sir," said Sergeant Rowe, "I think there's someone here you'd better see."

"Yes? Who is it?"

"A Mr Bruce Parkinson, sir. From what he tells me, I think he might know something about the car. You know, the one they used to take that young lass away."

Christ, it was coming in thick and fast now, the way it usually did after days of hard slog leading nowhere. "Hang onto him, Geoff," said Gristhorpe. "I'll be right down."

II

Dark satanic mills, indeed, thought DC Susan Gay as she approached Bradford. Even on a fine autumn day like this, even with most of the mills closed down or turned into craft shops or business centres, the tall, dark chimneys down in the valley still had a gloomy aspect.

Bradford had been cleaned up. It now advertised itself as the gateway to Brontë country and boasted such tourist attractions as Bolling Hall, the National Museum of Photography and even Undercliffe Cemetery. But as

Susan navigated her way through the one-way streets of the city centre, past the gothic Victorian Wool Exchange and the Town Hall, with its huge campanile tower, Bradford still felt to her like a nineteenth-century city in fancy dress.

After driving around in circles for what seemed like ages, she finally turned past St George's Hall and drove by the enormous Metro Travel Interchange onto Wakefield Road. The next time she had to stop for a red light, she consulted her street map again and found Hawthorne Terrace. It didn't seem too far away: a right, a left and a right again. Soon she found herself in an area of terrace back-to-backs, with washing hanging across rundown tarmac streets. The car bumped in potholes as she looked for the street name. There it was.

An old man in a turban and a long white beard hobbled across the street on his walking-stick. Despite the chill that had crept into the air that morning, people sat out on their doorsteps. Children played hand-cricket against wickets chalked on walls and she had to drive very slowly in case one of the less cautious players ran out in front of her chasing a catch. Some of the corner shops had posters in Hindi in their windows. One showed a golden-skinned woman apparently swooning in a rajah's arms—a new video release, by the look of it. She noticed the smells in the air, too: cumin, coriander, cardamom.

At last she bumped to a halt outside number six, watched by a group of children over the street. There were no gardens, just a cracked pavement beyond the kerb, then the houses themselves in an unbroken row. The red bricks had darkened over the years, and these places hadn't been sandblasted clean like the Town Hall. Like any other northern city, Bradford had its share of new housing, both council and private, but the Johnsons' part of town was pre-war, and here, old didn't mean charming, as it often did out in the country. Still, it was no real slum, no indication of abject poverty. As she locked her car door and looked around, Susan noticed the individualizing touches to some of the houses: an ornate brass door-knocker on one bright red door; a dormer window atop one house; double-glazing in another.

Taking a deep breath, Susan knocked. She knew that, even though the Johnsons had agreed to her coming, she would be intruding on their grief. No matter what the late Carl's police record said, to them he was a son who had been brutally murdered. At least she wasn't the one to break the news. The Bradford police had already done that. The upstairs curtains, she noticed, were drawn, a sign that there had been a death in the family.

A woman opened the door. In her late fifties, Susan guessed, she looked well preserved, with a trim figure, dyed red hair nicely permed and just the right amount of make-up to hide a few wrinkles. She was wearing a black skirt and a white blouse tucked in the waistband. A pair of glasses dangled on a cord around her neck.

"Come in, dearie," she said, after Susan had introduced herself. "Make yourself at home."

The front door led straight into a small living-room. The furniture was old and worn, but everything was clean and well cared for. A framed print of a white flower in a jar standing in front of a range of mountains in varying shades of blue brightened the wall opposite the window, which admitted enough sunlight to make the wooden surfaces of the sideboard gleam. Mrs Johnson noticed Susan looking at it.

"It's a Hockney print," she said proudly. "We bought it at the photography museum when we went to see his exhibition. It brightens up the place a bit, doesn't it? He's a local lad, you know, Hockney." Her accent sounded vaguely posh and wholly put-on.

"Yes," said Susan. She remembered Sandra Banks telling her about David Hockney once. A local lad he might be, but he lived near the sea now in southern California, a far cry from Bradford. "It's very nice," she added.

"I think so," said Mrs Johnson. "I've always had an cyc for a good painting, you know. Sometimes I think if I'd stuck at it and not. . . ." She looked around. "Well . . . it's too late for that now, isn't it? Cup of tea?"

"Yes, please."

"Sit down, dearie, there you go. Won't be a minute. Mr Johnson's just gone to the corner shop. He won't be long."

Susan sat in one of the dark blue armchairs. It was up-holstered in some velvety kind of material, and she didn't like the feel of it against her fingertips, so she folded her hands in her lap. A clock ticked on the man-telpiece. Beside it stood a couple of postcards from sunny beaches, and three cards of condolence, from neighbours no doubt. Below was a brown tiled hearth and fireplace, its grate covered by a gas-fire with fake glowing coals. Even though it was still warm enough in-doors, Susan could make out a faint glow and hear the hiss of the gas supply. The Johnsons obviously didn't want her to think they were stingy.

Before Mrs Johnson returned with the tea, the front door opened and a tall, thin man in baggy jeans and a red short-sleeved jumper over a white shirt walked in. When he saw Susan, he smiled and held out his hand. He had a narrow, lined face, a long nose, and a few fluffy grey hairs around the edges of his predominantly bald head. The corners of his thin lips were perpetually upturned as if on the verge of a conspiratorial smile.

"You must be from the police?" he said. "Pleased to

see you."

It was an odd greeting, certainly not the kind Susan was used to, but she shook his hand and mumbled her condolences.

"Fox's Custard Creams," he said.

"Pardon?"

"That's what Mother sent me out for. Fox's Custard Creams." He shook his head. "She thought they'd go nice with a cup of tea." Unlike his wife's, Mr Johnson's accent was clearly and unashamedly West Riding. "You think I could get any, though? Could I hell-as-like."

At that moment, Mrs Johnson came in with a tray bearing cups and saucers, her best china, by the look of it, delicate pieces with rose patterns and gold around the rims, and a teapot covered by a quilted pink cosy. She set this down on the low polished-wood table in front of the settee.

"What's wrong?" she asked her husband.

He glanced at Susan. "Everything's changed, that's what. Oh, it's been going on for years, I know, but I just can't seem to get used to it, especially as I'm home most of the time now."

"He got made redundant," said Mrs Johnson, whispering as if she were telling someone a neighbour had cancer. "Had a good job as a clerk in the accounts department at British Home Stores, but they had staff cutbacks. I ask you, after nearly thirty years' loyal service. And how's a man to get a job at his age? It's young 'uns they want these days." Her accent slipped as she expressed her disgust.

"Now that's enough of that, Edie," he said, then looked at Susan again. "I'm as tolerant as the next man—I don't want you to think I'm not—but I'd say things have come to a pretty pass when you can buy all the poppadoms and samosas you want at the corner shop but you can't get a packet of Fox's blooming Custard Creams. What'll it be next? that's what I ask myself. Baked beans? Milk? Butter? *Tea*?"

"Well, you'll have to go to Taylor's in future won't you?"

"Taylor's! Taylor's was bought out by Gandhi's or some such lot months back, woman. Shows how much shopping you do."

"I go to the supermarket down on the main road." She looked at Susan. "It's a Sainsbury's, you know, very nice."

"Anyway," said Mr Johnson, "the lass doesn't want to hear about our problems, does she? She's got a job to do." He sat down and they all waited quietly as Mrs Johnson poured the tea.

"We do have some ginger biscuits," she said to Susan, "if you'd like one."

"No thanks. Tea'll be fine, Mrs Johnson, honest."

"Where do you come from, lass?" asked Mr Johnson.

"Sheffield."

"I thought it were Yorkshire, but I couldn't quite place it. Sheffield, eh." He nodded, and kept on nodding, as if he couldn't think of anything else to say.

"I'm sorry to be calling at a time like this," Susan said, accepting her cup and saucer from Mrs Johnson, "but it's important we get as much information as we can as soon as possible." She placed the tea carefully at the edge of the low table and took out her notebook. In a crucial interrogation, either she would have someone along to do that, or she would be taking the notes while Banks asked the questions, but the Johnsons were hardly suspects, and all she hoped to get was a few names of their son's friends and acquaintances. "When did you last see Carl?" she asked first.

"Now then, when was it, love?" Mr Johnson asked his

wife. "Seven years? Eight?"

"More like nine or ten, I'd say."

"Nine years?" Susan grasped at a number. "You hadn't seen him in all that time?"

"Broke his mother's heart, Carl did," said Mr Johnson, with the incongruous smile hovering as he spoke. "He never had no time for us."

"Now that's not true," said Mrs Johnson. "He fell in with bad company, that's what happened. He was always too easily led, our Carl."

"Aye, and look where it got him."

"Stop it, Bert, don't talk like that. You know I don't like it when you talk like that."

Susan coughed and they both looked at her shame-facedly. "Sorry," said Mrs Johnson. "I know we weren't close, but he *was* our son."

"Yes," said Susan. "What I was wondering was if you could tell me anything about him, his friends, what he liked to do."

"We don't really know," said Mrs Johnson, "do we, Bert?" Her husband shook his head. "It was nine years ago, I remember now. His twenty-first birthday. That was the last time we saw him."

"What happened?"

"There was a local lass," Mr Johnson explained. "Our Carl got her . . . well, you know. Anyway, instead of doing the honourable thing, he said it was her problem. She came round, right at his birthday party, and told us. We had a barney and Carl stormed out. We never saw him again. He sent us a postcard about a year later, just to let us know he was all right."

"Where was it from?"

"London. It was a picture of Tower Bridge."

"Always did have a temper, did Carl," Mrs Johnson said.

"What was the girl's name?" Susan asked.

Mr Johnson frowned. "Beryl, if I remember correctly," he said. "I think she moved away years back, though."

"Her mum and dad still live round the corner," said Mrs Johnson. Susan got their address and made a note to call on them later.

"Did Carl keep in touch at all?"

"No. He wasn't even in much after he turned sixteen, but there's not been a dicky-bird since that postcard. He'd be thirty when he . . . when he . . . wouldn't he?"

"Yes," Susan said.

"It's awful young to die," Mrs Johnson muttered. "I blame bad company. Even when he was at school, whenever he got in trouble it was because somebody put him up to it, got him to do the dirty work. When he got caught shoplifting that time, it was that what's-his-name, you know, Bert, the lad with the spotty face."

"They all had spotty faces," said Mr Johnson, grinning at Susan.

"You know who I mean. Robert Naylor, that's the one. He was behind it all. He always looked up to the wrong people did our Carl. Always trusted the wrong ones. I'm sure he wasn't *bad* in himself, just too easily led. He always seemed to have this . . . this *fascination* for bad 'uns. He liked to watch those old James Cagney films on telly. Just loved them, he did. What was his favourite, Bert? You know, that one where James Cagney keeps getting these headaches, the one where he loves his mother."

"*White Heat*." Mr Johnson looked at Susan. "You know the one. 'Top of the world, Ma!'"

Susan didn't, but she nodded anyway.

"That's the one," said Mrs Johnson. "Loved that film, our Carl did. I blame the telly myself for a lot of the violence that goes on these days, I really do. They can get away with anything now."

"Did you know any of his other friends?" Susan asked her.

"Only when he was at school. He just wasn't home much after he left school."

"You don't know the names of anyone else he went around with?"

"Sorry, dearie, no. It's so long ago I just can't remember. It's a miracle Robert Naylor came back to me, and that's only because of the shoplifting. Had the police round then, we did."

"What about this Robert Naylor? Where does he live?"

Mrs Johnson shook her head. Susan made a note of the name anyway. It might be worth trying to track him down. If he was such a "bad 'un" he might even have a record by now. There didn't seem anything else to be gained from talking to the Johnsons, Susan thought. Best nip round the corner and find out about the girl Carl got pregnant, then head back to Eastvale. She finished her tea and stood up to leave.

"Nay, lass," said Mr Johnson. "Have another cup."

"No, I really must be going. Thank you very much."

"Well," he said, "I suppose you've got your job to do."

"Thank you for your time," Susan said, and opened the door.

"You can be sure of one thing, you mark my words," said Mrs Johnson.

Susan paused in the doorway. "Yes?"

"There'll be someone behind this had an influence on our Carl. Put him up to things. A bad 'un. A *real* bad 'un, with no conscience." And she nodded, as if to emphasize her words.

"I'll remember that," said Susan, then walked out into the cobbled street where bed-sheets, shirts and underclothes flapped on a breeze that carried the fragrances of the east.

III

The man sitting under a graphic poster about the perils of drunken driving had the irritated, pursed-lipped look of an accountant whose figures won't add up right. When he saw Gristhorpe coming, he got to his feet sharply.

"What are you going to do about it, then?" he asked.

Gristhorpe looked over to Sergeant Rowe, who raised his eyebrows and shook his head, then he led the man to one of the downstairs interview rooms. He was in his mid-thirties, Gristhorpe guessed, dressed neatly in a grey suit, white shirt and blue and red striped tie, fair hair combed back, wire-framed glasses, and his chin thrust out. His complexion had a scrubbed and faintly ruddy complexion that Gristhorpe always, rightly or wrongly, associated with the churchy crowd, and he smelled of Pears soap. When they sat down, Gristhorpe asked him what the problem was.

"My car's been stolen, that's what. Didn't the sergeant tell you?"

"You're here about a stolen car?"

"That's right. It's outside."

Gristhorpe rubbed his brow. "I'm afraid I don't understand. Can you explain it from the beginning?"

The man sighed and looked at his watch. "Look," he said, "I've been here twenty-two minutes already, first waiting to see the sergeant back there, then explaining everything to him. Are you telling me I have to go through it all again? Because if you are, you've got a nerve. I had trouble enough getting this time off from the office in the first place. Why don't you ask the other policeman what happened?"

Gristhorpe kept his silence throughout the tirade. He was used to impatient, precise and fastidious people like Mr Parkinson and found it best to let them carry on until they ran out of steam. "I'd rather hear it from you, sir," he replied.

"Oh, very well. I've been away for a while. When I—"

"Since when?"

"When what?"

"When did you go away?"

"Last Monday morning, a week ago. As I was saying, I left my car in the garage as usual, then I—"

"What do you mean, 'as usual'?"

"Exactly what I say. Now if—"

"You mean you were in the habit of doing this?"

"I think that's what 'as usual' means, don't you, Inspector?"

"Carry on." Gristhorpe didn't bother to correct him over rank. If the car turned out to be a useful lead, it would be important to find out how many people knew about Parkinson's habit of leaving his car for days at a time, and why he did so, but for now it was best to let him finish.

"When I returned this morning, it was exactly as I had left it, except for one thing."

"Yes?"

"The mileage. I always keep a careful record of how many miles I've done on each journey. I find it's important these days, with the price of petrol the way it is. Anyway, when I left, the mileometer stood at 7655. I know this for a fact because I wrote it down in the log I keep. When I got back it read 7782. Now, that's a difference of one hundred and twenty-seven miles, Inspector. Someone has driven my car one hundred and twenty-seven miles in my absence. How do you explain that?"

Gristhorpe scratched his bristly chin. "It certainly sounds as if someone borrowed it. If you—"

"*Borrowed*?" echoed Parkinson. "That implies I gave someone permission. I did no such thing. Someone stole my car, Inspector. *Stole* it. The fact that they returned it is irrelevant."

"Mm, you've got a point," said Gristhorpe. "Were there any signs of forced entry? Scratches around the door, that kind of thing?"

"There were scratches at the bottom of the chassis I'm positive weren't there before, but none at all around the door or windows. I imagine that today's criminal has more sophisticated means of entry than the wire coat-hanger some fools are reduced to when they lock themselves out of their cars?"

"You imagine right," said Gristhorpe. "Keys aren't hard to come by. And garages are easy to get into. What make is the car?"

"Make. I don't see—"

"For our records."

"Very well. It's a Toyota. I find the Japanese perfectly reliable when it comes to cars."

"Of course. And what colour?"

"Dark blue. Look, you can save us both a lot of time if you come and have a look yourself. It's parked right outside."

"Fine." Gristhorpe stood up. "Let's go."

Parkinson led. As he walked, he stuck his hands in his pockets and jingled keys and loose change. Outside the station, opposite the market square, Gristhorpe sniffed the air. His experienced dalesman's nose smelled rain. Already, clouds were blowing in from the north-west. He also smelled pub grub from the Queen's Arms, steak-and-kidney pie if he was right, and he realized he was getting hungry.

Parkinson's car was, indeed, a dark blue Toyota, illegally parked right in front of the police station.

"Look at that," Parkinson said, pointing to scratched paintwork on the bottom of the chassis, just behind the left front wheel. "Careless driving that is. Must have caught against a stone or something. Well? Aren't you going to have a look inside?"

"The fewer people do that, the better, sir," said Gristhorpe, looking to see what stones and dirt were trapped in the tread of the tires.

Parkinson frowned. "What on earth do you mean by that?"

Gristhorpe turned to face him. "You say you left last Monday?"

"Yes."

"What time?"

"I took the eight-thirty flight from Leeds and Bradford."

"To where?"

"I don't see as it's any of your business, but Brussels. EEC business."

Gristhorpe nodded. They were standing in the middle of the pavement and passers-by had to get around them somehow. A woman with a pram asked Parkinson to step out of the way so she could get by. A teenager with cropped hair and a tattoo on his cheek swore at him. Parkinson was clearly uncomfortable talking in the street. A mark of his middle-class background, Gristhorpe thought. The working classes—both urban and rural—had always felt quite comfortable standing and chatting in the street. But Parkinson hopped from foot to foot, glancing irritably from the corners of his eyes as people brushed and jostled past them to get by. His glasses had slipped down his nose, and a stray lock of hair fell over his right eye.

"How did you get to the airport?" Gristhorpe pressed on.

"A friend drove me. A business colleague. It's no mystery, Inspector, believe me. Long-term parking at the airport is expensive. My colleague drives a company car, and the company pays. It's as simple as that." He pushed his glasses back up to the bridge of his nose. "It's not that I'm overly concerned about saving money, of course. But why pay when you don't have to?"

"Indeed. Do you always do it that way?"

"What way?"

"Don't you ever take it in turns?"

"I told you. He has a company car. Look, I don't see—"

"Please bear with me. Did nobody notice the car was gone?"

"How could they? It was in the garage, and the garage door was locked."

"Have you asked if anyone heard anything?"

"That's your job. That's why—"

"Where do you live, sir?"

"Bartlett Drive. Just off the Helmthorpe road."

"I know it." If Gristhorpe remembered correctly, Bartlett Drive was close to the holiday cottage the Manleys had so suddenly deserted. "And the car was replaced as if it had never been gone?"

"That's right. Only they didn't bargain for my record-keeping."

"Quite. Look, I'll get someone to drive you home and take a full statement, then—"

"What? You'll do what?" A couple walking by stopped and stared. Parkinson blushed and lowered his voice. "I've already told you I've given up enough time already. Now why don't you—"

Gristhorpe held his hand up, palm out, and his innocent gaze silenced Parkinson just as it had put the fear of God into many a villain. "I can understand your feelings," Gristhorpe said, "but please listen to me for a minute. There's a chance, a very good chance, that your car was used to abduct a little girl from her home last Tuesday afternoon. If that's the case, it's essential that we get a forensic team to go over the car thoroughly. Do you understand?"

Parkinson nodded, mouth open.

"Now, this may mean some inconvenience to you. You'll get your car back in the same condition it's in now, but I can't say exactly when. Of course, we'll try to help you in any way we can, but basically, you're acting like the true public-spirited citizen that you are. You're generously helping us try to get to the bottom of a particularly nasty bit of business, right?"

"Well," said Parkinson. "Seeing as you put it *that* way." And the first drops of rain fell on their heads.

IV

Banks and Susan stood at the bar in the Queen's Arms that Monday lunch-time, wedged between two farmers and a family of tourists, and munched cheese-and-onion sandwiches with their drinks. Banks had a pint of Theakston's bitter, Susan a Slimline Tonic Water. A song about a broken love affair was playing on the jukebox in the background, and somewhere by the door to the toilets, a video game beeped as aliens went down in flames. From what he could overhear, Banks gathered that the farmers were talking about money and the tourists were arguing about whether to go home because of the rain or carry on to the Bowes Museum.

"So you found the girl's parents?" Banks asked.

"Uh-uh." Susan put her hand to her mouth and wiped away some crumbs, then swallowed. "Sorry, sir. Yes, they were home. Seems like everyone except the Pakistanis around there is unemployed or retired."

"Get anything?"

Susan shook her head. Tight blonde curls danced over her ears. Banks noticed the dangling earrings, stylized, elongated Egyptian cats in light gold. Susan had certainly brightened up her appearance a bit lately. "Dead end," she said. "Oh, it happened all right. Right charmer Carl Johnson was, from what I can gather. But the girl, Beryl's her name, she's been living in America for the past five years."

"What happened?"

"Just what his folks said. He got her in the family way, then dumped her. She came around to make a fuss, embarrass him like, at his twenty-first birthday party. He was still living at home then, off and on, and his parents invited a few close relatives over. There was a big row and he stormed out. Didn't even take any of his clothes with him. They never saw him again."

Banks sipped at his pint and thought for a moment. "So they've no idea who he hung around with, or where he went?"

"No." Susan frowned. "They know he went to London, but that's all. There was a chap called Robert Naylor. Mrs Johnson saw him as bad influence."

"Has he got form?"

"Yes, sir. I checked. Just minor vandalism, drunk and disorderly. But he's dead. Nothing suspicious. He was riding his motorbike too fast. He lost control and skidded into a lorry on the M1."

"So that's that."

"I'm afraid so, sir. From what I can gather, Johnson was the type to fall in with bad company."

"That's obvious enough."

"What I mean, sir, is that both his parents and Beryl's mother said he looked up to tough guys. He wasn't much in himself, they said, but he liked to be around dangerous people."

Banks took another sip of beer. One of the tourists bumped his elbow and he spilled a little on the bar. The woman apologized. "Sounds like the kind that hero-worships psychos and terrorists," Banks said. "He'd probably have been happy working for the Krays or someone like that back in the old days."

"That's it, sir. He was a weakling himself, but he liked to boast about the rough company he kept."

"It fits. Small-time con-man, wants to be in with the big boys. So you're thinking that might give us somewhere to look for his killer?"

"Well, there *could* be a connection, couldn't there?" Susan said, pushing her empty plate away.

Banks lit a cigarette, taking care that the smoke didn't drift directly into Susan's face. "You mean he might have been playing out of his league, tried a double-cross or something?"

"It's possible," said Susan.

"True. At least it's an angle to work on, and there don't seem very many. I dropped by The Barleycorn last night and found Les Poole. I just thought I'd mention Johnson to him, seeing as they're both in the same business, so to speak."

"And?"

"Nothing. Poole denied knowing him—well, of course he would—and he's not a bad liar. No signs in his voice or his body language that he wasn't telling the truth. But . . ." Banks shook his head. "I don't know. There was something there. The only way I can describe it is as a whiff of fear. It came and went in a second, and I'm not sure even Les was aware of it, but it was there. Anyway, no good chasing will-o'-the-wisps. Adam Harkness's Golf Club alibi checks out. I still think we might bring South Africa up whenever we question someone, though. Johnson *could* have been blackmailing Harkness, and Harkness could afford to pay someone to get rid of him. Have you had time to ask around the other flats?"

"Last night, sir. I meant to tell you, but I set off for Bradford so early. There's a student on the ground floor called Edwina Whixley. She heard male voices occasionally from Johnson's room. And she saw someone coming down the stairs one day she thought *might* have been visiting him."

"Did you get a description?"

"Yes." Susan fished for her notebook and found the page. "About five foot five, mid-thirties, cropped black hair and squarish head. He was wearing a suede zip-up jacket and jeans."

"That's all?"

"Yes, sir."

"Ring a bell?"

Susan shook her head.

"Me, neither. Maybe you can get her to come and look at some mug-shots. And you might as well check into Johnson's form, his prison mates, that kind of thing. See if you can come up with any local names, anyone fitting the description."

"Yes, sir." Susan picked up her bag and left.

She had a very purposeful, no-nonsense walk, Banks noticed. He remembered the trouble she had had not so long ago and decided it had actually done her good. Susan Gay wasn't the kind to throw her hands up in the air and surrender. Adversity strengthened her; she learned from her mistakes. Maybe that hardened her a bit, made her more cynical and less trusting, but perhaps they weren't such bad qualities for a detective. It was hard not to be cynical when you saw so much villainy and human misery, but in many cases the cynicism was just a shell, as the sick jokes at crime scenes and post-mortems were ways of coping with the horror and the gruesomeness of death, and perhaps, too, with the fact that it comes to us all at one time. The best coppers, Banks thought, are the ones who hang onto their humanity against all odds. He hoped he had managed to do that; he knew Gristhorpe had; and he hoped that Susan would. She was young yet.

The tourists decided to go home, partly because their youngest child was making a fearful racket, and the farmers had moved on to discuss the prospects for the three-forty at Newmarket. Banks drained his pint, then headed back to the office. There was paperwork to be done. And he would make an appointment to meet with Linda Fish, from the Writers' Circle, tomorrow, much as the thought made him wince, and see what light she could shed on Mr Adam Harkness.

V

The strange woman called on Brenda Scupham shortly after Les had left for the pub that Monday evening. She was washing the dishes and lip-synching to a Patsy Cline record when the doorbell rang. Drying her hands with the tea towel, she walked through and opened the door.

"Mrs Scupham? Brenda Scupham?"

The woman stood there in the rain, a navy-blue rain-coat buttoned up to her neck and a dark scarf fastened over her head. Wind tugged at the black umbrella she held. Beyond her, Brenda could see the nosy woman from number eleven across the street peeking through her curtains.

Brenda hugged herself against the cold and frowned. "Yes. What do you want?"

"I'm Lenora Carlyle," the woman said. "You might have heard of me?"

"Are you a reporter?"

"No. Can I come in?"

Brenda stood back, and the woman let down her umbrella and entered. Brenda noticed immediately in the hall light her intense dark eyes and Romany complexion. She unfastened her scarf and shook out her head of luxuriant, coal-black hair.

"I don't want anything," Brenda went on, suddenly nervous.

"I'm not a reporter, Brenda, and I'm not selling anything," the woman said in soft, hypnotic tones. "I'm a psychic. I'm here because of your daughter, Gemma. I want to help you."

Brenda just gaped and stood back as the woman unbuttoned her raincoat. Numbly, she took the umbrella and stood it on the rubber mat with the shoes, then she took the woman's coat and hung it up.

Lenora Carlyle was heavy-set, wearing a chunky-knit black cardigan covered with red and yellow roses, black slacks, and a religious symbol of some kind on a chain around her neck. Or so the odd-looking cross with the loop at the top seemed to Brenda. Lenora straightened her cardigan and smiled, revealing stained and crooked teeth.

Brenda led her into the living-room and turned off the music. She still felt a little frightened. The supernatural always made her feel that way. She wasn't sure if she believed in it or not, but she'd heard of enough strange things happening to people to make her wonder—like the time her old friend Laurie Burton dreamed about her father for the first time in years the very night he died.

After they had sat down, Brenda lit a cigarette and asked, "What do you mean, help? How can you help?"

"I don't know yet," Lenora said, "but I'm sure I can. If you'll let me."

"How much do you want?"

"I don't want anything."

Brenda felt suspicious, but you couldn't argue with that. "What do you want me to do?" she asked.

Lenora put a friendly hand on her knee. "Nothing, dear, except relax and be open. Are you a believer?"

"I . . . I don't know."

"It's all right. The Lord knows His own. Do you have something of Gemma's? Something personal."

"Like what?"

"Well, hair would be best, but perhaps an article of clothing, a favourite toy. Something she felt strongly about, touched a lot."

Brenda thought of the teddy bear one of her ex-boyfriends—Bob? Ken?—had bought Gemma some years ago. Even now she was older, Gemma never slept without it. Brenda felt a pang of guilt as she thought about it. If there were any chance that Gemma *was* alive, she would miss her teddy bear terribly. Being without it would make her so miserable. But no. Gemma was dead; she had to be.

She went upstairs to Gemma's room and Lenora Carlyle followed her. While Brenda walked to the tiny bed to pick up the bear, Lenora stood on the threshold and seemed to take several deep breaths.

"What is it?" Brenda asked.

Lenora didn't answer. Instead, she walked forward, reached out for the bear, and sat down on the bed with it. The bedspread had Walt Disney characters printed all over it: Mickey Mouse, Donald Duck, Bambi, Dumbo.

How Gemma loved cartoons. They were the only things that made her smile, Brenda remembered. But it was an odd, inward smile, not one to be shared.

Lenora clutched the bear to her breast and rocked slowly, eyes closed. Brenda felt a shiver go up her spine. It was as if the atmosphere of the room had subtly changed, somehow become thicker, deeper and colder. For what seemed like ages, Lenora hung onto the bear and rocked silently. Brenda clutched her blouse at her throat. Then finally, Lenora opened her eyes. They were glazed and unfocused. She began to speak.

"Gemma is alive," she said. "Alive. But, oh, she's so alone, so frightened. So much suffering. She wants you. She wants her mother. She *needs* you Brenda. You must find her."

Brenda felt light-headed. "She can't be," she whispered. "They've found her clothes . . . . I've seen them."

"She's alive, Brenda." Lenora turned and grasped Brenda's wrist. Her grip was tight.

Brenda steadied herself on the back of the small chair by Gemma's desk. She felt dizzy, her skin cold and clammy, as if she had had too much to drink and the world was spinning fast. "Where can I find her?" she asked. "Where do I look? Tell me, where do I look?"

8

I

By Tuesday morning, the searchers had turned up nothing buried in the garden of the holiday cottage; nor had anything of interest been discovered on the moors where Gemma's clothing had been found. Gristhorpe sat in his office going over the paperwork, waiting to hear from forensics about Parkinson's car. Outside, mucky clouds, like balls of black wool, started to attack from the west.

It was close to twelve when Vic Manson called.

"What did you find?" Gristhorpe asked.

"Plenty. The girl was in there all right. We found her prints. Windows, back of the front seat, all over. I checked them with the ones on file, and they match."

"Good work, Vic."

"And we found yellow fibres."

"The dungarees?"

"Looks like it. I'm still waiting for the confirmation."

"Anything else?"

"A bit of black hair-dye smeared on the driver's head-rest. Soil and gravel in the wheels, could have come from just about anywhere locally. Lay-by, track, drive, quarry."

"No particular kind of limestone deposit you only find

on Aldington Edge, or anything like that?"

Manson laughed. "Sorry, no. Look, remember that whitish powder I told you about on the kid's dungarees? It's a lime solution, most likely whitewash."

"Where from?"

"Same as the soil and gravel, it could have come from anywhere, really. A pub wall, a cellar, outhouse."

"You can't be more specific?"

"Whitewash is whitewash. Now if you'll kindly get off the bloody phone and let me get on with the confirmations, we'll have a pile of stuff that just might stand up in court when you catch the bastards."

"All right, all right. And Vic?"

"Yes."

"I'm eternally grateful."

"I'll remember that."

Gristhorpe hung up. He no longer had to sit around waiting for the phone to ring. There were things to do: question Parkinson again, and his neighbours; get in touch with the press and television. They could run this on "Crimewatch." And where had he seen whitewash recently? Calling for Richmond on his way, he swept down the corridor towards the stairs.

II

Why was it, Banks thought, as he sat in Corrigan's Bar and Grill on York Road near the bus station, that so many people gravitated towards these trendy, renovated pubs? What on earth was wrong with a down-to-earth, honest-to-goodness old pub? Just look at Le Bistro, that place he had met Jenny last week. All coral pink tablecloths, long-stemmed wine glasses and stiff napkins.

And now this: eighteenth-century Yorkshire translated

almost overnight into twentieth-century New York, complete with booths, brass rails, square Formica-top tables and waitresses who might bustle in New York, but in Yorkshire moved at their normal couldn't-care-less pace. At least some things didn't change.

And then there was the menu: a large, thin laminated card of bold, handwritten items with outrageous prices. Burgers, of course, club sandwiches, corned beef on rye (and they didn't mean Fray Bentos), and such delights for dessert as raspberry cheesecake, pecan pie and frozen yoghurt. All to the accompaniment (not *too* loud, thank the Lord) of Euro-pop.

Maybe he was getting conservative since the move to Yorkshire, he wondered. Certainly in London, Sandra and he had happily embraced the changes that seemed to happen so fast from the sixties on, delighted in the varieties of food and ambience available. But somehow here, in a town with a cobbled market square, ancient cross, Norman church and excavated pre-Roman ruins, so close to the timeless, glacier-carved dales and towering fells with their jagged limestone edges and criss-cross drystone walls, the phoney American theme and fashionable food seemed an affront.

The beer was a problem, too, just as it was in Le Bistro. Here was no Theakston's bitter, no Old Peculier, no Tetley's, Marston's or Sam Smith's, just a choice of gassy keg beer and imported bottled lagers from Germany, Holland, Mexico and Spain, all ice cold, of course. Funnily enough, he sat over a glass (they didn't serve pints, only tall heavy glasses that tapered towards their thick bases) of Labatt's, one of the less interesting lagers he remembered from his trip to Toronto.

Such were his thoughts as he puzzled over the menu waiting for Linda Fish, the Champagne socialist, to show. Corrigan's had been *her* choice, and as he wanted information, he had thought it best to comply. The sacrifices a copper makes in the course of duty, he thought to himself, shaking his head. At least there was an ashtray on the table. He looked out of the window at the lunchtime shoppers darting in and out of the shopping centre opposite in the rain. Raincoats, waxed-jackets, a chill in the air: it looked as if autumn had arrived at last.

Linda walked in after he had been musing gloomily for ten minutes or so. She packed up her telescope umbrella and looked around, then waved and came over to join him. She had always reminded Banks of an overgrown child. It was partly the way she dressed—today blue sweatpants and a matching sweatshirt with a pink teddy bear on its front—and partly the slightly unformed face, a kind of freckled, doughy blob on which had been stuck two watery eyes accentuated by blue shadow, a button nose and thin lips made fuller by lipstick. Her straw-coloured hair looked as if she had just cut it herself with blunt scissors in front of a funfair mirror. As always, she carried her oversized and scuffed leather shoulder-bag, something she had picked up in Florence, she had once told him, and with great sentimental value. Whether it was stuffed with bricks and toiletries or unpublished manuscripts, he had no idea, but it certainly looked heavy.

Linda squeezed her bulk into the booth opposite Banks. "I hope you don't mind meeting here," she said conspiratorially, "but I'm afraid I've become quite addicted to the chili-burgers."

"It's fine," Banks lied. She wasn't from Yorkshire, and her slight lisp seemed to make the Home Counties accent sound even posher. Whatever you might say or think about Linda, though, Banks reminded himself, she was far from stupid. Not only did she run the local Writers' Circle with such energy and enthusiasm that left most bystanders gasping, but she was indeed a *published* writer, not a mere hopeful or dilettante. She had, in fact, published a short novel with a large firm only a year ago. Banks had read it, and admitted it was good. Very good, in fact. No, Linda Fish was no fool. If she wanted to look ridiculous, then that was her business.

"I'm afraid I won't be able to tell you very much, you know," she said.

"Even a little will help." Banks flapped the menu. "Anything you'd recommend?"

Her blue eyes narrowed in a smile. "I can see you're uncomfortable," she said. "I'm sorry I suggested we meet here. Men are obviously much happier in pubs."

Banks laughed. "You're right about that. But let's see what I can salvage from the situation. Who knows, I might even find something I like."

"Good," said Linda. "Well, you know what I'm having. Are you not familiar with this kind of food?"

"American? Yes. I've never been to the States but I was in Toronto a couple of years ago. I think I can find my way around. I always found it was best to stick with the burgers."

"I think you're right."

A waitress ambled along, playing with her hair as she approached. "Yes?" She stood beside the booth, weight balanced on her left hip, order pad in one hand and pencil in the other. She didn't even look at them. Linda ordered her chili-burger and a bottle of San Miguel, and Banks went for the mushroom-and-cheese burger and another glass of Labatt's. He leaned back on the red vinyl banquette and lit a Silk Cut. The grill had filled up a bit since Linda arrived, mostly truant sixth-formers buzzing with conversation and laughter, and the Euro-pop droned on.

"Do you want to interrogate me before lunch or

after?" Linda asked.

Banks smiled. "I always find a full stomach helps. But if you're—"

She waved her hand. "Oh no, I'm not in a hurry or anything. I'm just interested." She stuck her hand deep in her bag and frowned, leaning slightly to the side, as she rummaged around in there like a kid at a fairground lucky-dip. "Ah, got them." She pulled out a packet of menthol cigarettes.

"You know," she said, lighting up, "I'd never really thought about it before, but you could be useful to me."

"Me? How?"

"I'm thinking of writing a detective story."

"Good Lord," said Banks, whose knowledge of detective fiction stopped at Sherlock Holmes.

"From what I've read," Linda went on, "it's clear that one can get away without knowing much police procedure, but a little realism does no harm. What I was thinking was—"

The waitress appeared with their food and drinks at that moment, and Linda's attention was diverted towards her chili-burger. Feeling relieved at the interruption, Banks bit into his burger. It was good. But his reprieve was only temporary.

"What I was thinking," Linda went on, wiping the chili sauce from her chin with a paper napkin, "was perhaps that you could advise me. You know, on police procedure. And maybe tell me a bit about some of your cases. Give me an insight into the criminal mind, so to speak."

"Well," said Banks, "I'd be glad to help if you have any specific questions. But I don't really think I can just sit down and tell you all about it."

Her eyes narrowed again, and she bit into her burger. When she had finished that mouthful, she went on. "I suppose that's a compromise of sorts. I'm sure your time is too valuable to waste on writers of fiction. Though I *did* get the impression that you are fairly well read."

Banks laughed. "I like a good book, yes."

"Well, then. Even Hardy and Dickens had to do their research, you know. They had to ask people about things."

Banks held up his hands. "All right, you've convinced me. Just give me specific questions and I'll do my best to answer them, OK?"

"Okay. I haven't got that far yet, but when I do I'll take you up on it."

"Now, what can you tell me about Adam Harkness?"

"Ah-hah, the interrogation at last. As I said, I can't tell you very much, really. But I don't believe all that phoney anti-apartheid rubbish, for a start."

"Why not?"

"Because it doesn't square with what I've heard. Oh, I'm sure he probably even believes it himself now, and it's a trendy enough position for white South African ex-patriates to take. But how do you think his father made his money? You can't tell me he didn't exploit the blacks. Everybody did. And you won't see Adam Harkness giving his money away to support the ANC."

"He told me he left South Africa because he didn't agree with the politics."

"That's not what I heard."

"What did you hear?"

"It's just rumours, but I've a friend lives there, a writer, and she said there was some kind of scandal about to break but the Harknesses hushed it up."

"What kind of scandal?"

"Nobody really knows. My friend suspects he killed someone, a black mine-worker, but there's no proof."

It was possible, Banks supposed, ten or more years

ago to cover up the murder of a black by a rich and powerful white man in South Africa. For all he knew, despite
the scrapping of racial classification, it probably still
was. Attitudes don't change overnight, whatever politi-
cians might decree.

"Have you ever heard of a man called Carl Johnson?"
Banks asked.

"Only from the papers. He was the one killed, wasn't
he, at the old lead mine?"

"That's right. He worked as a gardener for Harkness."

"Did he now?" She leaned forward. "And you think
there might be some connection?"

"There might be."

"You surely don't think Adam Harkness murdered
him?"

"Harkness has an alibi. But a man like him can afford
to have things done."

Her eyes opened wide. They looked like oysters on a
half-shell. "Do you mean that kind of thing really goes
on? In England? Hit men and contracts and all that."

Banks smiled. "It has been known."

"Well . . . there's obviously more to this crime business than I realized. But I'm afraid I can't help you any
further."

"Could you get in touch with your friend? Ask her for
more information?"

"I could try, but I got the impression they put a lid on
it pretty securely. Still, if it might help . . ."

"It might."

"I've just had a thought."

"Yes?"

"If the rumour's true, about Harkness and the black
miner, and if that Johnson person was killed at an old
mine, there's a sort of symmetry to that, isn't there?"

"I suppose there is," Banks agreed. Symmetry, for

Christ's sake, he thought. Plenty of it in books, but not in real life. "It's just a very isolated spot," he said.

"So why would anyone go there to meet a killer?"

"Obviously it was someone he trusted. He didn't have a car, so someone must have picked him up, or met him somewhere, and taken him there. Perhaps he thought he was going to get money."

"Oh, yes," said Linda. "I see. Well, I'd better leave the police work to you, hadn't I? But, you know, that's exactly the kind of thinking I'm interested in. Now, I'm going to have a chocolate sundae and you can tell me all about your most interesting case."

III

Gristhorpe and Richmond stood in the rain outside Parkinson's house. Semi-detached, with a frosted-glass door and a pebble-dash façade, it was more modern than the row of tiny limestone cottages that faced it across the lopsided square of unkempt grass. Gristhorpe hadn't realized that Parkinson's house was *so* close to the abandoned cottage. This was the extreme north-western edge of Eastvale, and both the new and the old houses shared a superb view west along the valley bottom. Not today, though; everything was lost in the grey haze of rain.

Richmond wore a belted navy-blue Aquascutum over his suit, and Gristhorpe a rumpled fawn raincoat with the collar turned up. Neither wore a hat. It was the kind of rain that you felt inside rather than out, Gristhorpe thought, already registering the aches in his joints. Outside you merely got beaded in moisture, but inside you were damp and chilled to the marrow.

They had already tried the semis to the west, the last pair, with only the Helmthorpe Road and a dry-stone wall between them and the open country, but found no-body home. In fact, as Gristhorpe stood there looking around, he noticed how quiet and secluded the area was. Given that Parkinson had kept his car in the garage at the back of his house, it wouldn't have been at all difficult for someone to "borrow" it without being seen. Apart from a few cars and delivery vans on the main road, thcrc was nothing else around.

They walked up the path and rang the bell of the semi adjoining Parkinson's. A few moments later a man an-swered and, after they had showed their identification, he invited them in.

"Come in out of the rain," he said, taking their coats. "I'll put the kettle on."

He was about forty, small and thick-set, with sparse fair hair and lively grey eyes. His right arm, encased in plaster, hung in a sling over the lower part of his chest.

They settled down in the cheerful living-room, where the element of an electric fire took some of the chill out of their bones, and their host, Mr David Ackroyd, came in with mugs of tea and joined them. Two women were talking on the radio about menopause. He turned it off and sat down. Richmond installed himself in the arm-chair opposite, long legs crossed, notebook and pen in hand.

"What happened?" Gristhorpe asked, indicating the arm.

"Broke it on Sunday. Doing a bit of climbing out Swainshead way." He shook his head. "Silly bugger I am. I ought to know I'm too old for that sort of thing."

"So you're not usually home weekdays?"

"Good lord, no. I'm a civil servant . . . well, civil as I can be to some of the riff-raff we get in the job centre these days." His eyes twinkled. "And servant to the devil, according to some. I'll be back at work again in a couple of days. The doctor says I just need a bit of a rest to get over the shock."

"Are you married?"

He frowned. "Yes. Why do you ask?"

"Does your wife work?"

"She's an auditor with the tax office."

"So she's usually out all day, too?"

"Yes. Most people around here are. Have to be to pay the mortgages, prices being the way they are. What's going on?"

"Just trying to feel out the lie of the land, so to speak," Gristhorpe said. "Did you know Mr Parkinson's car was stolen while he was away?"

"Yes. He came dashing in to tell me as soon as he checked the mileage. I told him to go to the police."

"Did you notice anything at all?"

"No. Of course, I was out at work all the time until the weekend. Everything seemed quite normal."

"Did he often make these trips?"

"Yes. Quite proud of himself he was about it too. He got a promotion in the company a short while ago. Exports. They do a bit of business with the Common Market countries. You know how it is, everything's Euro-this and Euro-that these days."

"And he always left his car in the garage?"

"Yes. Look, between you and me, Bruce is a bit tight. Short arms and deep pockets, if you know what I mean. He hasn't quite got to the company-car level yet but his boss, the bloke who usually goes with him, has. He lives a few miles north of here, so it's easy for him to pick Bruce up."

"How many people do you think knew about this arrangement?"

"I couldn't say."

"But Mr Parkinson was the sort to talk about such

things in public?"

"Well, I suppose so. I mean, it's nothing, is it, really? Just idle chatter, pub talk. He liked to let people know how important he was, how he got to travel to Europe on business and all that. I don't think he was worried that someone might overhear him and take off with his car."

"Could that have happened?"

"Easily enough, I suppose." He rubbed the plaster on his arm. Gristhorpe noticed that a couple of people had signed it in ball-point just below the elbow. "We ought to be more careful, oughtn't we?" Ackroyd went on. "Lord knows, we hear enough about crime prevention on telly, we should know better than to go blabbing all our holiday and business plans in a pub. You just don't think, do you?"

"Which pub is this, Mr Ackroyd?"

"Pub? Well, I was speaking figuratively, really, but there's a local in the next street. It's called The Drayman's Rest. Nothing special really, but they do a decent pint and the company's all right."

"Do you and Mr Parkinson go there regularly?"

"I suppose you could say that. Not that we're big drinkers, mind you." He laughed. "Bruce always drinks halves and makes them last. It's just the social thing, the local, isn't it? A chat and a few laughs with the lads after work, that sort of thing."

"Do you know most of the regulars?"

"Oh, aye. Except we get a few strangers in from the holiday cottages over the road. They never cause any trouble, though, and we make them welcome enough."

"Get friendly with them, do you?"

"Well, some are easier than others, if you know what I mean. Some just like to keep to themselves, grab a sandwich and a pint and sit in the corner reading the paper. But there's outgoing ones. I like talking to people. That's how you learn, isn't it?"

"Have you met any interesting strangers in there recently?"

"What?"

"The past couple of weeks. Anyone been especially friendly?"

Ackroyd rubbed his chin. "Aye, well now you mention it, there was Chris and Connie."

Gristhorpe looked over at Richmond. "The Manleys?"

"That's it. I always thought it a bit odd that they liked to stand at the bar and talk to the locals."

"Why?"

"Well, with a bird like her I wouldn't be in the pub in the first place," Ackroyd said, and winked. "But usually it's the couples tend to keep to themselves."

"They didn't?"

"No. Oh, they weren't pushy or anything. Just always there with a hello and a chat. Nowt special. It might be the weather, the news . . . that kind of thing."

"And Mr Parkinson's European business trips?"

"Well, he did go on a bit. . . . Now wait a minute, you can't be suggesting that Chris and Connie . . . ? No, I don't believe it. Besides, they had a car of their own. I saw them in it."

"A white Fiesta?"

"That's right."

"What kind of impression did they give you, Mr Ackroyd?"

"They just seemed like regular folk. I mean, Chris liked to talk about cars. Bit of a know-it-all, maybe. You know, the kind that likes to dominate conversations. And she seemed happy enough to be there."

"Did she say much?"

"No, but she didn't need to. I mean most of the men in that place would've given their right arms—" He stopped, looked at his cast and laughed. "No, that wasn't how I got it, honest. But what I'm trying to say is that it wasn't just that she was a looker, though she was that all right. The long blonde hair, those lovely red lips and the blue eyes. And from what I could tell she had all her curves in the right places, too. No, it wasn't just that. She was sexy. She had a presence. Like she didn't have to do anything. Just walk in, smile, stand there leaning on the bar. There was something about her you could feel, like an electric charge. I am rambling on, aren't I? Do you know what I mean?"

"I think so, Mr Ackroyd." Some women just gave out an aura of sex, Gristhorpe knew. That kind of sex appeal was common enough on screen—the way Marilyn Monroe's clothes always seemed to want to slip off her body, for example—but it also happened in real life. It was nothing to do with looks, though a combination of beauty and sex appeal could be deadly when it occurred, and some women didn't even realize they had it.

"How did Mr Manley act towards her?" he asked.

"No special way in particular. I mean, he wasn't much to look at himself. I got the impression he was sort of pleased that so many men obviously fancied her. You knew she was *his* and you could look but you couldn't touch. Now I think about it, he definitely seemed to be showing her off, like."

"Nobody tried to chat her up?"

"No." He scratched his cheek. "And that's a funny thing, you know. Now you've got me talking I'm thinking things that never really entered my head at the time. They were just an interesting couple of holidaymakers, but the more I think about them . . ."

"Yes?"

"Well, the thing that really struck you about Chris was his smile. When he smiled at you, you immediately wanted to trust him. I suppose it worked with the women too. But there was something . . . I mean, I can't put my finger on it, but you just sort of *knew* that if you really did try it on with Connie, outside a bit of mild flirting, that is, then he'd be something to reckon with. That's the only way I can express it. I suppose everyone picked up on that because nobody tried it on. Not even Andy Lumsden, and he goes after anything in a skirt as a rule."

"Where were they from?"

"Chris and Connie? Do you know, I couldn't tell you. He didn't have a Yorkshire accent, that's for certain. But it was hard to place. South, maybe. It was sort of characterless, like those television newsreaders."

"They didn't say where they were from?"

"Come to think of it, no. Just said they were taking some time off and travelling around for a while, having a rest from the fast lane. They never really said anything about themselves. Funny that, isn't it?"

"They didn't even say what they were taking time off from?"

"No."

Gristhorpe stood up and nodded to Richmond. He shook Mr Ackroyd's good hand and wished him well, then they walked back out into the drizzle.

"What now?" Richmond asked.

Gristhorpe looked at his watch. "It's half past two," he said. "I reckon we've just got time for a pint and a sandwich at The Drayman's Rest, don't you?"

IV

Susan Gay parked her red Golf outside and went up to her flat. She had had a busy day going over mug-shots with Edwina Whixley—to no avail—and questioning the

other occupants of 59 Calvin Street again. She had also
made an appointment to see the governor of Armley Jail,
where Johnson had served his time, at four-thirty the following afternoon. She knew she could probably have
asked him questions over the phone, but phone calls, she
always felt, were too open to interruptions, and too limit-
ing. If the governor needed to consult a warden for additional information, for example, that might prove
difficult over the phone. Besides, she was old-fashioned;
she liked to be able to watch people's eyes when she
talked to them.

She put her briefcase by the door and dropped her
keys on the hall table. She had made a lot of changes to
the place since her promotion to CID. It had once been
little more than a hotel suite, somewhere to sleep. But
now she had plants and a growing collection of books
and records.

Susan favoured the more traditional, romantic kind of
classical music, the ones you remember bits from and
find yourself humming along with now and then:
Beethoven, Tchaikovsky, Chopin, bits of opera from
films and TV adverts. Most of her records were "greatest
hits," so she didn't have their complete symphonies or
anything, just the movements everyone remembered.

Her reading was still limited mostly to technical stuff,
like forensics and criminology, but she made space on
her shelves for the occasional Jeffrey Archer, Dick
Francis and Robert Ludlum. Banks wouldn't approve of
her tastes, she was sure, but at least now she knew she
had tastes.

As usual, if she was in, she had "Calendar" on the
television as she fussed around in the kitchen throwing
together a salad. Normally, she would just be listening,
as the TV set was in the living-room, but this evening, an
item caught her attention and she walked through, salad

bowl in hand and stood and watched open-mouthed.

It was Brenda Scupham and a gypsyish looking woman on the couch being interviewed. She hadn't caught
the introduction, but they were talking about clairvoy-
ance. Brenda, in a tight lemon chiffon blouse tucked into
a black mini-skirt much too short for a worried mother,
sat staring blankly into the camera, while the other
woman explained how objects dear to people bear psychic traces of them and act as conduits into the extrasen-
sory world.

Brenda nodded in agreement occasionally. When
Richard Whiteley turned to her and asked her what she
thought, she said, "I don't know. I really don't know,"
then she looked over at the other woman. "But I'm convinced my Gemma is still alive and I want to beg whoever knows where she is to let her come back to her
mother, please. You won't be punished, I promise."

"What about the police?" he asked. "What do they
think?"

Brenda shook her head. "I don't know," she said. "I
think they believe she's dead. Ever since they found her
clothes, I think they've given up on her."

Susan flopped into her armchair, salad forgotten for
the moment. Bloody hell, she thought, Superintendent
Gristhorpe's going to *love* this.

9

I

Gristhorpe was indeed furious when he heard about Brenda Scupham's television appearance. As he had no TV set of his own, though, he didn't find out until Wednesday morning.

"It's been over a week now since Gemma Scupham disappeared," he said, shaking his head over coffee and toasted teacakes with Banks at the Golden Grill. "I can't say I hold out much hope. Especially since we found the clothes."

"I can't, either," Banks agreed. "But Brenda Scupham's got some bloody psychic to convince her that Gemma's alive. Who would you rather listen to, if you were her?"

"I suppose you're right. Anyway, it all connects: the abandoned cottage, the borrowed car, the hair-dye. We've got descriptions of the Manleys out—both as themselves and as Peterson and Brown. Somebody, somewhere must know them. How about you?"

Banks sipped some hot black coffee. "Not much. The lab finally came through with the scene analysis. The blood in the mill matched Johnson's, so we can be pretty certain that's where he was killed. Glendenning says it was a right-handed upthrust wound. Six-inch blade, single-edged. Probably some kind of sheath-knife, and you know how common those are. No handy footprints or tire tracks, and no sign of the weapon. I'm off to see Harkness again, though I don't suppose it'll do much good."

"You think he did it?"

"Apart from the mysterious stranger seen leaving Johnson's building, he's the only lead I've got. I keep telling myself that just because I didn't take to the man it doesn't mean he's a killer. But nobody gets that rich without making a few enemies. And Johnson was a crook. He *could* have been involved somewhere along the line."

"Aye, maybe you're right. Be careful, though, the last thing I need right now is the ACC on my back."

Banks laughed. "You know me. Diplomacy personified."

"Aye, well . . . I'd better be off to see Mrs Scupham. See if I can't talk some sense into her. I want a word with that bloody psychic, too. I've got Phil out looking for her." He looked outside. A fine mist nuzzled the window.

"Hang on a minute, sir," Banks said. "You know, Brenda Scupham might be right."

"What?"

"If Gemma *is* alive, a television appeal won't do any harm. It might even do some good."

"I realize that. We can't have any idea what the woman's going through. All I want to do is reassure her that we *are* doing the best we can. If Gemma is alive, we've more chance of finding her than some bloody tea-leaf reader. There's a trail to follow somewhere in all this, and I think we're picking it up. But these people, the Manleys or whatever they call themselves now, they talked to enough people, got on well enough with the locals, but they gave nothing away. We don't even know where they come from, and we can't be sure what they look like, either. They're still two-dimensional."

"What about the notes they used to pay for the cottage?"

"Patricia Cummings, the estate agent, said she paid the cash directly into the bank. Right now it's mixed up with all the rest of the money they've got in their vaults."

"How did they hear about the cottage? Did they say?"

"Told her they'd read about it in *The Dalesman*."

"You could get—"

"I know, I know—the list of subscribers. We're checking on it. But you can buy *The Dalesman* at almost any newsagent's, in this part of the country, anyway."

"Just a thought."

Gristhorpe finished his teacake and wiped his mouth with the paper serviette. "At the moment it looks like our best bet lies with the descriptions—if that's what they really look like. Christ knows, maybe they're Hollywood special-effects people underneath it all. We've got the artist working with Parkinson and the crowd in The Drayman's Rest. Should be ready for tomorrow's papers. And I was thinking about the whitewash they found on Gemma's clothes, too. I've seen it in two places recently: Melville Westman's, the Satanist, or whatever he calls himself, and the holiday cottage."

"I suppose the Manleys could have kept Gemma there," Banks said. "Perhaps they drugged her. She's not very big. It wouldn't be difficult to get her out of the cottage after dark."

"Aye, that's true enough. Still, I'm getting a warrant and sending a few lads to give Westman's place a good going-over."

"You don't like him any better than I like Harkness, do you?"

Gristhorpe grinned. "No," he said. "No, I don't." He

pushed his chair back. "Must be off. See you later, Alan." And he walked out into Market Street.

II

Adam Harkness's house clearly hadn't been vacuumed or tidied since Banks's last visit. At least a crackling fire took the chill out of the damp air in the library. The french windows were firmly closed. Beyond the streaked glass, drops of rain pitted the river's surface. Lyndgarth and Aldington Edge were shrouded in a veil of low grey cloud.

"Please, sit down," Harkness said. "Now what can I do for you, Chief Inspector? Have you found Carl's killer?"

Banks rubbed his hands in front of the fire, then sat. "Not yet," he said. "There's a couple of points you might be able to help me clear up, though."

Harkness raised a challenging eyebrow and sat in the chair opposite Banks. "Yes?"

"We've learned that Johnson might have met with a certain individual on a couple of occasions shortly before his murder. Did he talk to you about any of his friends?"

"I've already told you. He was my gardener. He came a couple of times a week and kept the garden in trim. That's all."

"Is it? Please think about it, Mr Harkness. Even if Johnson was only the hired help, it would be perfectly natural to have a bit of a chat now and then about innocuous stuff, wouldn't it?" He felt that he was giving Harkness a fair chance to come up with something he may have forgotten or chosen not to admit earlier, but it did no good.

Harkness folded his hands in his lap. "I knew nothing whatsoever about Carl Johnson's private life. The mo-

ment he left my property, his life was his own, and I neither know nor care what he did."

"Even if it was of a criminal nature?"

"You might believe he was irredeemably branded as a
criminal. I do not. Besides, as I keep telling you, I have
no knowledge of his activities, criminal or otherwise."

Banks described the man Edwina Whixley had seen
coming down the stairs of Johnson's building: thick-set,
medium height, short dark hair, squarish head. "Ever see
or hear about him?"

Harkness shook his head. "Carl always came here
alone. He never introduced me to any of his colleagues."

"So you never saw this man?"

"No."

"How did Johnson get here?"

"What?"

"Carl Johnson? How did he get here? He didn't have a
car."

"There are still buses, Chief Inspector, including a
fairly regular service from Eastvale to Lyndgarth.
There's a bus-stop just by the bridge."

"Of course. Did Johnson ever mention any of his old
prison friends?"

"What? Not to me. It would hardly have been appropriate, would it?" Harkness picked up the poker and
jabbed at the fire. "Look, why don't you save us both a
lot of wasted time and energy and accept that I'm telling
the truth when I say I knew *nothing* about Carl's private
life?"

"I don't know what gives you the impression I don't
believe you."

"Your attitude, for a start, and the questions you keep
on asking over and over again."

"Sir," said Banks, "you have to understand that this is
a murder investigation. People forget things. Sometimes

they don't realize the importance of what they know. All I'm doing is trying to jog your memory into giving up *something* that Johnson might have let slip in a moment of idle chatter. Anything. It might mean nothing at all to you—a name, a date, an opinion, whatever—but it might be vital to us."

Harkness paused. "Well . . . of course, yes . . . I suppose I see what you mean. The thing is, though, there really *is* nothing. I'm sure if he'd said anything I would have remembered it by now. The fact is we just didn't talk beyond discussing the garden and the weather. Basically, we had nothing else in common. He seemed a reticent sort of fellow, anyway, kept himself to himself, and that suited me fine. Also, remember, I'm often away on business."

"Was there ever any evidence that Johnson had used the house in your absence?"

"What do you mean, 'used the house'? For what purpose?"

"I don't know. I assume he had a key?"

"Yes. But . . ."

"Nothing was ever out of place?"

"No. Are you suggesting he might have been stealing things?"

"No. I don't think even Carl Johnson would have been that stupid. To be honest, I don't know what I'm getting at." Banks scratched his head and glanced at the river and the copper beech, leaves dripping, beyond the french windows. "This is a fairly out-of-the-way place. It could be suitable for criminal activities in any number of ways."

"I noticed nothing," Harkness said, with a thin smile. "Not even a muddy footprint on my carpet."

"You see," Banks went on, "Johnson's life is a bit of a mystery to us. We've got his record, the bald facts. But

how did he think? We don't seem to be able to find anyone who was close to him. And there are years missing.
He may have been to Europe, Amsterdam perhaps. He
may even have had friends from South Africa."

Harkness sat bolt upright and gripped the arms of the
chair. "What are you insinuating?"

"I've heard rumours of some sort of a scandal.
Something involving you back in South Africa. There
was some sort of cover-up. Do you know what I'm talking about?"

Harkness snorted. "There are always scandals sur-
rounding the wealthy, Chief Inspector. You ought to
know that. Usually they derive from envy. No, I can't say
I do know what you're talking about."

"But was there any such scandal involving you or your
family out there?"

"No, nothing that stands out."

Banks got that almost-infallible tingle that told him
Harkness was holding back. He gave his man-of-the-
world shrug. "Of course, I'm not suggesting there was
any truth in it, but we have to investigate everything that
comes up."

Harkness stood up. "It seems to me that you are
spending an unusual amount of time investigating *me*
when you should be looking for Carl Johnson's killer. I
suggest you look among his criminal cronies for your
killer."

"You've got a point, there. And, believe me, we're trying to track them down. Just out of interest, did Johnson
ever mention South Africa to you?"

"No, he did not. And don't think I don't know what
you're getting at. You're suggesting he was blackmailing
me over some secret or other, aren't you, and that I killed
him to silence him? Come on, is that what you're getting
at?"

Banks stood up and spoke slowly. "But you couldn't have killed him, could you, sir? You were dining at the Golf Club at the time of the murder. A number of very influential people saw you there." He regarded Harkness, who maintained an expression of outraged dignity, then said, "Thank you very much for your time," and left.

As he drove down to the main road with the wind-screen-wipers tapping time to Gurney's "Sleep," he smiled to himself. He had got at least some of what he had wanted: a sure sense that Harkness was holding something back; and the satisfying knowledge that the man, rich, confident and powerful notwithstanding, could be rattled. Time now to make a few overseas phone calls, then perhaps have another chat with Mr Adam Harkness.

III

"You think I acted dishonestly, is that what you're saying?"

"Irresponsibly is the word I had in mind," Gristhorpe replied. He was sitting opposite Lenora Carlyle in a small interview room at the station. A WPC sat by the window to take notes. With her wild black hair, her high, prominent cheekbones and blazing dark eyes, Lenora certainly looked dramatic. She seemed composed as she sat there, he noticed, arms folded across her jumper, a slightly superior smile revealing stained teeth. It was the kind of smile, Gristhorpe thought, that she probably reserved for the poor, lost disbelievers with whom she no doubt had to deal now and then.

"I do my job, Superintendent," she said, "and you do yours."

"And just what is your job? In this case it seems to

consist of giving a poor woman false hope." Gristhorpe
had just been to see Brenda Scupham, and he had noticed
the fervour in her eyes when she spoke of what Lenora
had told her.

"I can tell there's no convincing you, but I don't happen to believe it's false. Look, are you upset because
Brenda criticized you on television? Is that why you've
got me in here?"

"What was the source of your information about
Gemma Scupham?"

"I'm a psychic. You know that already."

"So the 'other side' is the source?"

"If you want to put it like that, yes."

"Are you sure?"

"What are you getting at?"

Gristhorpe leaned back and rested his forearms on the
table. "Ms Carlyle, we're investigating the abduction of a
child, a very serious crime, and one that happens to be
especially odious to me. All of a sudden, you walk into
Brenda Scupham's house and tell her you know the child
is still alive. I'd be a bloody idiot if I didn't ask you *how*
you know."

"I've told you."

"Aye. And, as you well know, I don't happen to believe in convenient messages from the other side."

She smiled. "It's stalemate, isn't it, then?"

"No, it isn't. Are you aware that I could hold you if I
wanted?"

"What do you mean?"

"You profess to have information about a missing
child, but you won't reveal your source. As far as I
know, you could have something to do with Gemma
Scupham's disappearance."

"Now look here—"

"No. *You* look here. If that child *is* alive and you know

something that could help us find her, you'd better tell me, because I'm getting tired of this."

"I only know what I told Brenda—that Gemma is alive, she's scared and she wants her mother. You know, you'd do much better with an open mind. The police *have* used psychics to help them in the past."

And a fat lot of good it's done, thought Gristhorpe, feeling himself being manipulated into the position of doing exactly that. The woman might know something, after all, and he couldn't dismiss that possibility, even if it meant playing her game. "All right," he sighed. "Did you get any impressions about where she is?"

Lenora shook her head.

"Any images, sounds, smells?"

"Nothing like that. Just an overwhelming emotional sense of her presence somewhere. Alive. And her fear."

"Near or far?"

"I can't say."

Gristhorpe scratched his chin. "Not much to go on, is it?"

"I can't help that. I'm merely a medium for the messages. Do you want to consult me professionally? Do you want me to try and help you?"

Gristhorpe noticed the smile of triumph. "Ms Carlyle," he shot back, "if you *fail* to help us, I'll make sure you're thrown in jail. Do you know Melville Westman?"

It was only fleeting, but he saw it, a split-second sign of recognition. It was second nature for him to notice the signs, the body language, the way eye-contact broke off. He could see her trying to decide how much to admit. "Well?" he prodded.

"The name sounds vaguely familiar," she said with a toss of her head. "I might have come across him."

"Let me fill you in. Melville Westman calls himself a magician. There have been incidents in the past few years of such groups using children in their rituals. Now, I don't know what you're up to, but if you and Westman have any involvement in Gemma's disappearance, direct or indirect, I'll find out about it."

"This is ridiculous!" Lenora said. "I've had enough of your accusations and insinuations." She tried to push the chair back to get to her feet, but forgot it was bolted to the floor and she got stuck, half-standing, between it and the table.

"Sit down." Gristhorpe waved his hand. "I haven't finished yet. What's your connection with Westman?"

She sat down, chewed on her lower lip for a moment, and answered, "I know him, that's all. We're acquaintances."

"Met at the magician's circle, did you?"

"You don't have to be sarcastic. It's a small community for anyone interested in the occult. We've had discussions, loaned one another books, that's all."

"I'm asking you if Westman has told you anything about Gemma Scupham's whereabouts. Are you some kind of messenger, some salve to the conscience come to spare the mother a little pain until you've finished with the child? Or are you just tormenting her?"

"Don't be absurd. What would Melville want with the child?"

"You tell me."

"He wouldn't. He's not that kind."

"What kind?"

"The kind that performs elaborate rituals, sacrifices animals and . . ."

"Children?"

"Look, I'm not denying there are lunatic fringes around, but Melville Westman doesn't belong to one."

"Is there anyone in the area you would associate with a lunatic fringe?"

"No."

"Ever heard of the Manleys? Chris and Connie. Or Miss Peterson and Mr Brown?"

"No."

"Did Melville Westman send you?"

"No, he bloody well didn't. I came forward to help the mother of my own free will," Lenora said through clenched teeth. "And this is how you treat me. I thought the police would—"

"You know nothing about the way we work, or you'd hardly have had Brenda Scupham shooting her mouth off on television."

"That wasn't my doing."

"It doesn't matter whose doing it was. It happened. And if that child *is* dead, I want you to think of how much harm you've done her mother."

Lenora put her fist to her heart. "The child is alive, Superintendent. I'm convinced of it."

For a moment, Gristhorpe was taken aback by the passion in her voice. After everything he had accused her of, she was still clinging to her original story. He let the silence stretch for a while longer, holding her intense gaze. He could feel something pass across the air between them. He couldn't put his finger on what it was, a tingling sensation, the hackles on his neck rising, and he certainly had no idea whether or not she was right about Gemma. He did know, though, that she was telling the truth as far as she knew it. The damn woman was genuine in her beliefs. He could see, now, how Brenda Scupham had been convinced.

"I want you to know," he said slowly, "that I'll check and double-check on everything you've told me." Then he broke off the staring match and looked towards the bare wall. "Now get out. Go on, get out before I change my mind." And he didn't even turn to watch her go. He knew exactly the kind of smile he would see on her face.

IV

Armley Jail was built in 1847 by Perkin and Backhouse. Standing on a low hill to the west of the city centre, it looks like a structure from the Middle Ages, with its keep and battlements all in dark, solid stone—especially in the iron-grey sky and the rain that swept across the scene. Eastvale Castle seemed welcoming in comparison, Susan thought. Even the modern addition to the prison couldn't quite overcome the sense of dank medieval dungeons she felt as she approached the gates. The architects could hardly have come up with a place more likely to terrify the criminals and reassure the good citizens, she thought, giving a shiver as she got out of the car and felt the rain sting her cheek.

She showed her warrant card, and at four-thirty on that dreary September afternoon, the prison gates admitted her, and a uniformed attendant led her to a small office in the administrative block to meet Gerald Mackenzie. She had found herself wondering on her way what kind of person felt drawn to prison work. It must be a strange world, she thought, locked in with the malcontents. Like the police, the prison service probably attracted its share of bullies, but it also had an appeal, she guessed, for the reformers, for people who believed in rehabilitation. For many, perhaps, it was just a job, a source of income to pay the mortgage and help feed the wife and kids.

Mackenzie turned out to be a surprisingly young man with thin brown hair, matching suit, a crisp white shirt and what she took to be a regimental or club tie of some kind. The black-framed glasses he wore gave him the look of a middle-management man. He was polite, offered coffee, and seemed happy enough to give her the time and information she wanted.

"From what I can remember," he said, placing a finger at the corner of his small mouth, "Johnson was a fairly unassuming sort of fellow. Never caused any trouble. Never drew attention to himself." He shook his head. "In fact, I find it very hard to believe he ended up the way he did. Unless he was the victim of some random crime?"

"We don't think so," Susan said. "How did he spend his time?"

"He was a keen gardener, I remember. Never went in much for the more intellectual pursuits or the team games."

"Was he much of a socializer in any way?"

"No. As I said, I got the impression he kept very much to himself. I must confess, it's hard to keep abreast of everyone we have in here—unless they're troublemakers of course. The well-behaved ones you tend to leave to themselves. It's like teaching, I suppose. I've done a bit of that, you know. You spend most of your energy on the difficult students and leave the good ones to fend for themselves. I mean, there's always far more to say about a wrong answer than a right one, isn't there?"

"I suppose so," said Susan. The memory of an essay she wrote at police college came to mind. When the professor had handed it back to her, it had been covered in red ink. "So Johnson was an exemplary prisoner?"

"Inmate. Well, yes. Yes, he was."

"And you don't know a lot more about him, his routine, his contacts here?"

"No. I don't actually spend much time on the shop floor, so to speak. Administration, paperwork . . . it all seems to take up so much time these days. But look, I'll see if I can get Ollie Watson to come in. He worked Johnson's wing."

"Would you?"

"No trouble."

Mackenzie ducked out of the office for a moment and Susan examined a framed picture of a pretty dark-skinned woman, Indian perhaps, with three small children. Mackenzie's family, she assumed, judging by the way the children shared both his and the woman's features: a certain slant to the nose here, a dimple there.

A few minutes later, Mackenzie returned with Ollie Watson. As soon as she saw the fat, uniformed man with the small black moustache, Susan wondered if the "Ollie" was a nickname because the man looked so much like Oliver Hardy. He pulled at the creases of his pants and sat down on a chair, which creaked under him.

"Mr Watson," Susan said after the introductions, "Mr Mackenzie tells me you're in the best position to give me some information about Carl Johnson's time in here."

Watson nodded. "Yes ma'm." He shifted in his seat. It creaked again. "No trouble, Carl wasn't. But you never felt you ever got to *know* him, like you do with some. Never seemed much interested in anything, 'cept the garden, I suppose."

"Did he have friends?"

"Not close ones, no. He didn't mix much. And people left him alone. Not because they were scared of him or anything. Just . . . there was something remote about him. It was as if they hardly even noticed him most of the time."

"What about his cell-mates? Did he share?"

"Most of the time, yes." He smiled. "As you probably know, it gets a bit overcrowded in here. Must be because you lot are doing such a good job."

Susan laughed. "Us or the courts. Was there anyone in particular?"

"Let me see . . ." Watson held out his hand and

counted them off on his fingers. "There was Addison, that's one. Basically harmless, I'd say. Business fraud. Then there was Rodgers. No real problems there, either. Just possession . . ."

"Johnson was brutally murdered," Susan butted in on Watson's leisurely thought process. "Did he meet anyone you think capable of doing that?"

"Good lord, no. Not in here," said Watson, as if prison were the last place on earth where one would expect to find real evil-doers. "He was never in with any of the really hard, serious lags. We keep them separate as best we can."

"But someone could have involved him in a criminal scheme, something that went wrong? Drugs, perhaps?"

"I suppose it's possible. But Rodgers was only in for possession of marijuana. He wasn't a dealer."

"What about the business fraud?"

"Like I said, he was harmless enough. Just the old purchasing scam."

Susan nodded. She had come across that before. A purchasing officer for a large company simply rents some office space, a phone and headed stationery, then he "supplies" his company with goods or services that don't exist and pockets the payment. He has to be careful to charge only small amounts, so the purchase orders don't have to go to higher management for signing. If it can be worked carefully and slowly over a number of years, the purchasing scam can prove extremely lucrative, but most practitioners get greedy and make mistakes.

"Could he have got Johnson involved in something more ambitious? After all, Johnson was a bit of a con-man himself."

Watson shook his head. "Prison took the life out of Addison. It does that to some people. You're on the job long enough you get to recognize the signs, who'll be back and who won't. Addison won't. He'll be straight as a die from now on. He was just a mild-mannered clerk fancied a crack at the high life."

Susan nodded, but she had already noted Addison's name in her book. "What about the others?"

"Aye." Watson lifted his hand again. "Who did we say . . . Addison, then the possession fellow, Rodgers. Then there was Poole. I wouldn't worry about him, either."

"Poole?" said Susan, suddenly alert. "What was his first name?"

"Leslie. But everyone called him Les. Funny-looking bloke, too. One of those old-fashioned Elvis Presley haircuts." Watson laughed. "Until the prison barber got to him, that is. From what he said, though, the women seemed—"

But Susan was no longer listening. She couldn't help but feel a sudden surge of joy. She had one-upped Richmond. With all his courses, caches and megabytes, he hadn't discovered what she had by sheer old-fashioned legwork. He was working on the Gemma Scupham case, of course, not the Johnson murder, but still . . .

"Sorry for interrupting," she apologized to Watson, then looked at Mackenzie. "May I use your phone, sir?"

10

I

In the evening beyond the venetian blinds in Banks's office, puddles gleamed between the cobbles, and water dripped from the crossbars of lamp-posts, from eaves and awnings. Muted light glowed behind the red and amber windows of the Queen's Arms, and he could hear the buzz of laughter and conversation from inside. The square itself was quiet except for the occasional click of high-heels on cobbles as someone walked home from work late or went out on a date. An occasional gust of cool evening air wafted through his partly open window, bringing with it that peculiar fresh and sharp after-the-rain smell. It made him think of an old John Coltrane tune that captured in music just such a sense of an evening after rain. He could make out the gold hands against the blue face of the church clock: almost eight. He lit a cigarette. The gaslights around the square—an affectation for tourists—came on, dim at first, then brighter, reflecting in twisted sheets of incandescent light among the puddles. It was the time of day Banks loved most, not being much of a morning-person, but his epiphany was interrupted by a knock at the office door, shortly followed by PC Tolliver and DC Susan Gay leading in an agitated Les Poole.

"Found him at the Crown and Anchor, sir," explained Tolliver. "Sorry it took so long. It's not one of his usual haunts."

"Bit up-market for you, isn't it, Les?" Banks said. "Come into some money lately?"

Poole just grunted and worked at his Elvis Presley sneer. Tolliver left and Susan Gay sat down in the chair beside the door, getting out her notebook and pen. Banks gestured for Poole to sit opposite him at the desk. Poole was wearing jeans and a leather jacket over a turquoise T-shirt, taut over his bulging stomach. Even from across the desk, Banks could smell the beer on his breath.

"Now then, Les," he said, "you might be wondering why we've dragged you away from the pub this evening?"

Les Poole shifted in his chair and said nothing; his features settled in a sullen and hard-done-by expression.

"Well, Les?"

"Dunno."

"Have a guess."

"You found out something about Gemma?"

"Wrong. I'm working on another case now, Les. The super's taken that one over."

Poole shrugged. "Dunno then. Look, shouldn't I have a brief?"

"Up to you. We haven't charged you with anything yet. You're just helping us with our enquiries."

"Still . . . what do you want?"

"Information."

"About what?"

"Can you read, Les?"

"Course I can."

"Read the papers?"

"Now and then. Sporting pages mostly. I mean, most

of your actual news is bad, isn't it? Why bother depressing yourself, I always say."

Banks scratched the thin scar beside his right eye. "Quite. How about the telly? That nice new one you've got."

Poole half rose. "Now look, if this is about that—"

"Relax, Les. Sit down. It's not about the Fletcher's warehouse job, the one you were going to tell me you know nothing about. Though we might get back to that a bit later. No, this is much more serious."

Poole sat down and folded his arms. "I don't know what you're on about."

"Then let me make it clear. I can do it in two words, Les: Carl Johnson. Remember, the bloke I asked you about a couple of days ago, the one you said you'd never heard of?"

"Who?"

"You heard."

"So what. I still don't know no Ben Johnson."

"It's Carl, Les. As in Carl Lewis. Better pay more attention to those sporting pages, hadn't you? And I think it was a bit too much of a slip to be convincing. Don't you, Susan?"

Banks looked over Poole's shoulder at Susan Gay, who sat by the door. She nodded. Poole glanced around and glared at her, then turned back, tilted his head to one side and pretended to examine the calendar on the office wall, a scene of the waterfalls at Aysgarth in full spate.

"According to the governor of Armley Jail," Susan said, reading from her notes to give the statement authority, "a Mr Leslie Poole shared a cell with a Mr Carl Johnson for six months about four years ago."

"Bit of a coincidence, isn't it, Les?" Banks said.

Poole looked up defiantly. "What if it is? I can't be expected to remember everyone I meet, can I?"

"Have we refreshed your memory?"

"Yeah, well . . . now you mention it. But it was a different bloke. Same name, all right, but a different bloke."

"Different from whom?"

"The one you mean."

"How do you know which one I mean?"

"Stands to reason, dunnit? The bloke who got killed."

"Ah. That's better, Les. And here was me thinking you weren't up on current affairs. How did you hear about it?"

"Saw it on the telly, didn't I? On the news. Someone gets croaked around these parts you can't help but hear about it somewhere."

"Good. Now seeing as this Carl Johnson you heard about on the news is the same Carl Johnson you shared a cell with in Armley Jail—"

"I told you, it was a different bloke!"

Banks sighed. "Les, don't give me this crap. I'm tired and I'm hungry. I haven't eaten since elevenses, and here I am sticking around out of the goodness of my heart just to talk to you. I'm trying to be very civilized about this. That's why we're in my nice comfortable office just having a friendly chat instead of in some smelly interview room. Listen, Les, we've got prison records, we've got fingerprints, we've got warders who remember. Believe me, it was the same person."

"Well, bugger me!" Les said, sitting up sharply. "What a turn-up for the book. Poor old Carl, eh? And here was me hoping it must have been someone else."

Banks sighed. "Very touching, Les. When did you last see him?"

"Oh, years ago. How long was it you said? Four years."

"You haven't seen him since you came out?"

"No. Why should I?"

"No reason, I suppose. Except maybe that you both live in the same town?"

"Eastvale ain't that small."

"Still," said Banks, "it's a bit of a coincidence, isn't it? He's been in Eastvale a few months now. It strikes me that, given your records, the two of you might have got together to do a little creative thievery. Like the Fletcher's warehouse job, for example. I'm sure Carl was versatile enough for that."

"Now there you go again, accusing me of that. I ain't done nothing."

"Les, we could drive down to your house right now, pick up the television and the compact music centre, maybe even the video, too, and likely as not *prove* they came from that job."

"Brenda bought those in good faith!"

"Bollocks, Les. What's it to be?"

Poole licked his lips. "You wouldn't," he said. "You wouldn't dare go and take them away, not after what's happened to poor Brenda." A sly smile came to his face. "Think how bad it would look in the papers."

"Don't push me, Les." Banks spoke quietly, but the menace in his voice came through clearly. "What we're dealing with here is a man who was gutted. Ever been fishing, Les? Ever cleaned a fish? You take one of those sharp knives and slit its gullet open to empty the entrails. Well, someone took a knife like that, someone who must have known Carl Johnson pretty well to get so close to him in such a remote spot, and stuck the knife in just above his balls and dragged it slowly up his guts, sliced his belly button in two, until it got stuck on the chest bone. And Carl's insides opened up and spilled like a bag of offal, Les. If his jacket hadn't been zipped up afterwards they'd have spilled all over the bloody dale." He pointed at Poole's beer-belly. "Do you know how many yards of intestine you've got in there? Are you seriously telling me that I'll let a few stolen electrical goods get in the way of my finding out who did that?"

Poole held his stomach and paled. "It wasn't me, Mr Banks. Honest, it wasn't. I've got to go to the toilet. I need a piss."

Banks turned away. "Go."

Poole opened the door, and Banks asked the uniformed PC standing there to escort him to the gents.

Banks turned to Susan. "What do you think?"

"I think he's close, sir," she said.

"To what?"

"To telling us what he knows."

"Mm," said Banks. "Some of it, maybe. He's a slippery bugger is Les."

He lit a cigarette. A short while later, Poole returned and resumed his seat.

"You were saying, Les?"

"That I'd nothing to do with it."

"No," said Banks. "I don't believe you had. For one thing, you haven't got the bottle. Just for the record, though, where were you last Thursday evening?"

"Thursday? . . . Let me see. I was helping my mate in his shop on Rampart Street."

"You seem to spend a lot of time at this place, Les. I never took you for a hard worker before, maybe I was wrong. What do you do there?"

"This and that."

"Be more specific, Les."

"I help out, don't I? Make deliveries, serve customers, lug stuff around."

"What's your mate's name again?"

"John."

"John what."

"John Fairley. It's just a junk shop. You know, old 78s,

second-hand furniture, the odd antique. Nothing really valuable. We empty out old people's houses, when they snuff it, like."

"Nothing new? No televisions, stereos, videos?"

"You're at it again. I told you I had nothing to do with that. Let it drop."

"What's he look like, this John Fairley?"

"Pretty ordinary."

"You can do better than that."

"I'm not very good at this sort of thing. He's strong, you know, stocky, muscular. He's a nice bloke, John, decent as they come."

"What colour's his hair?"

"Black. Like yours."

But Banks could see the guilt and anxiety in Poole's eyes. John's shop was where they fenced the stuff, all right, and John Fairley's description matched that of the man Edwina Whixley had seen coming down from Carl Johnson's flat, vague as it was.

"Do we know him, Les?"

"Shouldn't think so. I told you, he's straight."

"If I went to see this mate of yours, this John, he'd tell me you were in the shop all evening Thursday, would he?"

"Well, not *all* evening. We worked a bit late, unloading a van full of stuff from some old codger from the Leaview Estate who croaked a few weeks back."

"What time did you finish?"

"About seven o'clock."

"And where did you go after that?"

"Pub."

"Of course. Which one?"

"Well, first we went to The Oak. That's the nearest to Rampart Street. Had a couple there, just to rinse the dust out of my mouth, like, then later we went down the local,

The Barleycorn."

"I assume you were seen at these places?"

"I suppose so. That's what I did. Cross my heart and hope to die."

"I wouldn't do that, Les."

"What?"

"Hope to die. Look what happened to Carl Johnson."

Poole swallowed. "That's got nothing to do with me."

"But we don't know why he was killed, do we? Let's just take a hypothetical scenario, all right? A sort of falling out among thieves. Say Carl was involved in the Fletcher's warehouse job, and say there were two or three others in on it as well. Now, maybe Carl got too greedy, or maybe he tried to stick away a few pieces of merchandise for himself—like one of his accomplices might have done, too—you know, a nice new telly, and maybe a stereo. Follow my drift so far?"

Poole nodded.

"Good. So let's say one of these thieves doesn't have much regard for human life. He gets mad at Carl, arranges to meet him to discuss the problem, persuades him to go for a ride, then guts him. Now, what do you think this bloke, who's already killed once, might do if he gets wind there's a problem with *another* of his accomplices?"

Poole's jaw dropped.

"What's wrong, Les? Cat got your tongue?"

Poole shook his head. "Nothing. I ain't done nothing."

"So you keep saying. Say it often enough and *you* might believe it, but I won't. Are you sure there's nothing you want to tell me, Les? Maybe you met this bloke, or maybe Carl talked about him. I'd hate to have to hang around some filthy old lead mine while the doc tried to stuff you into a body sack without spilling your guts all over the dirt."

Poole put his hands over his ears. "Stop it!" he yelled. "It's not bloody fair. You can't do this to me!"

Banks slammed the desk. "Yes, I bloody well can," he said. "And I'll go on doing it until I find out the truth. If I have to, I'll lock you up. More likely I'll just let you go and tell the press you were kind enough to give us a few tips on the warehouse job. What's it to be, Les? Your choice."

Poole looked around the office like a caged animal. Seeing no way out, he sagged in his chair and muttered, "All right. You're a bastard, you know."

Banks glanced over at Susan Gay. She turned a page in her notebook.

"Look, about this 'ypo-whatsit story of yours," Poole said.

"Hypothetical."

"That's right. I mean, you can't pin owt on anyone for just telling an 'ypothetical story, can you?"

Banks grabbed his coffee mug, pushed his chair back, put his feet on the desk and lit a cigarette. "Maybe, maybe not," he said. "Just tell us about the bloke, Les. Talk to me. I'm listening."

"Yeah, well, I did bump into Carl a couple of times, accidental like. We had a jar or two now and then, talked about old times. There was this mate he mentioned. I didn't want to say before because I didn't want to get involved, not now that I'm going straight and all—What's up with you?"

"Sorry, Les," Banks said. "Just a bit of coffee went down the wrong way. Carry on. Tell me about this mate of Carl's."

Poole scowled. "Anyway, I remembered from the time inside, like, this bloke he used to talk about sometimes, like it was his hero or something. I never met him myself, but just hearing about him gave me the creeps.

Funny that, like Carl seemed to get some kind of kick out of telling me about this bloke and what he did and all that, but to me it was a bit over the top. I mean, I'm no fucking angel, I'll admit that, but I've got my limits. I never hurt anyone. Remember, this is all 'ypothetical."

"The man, Les."

"Hold on, I'm getting to him. Anyways, as I was saying, Carl said he was here in Eastvale. Well, that's when I cut out. I didn't want nothing to do with them. I didn't want to get mixed up in anything."

"What didn't you want to get mixed up in, Les?"

"You know, anything, like, criminal."

"I see. Were they in on the Fletcher's warehouse job? Johnson and this other bloke."

"I think so. But like I said, I stayed well away after I heard this bloke was in town."

"Tell me about him."

"Not much to tell. Like I said, I never met him. According to Carl, he's never been inside, yet he's been up to more evil than many as have."

"What kind of evil?"

"You name it. If what Carl says is right, this bloke worked with some of the London mobs, you know, peddling porn and hurting people who wouldn't pay up, but now he's gone freelance. Bit of a rover. Never stays in one place very long. Got lots of contacts."

"And he's never been inside?"

"Not as anyone knows of." Poole leaned forward. "Look, Mr Banks," he said, licking his lips. "This bloke's really nasty, know what I mean? Carl told me he was in a fish-and-chip shop once and got arguing with the woman in front. She was carrying a dog with her, like, one of those little Pekinese things, and this bloke just plucked it out of her arms and flung it in the frier then walked out cool as a cucumber. He's a nutter. I didn't want nothing to do with him."

"Can't say I blame you," said Banks. "What's his name?"

"Dunno. Carl never said."

"Les!"

"Look, I don't want anyone knowing I—"

"Just between you and me, Les. Off the record."

"You promise?"

"I'm in the business of preventing crime, remember? It'd hardly be in my interests to have another murder on my patch, would it? And you've no idea how much I'd miss you."

"Huh. Even so . . ."

"Les."

Poole paused. "All right, all right. I'll trust you—still 'ypothetical, like. All I know is his name is Chivers. It's pronounced with a 'sh', like in shivers. I don't know if it's his real name or a nickname."

"What does he look like?"

"I don't know. I told you, I never met him."

Banks wasn't convinced. For a start, he was certain that Poole *had* been connected with the Fletcher's warehouse job, and now it seemed a good bet that Johnson and this Chivers person had been involved, too, along with John Fairley, the junk-shop owner. He could understand Poole's not wishing to implicate himself, of course, especially as it was now a matter of murder.

The thing to remember about Les Poole was that he had spent time inside; he knew the value of information and of silence. He knew how to get as much slack as he could while giving as little as possible in return. Maybe he was a small-time crook, a coward and a bully, not too bright, but he knew the ropes; he knew how to duck and dodge to save his own neck, how to measure out exactly enough co-operation to get himself out of trouble. Banks sensed that he was holding back, that he *had* met this Chivers, but there was no percentage in pushing him yet. They needed more leverage, and Poole was right about one thing: impounding Brenda Scupham's television would look very bad indeed.

"Is he still in Eastvale?"

"Dunno. Don't think so."

"Is there anything else you can tell me about him?"

"No. 'Cept I'd stay out of his way if I were you. Carl said he had this bird and—"

"What bird's this, Les?"

"This bird Chivers had with him. Some blonde bint. Apparently, he always has a bit of spare with him. The lasses like him. Must be his unpredictable, violent nature."

They liked Les, too, Banks remembered, and wondered if there had been a spot of bother about this blonde. Maybe Les had made a pass and Chivers put a scare in him. Or maybe Carl Johnson had. It wasn't so difficult, he thought, to fill in the rest from the scraps Poole dished out.

"What did Carl say about Chivers's girlfriend?" he asked.

"Just that Chivers knifed a bloke once for looking at her the wrong way. Didn't kill him, like, just cut him up a bit. Anyway, like I said, he never had any shortage of birds. Not scrubbers either, according to Carl. Quality goods. Maybe it was his smile," Les added.

"What smile?"

"Nothing. Just that Carl said he had this really nice smile, like. Said his mates called him 'Smiler' Chivers."

When Banks heard Poole's last comment, the warning bells began to ring. "Susan," he said, looking over Poole's shoulder. "Do you know if the super's still here?"

II

Brenda Scupham couldn't concentrate on the television programme. For a moment she thought of going out, maybe to the pub, but decided she couldn't stand the questions and the looks people would give her. She hadn't enjoyed going out much at all since Gemma had gone. For one thing, people had given her dirty looks when they saw her, as if they blamed her or she wasn't obeying the proper rules of mourning or something. Instead, she took another tranquillizer and poured herself a small measure of gin. Again she wondered what the hell was going on.

All she knew was that the police had called at her house earlier that evening looking for Les. He'd been out of course, and she hadn't known where, though she was sure the policeman hadn't believed her. When she asked what they wanted, they wouldn't tell her anything. Surely, she thought, if it had anything to do with Gemma, they should tell her?

She looked over at the television and video. Maybe that's what it was all about? She knew they were stolen. She wasn't *that* stupid. Les hadn't said so, of course, but then he wouldn't; he never gave away anything. He had dropped them off in John's van one afternoon and said they were bankrupt stock. All the time the police had been coming and going because of Gemma, Brenda had been worried they would spot the stolen goods and arrest her. But they hadn't. Perhaps now they had some more evidence and had decided to arrest Les after all.

How her life could have changed so much in just one week was beyond her. But it had, and even the tranquillizers did no real good. She had enjoyed going on television with Lenora Carlyle—that had been the high spot of her week—but nothing had come of it. Just as nothing

had come of the police search, the "Crimewatch" recon-
struction, or her appeals through the newspapers. And
now, as she sat and thought about the police visit, she
wondered if Les might have been involved in some way
with Gemma's disappearance. She couldn't imagine how
or why—except he hadn't got on very well with
Gemma—but he *had* been acting strangely of late.

And the more she thought about it, the more she lost
faith in Lenora's conviction that Gemma was still alive.
She couldn't be. Not after all this time, not after the
bloodstained clothing they had brought for her to identify. And apart from that one statement, Lenora had come
up with nothing else, had she? Surely she ought to be
able to picture where Gemma was if she was any good as
a psychic? But no, nothing. And what if Gemma was
alive somewhere? It didn't bear thinking about. She felt
closer to her daughter now she was gone than she ever
had while Gemma had been around.

Time after time her thoughts circled back to Mr Brown
and Miss Peterson. Should she have known they weren't
who they said they were? And if she hadn't felt so guilty
about not loving Gemma the way a good mother should
and about shaking her the week before, would she have
let her go so easily? They had been so convincing, kind
and understanding rather than accusing in their approach.
They had looked so young, so official, so competent, but
how was she to know what child-care workers were supposed to look like?

Again she thought of the police officers who had come
to her house earlier. Maybe they had found Gemma and
some clue had led them to Les. But still she couldn't
imagine what he could possibly have to do with it. He
had been out when the child care workers called. Still,
there was no denying the police were after him. If he had
anything to do with Gemma's abduction, Brenda thought,

she would kill him. Damn the consequences. It was all his fault anyway. Yes, she thought, reaching for the gin bottle again. She would kill the bastard. For now, though, she was sick of thinking and worrying.

The only thing that worked, that took away the pain, even though it lasted such a short time, was the video. Slowly, she got up and went over to the player. The cassette was still in. All she had to do was rewind and watch herself on television again. She had been nervous, but she was surprised when she watched the playback that it didn't show so much. And she had looked so pretty.

Brenda poured herself another generous measure, turned on one element of the fire and reclined on the sofa with her dressing-gown wrapped around her. She had watched the video once and was rewinding for a second viewing when she heard Les's key in the door.

III

"You don't believe for a moment he told you everything, do you?" Gristhorpe asked Banks later in the Queen's Arms. It was a quiet Wednesday evening, a week since the first news of Gemma Scupham's disappearance—and despite the helicopters and search tactics learned from the North American Association of Search and Rescue, she still hadn't been found. Banks and Gristhorpe sat at a table near the window eating the roast beef sandwiches that they had persuaded Cyril, the landlord, to make for them.

Banks chewed and swallowed his mouthful, then said, "No. For a start, I'm sure he's seen this Chivers bloke, but he couldn't really admit to it without implicating himself in the warehouse job. We let him walk. For now. Les won't stray far. He's got nowhere to go."

"And then?"

Banks grinned. "Just an idea, but I'd like to find out if Les really does know anything about Gemma's abduction. I had a phone call just after I'd finished with Poole. Jim Hatchley's coming into town. Seems his mother-in-law's commissioned him to install a shower—"

Gristhorpe slapped the table. One of the customers at the bar turned and looked. "No, Alan. I'm not having any of Hatchley's interrogation methods in this one. If Gemma's abductors get off because we've bent the rules I'd never bloody forgive myself. Or Sergeant Hatchley, for that matter."

"No," said Banks, "that's not what I had in mind." He outlined his plan and both of them ended up laughing.

"Aye," said Gristhorpe, nodding slowly. "Aye, he'd be the best man for *that* job, all right. And it might work, at that. Either way, we've nothing to lose."

Banks washed his sandwich down with a swig of Theakston's bitter and lit a cigarette. "So where do we go now?" he asked.

Gristhorpe leaned back in his chair and folded his hands in his lap. "Let's start with a summary. I find it helps to get everything as clear as possible. In the first place, we know that a couple who called themselves Chris and Connie Manley rented a cottage and changed their appearance. Then they 'borrowed' a dark blue Toyota from Bruce Parkinson, passed themselves off as social workers called Mr Brown and Miss Peterson, and conned Brenda Scupham into handing over her daughter on Tuesday afternoon. After that, they drove a hundred and twenty-seven miles before returning the car to its owner.

"As far as we know, they left the cottage on Thursday in a white Fiesta. We don't have the number, and Phil's already checked and re-checked with the rental outlets.

Nothing. And it hasn't been reported stolen. We could check the ownership of every white Fiesta in the country, and we bloody well will if we have to, but that'll take us till doomsday. They might not be registered as owners, anyway. Nobody saw them with the child in Eastvale, and there was no evidence of a child's presence in the cottage, but she could have been there—the whitewash supports that—and we found her prints in Parkinson's car. Why they took her, we don't know. Or where. All we know is they most likely didn't bring her back, which to me indicates that she could well be lying dead and buried somewhere in a hundred-and-twenty-mile radius. And that includes the area of the North York Moors where we found the bloodstained clothes. Vic says there wasn't enough blood on them to cause death, but that doesn't mean the rest didn't spill elsewhere, or that she might not have died in some other way. Poole told you that this Chivers person was involved in the porn trade in London, so that's another ugly possibility to consider. I've been onto the paedophile squad again, but they've got nothing on anyone of that name or description.

"Anyway. Next we find Carl Johnson's body in the old lead mine on Friday morning. Dr Glendenning says he was probably killed sometime after dark on Thursday. You follow all the leads you can think of in the Johnson murder, and we arrive at this same man called Chivers with a smile that people notice, a blonde girlfriend and a nasty disposition. You think Poole knows a bit more. Maybe he does. There are too many coincidences for my liking. Chivers and the girl are the ones who took Gemma. Maybe one or both of them also killed Carl Johnson. Chivers, most likely, as it took a fair bit of strength to rip his guts open. But why? What's the connection?"

"Johnson could have double-crossed them on the warehouse job, or maybe he knew about Gemma and threatened to tell. Whatever Johnson was, he wasn't a paedophile."

"Assuming he found out they'd taken her?"

"Yes."

"That's probably our best bet. Makes more sense than killing over a bloody TV set, though stranger things have happened."

"Or it could have been over the girlfriend," Banks added. "Especially after what Poole told me about the knifing."

"Aye," said Gristhorpe. "That's another strong possibility. But let's imagine that Carl Johnson found out Chivers and his girlfriend had taken Gemma and . . . well, done whatever they did to her. Now Johnson's no angel, and he seems to have an unhealthy fascination with bad 'uns, from what you tell me, but somehow they've gone too far for him. He doesn't like child-molesters. He becomes a threat. They lure him out to the mine. Maybe the girl does it with promises of sex, or Chivers with money, I don't know. But somehow they get him there and . . ." Gristhorpe paused. "The mine might be a connection. I know the area's been thoroughly searched already, but I think we should go over it again tomorrow. There's plenty of spots around there a body could be hidden away. Maybe the clothes on the moors were just a decoy. What do you think, Alan?"

Banks frowned. "It's all *possible,* but there are still too many uncertainties for my liking. I'd like to know more about the girl's part in all this, for a start. Who is she? What's in it for her? And we've no evidence that Chivers killed Johnson."

"You're right, we don't have enough information to come to conclusions yet. But we're getting there. I thought you fancied Adam Harkness for the Johnson murder?"

"I did, though I'd no real reason to. Looks like I might have been wrong, doesn't it?"

Gristhorpe smiled. "Happens to us all, Alan. You always did have a chip on your shoulder when it came to the rich and influential, didn't you?"

"What?"

"Nay, Alan, I'm not criticizing. You're a working-class lad. You got where you are through brains, ability and sheer hard slog. I'm not much different myself, just a poor farm-boy at heart. I've no great love for them as were born with silver spoons in their mouths. And I don't mind sticking up for you when Harkness complains to the ACC about police harassment. All I'm saying is be careful it doesn't blur your objectivity."

Banks grinned. "Fair enough," he said. "But I haven't finished with Mr Harkness yet. I called the Johannesburg police and set a few enquiries in motion. You never know, there might be something to that scandal yet. And I called Piet in Amsterdam to see if he can track down Harkness's ex-wife. There's still a chance Harkness might have been involved somewhere along the line. What about your black magician, Melville Westman?"

"Nothing," said Gristhorpe. "The lads did a thorough job. He looks clean. It's my bet that Gemma was in the Manleys' cottage at some point, and that's where the whitewash on her clothes came from. That's not to say I won't be having another word with Mr Westman, though." Gristhorpe smiled. His own feelings about people like Melville Westman and Lenora Carlyle were not so different from Banks's feelings about the rich and powerful, he realized: different chip, different shoulder, but a prejudice, nonetheless.

"I'm going to call my old mate Barney Merritt at the

Yard first thing in the morning," Banks said. "He ought to be able to get something out of Criminal Intelligence about Chivers a damn sight quicker than the formal channels. The more we know about him, the more likely we are to be able to guess at the way he thinks. The bastard might never have been nicked but I'll bet a pound to a penny he's on the books somewhere."

Gristhorpe nodded. "Oh, aye. No doubt about it. And it looks as if we're all working on the same case now. You'd better get up to date on the Gemma files, and we'd better let Phil know so he can access his databases or whatever he does. I want this bloke, Alan. I want him bad. I mean I want him in front of me. I want to see him sweat. Do you know what I mean?"

Banks nodded and finished his drink. From the bar, they heard Cyril call time. "It's late," he said quietly. "Time we were off home."

"Aye. Everything all right?"

"Fine," said Banks. "Just think yourself lucky you don't have daughters."

Banks walked in the rain, coat buttoned tight, and listened to his Walkman. It was after eleven-thirty when he got home, and the house was in darkness. Sandra was already in bed, he assumed; Tracy, too. He knew he wouldn't be able to sleep just yet, after the conversation with Gristhorpe had got his mind working, and as he had drunk only two pints in the pub, he felt he could allow himself a small Scotch. What was it the medics said, three drinks a day is moderate? Some kind soul had brought him a bottle of Glen Garioch from a holiday in Scotland, so he poured himself a finger and sat down. Though he wasn't supposed to smoke in the house, he lit a cigarette anyway and put on a CD of Barenboim playing Chopin's Nocturnes. Even at low volume, the clarity of the sound was astonishing. He had hardly begun to let his mind roam freely over the image of Chivers he had created so far when he heard the front door open and close softly, then the creak of a stair.

He opened the living-room door and saw Tracy tiptoeing upstairs.

"Come down here a moment," he whispered, careful not to wake Sandra.

Tracy hesitated, halfway up, then shrugged and followed him into the living-room.

Banks held out his wristwatch towards her. "Know what time it is?"

"Of course I do."

"Where've you been?"

"Out with Keith."

"Where to?"

"Oh, Dad! We went to the pictures, then after that we were hungry so we went for a burger."

"A burger? At this time of night?"

"You know, that new McDonald's that's opened in the shopping centre. It's open till midnight."

"How did you get home?"

"Keith walked me."

"It's too late to be out on a weeknight. You've got school in the morning."

"It's only midnight. I'll get plenty of sleep."

There she stood, about seven stones of teenage rebellion, weight balanced on one hip, once long and beautiful blonde hair chopped short, wearing black leggings and a long, fawn cable-knit jumper, pale translucent skin glowing from the chill.

"You're too young to be out so late," he said.

"Oh, don't be so old-fashioned. *Everyone* stays out until midnight these days."

"I don't care what everyone else does. It's you I'm talking about."

"It would be different if it was Brian, wouldn't it? He could always stay out as late as he wanted, couldn't he?"

"He had to live with the same rules as you."

"Rules! I bet you've no idea what he's up to now, have you? Or what he got up to when he was still at home. It's all right for him. Honestly, it's not fair. Just because I'm a girl."

"Tracy, love, it's not a safe world."

Her cheeks blazed red and her eyes flashed dangerously, just like Sandra's did when she was angry. "I'm fed up of it," she said. "Living here, being interrogated every time I come in. Sometimes it's just absolutely fucking awful having a policeman for a father!"

And with that, she stormed out of the room and up the stairs without giving Banks a chance to respond. He stood there a moment, stunned by her language—not that she knew such words, even five-year-olds knew them, but that she would use them that way in front of him— then he felt himself relax a little and he began to shake his head slowly. By the time he had sat down again and picked up his drink, he had started to smile. "Kids . . ." he mused aloud. "What can you do?" But even as he said it, he knew that Sandra had been right: the problem was that Tracy wasn't a kid any more.

IV

Brenda had locked the door earlier, and slid the bolt and put the chain on, too. When the key wouldn't work, she could hear Les fumble around for a while, rattling it and mumbling. Brenda could see his silhouette through the frosted-glass panes in the door as she sat on the stairs and listened. He tried the key again, then she heard him swear in frustration and start knocking. She didn't answer.

"Brenda," he said, "I know you're in there. Come on, love, and open up. There's something wrong with my key."

She could tell by the way he slurred his words that he'd been drinking. The police either hadn't found him, then, or had let him go before closing time.

He rattled the door. "Brenda! It's fucking cold out here. Let me in."

Still she ignored him, sitting on the staircase, arms wrapped around herself.

The letter-box opened. "I know you're in there," he said. "Have a heart, Brenda."

She stood up and walked down the stairs to the door. "Go away," she said. "I don't want you here any more. Go away."

"Brenda!" He was still on his knees by the letter-box. "Don't be daft, love. Let me in. We'll talk about it."

"There's nothing to talk about. Go away."

"Where? This is my home. It's all I've got."

"Go back to the police. I'm sure they'll give you a bed for the night."

He was silent for a few moments. Then she heard shuffling outside. The letter-box snapped shut, then opened again. "It wasn't nothing, love," he said. "A mistake. It was some other bloke they were after."

"Liar."

"It was. Honest it was."

"What have you done with my Gemma?"

Another pause, even longer this time, then, "How could you think such a thing? It wasn't nothing to do with that. Look, let me in. It's raining. I'll catch cold. I'm freezing my goolies off out here."

"Good."

"Brenda! The neighbours are watching."

"I couldn't care less."

"What about my things?"

Brenda dashed up to the bedroom. Les's "things," such as they were, shouldn't take up much space. She was a bit unsteady on her feet, but she managed to stand on a chair and get an old suitcase down from the top of the wardrobe. First, she emptied out his underwear drawer. Shirts and trousers followed, then she tossed in his old denim jacket. He was wearing the leather one, she remembered. She dropped a couple of pairs of shoes on the top, then went into the bathroom and picked up his razor, shaving cream, toothbrush. For some reason, she didn't know why, she also picked up a package of tampons and put them in the suitcase, too, smiling as she did so. And on further thought, she took his condoms from the bedside drawer and put them in as well.

Enjoying herself more than she had since her TV appearance, Brenda searched around for anything else that belonged to him. A comb. Brylcreem. Half a packet of cigarettes. No, she would keep them for herself. Nothing else.

As she struggled to fasten the suitcase, she could hear him outside in the street yelling up at her: "Brenda! Come on, Brenda, let me in. Please. I'm freezing to death out here."

She walked over to the window. Les stood by the gate at the bottom of the path, partly lit by a nearby street-lamp. Across the street, lights came on as people opened their doors or peered through curtains to see what was going on. This would give the neighbours something to talk about, Brenda thought, as she opened the window.

Les looked up at her. For a moment, she remembered a scene in a play they'd taken her to see with the school years ago, where some wally in tights down on the ground had been chatting up a bird on a balcony. She giggled and swayed, then got a hold on herself. After all, she had an audience. "Bugger off, Les," she yelled. "I've had enough of you and your filthy ways. If it wasn't for you I'd still have my Gemma."

"Open the fucking door, cow," said Les, "or I'll kick it down. You never liked the little bitch anyway."

"I loved my daughter," said Brenda. "It was you used to upset her. Where is she, Les? What have you done with her?"

Another door opened down the street. "Be quiet," a woman shouted. "My husband's got to get up to go to work at five o'clock in the morning."

"Shut up, you stuck-up old bag," shouted someone else. "Your husband's never done a day's work in his life. This is the best show we've had in ages." Bursts of laughter echoed down the street.

A window slid open. "Give him hell, love!" a woman's voice encouraged Brenda.

"What's going on?" someone else asked. "Has anyone called the police yet?"

"See what you've started," Les said, looking around at the gathering of neighbours and trying to keep his voice down. "Come on, love, let me in. We'll have a cuddle and talk about it. I've done nowt wrong."

"And what about that telly?" Brenda taunted him. "Where did that come from, eh? Have you noticed the way the police look at it every time they come here?"

"Must be fans of 'The Bill,'" someone joked, and the neighbours laughed. "Anyone got a bottle," the joker continued. "I could do with a wee nip."

"Buy your own, you tight-fisted old bugger," came the reply.

"Open the door," Les pleaded. "Brenda, come on, love, have mercy."

"I'll not show no mercy for you, you snake. Where's

my Gemma?"

"I'll do you for bloody slander, I will," yelled Les. "Making accusations like that in front of witnesses." He turned to the nearest neighbour, an old woman in a dressing-gown. "You heard her, didn't you?"

"Maybe she's right," said the woman.

"Aye," said the man next door.

"Hey," said Les, "Now, come on." He looked up at the window again. "Brenda, let me in. I don't like the look of this lot."

"Too bad." Brenda swung the suitcase behind her as far as she could, then let it fly out the window. It hit the gatepost and burst open, showering its contents over the garden and street. Les put his hands up to try and stop it from hitting him, but all he managed to catch was the packet of tampons. It spilled its contents on him as he grasped it too tightly. One of the neighbours noticed and started laughing. Les stood there in the rain, half in shadow, surrounded by the flotsam and jetsam of his life and a packet of tampons spilled like cigarettes at his feet. He looked up at Brenda and shouted one last appeal. Brenda closed the window. Before she pulled the curtains on him, she noticed some of the neighbours edging forward in a semi-circle towards Les, who was backing down the street, looking behind him for a clear escape route.

11

I

"Les Poole's done a bunk, sir."

"Has he, now?" Banks looked up from his morning coffee at Susan Gay standing in his office door. She was wearing a cream skirt and jacket over a powder-blue blouse fastened at the neck with an antique jet brooch. Matching jet teardrops hung from her small ears. Her complexion looked fresh-scrubbed under the tight blonde curls that still glistened from her morning shower. Her eyes were lit with excitement.

"Come in and tell me about it," Banks said.

Susan sat down opposite him. He noticed her glance at the morning papers spread out on his desk. There, on the front pages of all of them, the police artist's impression of Smiler Chivers and his blonde girlfriend stared out.

"There was a bit of a barney last night on the East Side Estate," Susan began. "According to PC Evans, who walks the beat down there, Les Poole was out in the street yelling at Brenda to let him in."

"She locked him out?"

"Seems like it."

"Why?"

"Well, that's where it gets interesting. PC Evans talked

to some of the neighbours. Most of them were a bit tight-lipped, but he found one chap who'd been watching it all from his bedroom window down the street. He said it looked like the others had turned into a mob and were about to attack Poole. That's why he ran off."

"Any idea why, apart from his sparkling personality?"

"While they were yelling at each other, Brenda apparently made some comment about Poole being responsible for Gemma's disappearance."

"What?"

"That's all he heard, sir, the neighbour. Brenda kept asking Poole what he'd done with Gemma."

Banks reached for a cigarette, his first of the day. "What do you think?" he asked.

"About Poole?"

"Yes."

"I don't know. I mean it could just have been something Brenda thought up on the spur of the moment to hit out at him, couldn't it?"

"I know Poole's been holding something back," Banks said. "That's just his nature. But I never really thought . . ." He stubbed out his unfinished cigarette and stood up. "Come on. First, let's send some of the lads out looking for him. And then we'd better have another word with Brenda." He picked up one of the newspapers. "We'll see if she recognizes the artist's impression, too."

They drove in silence to East Side Estate. It was a blustery morning, with occasional shafts of sunlight piercing the clouds and illuminating a bridge, a clump of trees or a block of maisonettes for a few seconds then disappearing. There ought to be a shimmering dramatic soundtrack, Banks thought, something to harmonize with the odd sense of revelation the fleeting rays of light conveyed.

Banks knocked on the frosted pane of Brenda's door,

but no one answered. He knocked harder. Across the street, a curtain twitched. Discarded cellophane wrapping and newspaper blew across the road, scraping against the tarmac.

"They'll be having the time of their lives," Susan said, nodding towards the houses opposite. "Twice in two days. A real bonanza."

Banks renewed his efforts. Eventually he was rewarded by the sight of a blurry figure walking down the stairs.

"Who is it?" Brenda asked.

"Police."

She fiddled with the bolts and chain and let them in.

"Sorry," she said, rubbing the back of her hand over her eyes. "I was fast asleep. Must have been those pills the doctor gave me."

She looked dreadful, Banks thought: knotted and straggly hair in need of a good wash, puffy complexion, mottled skin, red eyes. She wore a white terry-cloth robe, and when she sat down in the living-room under the gaze of Elvis, it was clear she wore nothing underneath. As she leaned forward to pick up a cigarette from the table, the bathrobe hung loose at the front, revealing her plump, round breasts. Unembarrassed, she pulled the lapels together and slouched back in the chair. Banks and Susan sat on the sofa opposite her.

"What is it?" Brenda asked after she had exhaled a lungful of smoke. "Have you found Gemma?"

"No," said Banks. "It's about Les."

She snorted. "Oh, him. Well, he's gone, and good riddance, too."

"So I heard. Any idea *where* he's gone?"

She shook her head.

"Why did you throw him out, Brenda?"

"You should know. It was you lot had him at the

station last night, wasn't it?"

"Did you know the neighbours nearly lynched him?"

"So what?"

"Brenda, it's dangerous to make accusations like the one you did, especially in front of a crowd. You know from experience how people feel whenever children are involved. They can turn very nasty. There's records of people being torn apart by angry mobs."

"Yes, I know. I know all about what people do to child-molesters. They deserve it."

"Did Les molest Gemma? Is that it?"

Brenda blew out more smoke and sighed. "No," she said. "No, he never did anything like that."

"Maybe when you weren't around?"

"No. I'd have known. Gemma would have . . ." She paused and stared at the end of her cigarette.

"Perhaps Gemma wouldn't have mentioned it to you," Banks suggested. "You told us yourself she's a quiet, secretive child. And children are almost always afraid to speak out when things like that happen."

"No," Brenda said again. "I would have known. Believe me."

Whether he believed her or not, Banks felt that line of questioning had come to a dead end. "What reason do you have to think Les was involved in her disappearance, then?" he asked.

Brenda frowned. "You had him in for questioning, didn't you?"

"What made you think that had anything to do with Gemma?"

"What else would it be about?"

"So you just assumed. Is that it?"

"Of course. Unless . . ."

"Unless what?"

Brenda reddened, and Banks noticed her glance towards the television set.

"Did you think it was about the Fletcher's warehouse job?"

Brenda shook her head. "I . . . I don't know."

"Did Les ever mention an acquaintance named Carl Johnson to you?"

"No. He never talked about his pub mates. If I ever asked him where he'd been or who he'd been with, he just told me to mind my own business."

"Look, this is important," Banks said slowly. "Think about it. When you accused Les out in the street, did you have any other basis for doing so other than the fact that we'd taken him in for questioning?"

"What?"

Banks explained. Brenda leaned forward to put out her cigarette. She held her robe closed this time. "That and the way he's been acting," she said.

"What do you mean?"

"It's hard to put into words. Ever since Gemma . . . well, things haven't been the same between us. Do you know what I mean?"

Banks nodded.

"I don't know why, but they haven't. And he just looks so sheepish, the way he creeps around all the time, giving me guilty smiles. Mostly, though, he's been keeping out of my way."

"In what way could he have been involved, Brenda?" Susan asked.

Brenda looked sideways towards her, as if seeing her for the first time. "How should I know?" she said. "I'm not the detective, am I?" She spoke more harshly than she had to Banks. Woman to woman, he thought, Brenda Scupham was uncomfortable.

Banks gently took the focus away from Susan. "Brenda, have you any proof at all that Les had something to do with Gemma's disappearance?"

"No. Just a feeling."

"Okay. I'm not dismissing that. What you told us, about this Mr Brown and Miss Peterson, that was all true, wasn't it?"

"Yes. That's how it happened."

Banks showed her the newspaper pictures of Chivers and the blonde. "Do you recognize these people?"

She squinted at the pictures. "It could be him. The hair's sort of the same, but a different colour. I don't know about her, though. People look so different with their hair up. Him, though . . . I think . . . yes . . . I think it might be."

Banks put the paper aside. "You told us Les wasn't in when they came."

"That's right. He was at the pub."

"How did he react when you told him?"

"I don't know what you mean."

"Did he seem shocked, upset, what?"

Tears came to Brenda's eyes. "He said I was a stupid cow for letting them take her . . . but . . ."

"But what?"

She rubbed the backs of her hands across her eyes. "I need a cup of tea. I can't really get started without my cup of tea in a morning. Do you want some?"

"All right," said Banks. It wouldn't be a bad idea to give her a couple of minutes to mull over his question.

He and Susan waited silently while Brenda went into the kitchen and made tea. Outside, a car went by, a dog barked, and two laughing children kicked a tin can down the street. The wind shrilled at the ill-fitting windows, stirring the curtains in its draught. Banks studied the portrait of Elvis. It really was grotesque: a piece of kitsch dedicated to a bloated and gaudy idol.

As a teenager, he had been a keen Elvis fan. He had

seen all those dreadful movies of the early sixties, where Elvis usually played a slightly podgy beach-bum, and he had bought all the new singles as soon as they came out. Somehow, though, after The Beatles, Bob Dylan, The Rolling Stones and the rest, Elvis had never seemed important again.

Still, he remembered how he had listened to "They Remind Me Too Much of You" over and over again the night June Higgins chucked him for John Hill. He had been assembling a model Messerschmitt at the time, so maybe it was the glue fumes that had made his eyes water. Glue-sniffing hadn't been invented back then. He had been thirteen; now Elvis was dead but lived on in garish oils on walls like this.

The whistle blew. When it stopped, Banks heard Brenda go upstairs. A few moments later she came in with the teapot and three mugs. She had taken the opportunity to get dressed, run a brush through her hair and put on a bit of make-up.

"Where were we?" she asked, pouring the tea. "There's milk and sugar if you want it." Susan helped herself to a splash of milk and two teaspoons of sugar. Both Banks and Brenda took theirs as it came.

"Les's reaction when you told him about Gemma."

"Yes. I've been thinking about it while the tea was mashing," Brenda said. "He didn't believe me at first. I'd say more than anything he was surprised. It's just that . . . well, he turned away from me, and I couldn't see his face, but it was like he knew something or he suspected something, like he was frowning and he didn't want me to see his expression. Do you know what I mean?"

"I think so."

"I could just feel it. I know I've not got any proof or anything, but sometimes you can sense things about people, can't you? Lenora says she thinks I'm a bit psychic, too, so maybe that's it. But I never thought for a moment he had anything to do with it. I mean, how could I? What could Les have had to do with those two well-dressed people who came to the door? And we lived together. I know he didn't care for Gemma much, she got on his nerves, but he wouldn't hurt her. I mean he *was* surprised, shocked, I'm sure of that, but when it sank in, he seemed to be *thinking,* puzzling over something. I put it out of my mind, but it nagged. After that we never really got on well. I'm glad he's gone." She paused, as if surprised at herself for saying so much, then reached for a second cigarette.

"What made you accuse him last night?" Banks asked.

"It's just something that had been at the back of my mind, that's all. Like I said, I never really believed he had anything to do with it. I just had this nagging feeling something wasn't right. I suppose I lashed out, just for the sake of it. I couldn't help myself."

"What about now?"

"What?"

"You said you didn't think Les had anything to do with Gemma's disappearance at first. What do you think now?"

Brenda paused to blow on her hot tea, cradling the mug in her palms, then she turned her eyes up to Banks and shook her head. "I don't know," she whispered. "I just don't know."

II

Banks and Jenny dashed across the cobbles in the rain to the Queen's Arms. Once through the door, they shook their coats and hung them up.

"Double brandy, then?" Banks asked.

"No. No, really, Alan. I didn't mean it," Jenny said. "Just a small Scotch and water, please."

Now she was embarrassed. She put her briefcase on the chair beside her and sat down at a table near the window. She had been in Banks's office going over all the material on the Carl Johnson murder—statements, forensic reports, the lot—and when she got to the photographs of his body, she had turned pale and said she needed a drink. She didn't know why they should affect her that way—she had seen similar images in textbooks—but suddenly she had felt dizzy and nauseated. Something about the way the belly gaped open like a huge fish-mouth . . . no, she wouldn't think about it any more.

Banks returned with their drinks and reached for his cigarettes.

"I'm sorry," she said. "You must think I'm a real idiot."

"Not at all. I just wasn't thinking. I should have prepared you."

"Anyway, I'm fine now." She raised her glass. "Cheers."

"Cheers."

She could see Market Street through a clear, rain-streaked pane. Young mothers walked by pushing prams, plastic rainhats tied over their heads, and delivery vans blocked the traffic while men in white smocks carried boxes in and out of the shops, oblivious to the downpour. All the hurly and burly of commerce so essential to a thriving English market town. So normal. She shivered.

"I take it you're assuming the crimes are related now?" she asked.

Banks nodded. "We are for the moment. I've read over the paperwork on the Gemma Scupham case, and I've filled the super in on Johnson. How are you getting on with him, by the way?"

Jenny smiled. "Fine. He doesn't seem like such an ogre when you get to know him a bit."

"True, he's not. Anyway, we know that the Manleys abducted Gemma, and that in all likelihood the man's real name is Chivers. We still don't know who the woman is."

"But you don't know for sure that this Chivers killed Carl Johnson?"

"No. I realize it's a bit thin, but when you get connections like this between two major crimes you can't overlook them. Maybe in a big city you could, but not in Eastvale."

"And even if he did it, you don't know if the woman was present?"

"No."

"Then what do you want from me?"

"For a start, I want to know if you think it could be the same person, or same people, psychologically speaking."

Jenny took a deep breath. "The two crimes are so different. I can't really find a pattern."

"Are there no elements in common?"

Jenny thought for a moment, and the images of Johnson's body came back. She sipped at her drink. "From all I've seen and heard," she said, "I'd say that the two crimes at least demonstrate a complete lack of empathy on the criminal's part, which leans towards the theory of the psychopath. If that's the case, he probably wasn't sexually interested in Gemma, only in his power over her, which he may have been demonstrating to the woman, as I said to the superintendent last time we met." She ran her hand through her hair. "I just don't have anything more to go on."

"Think about the Johnson murder."

Jenny leaned forward and rested her hands on the table. "All right. The couple who took Gemma showed no feeling for the mother at all. Whoever killed Johnson didn't feel his pain, or if he did, he enjoyed it. You know even better than I do that murder can take many forms—there's the heat of the moment, and there's at least some distancing, as when a gun's used. Even the classic poisoner often prefers to be far away when the poison takes effect. But here we have someone who, according to all the evidence you've shown me, must have stood very close indeed to his victim, looked him in the eye as he killed slowly. Could you do that? Could I? I don't think so. Most of us have at least some sensitivity to another's pain—we imagine what it would feel like if we suffered it ourselves. But one class of person doesn't—the psychopath. He can't relate to anyone else's pain, can't imagine it happening to him. He's so self-centred that he lacks empathy completely."

"You keep saying 'he.'"

Jenny slapped his wrist playfully. "You know as well as I do that, statistically speaking, most psychopaths are men. And it might be pretty interesting to try to find out why. But that's beside the point. That's what the two crimes, what I know of them, have in common. There are other elements that fit the psychopath profile, too: the apparent coolness and bravado with which Gemma was abducted; the charm Chivers must have exhibited to her mother; the clever deceit he must have played to get Johnson out to the mill, if that's what he did. And you can add that he's also likely to be manipulative, impulsive, egocentric and irresponsible. You're nursing your pint, Alan. Anything wrong?"

"What? Oh, no. I'm just preserving my liver. I have to meet Jim Hatchley for dinner in a couple of hours."

"So he's in town again, is he?"

"Just for a little job."

Jenny held her hand up. "Say no more. I don't want to

know anything about it. I can't understand why you like that man."

Banks shrugged. "Jim's all right. Anyway, back to Chivers. What if he committed the Carl Johnson murder out of self-preservation?"

"The method was still his choice."

"Yes." Banks lit another cigarette. "Look, I'll tell you what I'm getting at. Just before you arrived, I talked to my old friend Barney Merritt at the Yard, and he told me that Criminal Intelligence has got quite a file on Chivers. They've never been able to put him away for anything, but they've had reports of his suspected activities from time to time, and they've usually had some connection with organized crime. The closest they came to nabbing him was four years ago. An outsider trying to muscle in on a protection racket in Birmingham was found on a building site with a bullet in his brain. The police knew Chivers was connected with the local mob up there, and a couple of witnesses placed him with the victim in a pub near the site. Soon as things got serious, though, the witnesses started to lose their memories."

"What are you telling me, Alan, that he's a hit man or something?"

Banks waved his hand. "No, hold on, let me finish. Most of the information in the CI files concerns his suspected connection with criminal gangs in London and in Birmingham, doing hits, nobbling witnesses, enforcing debt-collection and the like. But word has it that when business is slack, Chivers is not averse to a bit of murder and mayhem on the side, just for the fun of it. And according to Barney, his employers started to get bad feelings about him about a year ago. They're keeping their distance. Again, there's nothing proven, just hearsay."

"Interesting," said Jenny. "Is there any more?"

"Just a few details. He's prime suspect—without a

scrap of proof—in three murders down south, one involving a fair amount of torture before death, and there are rumours of one or two fourteen-year-old girls he's treated roughly in bed."

Jenny shook her head. "If you're getting at some kind of connection between that and Gemma, I'd say it's highly unlikely."

"But why? He likes his sex rough and strange. He likes them young. What happens when fourteen isn't enough of a kick any more?"

"The fact that he likes having sex with fourteen-year-old girls in no way indicates, psychologically, that he could be interested in seven-year-olds. Quite the opposite, really."

Banks frowned. "I don't understand."

"It was something else I discovered in my research. According to statistics, the younger the child, the older the paedophile is likely to be. Your Chivers sounds about the right age for an unhealthy interest in fourteen-year-olds, but, you know, if you'd given me no information at all about Gemma's abduction, I'd say you should be looking for someone over forty, most likely someone who knew Gemma—a family friend, neighbour or even a relative—who lives in the area, or not far away, and probably lives alone. I certainly wouldn't be looking for a young couple from Birmingham, or wherever."

Banks shook his head. "Okay, let's get back on track. Tell me what you think of this scenario. We know that plenty of psychopaths have found gainful employment in organized crime. They're good at frightening people, they're clever, and they make good killers. The problem is that they're hard to control. Now, what do you do with a psychopath when you find him more of a business liability than an asset? You try to cut him loose and hope to hell he doesn't bear a grudge. Or you have him killed, and so the cycle continues. His old bosses don't trust Chivers any more, Jenny. He's *persona non grata*. They're scared of him. He has to provide his own entertainment now."

"Hmm." Jenny swirled her glass and took another sip. "It makes some sense, but I doubt that it's quite like that. In the first place, if he's hard to control, it's more likely to mean that he's losing control of himself. From what you told me, Chivers must have been a highly organized personality type at one time, exhibiting a great deal of control. But psychopaths are also highly unstable. They're prone to deterioration. His personality could be disintegrating towards the disorganized type, and right now he might be in the middle, the mixed type. Most serial killers, for example, keep on killing until they're caught or until they lose touch completely with reality. That's why you don't find many of them over forty. They've either been caught by then, or they're hopelessly insane."

Banks stubbed out his cigarette. "Are you suggesting that Chivers could be turning into a serial killer?"

Jenny shrugged. "Not necessarily a serial killer, but it's possible, isn't it? He doesn't fit the general profile of a paedophile, and he's certainly changing into *something*. Yes, it makes sense, Alan. I'm not saying it's true, but it's certainly consistent with the information you've got."

"So what next?"

Jenny shuddered. "Your guess is as good as mine. Whatever it is, you can be sure it won't be very pleasant. If he is experiencing loss of control, then he's probably at a very volatile and unpredictable stage." She finished her drink. "I'll give you one piece of advice, though."

"What's that?"

"If it is true, be very careful. This man's a loose cannon on the deck. He's very dangerous. Maybe even more so than you realize."

III

"Congratulations," said Banks. "I really mean it, Jim. I'm happy for you. Why the hell didn't you tell me before?"

"Aye, well . . . weren't sure." Sergeant Hatchley blushed. A typical Yorkshireman, he wasn't comfortable with expressions of sentiment.

The two of them sat in the large oak-panelled dining-room of the Red Lion Hotel, an enormous Victorian structure by the roundabout on the southern edge of Eastvale. Hatchley was looking a bit healthier than he had on his arrival that afternoon. Then the ravages of a hangover had still been apparent around his eyes and in his skin, but now he had regained his normal ruddy complexion and that tell-me-another-one look in his pale blue eyes. Just for a few moments, though, his colour deepened even more and his eyes filled with pride. Banks was congratulating him on his wife's pregnancy. Their first.

"When's it due?" Banks asked.

"I don't know. Don't they usually take nine months?"

"I just wondered if the doctor had given you a date."

"Mebbe Carol knows. She didn't say owt to me, though. This is a good bit of beef." He cut into his prime-rib roast and washed it down with a draught of Theakston's bitter. "Ah, it's good to be home again."

Banks was eating lamb and drinking red wine. Not that he had become averse to Theakston's, but the Red Lion had a decent house claret and it seemed a shame to ignore it. "You still think of Eastvale as home?" he asked.

"Grew up here," replied Hatchley around a mouthful of Yorkshire pudding. "Place gets in your blood."

"How are you liking the coast?"

"It's all right. Been a good summer." Sergeant

Hatchley had been transferred to Saltby Bay, between Scarborough and Whitby, mostly in order to make way for Phil Richmond's boost up the promotion ladder. Hatchley was a good sergeant and always would be; Richmond, Banks suspected, would probably make at least Chief Inspector, his own rank, and might go even further if he kept on top of the latest computer technology and showed a bit more initiative and leadership quality. Susan Gay, their most recent DC, was certainly demonstrating plenty of initiative, though it didn't always lead where it should.

"Do I detect a note of nostalgia?" Banks asked.

Hatchley grinned. "Let me put it this way. It's a bit like a holiday. Trouble is—and I never thought I'd be complaining about *this*—it's a holiday that never bloody ends. There's not much goes on for CID to deal with out there, save for a bit of organized pickpocketing in season, a few B-and-Es, or a spot of trouble with the bookies now and then. It's mostly paperwork, a desk job." Hatchley uttered those last two words with flat-vowelled Yorkshire contempt.

"Thought you'd be enjoying the rest."

"I might be a bit of a lazy sod, but I'm not bloody retiring age yet. You know me, I like a bit of action now and then. Out there, half the time I think I've died and gone to Harrogate, only by the sea."

"What are you getting at, Jim?"

Hatchley hesitated for a moment, then put his knife and fork down. "I'll be blunt. We're all right for now, Carol and me, but after the baby's born, do you think there's any chance of us getting back to Eastvale?"

Banks sipped some wine and thought for a moment.

"Look," Hatchley said, "I know the super doesn't like me. Never has. I knew that even before you came on the scene."

Three and a half years ago, Banks thought. Was that all? So much had happened. He raised his eyebrows.

"But we get on all right, don't we?" Hatchley went on. "I mean, it took us a while, we didn't have the best of starts. But I know my faults. I've got strengths, too, is all I'm saying."

"I know that," Banks said. "And you're right." He remembered that it had taken him two years to call Sergeant Hatchley by his first name. By then he had developed a grudging respect for the man's tenacity. Hatchley might take the easy way out, act in unorthodox ways, cut corners, take risks, but he generally got what he set out to get. In other words, he was a bit of a maverick, like Banks himself, and he was neither as thick nor as thuggish as Banks had first thought.

Apart from Gristhorpe, Banks felt most comfortable with Hatchley. Phil Richmond was all right, pleasant enough, but he always seemed a bit remote and self-absorbed. For God's sake, Banks thought, what could you expect from a man who read science fiction, listened to New Age music and spent half his time playing computer games? Susan Gay was too prickly, too over-sensitive to feel really at ease with, though he admired her spunk and her common sense.

"It's not up to me," Banks said finally. "You know that. But the way Phil's going it wouldn't surprise me if he went in for a transfer to the Yard before long."

"Aye, well, he always was an ambitious lad, was Phil."

It was said without rancour, but Banks knew it must have hurt Hatchley to be shunted to a backwater so as not to impede a younger man's progress up the ranks. Transfer to CID was no more a "promotion" *per se* than transfer to Traffic and Communications —a sergeant was a sergeant, whether he or she had the prefix "detective" or not—though some, like Susan Gay, actually saw it that way, as a mark of recognition of special abilities. Some detectives were transferred back to uniform; some returned from choice. But Banks knew that Hatchley had no desire to walk the beat or drive the patrol cars again. What he wanted was to come back to Eastvale as a Detective Sergeant, and there simply wasn't room for him with Richmond at the same rank.

Banks shrugged. "What can I say, Jim? Be patient."

"Can I count on your support, if the situation arises?"

Banks nodded. "You can." He smiled to himself as the unbidden image of Jim Hatchley and Susan Gay working together came to mind. Oh, there would be fun and games ahead if Sergeant Hatchley came back to Eastvale.

Hatchley finished his pint and looked Banks in the eye. "Aye, well that's all right then. How about a sweet?"

"Not for me."

Hatchley caught the waiter's attention and ordered Black Forest gateau, a cup of coffee and another pint of Theakston's. Banks stayed with his glass of red wine, which was still half-full.

"Down to business, then," Hatchley said, as he tucked into the dessert.

Banks gave him a summary of the case and its twists and turns so far, then explained what he wanted him to do.

"A pleasure," said Hatchley, smiling.

"And in the meantime, you can concentrate on installing that shower or whatever it is. I can't say how long we'll be. It depends."

Hatchley pulled a face. "I hope it's sooner rather than later."

"Problem?"

"Oh, not really. As you know, I've got a few days leave. There's not a lot on in Saltby at the moment, anyway, and Carol will be all right. She's built up quite a gaggle of mates out there, and there'll be no keeping them away since we heard about the baby. You know how women get all gooey-eyed about things like that. You can almost hear the bloody knitting needles clacking from here. No, it's just that it might mean staying on longer than I have to at the in-laws, that's all."

"You don't get on?"

"It's not that. We had them for two weeks in July. It's just . . . well, you know how it is with in-laws."

Banks remembered Mr and Mrs Ellis from Hatchley's wedding the previous Christmas. Mrs Ellis in particular had seemed angry that Hatchley stayed at the reception too long and drank too much. But then, he thought, she had every right to be annoyed. "They don't approve of your drinking?" he guessed.

"You make it sound as if I'm an alcoholic or something," Hatchley said indignantly. "Just because a bloke enjoys a pint or two of ale now and then. . . . No, they're religious, Four Square Gospel," he sighed, as if that explained it all. "You know, Chapel on Sundays, the whole kit and caboodle. Never mind." He sat up straight and puffed out his chest. "A man's got to do what a man's got to do. Just hurry up and find the bugger. What about this Chivers bloke? Any leads?"

"According to Phil, we've already had sightings from St Austell, King's Lynn, Clitheroe and the Kyle of Lochalsh."

Hatchley laughed. "It was ever thus. Tell me about him. He sounds interesting."

Banks told him what Barney Merritt had said and what he and Jenny had discussed late afternoon.

"Reckon he's done her, the kid?"

Banks nodded. "It's been over a week, Jim. I just don't like to think about what probably happened *before* he killed her."

Hatchley's eyes narrowed to slits. "Know who the tart is? The blonde?"

"No idea. He picks them up and casts them off. They're fascinated by him, like flies to shit. According to what Barney could dig up, his full name's Jeremy Chivers, called Jem for short. He grew up in a nice middle-class home in Sevenoaks. No record of any trouble as a kid. No one can figure out how he got hooked up with the gangs. He had a good education, moved to work for an insurance company in London, then it all started."

"It's not hard for rats to find the local sewer," said Hatchley.

"No. Anyway, he's twenty-eight now, apparently looks even younger. And he's no fool. You've got to be pretty smart to keep on doing what he does and get away with it. It all satisfies whatever weird appetites he's developing."

"If you ask me," said Hatchley, "we'd all be best off if he found himself at the end of a noose."

Banks remembered his early feelings about Hatchley. That comment, so typical of him and so typical of the burned-out, cynical London coppers Banks had been trying to get away from at the time, brought them all back.

Once, Banks would have cheerfully echoed the sentiment. Sometimes, even now, he felt it. It was impossible to contemplate someone like Chivers and what he had done to Carl Johnson—if he had done it—and, perhaps, to Gemma Scupham, without wanting to see him dangling at the end of a rope, or worse, to make it personal, to squeeze the life out of him with one's own hands. Like everyone who had read about the case in the newspapers, like everyone who had children of his own, Banks could easily give voice to the outraged cliché that hanging was too good for the likes of Chivers. What was even worse was that Banks didn't know, could not predict for certain, what he would do if he ever did get Chivers within hurting distance.

The conflict was always there: on the one hand, pure atavistic rage for revenge, the gut feeling that someone who did what Chivers did no longer deserved to be a member of the human race, had somehow, through his monstrous acts, forfeited his humanity; and on the other hand, the feeling that such a reaction makes us no better than him, however we sugar-coat our socially sanctioned murders, and with it the idea that perhaps more insight is to be gained from the study of such a mind than from its destruction, and that knowledge like that may help prevent Chiverses of the future. There was no easy solution for him. The two sides of the argument struggled for ascendancy; some days sheer outrage won out, others a kind of noble humanism took supremacy.

Instead of responding to Hatchley's comment, Banks gestured for the bill and lit a cigarette. It was time to go home, perhaps listen to Mitsuko Uchida playing some Mozart piano sonatas and snuggle up to Sandra, if she was in.

"Ah well," sighed Hatchley. "Back to the in-laws, I suppose." He reached into his pocket, pulled out a packet of extra-strong Trebor mints and popped one in his mouth. "Once more unto the breach, dear friends. . . ."

IV

The piece of luck that Banks had been hoping for came at about six-thirty in the morning. Like most police luck, it was more a result of hard slog and keen observation than any magnanimous gesture on the part of some almighty deity.

The telephone woke Banks from a disjointed dream

full of anger and frustration. He groped for the receiver in the dark. Beside him, Sandra stirred and muttered in her sleep.

"Sir?" It was Susan Gay.

"Mmm," Banks mumbled.

"Sorry to wake you, sir, but they've found him. Poole."

"Where is he?"

"At the station."

"What time is it?"

"Half past six."

"All right. Phone Jim Hatchley at Carol's parents' place and get him down there, but keep him out of sight. And—"

"I've already phoned the super, sir. He's on his way in."

"Good. I'll be there as soon as I can."

Sandra turned over and sighed. Banks crept out of bed as quietly as he could, grabbed the clothes he had left folded on a chair and went into the bathroom. He still couldn't shake the feeling the dream had left him with. Probably something to do with the row he had with Tracy after he got back from dinner with Jim Hatchley. Not even a row, really. Trying to be more understanding towards her, he had simply made some comment about how nice it was to have her home with the family, and she had burst into tears and dashed up to her room. Sandra had shot him a nasty look and hurried up after her. It turned out her boyfriend had chucked her for someone else. Well, how was he supposed to know? It all changed so quickly. She never told him about anything these days.

As soon as he had showered and dressed, he went out to the car. The wind had dropped, but the pre-dawn sky was overcast, a dreary iron grey, except to the east where it was flushed deep red close to the horizon. For the first time that year, Banks could see his breath. Already, lights were on in some of the houses, and the woman in the newsagent's at the corner of Banks's street and Market Street was sorting the papers for the delivery kids.

Inside the station, an outsider would have had no idea it was so early in the morning. Activity went on under the fluorescent lights as usual, as it did twenty-four hours a day. Only a copper would sense that end-of-the-night-shift feel as constables changed back into civvies to go home and the day shift came in bright-eyed and bushy-tailed, shaved faces shining, or make-up freshly applied.

Upstairs, where the CID had their offices, was quieter. They hardly had a need for shift work, and their hours varied depending on what was going on. This past week, with a murder and a missing child, long hours had been taking their toll on everyone. Richmond was there, looking red-eyed from too much staring at the computer screen, and Susan Gay had dark blue smears under her eyes.

"What happened?" Banks asked her.

"I'd just come in," she said. "Couldn't sleep so I came in at six and thought I'd have another look at the forensic reports, then they brought him in. Found him sleeping in a ditch a mile or so down the Helmthorpe Road."

"Jesus Christ," said Banks. "It must have been cold. Where is he?"

"Interview room. PC Evans is with him."

"Sergeant Hatchley?"

"Got here just before you. He's in position."

Banks nodded. "Let's wait for the super."

Gristhorpe arrived fifteen minutes later, looking brighter than the rest of them. His hair was a mess, as usual, but his innocent blue eyes shone every bit as alert and probing as ever.

"Let's have at him, then," he said, rubbing his hands. "Alan, would you like to lead, seeing as you know him so well? Let me play monster in reserve."

"All right."

They headed for the small interview room. Before they went in, Banks asked Richmond if he would get them a large pot of tea.

The drab room seemed overcrowded with four of them, and the heat was turned too high. PC Evans went and sat in the corner by the window, ready to take notes, Banks sat opposite Poole, and Gristhorpe at right angles.

Poole licked his lips and looked around the room.

"You look like you've been dragged through a hedge backwards, Les," Banks said. "What happened?"

"Sleeping rough. Nowhere to go, had I?"

He was unshaven, his leather jacket was scuffed and stained with mud, his greasy hair bedraggled and matted. He also had a black eye and a split lip. The tea arrived. Banks played mother and passed a large steaming mug over to Les. "Here, have a cuppa," he said. "You don't look like you've had your breakfast yet."

"Thanks." Poole grasped the mug with both hands.

"How'd you get the war wounds?"

"Bloody mob, wasn't it? I need protection, I do."

"From your neighbours?"

"Bloody right." He pointed to his face. "They did this to me before I managed to run off. I'm a victim. I should press charges." Poole slurped some tea.

"Be our guest," said Banks. "But later. There's a few other things to deal with first."

Poole frowned. "Oh? Like what?"

"Like why did you run?"

"That's a daft question. You'd bloody run if you had a mob like that after you."

"Where were you heading?"

"Dunno. Anywhere. I'd got no money so I could hardly stay in a bleeding hotel, could I?"

"What about your mate at the shop?"

"Wasn't in."

"What did the mob want with you, Les?"

"It was all that silly bitch Brenda's fault. Put on a right show, she did, chucking my stuff at me like that. And that's another thing. I'll bloody sue her for damage to property."

"You do that, Les. She'd probably have to sell the telly and that nice little stereo system to pay her costs. Why did they turn on you?"

Les glanced nervously at Gristhorpe, then said to Banks, "Is he going to stay here all the time?"

Banks nodded. "If I can't get the truth out of you, he takes over. Believe me, you'll be a lot happier if that never happens. We were talking about your neighbours. Look at me."

Poole turned back. "Yeah, well, Brenda yelled some stupid things out the window. It was her fault. She could have got me killed."

"What did she yell?"

Banks could see Poole weighing him up, gauging what he knew already. Finally, he said, "Seeing as she's probably already told you, it doesn't matter, does it?" He kept glancing at Gristhorpe out of the corner of his eye.

"It matters a lot," Banks said. "It's a very serious allegation, that is, saying you were mixed up with Gemma's disappearance. They don't take kindly to child-molesters in prison, Les. This time it won't be as easy as your other stretches inside. Why don't you tell us what you know?"

Poole finished his tea and reached for the pot. Banks let him pour another large mug. "Because I don't know anything," he said. "I told you, Brenda was out of line."

"No smoke without fire, Les."

"Come on, Mr Banks, you know me. Do I look like a child-molester?"

"How would I know? What do you think they look like? Ogres with hairs growing out of their noses and warts on their bald heads? Do you think they go around carrying signs?"

"She was trying to stir it, to wind me up. Honest. Ask her. Ask her if she *really* thinks I had anything to do with it."

"I have, Les."

"Yeah? And what did she say?"

"How did you feel when she told you Gemma had been abducted?"

"Feel?"

"Yes, Les. It's something people do. Part of what makes them human."

"I know what it means. Don't think I don't have feelings." He paused, and gulped down more tea. "How did I feel? I dunno."

"Were you upset?"

"Well, I was worried."

"Were you surprised?"

"Course I was."

"Did anything spring to mind, anything to make you wonder maybe about what had happened?"

"I don't know what you mean."

"I think you do, Les."

Banks looked over at Gristhorpe, who nodded grimly.

Poole licked his lips again. "Look, what's going on here? You trying to fit me up?"

Banks let the silence stretch. Poole squirmed in his hard chair. "I need a piss," he said finally.

Banks stood up. "Come on, then."

They walked down the corridor to the gents and Banks stood by the inside of the door while Poole went to the urinal.

"Tell us where Gemma is, Les," Banks said, as Poole relieved himself. "It'll save us all a lot of trouble."

All of a sudden, the stall door burst open. Poole turned. A red-faced giant in a rumpled grey suit with short fair hair and hands like hams stood in front of him. Poole pissed all over his shoes and cursed, cringing back against the urinal, holding his arms out to ward off an attack.

"Is that him?" the giant said. "Is that the fucking pervert who—"

Banks dashed over and held him back. "Jim, don't. We're still questioning—"

"Is that the fucking pervert or isn't it?"

Hatchley strained to get past Banks, who was backing towards the door with Poole scrabbling behind him. "Get out, Les," Banks said. "While you can. I'll keep him back. Go on. Hurry!"

They backed into the corridor and two uniformed constables came to hold Hatchley, still shouting obscenities. Banks put a protective arm around Poole and led him back to the interview room. On the way, they passed Susan Gay, who looked at Poole and blushed. Banks followed her gaze. "Better zip it up, Les," he said, "or we'll have you for indecent exposure as well."

Poole did as he was told and Banks ushered him back into the room, Hatchley cursing and shouting behind them, held back by the two men.

"What the hell's going on?" Gristhorpe asked.

"It's Jim," Banks explained, sitting Poole down again. "You know what he's been like since that bloke interfered with his little girl."

"Aye," said Gristhorpe, "but can't we keep a leash on him?"

"Not easy, sir. He's a good man. Just a bit unhinged at

the moment."

Poole followed the exchange, paling.

"Look," he said, "I ain't no pervert. Tell him. Keep him away from me."

"We'll try," Banks said, "but we might have a hard time getting him to believe us."

Poole ran a hand through his greasy hair. "All right," he said. "All right. I'll tell you all I know. Okay? Just keep him off me."

Banks stared at him.

"Then you can tell them all I'm not a pervert and I had nothing to do with it, all right?"

"If that's the way it turns out. If I believe you. And it's a big if, Les, after the bollocks you've been feeding us this past week."

"I know, I know." Poole licked his lips. "Look, first off, you've got to believe me, I had nothing to do with what happened to Gemma. Nothing."

"Convince me."

Outside, they could hear Hatchley bellowing about what he would do to perverts if he had his way: "I'd cut your balls off with a blunt penknife, I bloody would! And I'd feed them down your fucking throat!" He got close enough to thump at the door and rattle the handle before they could hear him being dragged off still yelling down the corridor. Banks could hardly keep from laughing. Jim and the uniforms sounded like they were having the time of their lives.

"Christ," said Les, with a shudder. "Just keep him off me, that's all."

"So you had nothing to do with Gemma's disappearance?" Banks said.

"No. See, I used to talk about the kid down the pub, over a jar, like. I admit I wasn't very flattering, but she was a strange one was Gemma. She could irritate you just by looking at you that way she had, accusing like. Make you feel like dirt."

"So you complained about your girlfriend's kid. Nothing odd in that, is there, Les?"

"Well, that's just it, isn't it? What I've been saying. It was just pub talk, that's all. Now, I never touched her, Mr Banks. Never. Not a word of a lie. But Brenda got pissed off that time after Gemma spilled her paints on my racing form and gave her a bloody good shaking. First time I seen her do it, and it scared me, honest it did. Left big bruises on the kid's arm. I felt sorry for her, but I'm not her fucking father, what am I supposed to do?"

"Get to the point, Les. Those lads out there can't hold Sergeant Hatchley down forever."

"Aye, well, I didn't exactly tell you the truth before. You see, I did meet this Chivers and his bird a couple of times, with Carl at the pub. Never took to him. She wasn't a bad-looking bint, mind you. A bit weird, but not bad. He thought I was coming on to her once and warned me, all quiet and civilized, like, that if I went so much as with a yard of her he'd cut off my balls and shove them up my arse." Poole paused and swallowed. No doubt he was realizing, Banks thought, that threats to his privates were coming thick and fast from all sides. "He gave me the creeps, Mr Banks. There was something not right about him. About the pair of them, if you ask me."

"Did this Chivers seem interested when you talked about Gemma?"

"Well, yeah, about as interested as he seemed in anything. He was a cool one. Cold. Like a fucking reptile. There was just no reading him. He'd ask about her, yeah, just over a few drinks, like, but I thought nothing of it. And once he told me about a case he'd read in the papers where some couple had pretended to be child-care workers and asked to examine a child. Thought that was

funny, he did. Thought it showed bottle. I put it out of
my mind. To be honest, soon as we'd done the Fl—soon
as we'd finished our bit of business, I wouldn't go near
him or her. I can't explain it. They seemed nice and normal enough on the surface, all charm and that nice smile
of his, but inside he was hard and cold, and you never
knew what he was going to do next. I suppose that's the
kind of thing she liked. There's no figuring out some
women's taste."

"So Chivers showed some interest in Gemma and he
told you about the newspaper story, right?"

"Right. And that's as far as it went."

"Did Chivers give you any reason to believe he was
interested in little children?"

"Well, no, not directly. I mean, Carl told me a few stories about him, how he'd been involved in the porn trade
down The Smoke and how he wasn't averse to a bit of
bondage and that. Just titillating stories, that's all. And
when you saw him and his bird together, they were
weird, like they had something going that no one could
get in on. She hung on his every word and when he told
her to do something, she did. I mean . . . it was . . . Once,
we was in the car, like, plann—, just talking, with them
two in the front and me and Carl in the back, and he told
her to suck him off. She got right down there and did it,
and all the time he kept talking, just stopping once, like,
to give a little sigh when he shot his load. Then she sat
back up again as if nothing had happened."

"But they never made any direct reference to children?"

"No. But you see what I mean, don't you, Mr Banks? I
mean, as far as I'm concerned, them two was capable of
anything."

"I see what you mean. What did you do?"

"Well, I kept quiet, didn't I? I mean, there was no way

of knowing it was them took Gemma. The descriptions weren't the same. And then when Carl turned up dead, I had a good idea who might have liked killing someone that way and . . . I was scared. I mean, wouldn't you be? Maybe Carl had made the same connection, too, and Chivers had offed him while the bint looked on and laughed. That's the kind of feeling they gave you."

"Do you have any evidence that Chivers killed Carl?"

"Evidence? That's down to you lot, isn't it? No, I told you. I kept away from him. It just seemed like something he would do."

"Where are they now, Les?"

"I've no idea, honest I don't. And you can turn your gorilla on me and I can't tell you any different. I haven't seen nor heard of them since last week. And I don't want to."

"Do you think they're still in Eastvale, Les?"

"Be daft if they were, wouldn't they? But I don't mind saying I was scared shitless those two nights sleeping out. I kept thinking there was someone creeping up on me to cut my throat. You know what it's like out in the country, all those animal noises and the wind blowing barn doors." He shuddered.

"Is that everything, Les?"

"Cross my heart."

Banks noticed he didn't say "hope to die" this time. "It'd better be," said Banks, standing and stretching. He walked over to the door and peered outside, then turned to Gristhorpe. "Looks like they've got Jim away somewhere. What shall we do now?"

Gristhorpe assessed Poole with a steady gaze. "I think he's told us all he knows," he said finally. "We'd better take him to the charge room then lock him up."

"Good idea," Banks said. "Give him a nice warm cell for the day. For his own safety."

"Aye," said Gristhorpe. "What'll we charge him with?"

"We could start with indecent exposure."

They spent another hour or so going over Poole's statement with him, and Poole made no objections as the constable finally led him down to the charge room. He just looked anxiously right and left to make sure Hatchley wasn't around. Banks wandered to his office for a cigarette and another cup of coffee. Gristhorpe joined him there, and a few minutes later Jim Hatchley walked in with a big grin on his face.

"Haven't had as much fun since the last rugby club trip," he said. "How did you know he'd be going for a piss anyway? I was getting a bit fed up stuck in there. I'd read the *Sport* twice already."

"People want to urinate a lot when they're anxious," Banks said. "He did before. Besides, tea's a diuretic, didn't you know that?"

Hatchley shook his head.

"Anyway, he'd have wanted to go eventually. We'd just have kept him as long as necessary."

"Aye," said Hatchley, "and me in the fucking shit-house."

Banks smiled. "Effective, though, wasn't it? More dramatic that way."

"Very dramatic. Thinking of doing a bit of local theatre, are you?"

Banks laughed. "Sometimes that's what I think I am doing already." He walked over to the window and stretched. "Christ, it's been a long morning," he muttered.

The gold hands against the blue face of the church clock stood at ten-twenty. Susan Gay walked in and out with the latest developments. Not much. There had been more reports of Chivers, from Welshpool, Ramsgate and

Llaneilian, and all had to be checked out by the locals. So far, they didn't have one clear lead. Just after eleven, the phone rang, and Banks picked it up.

"Detective Inspector Loder here. Dorset CID."

Banks sighed. "Not another report of Chivers?"

"More than that," said Loder. "In fact, I think you'd better get down to Weymouth if you can."

Banks sat upright. "You've got him?"

"Not exactly, but we've got a dead blonde in a hotel room, and she matches the description you put out."

12

I

Gristhorpe sat in the passenger seat of the unmarked police car with a road map spread out on his knees. Banks drove. He would have preferred his own Cortina, mostly because of the stereo system, but Sandra needed it for all her gallery work. Besides, Gristhorpe was tone deaf; for all his learning, he couldn't appreciate music. Banks had packed his Walkman and a couple of tapes in his overnight bag; he knew it wouldn't be easy getting to sleep in a strange hotel room, especially after what awaited them in Weymouth, and music would help.

They were heading down the M1 past Sheffield with its huge cooling towers, shaped like giant whalebone corsets, and its wasteland of disused steel factories. It was almost one-thirty in the afternoon, and despite the intermittent rain they were making good time.

Gristhorpe, after much muttering to himself, decided it would be best to turn off the motorway just south of Northampton and go via Oxford, Swindon and Salisbury. Banks drove as fast as he could, and just over an hour later they reached the junction with the A43. They skirted Oxford in the late afternoon and didn't get held up until they hit Swindon at rush-hour.

After Blandford Forum, they passed the time reading signposts and testing one another on Hardy's names for the places. They managed to keep abreast until Gristhorpe went ahead with Middleton Abbey for Milton Abbas.

After a traffic snarl-up in the centre of Dorchester, they approached Weymouth in the early evening. Loder had given clear directions to the hotel, and luckily it was easy to spot, one of the Georgian terraces on the Dorchester Road close to the point where it merged with The Esplanade.

A plump, curly-haired woman called Maureen greeted them in the small lobby and told them that Inspector Loder and his men had been gone for some time but had left a guard outside the room and requested she call them at the station as soon as Banks and Gristhorpe arrived. Their booking for the night had already been made: two singles on the third floor, one floor down from where the body had been discovered.

Out of courtesy, Banks and Gristhorpe waited for Loder to arrive before going up to the room. They had requested that, as far as possible, things should be left as they were when the chambermaid discovered the body that morning. Of course, Loder's scene-of-crime men had done their business, and the Home Office pathologist had examined the body *in situ*, but the corpse was still there, waiting for them, in the position she been found.

Loder walked in fifteen minutes later. He was a painfully thin man with a hatchet face and a sparse fuzz of grey hair. Close to retirement, Banks guessed, and tired. His worn navy blue suit hung on him, and his wire-rimmed glasses seemed precariously balanced near the end of his long, thin nose. As he spoke, his grey-green eyes peered over the tops of the lenses.

After the formalities were over, the three men headed

up the thickly carpeted stairs to room 403.

"We tried to do as you asked," Loder said as they climbed. "You might see some traces of the SOCO team's presence, but otherwise . . ." He had a local accent, a kind of deep burr like a mist around his vowels, and he spoke slowly, pausing between thoughts.

The uniformed constable stepped aside at Loder's gesture, and they entered the room and turned on the light. They had no need to wear surgical gloves, as the forensic scientists had already been over the scene. What they were getting was part preservation, part re-creation.

First, Banks studied the room in general. It was unusually spacious for a seaside hotel room, with a high ceiling, ornate moulding and an oriel window overlooking the sea, now only a dim presence beyond the Esplanade lights. The window was open a fraction and Banks felt the pleasant chill of the breeze and heard the distant wash of waves on the beach. Gristhorpe stood beside him, similarly watchful. The wallpaper, a bright flower pattern, gave a cheerful aura, and a framed watercolour of Weymouth's seafront hung over the writing-desk. There was little other furniture: armchair, television, dressing-table, wardrobe and bedside tables—and the large bed itself. Banks left that until last.

The shape of a woman's body was clearly defined by the twisted white sheet that covered it. At first glance, it looked like someone sprawled on her back in the morning just before stretching and getting up. But instead of her head resting on the pillow, the pillow was resting on her head.

"Is this how you found her?" Banks asked Loder.

He nodded. "The doc did his stuff, of course, but he tried not to disturb her too much. We put the body back much as it was, as you requested."

There was an implied criticism in his tone. Why on

earth, Loder seemed to be asking, did you want us to leave the body? But Banks ignored him. He always liked to get the feel of a scene; somehow it told him much more than photographs, drawings and reports. There was nothing morbid in his need to *see* the body where it lay; in fact, in many instances, this included, he would far rather not. But it did make a difference. Not only did it give him some sort of contact with the victim, the symbolism of having *touched* the corpse, something he needed to fuel him through a murder investigation, but it also sometimes enabled him to enter the criminal's and the victim's minds. He didn't think there was anything particularly psychic about this; it was more a Holmesian manner of working back from the little things one observed to the circumstances that created them. There was no denying, though, that sometimes he did get a true *feel* for the way the killer thought and what his next moves might be.

From the disapproval in his tone, Banks formed the impression that Loder was a highly moral man, outraged not only by the murder but by the delay in getting the corpse to its proper place. It was a woman's body, too, and that seemed to embarrass him.

Slowly, Banks walked over to the bed and picked up the pillow. Gristhorpe stood beside him. The woman's long blonde hair lay spread out on the undersheet. She had been beautiful, no doubt about that: fine bone structure, a clear complexion, full lips. Apart from her head, only her neck and shoulders were exposed, alabaster skin clouded with the bluish tinge of cyanosis.

Her left hand grasped the top of the sheet and bunched it up. She wore red nail polish, but Banks thought he could also detect traces of blood around the tips of her fingers and smeared on the white sheet. He lifted the sheet. She was naked underneath. Carefully, he replaced it, as if to avoid causing her further embarrassment. Loder wasn't the only sensitive one, no matter what he thought.

Gristhorpe opened one of her eyelids. "See that," he said pointing to the red pinpricks of blood in the once-blue eye.

Banks nodded. It was a petechial haemorrhage, one sign of asphyxiation, most likely in this case caused by the pillow.

Banks touched her right hand and shivered; it was cold and stiff with rigor.

"We've got the skin and blood samples, of course," said Loder, when he saw Banks examining the nails. "Looks like she put up a bit of a struggle. We should be able to type the killer, maybe even do a DNA profile."

"We don't have time for that," Gristhorpe said. "This one's got to be stopped fast."

"We-ell," said Loder, in his slow burr, "at least it'll come in useful in court. Is it her, the one you're looking for?"

"We didn't have a very good description," Gristhorpe answered. "Alan?"

"Couldn't say." Banks turned to Loder. "She was with the man, though, you said?"

"Yes. The one with the nice smile. You mentioned it specifically in the papers. That's why we called you boys in."

"Any identification?" Gristhorpe asked.

Loder shook his head. "Nothing. Whoever did it took everything. Clothes, handbag, the lot. We tried her fingerprints but they're not on file." He paused. "It looks as if she was killed here, and the doc says she certainly hasn't been moved since she died. He's anxious to get to the PM, of course, but ruling out drugs, his findings so far are consistent with asphyxiation."

"Any idea of the time?"

"Doc puts it between six and nine in the morning."

"Anything else we should know?"

Loder glanced towards the body and paused for a moment before speaking. "Nothing else unusual about the body," he said, "unless you count the fact that she'd had sex around the time she was killed."

"Forced?"

"Not so far as the doc could make out." Loder walked towards the window, leaned on the sill and looked out over the Esplanade lights. "But it probably wouldn't be, would it, if she was sleeping with the bloke. Now, if you gentlemen are through, could we possibly get out of here? I seem to have spent far too much time with her already today." He sounded weary, and Banks wondered if he were not only tired but ill; he certainly seemed unusually thin and pale.

"Of course," said Gristhorpe, looking over at Banks. "Just a couple more questions first, while they're fresh in my mind."

Loder sighed. "All right."

"I don't suppose the chambermaid actually cleaned the room, did she, given what she found here?"

"No," said Loder, a thin smile on his lips. "No, she didn't. I'm sure you'll want to talk to her yourselves, but the one odd thing—and I noticed it, too—was that room looked as if it *had* just been cleaned. The SOCO team tried to disturb things as little as possible. They took their samples, dusted for prints and so on, but you can see what it was like."

Indeed they could. The room looked spotless, clean and tidy. Under the thin patina of fingerprint powder, wood surfaces gleamed with recent polishing. Gristhorpe glanced in the small bathroom toilet, and it was the same, as if the fixtures and fittings had been scrubbed with

Ajax, the towels hung neatly on the racks. There wasn't a smear of toothpaste or a trace of stubble stuck to the sides of the sink.

"The cottage the Manleys left in Eastvale was just the same," Gristhorpe said. "What do you make of it, Alan?"

Banks shrugged. "Partly getting rid of evidence, I suppose," he said. "Though he kindly left us semen samples, not to mention blood and skin under her fingernails. Maybe he's got a pathological obsession with cleanliness and neatness. I've heard it's not uncommon among psychopaths. Something to ask Jenny about, anyway." He pointed to two thin, glossy leaflets on the dressing-table. "Were those there when the chambermaid came in?"

"No," said Loder. "Sorry. One of the crime-scene boys found them and forgot to put them back."

"Would you show us where?"

Loder opened one of the drawers, which was lined with plain paper, and slipped the brochures under. "Like this," he said. "I thought maybe he'd forgotten them, or they slipped under the lining by accident. The chambermaid said she cleans out the drawers thoroughly between guests, so they can't have been there before. They're ferry timetables, see. For Cherbourg and the Channel Islands. We reckon that's where he must have gone."

"What time do the ferries start?"

"Early enough."

"Did he have a car?"

"Yes, parked out back. A white Fiesta. See, he wouldn't need it to get to the ferry dock, and once he gets over to the Channel Islands or France, well . . . Anyway, our lads have taken it to the police garage."

"Is there anything else?" Gristhorpe asked.

Loder shook his head.

"All right, let's get out of here. Tell your boys they can get her to the mortuary. Will the pathologist be able to start the autopsy tonight?"

"I think so." Loder closed the door behind them. "As I said, he's been chomping at the bit all day as it is." The police guard resumed his post and Loder led the way downstairs.

"Good," said Gristhorpe. "I think we can leave it till morning to talk to the hotel staff. I trust your lads have already taken statements?"

Loder nodded.

"We'll see what a good night's sleep does for their memories then. Anything else you can think of, Alan?"

Banks shook his head, but couldn't prevent his stomach from rumbling.

"Oh, aye," said Gristhorpe. "I forgot we hadn't eaten all day. Better see what we can rustle up."

II

"Is this the place?" Susan Gay asked.

Richmond nodded. "Looks like it."

Rampart Street sounded as if it should have been situated near the castle, but instead, for reasons known only to town planners, it was a nondescript cul-de-sac running south off Elmet Street in Eastvale's west end. One side consisted of pre-war terrace houses without gardens. Mostly they seemed in a state of neglect and disrepair, but some tenants had attempted to brighten things up with window-boxes and brass door-knockers.

The other side of the street, with a small Esso garage on the corner, consisted of several shops, including a greengrocer's with tables of fruit and vegetables out front; a betting shop; a newsagent-cum-video rental outlet; and the incongruously named Rampart Antiques. However one defines "antique," whether it be by some kind of intrinsic beauty or simply by age, Rampart Antiques failed on both counts.

In the grimy window, Susan spotted a heap of cracked Sony Walkmans without headphones, two stringless acoustic guitars and several dusty box-cameras, along with the occasional chipped souvenir plate with its "hand-painted" scene of Blackpool tower or London Bridge wedged among them. One corner was devoted to old LPs—Frank Sinatra, the Black Dyke Mills Band, Bobby Vinton, Connie Francis—covers faded and curled at the edges after too long in the sun. An old Remington office typewriter, which looked as if it weighed a ton, stood next to a cracked Coronation mug and a bulbous pink china lamp-stand.

Inside was no less messy, and the smell of dust, mildew and stale tobacco made Susan's nose itch.

"Can I help you?"

The man sat behind the counter, a copy of *Penthouse* open in front of him. It was hard to tell how tall he was, but he certainly had the short black hair, the squarish face and the broken nose that the woman in Johnson's building had mentioned.

"John Fairley?" Richmond asked.

"That's me."

Richmond and Susan showed their warrant cards, then Richmond said, in his formal voice, "We have received information which leads us to believe that there may be stolen property on these premises." He handed over a copy of the search warrant they had spent all afternoon arranging. Fairley stared at it, open-mouthed.

By then, both Richmond and Susan were rummaging through the junk. They would find nothing on display, of course, but the search had to be as thorough as possible. Susan flipped through the stacks of old 45s on wobbly tables—Ral Donner, B. Bumble and the Stingers, Karl

Denver, Boots Randolph, the Surfaris, names she had never heard of. One table groaned under the whole of Verdi's *Rigoletto* on 78s. There were also several shelves of books along one wall: *Reader's Digest* condensed editions; old Enid Blytons with torn paper covers that said 2/6 on the front; books with stiff pages and covers warped and stained by water-damage, most by authors she had never heard of. She doubted whether even Banks or Gristhorpe would have heard of them, either. Who on earth would want to buy such useless and smelly junk?

When they were satisfied that there were no videos or stereos hidden among the cracked figurines and rusted treadle sewing-machines, they asked Fairley if he would show them the rest of the premises. At first he hesitated, then he shrugged, locked the front door, turned the sign to read CLOSED, and led them through the moth-eaten curtain behind the counter. Silent so far, he seemed resigned to his fate.

The curtain led into a corridor with a filthy sink piled with cups growing mould from old tea leaves. Next to the sink was a metal counter-top streaked with rust, on which stood, among the mouse-droppings, a bottle of Camp coffee, a quarter of Typhoo tea, some curdled milk and a bowl of sugar lumps.

The corridor ended in a toilet with a stained bowl and washbasin, flaking plaster and spider-webs in the corners. It was almost impossible to open the door to the other room on the ground floor, but slim Richmond managed to slip in and discover that it was packed mostly with collapsed cardboard boxes. There were also some books, video cassettes and magazines of a slightly suspect eroticism, though perhaps not the more prosecutable variety of pornography.

After he had finished there, Richmond pointed to the other door off the corridor. "Where's that lead?" he asked.

Fairley tried to bluff his way out of opening it. He said it led nowhere, wasn't part of the premises, but Richmond persisted. They soon found themselves following Fairley down to a cellar with whitewashed walls. There, lit by a bare bulb, stood what looked like the remnants of the Fletcher's warehouse job. Two television sets, three videos and a compact-disc player.

"Bankrupt stock," said Fairley. "I was going to put them in the window when I've got room."

Richmond ignored him and asked Susan to check the serial numbers on the cartons with the list that the manager of Fletcher's had supplied. They matched.

"Right," said Richmond, leaning back against the stack of cartons. "Before we go down to the nick, I'd like to ask you a few questions, John."

"Aren't you going to charge me?"

"Later."

"I mean, shouldn't I have a solicitor present or something?"

"If you want. But let's just forget the stolen goods for the moment, shall we? Have you got any form, John?"

Fairley shook his head.

"That's good," Richmond said. "First offence. It'll go better for you if you help us. We want to know about Carl Johnson."

"Now look, I didn't have nothing to do with that. You can't pin that on me."

It was interesting to watch Richmond at work, Susan thought. Cool, relaxed and looking as elegant as ever in the dingy room, careful not to lean against the wall for fear of marking his suit, he set Fairley at ease and led him gently through a series of preliminary questions about his relationship with Johnson and Poole before he got to Chivers. At the mention of the name, Fairley became obviously nervous.

"Carl brought him here," he said, squatting miserably on a box. "I never liked him, or that girlfriend of his. They were both a bit doolally, if you ask me."

"What do you mean?"

"Just that look he got in his eyes sometimes. Oh, he could be pleasant enough on the surface, but when you saw what was underneath, it was scary. I couldn't look him in the eye without trembling."

"When did you see him last?"

"Couple of weeks ago."

"Did you ever think he might be concerned with Carl's death?"

"I . . . well, to be honest, it crossed my mind. I don't know why. Just the kind of person he seemed."

"Yet you didn't come forward?"

"Do you think I'm crazy or something?"

"Did you know of any reason he might have had for killing Johnson?"

Fairley shook his head. "No."

"There was no falling out over the loot?"

"What loot?"

Richmond kicked a box. "The alleged loot."

"No."

"What about the girl? Did Johnson make a play for her?"

"Not that I know of. She was sexy enough, and she knew it, but she was Chivers's property, no mistaking that. NO ENTRY signs on every orifice. Sorry, love." He looked at Susan, who simply gave him a blank stare. "No," he went on, turning back to Richmond, "I don't think Carl was daft enough to mess with her."

"What about Gemma Scupham?"

Fairley looked surprised. "The kid who was abducted?"

"That's her."

"What about her?"

"You tell me, John."

Fairley tensed. A vein throbbed at his temple. "You can't think I had anything to do with that? Oh, come on! I don't go in for little girls. No way."

"What about Chivers?"

"Nothing about him would surprise me."

"Did he ever mention her?"

"No. I mean, I *had* heard of her. Les complained about her sometimes and Carl sympathized. Chivers just seemed to be standing back, sort of laughing at it all, as if such a problem could never happen to him. He always seemed above everything, arrogant like, as if we were all just petty people with petty concerns and he'd think no more about stepping on us if he had to than he would about swatting a fly. Look, why are you asking me about Gemma? I never even met the kid."

"She was never in this shop?"

"No. Why should she have been?"

"Where is Chivers now?"

"I don't know and I don't want to know. He's bad news."

Richmond sat down carefully on a box. "Has it never struck you," he said, "that if he did kill Johnson, then you and Les might be in danger, too?"

"No. Why? We didn't do nothing. We always played square."

"So did Carl, apparently. Unless there's something you're not telling me. It doesn't seem to matter with Chivers, does it? Why do you think he killed Carl, if he did?"

"I told you, I don't know. He's a nutter. He always seemed to me like he was on the edge, you know, ready to go off. People like him don't always need reasons.

Maybe he did it for fun."

"Maybe. So why not kill you, too? Might that not be fun?"

Fairley licked his lips. "Look, if you're trying to scare me you're doing a damn good job. Are you trying to warn me I'm in danger or just trying to make me talk? I think it's about time I saw a solicitor."

Richmond stood up and brushed off the seat of his pants with his palm. "Are you sure you have no idea where Chivers went after he left Eastvale?"

"None."

"Did he say anything about his plans?"

"Not to me."

"Where did he come from?"

"Dunno. He never talked about himself. Honest. Look, are you winding me up about all this?" Fairley had started to sweat now.

"We need to find him, John," said Richmond quietly. "That's all. Then we'll all sleep a little easier in our beds." He turned to Susan. "Let's take him to station now and make it formal, shall we?" He rubbed the wall and held up his forefinger. "And we'd better get a SOCO team down here, too. Remember that whitewash on Gemma's clothing?"

Susan nodded. As they left, she noticed that John Fairley seemed far more willing to accompany them to the station than most villains they arrested.

"I'll tell you one thing for free," he said as they got in the car.

"What's that?" said Richmond.

"He had a gun, Chivers did. I saw it once when he was showing off with it in front of his girlfriend."

"What kind of gun?"

"How would I know? I don't know nothing about them."

"Big, small, medium?"

"It wasn't that big. Like those toy guns you play with when you're a kid. But it weren't no toy."

"A revolver?"

"What's the difference?"

"Never mind."

"Isn't it enough just to know the bastard's got a gun?"

"Yes," sighed Richmond, looking over at Susan. "Yes, it is."

III

Banks and Gristhorpe leaned on the railings above the beach and ate fish and chips out of cardboard cartons. The hotel didn't do evening meals, and, as in most seaside towns, all the cafés seemed to close at five or six.

"Not bad," said Gristhorpe, "but they do them better up north."

"If you like them greasy."

"Traitor. I keep forgetting you're still just a southerner underneath it all."

Banks tossed his empty carton into a rubbish-bin and looked out to sea. Close to shore, bright stars shone through gaps in the clouds and reflected in the dark water. Farther out, the cloud-covering thickened and dimmed the quarter moon. The breeze that was slowly driving the clouds inland carried a chill, and Banks was glad he had put on a pullover under his sports jacket. He sniffed the bracing air, sharp with ozone. A few cars droned along The Esplanade, and the sound of people talking or laughing in the night drifted on the air occasionally, but mostly it was quiet. Banks lit a cigarette and drew deep. Silly, he thought, but it tasted better out here in the sea air pervaded with the smells of saltwater and seaweed.

"Do you know," said Banks finally, "I think I'm developing a feel for Chivers. I *know* he's been here. I know he killed the girl."

Gristhorpe gave him a steady, appraising look. "Not turning psychic on me, are you, Alan?"

Banks laughed. "Not me. Look, there's the white Fiesta, the smile, the blonde, the neatness of the hotel room. You'll agree the incidents have those things in common?"

"Aye. And tomorrow morning we'll have a word with the hotel staff and look over Loder's reports, see if we can't amass enough evidence to be *sure*. Maybe then we'll know what the next move is. If that bastard's slipped away abroad . . ." Gristhorpe crumpled up his cardboard box and tossed it in the bin.

"We'll get him."

Gristhorpe raised an eyebrow. "More intuition?"

"No. Just sheer dogged determination."

Gristhorpe clapped Banks lightly on the shoulder. "That I can understand. I think I'll turn in now. Coming?"

Banks sniffed the night air. He felt too restless to go to bed so soon. "Think I'll take a walk on the prom," he said. "Just to clear out the cobwebs."

"Right. See you at breakfast."

Banks watched Gristhorpe, a tall, powerful man in a chunky Swaledale sweater, cross the road, then he started walking along the promenade. A few couples, arms around one another, strolled by, but Weymouth at ten-thirty that Friday evening in late September was as dead as any out-of-season seaside resort. Over the road stood the tall Georgian terrace houses, most of them converted into hotels. Lights shone behind some curtains, but most of the rooms were dark.

When he got to the Jubilee Clock, an ornate structure built to commemorate Queen Victoria's Diamond Jubilee, Banks took the steps down to the beach. The tide hadn't been out long and the glistening sand was wet like a hardening gel under his feet. The footprints he made disappeared as soon as he moved on.

As he walked, it was of John Cowper Powys he thought, not Thomas Hardy. Somebody had mentioned *Weymouth Sands* to him around Christmas time and, intrigued, he had bought a copy. Now, as he actually trod Weymouth sands himself for the first time since he was a child, he thought of the opening scene where Magnus Muir stood meditating on the relationship between the all-consuming unity of the sea and the peculiar and individual character of each wave. The Esplanade lights reflected in the wet sand, which sucked in the remaining moisture with a hissing sound every time a wave retreated.

Heady thoughts for a lowly chief inspector. He stood for a moment and let the waves lick at his shoes. Farther south, the lights of the car ferry terminal seemed to hang suspended over the water. Loder was right, he thought: Chivers would have been a fool to take his car. Much easier to mingle with the foot-passengers and rent one wherever he went. Or, even more anonymous, travel by train if he got to France.

Seeing the dead woman in the hotel had shaken Banks more than he realized. Wondering why, as he doubled back along the ribbed sand at the edge of the beach, he felt it was perhaps because of Sandra. There was only a superficial resemblance, of course, but it was enough to remind him of Sandra in her twenties. Though Sandra had ridiculed the idea, the photo of Gemma Scupham had also reminded him of a younger Tracy, albeit a less doleful-looking one. Tracy took after Sandra, whereas

Brian, with his small, lean, dark-haired Celtic appearance, took after Banks. There were altogether too many resemblances for comfort in this case.

Banks thought about what he had said earlier, the *feel* he was developing for the way Chivers operated. Then he thought about what he *hadn't* told Gristhorpe. Standing in that room and looking down at the dead woman, Banks had known, as surely as he knew what happened at Johnson's murder, that Chivers had been making love to her, smiling down, and that as he was reaching his climax—that brief pause for a sigh that Les Poole had mentioned—he had taken the pillow and held it over her face. She had struggled, scratching and gouging his skin, but he had pushed it down and ejaculated as she died.

Was he really beginning to understand something of Chivers's psychopathic thought processes? It was a frightening notion, and for a moment he felt himself almost pull in his antennae and reject the insight. But he couldn't.

The blonde woman—he wished he knew her name—must somehow have started to become a liability. Perhaps she was having second thoughts about what they'd done to Gemma; maybe she was overcome by guilt and had threatened to go to the police. Perhaps Chivers had conned her into thinking they were taking the child for some other reason, and she had found out what really happened. She could have panicked when she saw the newspaper likenesses, and Chivers didn't feel he could trust her any longer. Or maybe he just grew tired of her. Whatever the reason, she ceased to be of use to him, and someone like Chivers would then start to think of an *interesting* way to get rid of her.

He must be easily bored, Banks thought, remembering what he and Jenny had talked about in the Queen's

Arms. A creative intelligence, though clearly a warped one, he showed imagination and daring. For some years, he had been able to channel his urges into legitimate criminal activity—a contradiction in terms, Banks realized, but nonetheless true. Chivers had sought work from people who had logical, financial reasons for what they employed him to do, and however evil they were, whatever harm they did, there was no denying that at bottom they were essentially businessmen gone wrong, the other side of the coin, not much different from insider traders and the rest of the corporate crooks.

Now, though, perhaps because he was deteriorating, losing control, as Jenny had said, Chivers was starting to create his own opportunities for pleasure, financed by simple heists like the Fletcher's warehouse job. The money he got from such ventures would allow him the freedom to roam the country and follow his fancy wherever it led him. And by paying cash, he would leave no tell-tale credit-card traces.

Now, it seemed, Chivers was escalating, craving more dangerous thrills to satiate his needs. He was like a drug addict; he always needed more to keep him at the same level. Gemma Scupham, Carl Johnson, the blonde. How quickly was he losing control? Was he starting to get careless?

A wave soaked one foot and the bottom of his pant leg. He stepped back and did a little dance to shake the water off. Then he reached for a cigarette and, for some reason, thought of Brian, not more than seventy miles east of him, in Portsmouth. College had only just started, and he might be feeling lonely and alien in a strange city. It was so close, yet Banks wouldn't be able to visit.

He missed his son. Much as Tracy had always seemed the favourite, with her interests in history and literature, her curiosity and intelligence, and Brian always the outsider, the rebel, with his loud rock music and his lack of interest in school, Banks missed him. Certainly he felt the odd one out now that Tracy was only interested in boys and clothes.

Brian was eighteen, and Banks had turned forty in May. With a smile, he remembered the compact disc of Nigel Kennedy playing the Brahms violin concerto that Brian had bought him for his birthday. Well, at least the thought was there. And he also remembered his recent row with Tracy. In a way, she had been right: Brian *had* got away with a lot, especially that summer, before he had left for the polytechnic: late-night band practices; a week-long camping trip to Cornwall with his mates; coming in once or twice a little worse for drink. But of one thing Banks was certain: Brian wasn't taking drugs. As an experienced detective, he knew the signs, physical and psychological, and had never observed them in his son.

He turned from the beach and found a phonebox on The Esplanade. It was eleven o'clock. Would he be in? He put his phonecard in and punched in the number Brian shared with the other students in the house. It started to ring.

"Hello?"

A strange voice. He asked for Brian, said it was his father.

"Just a minute," the voice mumbled.

He waited, tapping his fingers against the glass, and after a few moments Brian came on the line.

"Dad! What is it? What's wrong?" he asked.

"Nothing. I'm just down the coast from you and I wanted to say hello. How are you doing?" Banks felt choked, hearing Brian's voice. He wasn't sure his words came out right.

"I'm fine," Brian answered.

"How's college?"

"Oh, you know. It's fine. Everything's fine. Look, are you sure there's nothing wrong? Mum's okay, isn't she?"

"I told you, everything's all right. It's just that I won't be able to make the time to drop by and I thought, well, being so close, I'd just give you a ring."

"Is it a case?"

"Yes."

Silence.

"Are you still there, Dad?"

"Of course I am. When are you coming up to visit us again?"

"I'll be up at Christmas. Hey, I've met some really great people down here. They play music and all. There's this one guy, we're going to form a band, and he's been playing some great blues for me. You ever heard of Robert Johnson? Muddy Waters?"

Banks smiled to himself and sighed. If Brian had ever taken the trouble to examine his collection—and of course, no teenager would be seen dead sharing his father's taste in music—he would have found not only the aforementioned, but Little Walter, Bessie Smith and Big Bill Broonzy, among several dozen others.

"Yes, I've heard of them," he said. "I'm glad you're having a good time. Look, keep in touch. Your mother says you don't write often enough."

"Sorry. There's really a lot of work to do. But I'll try to do better, promise."

"You do. Look—"

His time ran out and he didn't have another card. Just a few more seconds to say hurried goodbyes, then the electronic insect sound of a dead line. When he put the phone down and started walking back to the hotel, Banks felt empty. Why was it always like that? he wondered. You call someone you love on the phone, and when you've finished talking, all you feel is the bloody distance between you. Time to try sleep, perhaps, after a little music. Sleep that knits up the ravell'd sleave of care. Some hope.

13

I

Hotel or bed and breakfast, it didn't seem to make much difference with regard to the traditional English breakfast, thought Gristhorpe the following morning. Of course, there was more choice at the Mellstock Hotel than there would be in a typical B and B, but no one in his right mind would want to start the day with a "continental" breakfast—a stale croissant and a gob of strawberry jam in a plastic container. As it was, Banks sat struggling over a particularly bony kipper while Gristhorpe stuck to bacon and eggs and wished he hadn't. Between them, they shared a rack of cold toast and a pot of weak instant coffee.

Gristhorpe felt grumpy. He hadn't slept well; the mattress had been too soft, and his back was bothering him. The breakfast didn't help either, he realized, feeling the onset of heartburn.

"I dropped in at the hotel bar for a nightcap yesterday," he said, pushing the plate aside and pouring more coffee. "Thought I might be able to get something out of the regulars."

"And?" asked Banks, pulling a bone from the corner of his mouth.

"Nothing much. There's a couple from Wolverhampton staying the week, and they said the Barlows, as they called themselves, were in once or twice. Always pleasant. You know, nodded and said hello, but never got into any conversations. The missis thought they were a honeymoon couple."

"You know," said Banks, "he's really starting to get on my nerves, Chivers. He turns up somewhere, goes around smiling like Mr Clean, and people die."

"What do you expect?"

"It's just his bloody nerve. It's as if he's challenging us, playing catch-me-if-you-can."

"Aye, I know what you mean," said Gristhorpe, with a scowl. "And we won't catch him sitting here picking at this fine English cuisine. Come on." He pushed his plate away and stood up abruptly, leaving Banks to follow suit.

The hotel manager had provided a small room on the ground floor for them to conduct interviews. First, they read over the statements that DI Loder and his men had taken from the hotel staff, then asked to see Meg Wayne, the chambermaid.

She looked no older than fourteen or fifteen, a frightened schoolgirl with her uniform and starched cap that couldn't quite contain her abundant golden hair. She had a pale, clear complexion, and with a couple of red spots on her cheeks, Gristhorpe thought, she could probably pass herself off as one of Tess's milkmaid friends in Hardy's book. Her Dorset burr was even more pronounced than Loder's, her voice soft and surprisingly low.

"Mr Ballard, the manager, said I could take the day off," she said, "but I don't see the point, do you? I mean, the rooms need doing every day no matter what happens, and I could certainly do with the money."

"Still," said Gristhorpe, "it must have been a shock?"

"Oh yes. I've never seen a dead body before. Only on telly, like."

"Tell us what you saw yesterday, Meg."

"We-ell, I opens the door as usual, and as soon as I does I knows something's wrong."

"Were the curtains open?"

"Part way. Enough to see by."

"And the window?"

"Open a bit. It was chilly." She fiddled with a set of room keys on her lap as she spoke.

"Did you go into the room?"

"Not right in. I just stood in the doorway, like, and I could see her there on the bed, with her head all covered up."

"Tell me exactly what you saw," said Gristhorpe. He knew that people tend to embellish on what they have observed. He also wanted to be certain that Loder and his SOCO team had restored the room to the way it had been when Meg opened the door. He grimaced and rubbed his stomach; the heartburn was getting worse.

"It looked like just twisted sheets at first," she said, "but then, when my eyes grew more accustomed, I could tell it was someone under there. A shape." She blushed and looked down at her lap. "A woman's shape. And the pillow was over her head, so I knew she was . . . dead."

"It's all right, Meg," said Gristhorpe. "I know it's upsetting. We won't be much longer."

Meg nodded and took a deep breath.

"Did you see the woman's face?"

"No. No, I just knew it was a woman by the outline of the sheets."

"Did you disturb anything in the room?"

"Nothing. Like I told Mr Loder, I ran straight off to Mr Ballard and he sent for the police. That's God's honest truth, sir."

"I believe you," said Gristhorpe. "We just have to make certain. You must have been upset. Maybe there's something you forgot?"

"No, sir."

"All right. Did you ever see the people who were staying in that room?"

"Not as far as I know. I don't see many guests, sir. I have to do my job when they're out."

"Of course. Now think, Meg, try to remember, was there anything else about the scene that struck you at the time?"

Meg squeezed her eyes shut and fiddled with the keys. Finally, she looked at Gristhorpe again. "Just how tidy it was, sir. I mean, you wouldn't believe the mess some guests leave you to clean up. Not that I mind, like. I know they pay for the service and it's my job, but . . ."

"So this room was unusually tidy?"

"Yes."

"Did you see anything at all on the table or the dresser?"

She shook her head. "Nothing. They were empty."

"All right, Meg, we're just about finished now. Can you remember anything else at all?"

"Well, it's funny," she said, "but just now when I had my eyes closed I did remember something. I never really paid it any mind at the time, though I must have noticed, but it stuck."

"What is it?"

"I don't think it can be important, but it was the smell. I use Pledge Natural on the furniture. I'd know that smell anywhere. Very clean and. . . . But this was something else . . . a sort of pine-scented polish . . . I don't know. Why would anybody want to polish furniture in a hotel room?"

"Thank you, Meg," said Gristhorpe. "You can go now. You've been a great help."

"I have? Thank you." She went to the door and turned with her fingers touching the handle. "I'm not looking forward to this, sir," she said. "Between you and me, I'm not looking forward to opening any doors in this hotel this morning." And she left.

Gristhorpe reached into his side pocket, took out a pack of Rennies he carried for such emergencies as English breakfasts and southern fish and chips, and chewed two of them.

"All right?" Banks asked.

"Aye." Gristhorpe pulled a face. "Just ought to watch my diet, that's all."

Next they saw the receptionist, Maureen, rather prickly at being called away from her domain. Gristhorpe basked in antacid relief and left Banks to do most of the questioning. She had very little to tell them save that the Barlows had checked in the evening of Wednesday, September 24, at about six o'clock with just one tan suitcase between them. She had told them about parking and got their car licence number, then he had signed the register Mr and Mrs Barlow and given an address in Lichfield. Loder had already checked this and found it didn't exist. No, Maureen hadn't asked for any identification. Why should she? And yes, of course he had skipped out on his bill. If you'd just murdered your lover, you'd hardly stop at the front desk and pay your hotel bill, would you? No, nobody had seen him leave. It wasn't a prison camp or one of those Russian gulags, you know. What did she think of them? Just ordinary, no one you'd look twice at if you saw them in the street. Her, maybe, but he was just a nondescript bloke with a nice smile. In fact, Maureen remembered wondering what an attractive, if rather stuck-up, girl like her was doing with the likes of him.

And that was it. They talked briefly with Mr Ballard, who didn't remember seeing the Barlows at all, and to the bellboy who had carried their suitcase to their room and remembered nothing but the pound tip the bloke had given him. Nobody knew what they did with their time. Went for walks, the cinema in the evening, or to a pub. Nothing unusual about them. Nothing much else to do in Weymouth.

By the time they had finished the interviews, it was eleven-thirty. DI Loder had said he would drop by that morning as soon as the autopsy results became available, and they met him walking into the lobby. He looked as if he had slept badly, too, Gristhorpe thought, with bags under his eyes and his long face pale and drawn. The three of them decided to take some fresh air on the prom while they discussed the results.

"Anything?" Gristhorpe asked as they leaned on the railings. A faint breeze ruffled his thick grey hair. The weather was overcast, but reasonably warm. Seagulls squawked overhead.

Loder shook his head slowly. "First, we've made enquiries at the ferry dock and no one remembers anyone of his description. We can't really make too much of that, though, as it's very busy down there. And the autopsy findings bear out what the doc suspected. She died of asphyxiation, and the pillow fibres in her lungs indicate that's how it happened. No sign of drugs or anything, though it'll be a while before all the test results come back. We've sent the tissue for DNA testing—it looks like our man's Group O, by the way—but that'll take some time. She did have sex prior to death, and there were no signs of sexual assault, so we assume it was by consent. Otherwise healthy. Poor woman, we don't even know her name yet. Only one surprise: she was eight weeks pregnant."

"Hmm," said Gristhorpe. "I wonder if Chivers knew that."

Loder shrugged. "Hardly a motive for murder."

"I don't think he needs much of a motive. It could have pushed him over the edge."

"Or maybe it made her a liability," Banks suggested. "Not so much just because she was pregnant but because it softened her, brought out the guilt over what they'd done? If she found out she was going to have a child of her own . . ."

"There's no point in speculating," said Gristhorpe. "It's something we might never know. Anything else?"

"Nothing from the car," Loder said. "A few partials . . . fibres and the like, but you know as well as I do most stuff's mass-produced these days. Could have come from almost any blue cotton shirt. There's not a lot else to say. We've got men asking around about him, if anyone saw him after he left the hotel. Nothing so far. Oh, and I informed Interpol and the authorities on the Channel Islands."

"Good," said Gristhorpe. "That seems to cover it all."

"What next?" asked Loder.

"We can only wait, can't we?"

"Looks like it. I'd better be off back to the station, keep on top of it."

"Thanks." Gristhorpe shook his hand. "Thanks a lot."

They watched Loder walk off towards his car. "He's got a point," said Gristhorpe. "What *do* we do next?"

Banks shrugged. "I can only speculate."

"Go ahead."

Banks watched a ferry steam out of the dock. The flock of gulls swooped on a dead fish on the beach. "I've been thinking about Chivers," he said, lighting a cigarette and looking out to sea. "Trying to fathom his thought processes."

"And?"

"And I'm not sure, but . . . look, he must know we're after him by now. Surely he's seen the stuff in the newspapers. What does he do? He kills the woman, too much extra baggage, and he takes off. Now a normal criminal would certainly head for the continent and disappear. But we know Chivers isn't normal."

"I think I follow your train, Alan. I've had the same thought myself. He's playing a game, isn't he? Laughing at us."

Banks nodded. "And he likes the attention. Jenny said he's likely to be egocentric, but he's also probably impulsive and irresponsible. I've thought about that a lot."

"So where would he head, given the way he thinks?"

"Back to where it started, I think," said Banks. "I'll bet you a pound to a penny the bastard's back in Eastvale."

II

It was late that Saturday evening when Banks and Gristhorpe arrived back in Eastvale. They were delayed by a six-car pile-up into a jackknifed lorry on the M1 just south of Leicester, and as they passed by Pontefract and Castleford on the A1, the rain fell in buckets, slowing traffic to a crawl.

So it was that on Sunday morning, as the bells rang in the church and people crossed the market square in their Sunday best for the morning service, the members of Eastvale CID sat in the conference room around the large circular table drinking coffee and pooling their findings.

Richmond and Susan brought the others up to date on John Fairley's information about Chivers and the fact that he owned a gun.

"Fairley seems the least involved of them all," said Richmond. "We had a good long chat when we brought him in. He's got no prior form. I'm sure he's dealt with stuff that fell off the back of a lorry before, but the Fletcher's warehouse job is his first big bit of fencing, we're sure of that. Susan?"

"I agree," said Susan Gay, looking up from the notes in front of her. "Seems it was Johnson's idea, and he recruited Les Poole easily. They were mates of Fairley's, genuinely helping out at the shop for a bit of under-the-counter pocket money. Chivers was the prime mover. Without him, I don't reckon the others would have had the guts to go through with it. It was Chivers drugged the guard dogs and cut through the chain-link fence. Poole drove the van, backed it up to the loading bay and away they went. The back of Fairley's shop is just a quiet backstreet, so they got unloaded without any trouble. It wasn't too hard to make a few sales through their pub mates, word of mouth, and they'd already got rid of most of the stuff by the time we called."

"Was there any falling out over the loot?" Banks asked.

"No," said Richmond. "Not as far as we could tell. Everyone seemed happy with his share. Poole took the television and stereo as part of his cut. Johnson got a thousand in cash. Fairley's got no idea why Johnson was killed, though he said he wouldn't be surprised to hear that Chivers had done him. Chivers scared him, seemed the type who'd do it for fun."

"And he's seen or heard nothing of him since?"

"No, sir. And doesn't want to."

"What about Gemma?" Banks asked. "Does Fairley know anything about what happened to her?"

"Just confirms what Poole told us, that's all," said

Richmond. "After we spotted the whitewash in the cellar, we had the team do a thorough search last night, but they've turned up nothing to indicate Gemma was there."

"Right," said Gristhorpe, standing up and looking at his watch. "I've told you what Alan thinks about Chivers being in the area, and I agree with him. What I propose is that we start trying to flush him out. Phil, I'd like you to muster as many men as you can and start knocking on doors, asking questions. Somebody must have seen the bastard. The station and the bus station are obvious places to start. He left his car in Weymouth and unless he stole one, the odds are that he took some other form of transport. The lads down there are doing their bit, too. We're co-ordinating with a DI Loder. I'll get in touch with the media and we'll see if we can't get something on the local news tonight. I want it all in the open. If he is here, I want him to know we're closing in on him. I want him to panic and make a run for it.

"Susan, get in touch with as many of those concerned citizens who helped in the search for Gemma and get them to ask around. Tell them to make sure they don't take any risks, though. This one's dangerous. You know the kind of thing to ask about. Smoke from a cottage that's supposed to be empty, odd noises, suspicious strangers, that kind of thing. Especially anyone who insists on paying cash in large amounts. We'd better put a watch on Fairley's shop, Brenda Scupham's place and the holiday cottage, too, just in case. And we'll ask around the pubs. He's not the type to lie low. He'll be wanting to see the effect he's having. And remember, he may have altered his appearance a bit. He's done it before, so don't rely on hair colour. The one thing he can't change is that bloody smile. All right?"

Everyone nodded and dispersed. Banks returned to his office and looked out on the church-goers pouring into the market square: women in powder blue suits holding onto their broad brimmed hats in the wind, clutching handbags; husbands in dark suits at their sides, collars too tight, shifting from foot to foot as their wives chatted, thinking maybe now they'd done their duty they'd be able to sneak off to the Queen's Arms or the Crooked Billet for a quick one before dinner; restless children dreaming of an afternoon at Kinley Pond catching frogs, or climbing trees to collect birds' eggs in Brinely Woods—either that or sniffing glue under the railway bridge and planning a bit of recreational B and E. And somewhere, in the midst of all that quotidian human activity and aspiration, was Jeremy Chivers.

Banks didn't notice Susan in his doorway until she cleared her throat. He turned.

"Sorry, sir," she said, "it slipped my mind at the meeting, but you had a call from Piet Kuypers, Amsterdam police. Said to call him back, you'd know what it was about."

"Did he leave a message?"

"No. Just said he had a few interesting speculations for you." Susan handed him a piece of paper. "The top's his work number," she said, pointing, "and that one's home."

"Thank you." Banks took the paper and sat down. In the excitement of the chase for Chivers, he realized, he had quite forgotten asking Piet to check up on Adam Harkness. He hadn't liked the man much, but as soon as it became clear that Chivers had more than likely killed Carl Johnson, there had seemed no real reason to consider Harkness any longer.

Puzzled, he dialled Piet's home number. A child's voice answered. Banks couldn't speak Dutch, and the little girl didn't seem to understand English. The phone banged down on a hard surface and a moment later a man's voice came over the line, again in Dutch.

"Piet? It's me. Alan Banks in Eastvale?"

"Ah, Alan," said Piet. "That was my daughter, Eva. She only began to learn her English this year." He laughed. "How are you?"

"I'm fine, Piet. Hope I didn't disturb your lunch but I've been out of town and I got a message to call you."

"Yes. You have a moment?"

"Yes, of course."

Banks heard the receiver placed, more gently this time, on the hard surface, and he put his feet on the desk and lit a cigarette while he waited for Piet to come back. He realized he had been talking too loudly, as one does on the telephone to foreigners, and reminded himself that Piet's English was almost as good as his own.

"Sorry about that," said Piet. "Yes, I did a little snooping, as you call it, about that man Harkness." His voice bore only traces of a Dutch accent.

"Anything interesting?"

"Interesting, yes, I think so. But nothing but rumours, you understand. Hearsay. I found his wife. She has since remarried, and she didn't want to talk about her relationship with Harkness, but she hinted that part of the reason they separated was that he had what she called filthy habits."

"Filthy habits?"

"Yes. Like what, I thought? What do you English regard as a filthy habit? Picking his nose in bed? But I couldn't get her to say any more. She is very religious. She had a strict Dutch Protestant upbringing in a small town in Friesland. I'm sorry, Alan, but I couldn't force her to talk if she did not want to."

Banks sighed. "No, of course not. What happened next?"

"I talked to some of my colleagues on drugs and vice, but they don't know him. Mostly they're new. You don't last that long working on drugs and vice, and Harkness has been gone, how long did you say, two years?"

"Something like that," said Banks.

"So I had an idea," Piet went on. "I went to see Wim Kaspar. Now Wim is a strange man. Nobody really knows how far it all went, but he was, how do you English say, made to leave work early?"

"Fired?"

"No. I know that word. Not exactly fired."

"Made redundant?"

Piet laughed. "Yes, that's it. Such an odd phrase. Well, there was something of a cloud over Wim, you see. Nobody could prove anything, but it was suspected he took bribes and that he was involved with the drugs and girls in the Red Light district. But Wim worked many years in the Red Light district, ever since patrolman, and he knows more than anybody else what goes on there. And I don't care what people say—maybe it is true—but he is a good man in many ways. Do you understand?"

"I think so," said Banks, remembering now that Piet was a nice bloke but took ages getting to the bloody point.

"Wim heard and saw many things that went no further. It's give and take in that world. You scratch my back and I'll scratch yours. Especially if what they say about him is true. So I talked to him and he remembers something. Now you must understand, Alan, that there is no proof of this. It's just rumours. And Wim will never repeat officially what he told me."

"Tell me, Piet."

"According to Wim's contacts, your Mr Harkness visited the Red Light district on several occasions."

"Piet, who doesn't visit the Red Light district? It's one of your main tourist attractions."

"No, wait. There's more. There are some places, very

bad places. Not just the pretty women in the windows, you understand?"

"Yes?"

"And Wim told me that your Mr Harkness visited one of these places."

"How did your source know who he was?"

"Alan, you must remember Mr Harkness is well known in Amsterdam, and not without influence. Do you want me to go on?"

"Yes, please."

"It was a very bad place," Piet continued. "You understand prostitution is not illegal here, that there are many brothels?"

"Yes."

"And the live sex shows and the whips and chains and all the rest. But this one brothel, Wim says, was a very special place. A place that caters for people who like little girls."

"Jesus Christ!"

"It happens, Alan. What can I say? Girls disappear from the big cities, they turn up in these places. Sometimes they are used for snuff films. You know what they are?"

"I know. Why wasn't he arrested?"

"Sometimes it is better to leave the little fish. Also, Harkness was an important man and, how shall I say, perhaps pressure could be brought to bear. He could have been useful."

Banks sighed. He knew the scenario. Get something on a man like Harkness and you've got him in your pocket: the police version of blackmail.

"Alan, in Amsterdam, just as, I suspect, in your London, you can get anything you want if you have the money to pay for it. Anything. If we can find these places and find evidence, we close them down and arrest the people responsible. But these men are very clever. And sometimes policemen can be bought, protection can be paid. Or blackmailed. We all have skeletons in our closets. Alan? Are you still there?"

"Yes. Yes, Piet, I know. I was thinking. Listen, I'd like you to do me a big favour. I assume places like this are still in existence?"

"There is one place now we are suspicious of. On the surface, it seems like an ordinary brothel, but rumour has it that young girls can be had there, for a price. Our undercover men are watching, but we have no proof yet."

"I'd like you to find out if there are any new girls." He gave Piet Gemma's description, praying he was wrong. At least it meant she might still be alive, if Harkness kept his connections in Amsterdam. He still couldn't work out the whys and the wherefores, how everything linked up, but he knew it would not have been so difficult for Harkness or someone else to smuggle Gemma out of the country, even during the search. The ferry from Immingham, for example, was always crowded; it would be easy enough to slip in among the other families with a sleeping child on the overnight journey, when everyone was tired. "I don't care whether you get enough proof to lock them up or not. Rumours will do fine for me. Use your contacts, informers. Maybe even your friend Wim might be able to help?"

"Yes," said Piet slowly. "I understand. I'll try. What more can I say?"

"And Piet."

"Yes?"

"Thanks. Thanks a lot. You did a great job." Then Banks slammed down the receiver and rushed to find Gristhorpe.

III

It was about time the place had a good cleaning, Brenda thought, wielding the Hoover like a lawnmower. She knew she wasn't good at housekeeping, but now she had so much time on her hands and nothing but bad thoughts and terrifying dreams, she had to do something or she would fall apart. The ground-in dirt and the food stains wouldn't come out, of course, they would need shampooing, but the dust would. At least it was a start.

The vacuum was so noisy that she didn't hear the bell. It was only the steady thumping on her door that broke through. She turned off the machine and listened again. Another knock. For a moment she just stood there, worried it might be Les. She wasn't frightened of him—she knew he was a coward at heart—but she didn't feel like another public row and she was damned if she was going to let him in. On the other hand, it might be the police with news of Gemma. She glanced out of the window but couldn't see a police car. That didn't matter, she realized. The plain-clothes men drove ordinary cars.

She sighed and stood the Hoover in the corner. Well, if it *was* Les, she'd just have to tell him to stay away and call the police if he insisted on pestering her. The blurred figure through the frosted glass wasn't Les, that was for certain, but she couldn't tell who it was until she opened the door and saw Lenora Carlyle standing there with her long black hair and penetrating eyes. She didn't want to let Lenora in. Somehow, she thought, that entire episode had been a weakness, a mistake. She had been grasping at straws. And look what she was left with: nothing but a video of herself, which was already beginning to feel like an embarrassment. But she stood aside politely. Lenora hung up her coat and followed her into the front room.

"Tea?" said Brenda, feeling like a cup herself.

"Yes, please, dear, if it's no trouble." Lenora sat on the sofa and brushed down her skirt. "Been cleaning, I see."

"Yes." Brenda shrugged and went to make the tea. When it was ready, she brought it in on a tray and poured, then lit a cigarette.

"I sense there's been some great change," Lenora said, frowning with concentration. "Some sort of upheaval."

"If you mean I chucked Les out, I suppose you're right."

Lenora looked disappointed at such a prosaic explanation. "Any news?"

Brenda shook her head.

"Well, that's why I'm here, really. You remember what I said before?"

"That Gemma's still alive?"

"That's right." Her eyes glittered. "More than ever I'm convinced of it, Brenda."

"I don't think so." Brenda shook her head. "Not after all this time."

"But you must have faith. She's frightened and weak. But she's alive, Brenda."

"Don't."

"You must listen." Lenora put her mug down and leaned forward, clasping her hands. "I saw animals. Jungle animals, Brenda. Lions, tigers, leopards. They're connected with Gemma somehow."

"What are you saying? She's been taken to Africa or something?"

Lenora flopped back on the sofa. "I don't know. The message is very weak. That's all I see. Gemma and animals."

"Look, I really don't—"

"They're not harming her, Brenda."

"I don't believe you."

"But you *must* believe!"

"Why must I believe? What good has it done me?"

"Don't you want to see your Gemma again?"

Brenda stood up. "Of course I want to see Gemma again. But I can't. She's dead. Can't you understand? She's dead. She must be. If she's not dead by now she must be suffering so much. It's best that she's dead." The tears and grief she had felt welling up for so long were breaking the dam.

"We must cling to the gift of life, Brenda."

"No. I don't want to listen to this. You're frightening me. Go away. Leave me alone."

"But Brenda, I—"

"Go on." Brenda pointed at the door, tears burning her eyes. "Go away. Get out!"

Lenora shook her head slowly, then, shoulders slumped, she got up and left the room. When Brenda heard the door close, she sank back into her chair. She was shaking now and tears burned down her cheeks. Dammit, why wouldn't they all leave her alone? And why couldn't she know for sure? Every day that Gemma stayed missing was more like hell. Why couldn't they find her body, then Brenda could get her grieving done with, organize the funeral, move on. But no. Just day after day of misery. And it was all her fault, all Brenda's fault for not loving her daughter enough, for losing control and shaking her so much she was terrified what she might do the next time.

She stared at the large TV screen and saw her own reflection distorted through her tears. She remembered the interview she had watched over and over again. Vanity. Madness. It had all been madness. In a sudden burst of rage, she drew back her arm and flung her mug as hard as she could at the screen.

IV

Just a few hours ago the wind had been cool, and there had been only enough blue sky to make baby a new bonnet. Now, as Banks and Susan drove to Harkness's, the wind had dropped, the sun had come out and the afternoon had turned out fine. Gristhorpe had been out when Banks went to find him, so he had left a message and found Susan, who happened to be in the corridor at the time.

Enjoying probably the last fine weekend of the season, families sat out on the green at Fortford eating picnics, even though it wasn't particularly warm and the grass must still be damp. Banks turned right on the Lyndgarth road, and as they approached the bridge, they saw even more people ambling along The Leas or sitting on the riverbank fishing.

Banks drove in silence, tense and angry over the forthcoming confrontation. They turned in the drive just before the old pack-horse bridge, and the car flung up gravel as they stopped. They had no evidence, he reminded himself, only supposition, and everything depended on bluffing and scaring Harkness into blabbing. It wouldn't be easy; it never was with those so used to having things their own way. Piet's information wasn't anywhere near enough to get him in court. But Harkness *had* known Johnson, and Johnson had known Chivers. Jenny said the paedophile was likely to be over forty, lived alone, and probably knew Gemma. Well, Harkness hadn't known Gemma, but he could have heard of her through Johnson and Chivers. It made sense.

After the conversation, Banks had checked the time and, finding they were only two hours ahead, tried the South African police again. They still had nothing to report, and he got the impression they were dragging their feet. He could only speculate on the nature of the crime there, and on the depth of the cover-up. He had tried Linda Fish from the Writers' Circle again, too, but she had heard no more from her writer friend. He had felt too edgy simply to wait around for more information to come in.

Harkness answered the door at the first ring. He seemed nervous to see them, Banks thought, fidgety and too talkative as he led them this time into the living-room and bade them sit.

"Have you found out who killed Carl?"

"We're looking for a man called Jeremy Chivers," Banks said. "Someone Johnson knew. Did he ever mention the name?"

"Let's not go through all that again." Harkness walked over to the mantelpiece. "Who is this Chivers?"

"A suspect."

"So why have you come to pester me again?"

Banks scratched the little scar by his right eye. It wasn't always reliable, but it did have a tendency to itch in warning when he hadn't quite realized that something was wrong. "Well, I'll tell you, Mr Harkness. I've just had a chat with a friend of mine on the Amsterdam police, and he told me some very odd things."

"Oh?"

"Yes. You lived there for some time, didn't you?"

"Yes, you know I did. But I can assure you I never came into contact with the police."

"Clever there, sir, weren't you?" said Susan suddenly.

Harkness looked from one to the other, reddening. "Look, what is this?" he said. "You can't just come in here—"

Banks waved him to silence, ready to make his accusation. But just before he opened his mouth to speak, he paused. Something was definitely bothering him. Even now, he didn't know what it was: tension in the air, a feeling of *déjà vu*, or that little shiver when someone steps on your grave. It would come. He went on, "Everyone knows you can get anything you want in Amsterdam. If you know where to go. If you can pay for it."

"So what? It's hardly different from any other city in that way, I should think." Harkness paced, hands in his pockets.

"True," said Banks, "though it does have something of a reputation for sex in various forms, straight and other."

"What are you suggesting? Get to the point."

"That's just it. We have information leading us to believe that you frequented a brothel. A very special kind of brothel. One that made young children available to its customers."

"What! This is monstrous. I've already told you the Assistant Chief Commissioner is a good friend of mine, the Commissioner, too. If you don't take back your slanderous allegations, I'll make sure you're out of the force before bedtime tonight. Damn it, I think I'll do it anyway."

"I don't think so," said Banks. "The Commissioner is particularly upset about this case. He has grandchildren the same age as Gemma Scupham, so I don't think the fact that you belong to the same golf club will cut a lot of ice with him, sir."

"But this is preposterous! You can't possibly be suggesting that I had anything to do with that?"

"Well, I—" Banks stopped, suddenly aware of what was bothering him. He shot Susan a quick glance and stood up. Looking puzzled, she followed suit. "Probably not," he said, "But I had to find out. I'm sorry, Mr Harkness. I just wanted to test your reaction to the allegations."

"You've got a damned nasty way of going about your business, Banks. I most certainly will be talking to your superior."

"As you wish." Banks followed Susan to the door. "But please understand, we have to follow every lead, however incredible, however distasteful. I'm very sorry to have bothered you, sir. I think I can safely say we won't be troubling you again."

"Well . . ." Harkness looked confused. He opened his mouth as if to complain more, then seemed to think better of it, realizing they were leaving, and stood there gulping like a fish. "I should damn well think so," he muttered finally. "And don't think I don't mean it about talking to the Commissioner."

"What is it?" Susan asked as they drove back onto the road. "Sir? Why did you do that?"

Banks said nothing. When they were out of the sight of the house, about half a mile down the road, hidden by the roadside trees, he pulled into a lay-by.

"What is it?" Susan asked again. "I picked up the signal to get out, but why? You were rattling him. We could have had him."

"This is the third time I've visited Harkness," Banks said slowly, hands still gripping the wheel. "Both times before the place has been a bit of a mess—dusty, untidy, a typical bachelor dwelling."

"So?" said Susan. "He's had the cleaning lady in."

"I don't think so. He said he didn't employ one. Notice how clean the surfaces were, and that silver goblet on the coffee-table?"

"Yes. Polished so you could see your face."

"You weren't there," Banks said, "but it's the same polish smell as in the Weymouth hotel room, something with a strong scent of pine."

"You can't be thinking . . . surely?"

Banks nodded. "That's just what I am thinking, Susan. We've got to radio for help." He gestured with his thumb back towards the house. "I think Chivers is in there somewhere, and he's armed."

14

I

To the casual observer, nothing unusual occurred around The Leas and Devraulx Abbey that fine Sunday afternoon in late September. If one fisherman approached another, had a chat, then replaced him at the riverbank, or if a picnicking family, shortly after having a few words with a passing rambler complete with rucksack and stick, decided to pack up and leave because the wasps were bothering them, then what of it? The Abbey closed early, and there were a few more cars on the road than usual, but then it was such a surprisingly beautiful afternoon that everyone wanted to enjoy a bit of it before the rain and wind returned.

Still in the same position, about half a mile down the road, out of sight of the Harkness house, Banks and Susan waited. Birds called, insects hummed, a light breeze hissed through the trees. At last, another car joined them, and Superintendent Gristhorpe got out, along with DS Richmond, and strode purposefully over to Banks's Cortina. There wasn't much to say; everything had been taken care of on the radio. The replacement fishermen were policeman in plain clothes; the picnicking families had all been cleared from the area, and a tight circle had been drawn around Harkness's house and grounds.

"If he's in there," Gristhorpe said. "He won't get away. Alan, let's you and I go back to the house, say we have a few more questions. Let's see if we can't defuse this mess before it blows up."

"But sir," said Susan. "I think I should go, too."

"No," said Gristhorpe. "Stay here with Phil."

"But—"

"Look. I'm not doubting your competence, Susan. But what we need here is experience. Alan?"

"I agree," said Banks.

Gristhorpe took a .38 Smith and Wesson from his pocket and handed it to Banks, who automatically checked it, though he knew Gristhorpe would have already done so. Susan's lips drew tight and Banks could feel the waves of humiliation flowing from her. He knew why—she had potential, but she was young, inexperienced, and she had made mistakes before—and he agreed completely with the superintendent's judgment. There was no room for error in dealing with someone like Chivers.

"Ready?" said Gristhorpe.

Banks nodded and joined him in the unmarked Rover, leaving Susan to fume and Richmond to console her in Banks's own Cortina.

"How do you read it?" Gristhorpe asked, as Banks drove slowly back towards the pack-horse bridge.

"Harkness is nervous, and I think he's shit-scared, too. And it's not just because of what I think he's done to Gemma Scupham. If I had to guess, I'd say Chivers is either in the house somewhere, or he's been there and he's hiding out nearby. And Harkness isn't harbouring him out of the kindness of his heart. He's damn close to being held hostage. There's nothing he can do, though, without incriminating himself."

"All right," said Gristhorpe. "Let me do the talking. Keep your eyes peeled. We'll try and get Harkness out of there if we can."

Banks nodded, turned into the driveway and crunched over the gravel. He felt a claw tighten at the pit of his stomach; the gun hung heavy in his pocket.

They rang the doorbell. Harkness flung the door open and growled, "You again? What the bloody hell do you want this time?"

Gristhorpe introduced himself. "I think it might be best if we did this at the station," he said to Harkness.

"Am I under arrest? You can't be serious. This is nothing but a tissue of unsubstantiated lies."

He was sweating.

"I think it would be best, sir," said Gristhorpe. "Of course, you have the right to consult your solicitor."

"I'll sue the both of you for wrongful arrest. I'll have you off the force. I'll—"

Banks thought he noticed a flash of movement behind Harkness on the staircase, but it was hard to see into the house clearly. What followed next was so sudden and so unexpected, he realized in retrospect that there was nothing he could have done to prevent it.

They heard a sound like a dull pop and Harkness's eyes seemed to fill with blood. His forehead opened like a rose in time-lapse photography. Both Banks and Gristhorpe flung themselves out of the way by instinct. As Banks flattened himself against the wall of the house, he became aware of the blood and tissue on his face and chest. Harkness's. He wanted to be sick.

Time seemed to hang like over-ripe fruit ready to fall at any moment. Harkness lay half in and half out the door, only a small hole showing in the back of his closely cropped skull and a pool of dark blood thicken-

ing under his face around his head. Gristhorpe stood
back, flat against the wall on one side of the door, Banks
on the other. From inside, they heard nothing but silence.
Then, it could have been minutes or just seconds after
the shooting, they heard a crash from the far side of the
house, followed by a curse and the sound of someone
running.

They glanced quickly at one another, then Gristhorpe
nodded and swung himself into the doorway first, gun
sweeping the hall and stairwell. Nothing. Banks followed, adopting the stance he had learned in training:
gun extended in one hand, other hand gripping the wrist.
They got to the front room and found no one. But there,
beyond the french windows, one of which had been
smashed by a careless elbow as he dashed by, they saw
Chivers running down the lawn towards the riverbank.

"Get on the radio, Alan," said Gristhorpe. "Tell them
to close in. And tell them to be bloody careful. Get an
ambulance here, too."

Banks dashed to the car and gave the message to the
plain-clothes watchers, all of whom carried police radios
in their fishing boxes or picnic hampers. After he had ra-
dioed headquarters for an ambulance, he hurried through
the house after Gristhorpe and Chivers.

Chivers was in the garden, heading for the river. As he
ran, he turned around and fired several times. A window
shattered, slate chips showered from the roof, then
Gristhorpe went down. Banks took cover behind the copper beech and looked back at the superintendent's body
sprawled on the lawn. He wanted to go to him, but he
couldn't break cover. Carefully, he edged around the tree
trunk and looked for Chivers.

There weren't many places Chivers could go. Fences
and thick hedges blocked off the riverbank to the east
and west, enclosing Harkness's property, and ahead lay

the water. With a quick glance right and left and a wild shot, Chivers charged into the water. Soon it was up to his hips, then his waist. He aimed towards the tree and fired again. The bullet thudded into the bark. When Banks looked around the trunk again, he saw the other police in a line across the river, all with guns, closing fast. Gristhorpe must have commandeered the whole bloody dale, he thought. Glancing back towards the house, he saw Susan Gay and Phil Richmond framed by the french window staring at Gristhorpe. He waved to them to take cover.

Chivers stopped when the water came up to his armpits and fired again, but the hammer fell with an empty click. He tried a few more times, but it was empty. Banks shouted for Richmond and Susan to see to the superintendent, then he walked down the slope.

"Come on," he said. "Look around you. It's over."

Chivers looked and saw the men lining the opposite bank. They were in range now. He looked again at Banks. Then he shrugged, tossed the gun in the water, and smiled.

II

Everything had been done by the book; Banks saw to that. Thus, when they finally got to talk to Chivers, the custody record had been opened; he had been offered the right to legal advice, which he had repeatedly refused; offered the chance to inform a friend or relative of his arrest, at which he had laughed; and even offered a cup of tea, which he had accepted. The desk sergeant had managed to rustle up a disposable white boiler suit to replace his wet clothes, as according to the Police and Criminal Evidence Act, "a person may not be interviewed unless

adequate clothing has been offered to him." And the interview room they sat in, while not especially large, was
at least "adequately heated, lit and ventilated" according
to the letter of the law. If questioning went on for a long
time, Chivers would be brought meals and allowed peri-
ods of rest.

In addition, Jenny Fuller had turned up at the station
and asked if she could be present during the questioning.
It was an unusual request, and at first Banks refused.
Jenny persisted, claiming her presence might even help,
as Chivers seemed to like to show off to women. Finally,
Banks asked Chivers's permission, which galled him,
and Chivers said, "The more the merrier."

Back at Harkness's house, Banks knew, the SOCO
team would be collecting evidence, Glendenning poring
over Harkness's body, a group of constables digging up
the garden that Carl Johnson had so lovingly tended, and
police frogmen searching the river.

Sometimes, thought Banks, the creaking machinery of
the law was a welcome prophylactic on his desire to
reach out and throttle someone. Hampered as he had often felt by the Act, today, ironically enough, he was glad
of it as he sat across the table looking at the man who
had murdered at least three people, wounded Superintendent Gristhorpe and abducted Gemma Scupham.

As he looked, he certainly felt the impulse to kill
Chivers, simply to swat him as one would a troublesome
wasp. But it wasn't an impulse he was proud of. All his
life, both in spite of and because of his job, Banks had
tried to cultivate his own version of compassion. If crime
really was part of what made us human, he thought, then
it merited deep study. If we simply kill off the pests that
bother us, we make no progress at all. He knew that he
could, in some strange way, *learn* from Chivers. It was a
knowledge he might deeply wish to reject, but spiritual

and intellectual cowardice had never been among his failings.

Banks sat opposite Chivers, Richmond stood behind him, by the door, and Jenny sat by the window, diagonally across from him.

Close up, the monster didn't look like much at all, Banks noted. About Banks's height, and with the same kind of lean, wiry strength, he sat erect, hands placed palms down on the table in front of him, their backs covered with ginger down. His skin was pale, his hair an undistinguished shade of sandy brown, and his general look could only be described as boyish—the kind of boy who pulled pranks and was amused to see their effects on the victims.

If there was anything outstanding about him at all, it was his eyes. They were the kind of green the sea looks sometimes, and when he wasn't smiling they looked just as cold, as deep and as unpredictable as the ocean itself. When he did smile, though, they lit up with such a bright, honest light you felt you could trust him with anything. At least, it was *almost* like that, Banks thought, if it weren't for that glint of madness in them; not quite insanity, but close enough to the edge. Not everyone would notice, but then not everyone was looking at him as a murderer.

Banks turned on the tape-recorder, repeated the caution and reminded Chivers of his rights. "Before we get onto the other charges against you," he said, "I'd like to ask you a few questions about Gemma Scupham."

"Why not?" said Chivers. "It was just a lark really." His voice, a little more whiny and high-pitched than Banks had expected, bore no trace of regional accent; it was as bland and characterless as a BBC 2 announcer's.

"Whose idea was it?"

"Mr Harkness wanted a companion."

"How did he get in touch with you?"

"Through Carl Johnson. We'd known each other for a while. Carl was . . . well, between you and me he wasn't too bright. Like that other chap, what's his name?"

"Poole?"

"That's right. Small-time, the two of them. Low-lifes."

"How did you first meet Harkness?"

"Look, does any of this really matter? It's very dull stuff for me, you know." He shifted in his chair, and Banks noticed him look over at Jenny.

"Humour us."

Chivers sighed. "Oh, very well. Harkness knew Carl was a gutless oaf, of course, but he had contacts. Harkness needed someone taken care of a couple of months ago." He waved his hand dismissively. "Someone had been stealing from him in the London office, apparently, and Harkness wanted him taught a lesson. Carl got in touch with me."

"What happened?"

"I did the job, of course. Harkness paid well. I got an inkling from our little chats that this was a man with unusual tastes and plenty of money. I thought a nice little holiday in Yorkshire might turn out fruitful." He smiled.

"And did it?"

"Of course."

"How much?"

"Please. A gentleman never discusses money."

"How much?"

Chivers shrugged. "I asked for twenty thousand pounds. We compromised on seventeen-fifty."

"So you abducted Gemma Scupham just for money?"

"No, no. Of course not. Not just for the money." Chivers leaned forward. "You don't understand, do you? It sounded like fun, too. It had to be interesting."

"So you'd heard about Gemma through Les Poole and

thought she would be the perfect candidate?"

"Oh, the fool was always moaning about her. Her mother sounded as thick as two short planks, and she clearly didn't care much about the child anyway. They didn't want her. Harkness did. It's a buyer's market. It was almost too easy. We picked her up, drove around for a while just to be on the safe side, then dropped her off at Harkness's after dark and returned the car." He smiled. "You should have seen his face light up. It was love at first sight."

"Did either Johnson or Poole know about this?"

"I'm not stupid. I wouldn't have trusted either of them."

"So what went wrong?"

"Nothing. It was the perfect crime," Chivers mused. "But Carl got foolish and greedy. Otherwise you'd never have gone anywhere near Harkness."

"But we did."

"Yes. Carl suspected something. Maybe he actually saw the child, I don't know. Or perhaps he caught Harkness drooling over his kiddie porn and put two and two together. That surprised me, that did. I never thought him capable of that. Putting two and two together and coming up with the right answer. I must admit I underestimated him."

"What happened?"

Chivers made a steeple with his hands and his eyes glazed over. He seemed lost in his own world. Banks repeated the question. Chivers seemed to come back from a great distance.

"What? Oh." He gave a dismissive wave of the hand. "He tried to put the touch on Harkness. Harkness got worried and called me again. I said I'd take care of it."

"For a fee?"

"Of course. I wouldn't say I'm in it for the money, but

I need a fair bit to keep me in the style to which I'm accustomed. Harkness arranged to meet him at the old lead mine to pay him off and Chelsea and I gave him a lift there. Poor bastard, he never suspected a thing."

"Chelsea?"

He stared at a spot above Banks's left shoulder. "Yes. Silly name, isn't it? Fancy naming someone after a flower show, or a bun. Poor Chelsea. She just couldn't quite understand."

"Understand what?"

"The beauty of it all." Chivers's eyes turned suddenly back on Jenny. They looked like a dark green whirlpool, Banks thought, with blackness at its centre, evil with a sense of humour. "She liked it at the time, you know, the thrill. And she never liked poor Carl anyway. She said he was always undressing her with his eyes. You should have seen the look in *her* eyes when I killed him. She was standing right next to me and I could smell her sex. Needless to say, we had a *lot* of fun later that night. But she got jittery, read the newspapers, began to wonder, asked too many questions . . . . As I said, she didn't fully comprehend the beauty of it all."

"Did you know she was pregnant?"

He turned his eyes slowly back to Banks. "Yes. That was the last straw. It turned her all weepy, the sentimental fool. I had to kill her then."

"Why?"

"Wouldn't want another one like me in this universe, would we?" He winked. "Besides, it was what she wanted. I have a knack of knowing what people really *want*."

"What did she want?"

"Death, of course. She enjoyed it. I know. I was there. It was glorious, the way she thrust and struggled." He looked over at Jenny again. "*You* understand, don't you?"

"And Harkness?" Banks said.

"Oh, it was very easy to see into his dirty soul. Little children. Little kiddies. He'd had it easy before. South Africa, Amsterdam. He found it a bit difficult here. He was getting desperate, that's all. It's simply a matter of knowing the right people."

Banks noticed that Chivers had dampened a part of his cuff and was rubbing at an old coffee ring on the desk. "What happened to Gemma?" he asked.

He shrugged. "No idea. I completed my side of the bargain. I suppose when the old pervert had finished with her he probably killed her and buried the body under the petunia patch or something. Isn't that what they do? Or maybe he sold her, tried to recoup what he'd spent. There's plenty in the market for that kind of thing, you know."

"What about the clothing we found?"

"You want me to do your job for you? I don't know. I suppose as soon as things got too hot for him he wanted to put you off the scent. Does that sound about right?"

"Why did you come back to Eastvale? You could probably have got away, you know."

Chivers's eyes dulled. "Fatal flaw, I suppose. I can't bear to miss anything. Besides, you only caught me because I wanted you to, you know. I've never been on trial, never been in jail. It might be interesting. And, remember, I'm not there yet." He shot Jenny a quick smile and began to rub harder at the coffee stain, still making no impression. He was clearly uncomfortable in the boiler suit they had found for him, too, scratching now and then where the rough material made his skin itch.

Banks walked over to the door and opened it to the two uniformed officers who stood outside and nodded for them to take Chivers down to the holding cells for the time being.

Chivers sat at the desk staring down at the stain he was rubbing and rubbing. Finally, he gave up and banged the table once, hard, with his fist.

III

Banks stood by his office window with the light off and looked down on the darkening market square again, a cigarette between his fingers. Like Phil and Jenny, he had felt as if he needed a long, hot bath after watching and listening to Chivers. It was odd how they had drifted away to try to scrub themselves free of the dirt: Jenny, pale and quiet, had gone home; Richmond had gone to the computer room. They all recognized one another's need for a little solitude, despite the work that remained.

Little people like Les Poole and others Banks had met in Eastvale sometimes made him despair of human intelligence; someone like Chivers made him wonder seriously about the human *soul*. Not that Banks was a religious man, but as he looked at the Norman church with its low square tower and the arched door with its carvings of the saints, he burned with unanswered questions.

They could wait, though. The hospital had called to tell him that Gristhorpe had a flesh wound in his thigh and was already proving to be a difficult patient. The SOCOs had called several times from The Leas area; no luck so far in finding Gemma's body, and it was getting dark. The frogmen had packed up and gone home. They had found Chivers's gun easily enough, but no trace of Gemma. They would be back tomorrow, though they didn't hold out much hope. The garden was in ruins, but so far the men had uncovered nothing but stones and roots.

Harkness's body lay in the mortuary now, and if anyone had to make him look presentable for the funeral, good luck to them. Banks shuddered at the memory. He had washed and washed his face, but he could still smell the blood, or so he thought. And he had tossed away his jacket and shirt, knowing he could never wear them again, and changed into the spares he always kept at the station.

And he thought of Chelsea. So that was her name, the poor twisted shape on the hotel bed in Weymouth. Why had she been so drawn to a monster like Chivers? Can't people *see* evil when it's staring them right in the face? Maybe not until it's too late, he thought. And the baby. Chivers knew his own evil, revelled in it. Chelsea. Who was she? Where did she come from? Who were her parents and what were they like? Bit by bit, he would find out.

He had been alone with his thoughts for about an hour, watching dusk fall slowly on the cobbled square and the people dribble into the church for the evening service. The glow from the coloured-glass windows of the Queen's Arms looked welcoming on the opposite corner. God, he could do with a drink to take the taste of blood out of his mouth, out of his soul.

The harsh ring of the telephone broke the silence. He picked it up and heard Gristhorpe say, "The buggers wouldn't let me out to question Chivers. Have you done it? Did it go all right?"

Banks smiled to himself and assured Gristhorpe that all was well.

"Come and see me, Alan. There's a couple of things I want to talk about."

Banks put on his coat and drove over to Eastvale General. He hated hospitals, the smell of disinfectant, the starched uniforms, the pale shadows with clear fluid dripping into them from plastic bags being pushed on trolleys down gloomy hallways. But Gristhorpe had a pleasant enough private room. Already, someone had sent flowers and Banks felt suddenly guilty that he had come empty-handed.

Gristhorpe looked a little pale and weak, mostly from shock and blood loss, but apart from that he seemed in fine enough fettle.

"Harkness never expected any trouble from the police over Gemma's abduction, did he?" he asked.

"No," said Banks. "As Chivers told us, why should he? It was almost the perfect crime. He'd managed to keep a very low profile in the area. Nobody knew how sick his tastes really were."

"Aye, but everything changed, didn't it, after Johnson's murder?"

"Yes."

"And you were a bit hard on Harkness, given that chip on your shoulder, weren't you?"

"I suppose so. What are you getting at?"

Gristhorpe tried to sit up in bed and grimaced. "So much so that he might think we'd get onto him?" he said.

"Probably." Banks rearranged the pillows. "I think he felt quite certain I'd be back." The superintendent was wearing striped pyjamas, he noticed.

"And he claimed harassment and threatened to call the Commissioner and probably the Prime Minister for all I know."

"Yes." Banks looked puzzled. What was Gristhorpe getting at? It wasn't like him to beat about the bush. Had delirium set in?

"Let's assume that Chivers is telling the truth," Gristhorpe went on, "and he delivered Gemma to Harkness on Tuesday evening and killed Johnson on Thursday evening. Now Harkness *could* have spirited

Gemma out of the house, say to Amsterdam, before Johnson's murder, but why should he? And if he hadn't done it by then, he'd probably be too nervous to make such a move later."

"I suppose he would," Banks admitted. "And he could have taken her clothes up to the moors to put us off the scent on Thursday evening or Friday, whenever Chivers told him Johnson was dead and came to collect his fee. Harkness must have known we'd visit him then, given his connection with Johnson. But he could have buried her anywhere. It's a very isolated house, and pretty well sheltered by trees. I mean, even someone passing by on the road wouldn't notice him burying a body in the garden, would they?"

"But our men have found nothing so far."

"You know it can take time. It's a big garden. If she's there, they'll find her. Then there's the river."

"*If* she's there."

Banks watched the blood drip slowly into Gristhorpe's veins. "What do you mean?"

"This." Gristhorpe rolled over carefully and took something out of his bedside cabinet. "I got one of the lads to tag it as evidence and bring it here to me."

Banks stared at the polished silver. "The goblet?"

"Yes. It's a chalice actually, sixteenth-century, I think. Remember when Phil and Susan took me into Harkness's living-room and laid me on the couch till the ambulance came? That's when I noticed it. I could hardly miss it, it was right at eye-level."

"I still don't see what that's got to do with Gemma," said Banks, who was beginning to worry that Gristhorpe was more seriously injured than he let on.

"Don't you?" Gristhorpe passed him the chalice. "See those markings?"

Banks examined it. "Yes."

"It's the banner of the Pilgrimage of Grace. See where it shows the five wounds of Christ? I'll explain it, then you can go see if I'm right."

Puzzled, Banks crossed his legs and leaned back in his chair.

IV

It was late twilight as Banks drove: the time of evening when the greens of the hillsides and the grey of the limestone houses and walls are all just shades of darkness. But the river seemed to glow with a light of its own, hoarded from the day, as it snaked through the wooded river meadows known as The Leas.

As he drove, Banks remembered Gristhorpe's words: "In Yorkshire history, The Pilgrimage of Grace started as a religious uprising against Henry VIII, sparked by the closing of the monasteries in 1536. Harkness's house was built later, so this chalice would probably be a precious family heirloom and a powerful symbol to whoever owned it. In the seventeenth century, it was often dangerous to be a Roman Catholic in this part of the country, but they persisted. They didn't take unnecessary risks, though. So while they would invite some wandering incognito priest around to perform mass or take confession in their houses, they knew they might hear the soldiers hammering on the door at any moment, so they built priest holes, cavities in the walls where the priests could hide. Some were even more elaborate than that. They led to underground passages and escape routes.

"I grew up in Lyndgarth, just up the hill from Harkness's," Gristhorpe had continued, "and when we were kids there were always rumours about the old De Montfort house, as it was called then. We thought it was haunted, riddled with secret passages. You know how kids dream. We never went inside, of course, but we made up stories about it. I'd forgotten all about it until we went there tonight—and I must admit things happened quickly enough to put it right out of my mind again. Until I saw this chalice. It started me thinking. The date's right, the history, so it's worth a try, don't you think?"

Banks had agreed. He turned into the drive and stopped at the police tape. The man on duty came forward, and when he recognized Banks he let him through.

Banks nodded greetings as he passed the SOCO team at work in the garden, receiving shakes of the head to indicate that nothing new had been discovered. The grounds looked like a film set, with the bright arc-lights casting shadows of men digging, and it was loud with the sound of drills, the humming of the generator van and instructions shouted above the noise. Inside the house, men examined the corners of carpets and settees, sticking on pieces of Sellotape and lifting off fibres, or running over areas with compact hand-vacuums.

First, Banks checked the kitchen, behind the fridge and cooker, then the dining-room, getting help to move out the huge antique cabinet that held cutlery and crystal glasses. Nothing.

The library yielded nothing either, so he went next to the living-room, where he had first noticed the grimy, tarnished chalice on the coffee-table. It was partly seeing it again and noticing how clean it was that had first made him uneasy earlier that day, on his visit with Susan.

The bookcase opposite the fireplace looked promising, and Banks started pulling out the old *National Geographics*, looking for some kind of lever or button to press, and feeling, as he did so, more than a little foolish. It was like something out of Edgar Allan Poe, he thought.

Then he found it: a brass bolt sunk perfectly in the wood at the back of the central shelf, on the left. It slid back smoothly, as if recently oiled, and the whole bookcase swung away from the wall on hinges, just like a door. Before him loomed a dark opening with a flight of worn stone steps leading down.

Banks called for a torch, and when he had one, he stepped into the opening. On a hook to his left hung two keys on a ring. He plucked them off as he went by.

At the bottom of the stairs, a rough, dank passage led on, probably far away from the house to provide an escape for the itinerant priest. Banks shone his torch ahead and noticed that the passage was blocked by rubble after a few yards. But the two heavy wooden doors, one on either side of the passage, looked more interesting. Banks went to the one on his right and tried to open it. It was locked. Holding his breath, heart pounding, he tried the keys. The second one worked.

The hinges creaked a little as he slowly pushed the door open. Groping in the dark, he found a light switch, and a bare bulb came on, revealing a small, square room with whitewashed walls. At the centre of the room stood a leather armchair, the kind with a footrest that slides out as you sit in it, and in front of that stood a television set attached to a video. Banks doubted that priest holes had electricity, so Harkness must have gone to all the trouble of wiring his private den himself. In a rack beside the chair, Banks found a range of pornographic magazines, all of them featuring children being subjected to disgusting and degrading acts. In the cabinet under the video were a number of video cassettes of a similar nature.

Afraid of what he might find, Banks crossed the passage and fitted the other key in the lock. It opened easily. This time, he had no need to grope for a light switch.

Beside the narrow bed stood a small orange-shaded table-lamp. Next to it sat a book of *Thomas the Tank Engine* stories and a bottle of pills. The walls were painted with the same whitewash as the other room, but a quilt decorated with stylized jungle animals—lions, tigers and leopards with friendly human expressions— covered the small, still shape on the bed.

It was Gemma Scupham, no doubt about it. From what Banks could see of her face between the dirty patches, it looked white, and she lay motionless on her back, her right arm raised above her head. The scar of a thin cut ran across the pale flesh of her inner arm.

Banks could sense no breath, no life. He bent over to look more closely. As he leaned over Gemma, he fancied he noticed one of her eyelids twitch. He froze. It happened again.

"My God," he muttered to himself, and gazed down in awe as a tear formed and rolled out of the corner of Gemma's eye, leaving a clean and shining path through the grime.

Gallows View
by Peter Robinson

Short-listed for the John Creasy Award

Chief Inspector Alan Banks of the Criminal Investigation
Department has been recently transferred from London
to Eastvale, a town in the Yorkshire Dales. His desire to
escape the stress of city life appears to be satisfied by
Eastvale's cobbled market square, its tree-shaded river
and its picturesque castle ruins. But the village begins to
show a more dangerous side...

As a Peeping Tom disturbs the peace of Eastvale's
women, police are accused of underestimating the
seriousness of the crime. At the same time, Banks is also
investigating the case of two local teenagers whose
crimes are escalating from theft to violence. The two
cases weave together as this tough, gritty novel of power
and suspense reaches a terrifying and surprising climax.

"This is a first novel that will knock you over
with its maturity."
- Howard Engel

"Offers all the suspense and local colour that anyone
could expect, plus a few surprises."
- The Toronto Star

"A fast-moving, gripping mystery story."
- Winnipeg Free Press

 ISBN 0-14-009663-9

A Dedicated Man
by **Peter Robinson**

It was a perfect summer. The weather was unusually warm for the Dales, and Harry Steadman, who was preparing a book on the area, and his wife, Emma, enjoyed their holiday at the Ramsden Bed and Breakfast.

But ten years later the memories of that peaceful summer are shattered by Harry Steadman's brutal murder. Inspector Banks is back, and investigating a case just as confounding as his first. Who would kill the kindly scholar? Penny Cartwright, a beautiful woman with a disturbing past? Harry's editor or the shady land developer? And is it possible that young Sally Lumb, locked in her lover's arms on the night of the murder, could unknowingly hold the key to the case?

"A perfect little portrait of a village in the Yorkshire dales...First-rate stuff for the detective story buff."
- Province (Vancouver)

"A cast of interesting, human characters—especially his wry and introspective hero."
- Star Phoenix (Saskatoon)

"The atmosphere of the English dales is perfectly captured."
- The Edmonton Journal

"A first-class story."
- The Toronto Star

 ISBN 0-14-009665-5

The Hanging Valley
by Peter Robinson

"A terrific book with a complex plot about murder and
madness in the Yorkshire Dales."
- The Globe and Mail

It began with a faceless, maggot-ridden corpse in a
tranquil, hidden valley above the village of
Swainshead.... Or did it really begin with an unsolved
murder in the same area over five years ago?
The people of the village, especially those who frequent
the White Rose, are annoyingly silent.

Among the suspects are the Collier brothers, Stephen
and Nicholas, the wealthiest and most powerful family
in Swainsdale; John Fletcher, a local farmer; Sam
Greenock, owner of the village's best guest house;
and his unhappy wife, Katie, who knows more
than she realizes.

When the Colliers use their influence to slow down the
investigation and the others clam up, Inspector Banks
heads for Toronto to track down the killer. He soon finds
himself in a race against time as events rush towards the
shocking conclusion.

"[Peter Robinson] knows how to write an extremely
good mystery and keep the reader hopping
from page to page."
- The Hamilton Spectator

 ISBN 0-14-011544-7

A Necessary End
by Peter Robinson

One rainy March evening, an anti-nuclear demonstration outside the Eastvale Community Centre turns nasty: the mood of the crowd begins to darken as the weather worsens. Finally the police lose control and violence erupts, leaving one policeman dead and almost a hundred suspects.

Detective Chief Inspector Banks is back, investigating his third case in Yorkshire. But things are made difficult for Banks when Superintendent Richard "Dirty Dick" Burgess is sent from London, for political reasons, to lead the investigation. Sifting through a host of unusual suspects and disturbing discoveries about the police themselves, Banks is finally warned off the case. And the only way he can salvage his career is by beating Burgess to the killer. As the two head for a final confrontation, Banks pieces together the full story behind his most tragic case so far.

"A good mystery and a contemporary variation.... With the publishing of *A Necessary End*, I think we can now be assured that we have a series that is going to be with us for a long time to come."
- The Vancouver Sun

"Well-written, and with a rich and varied cast of believable characters, *A Necessary End* is Robinson's best novel to date."
- The London Free Press

 ISBN 0-14-011545-5

Past Reason Hated
by Peter Robinson

"The best book yet in this superior series...intriguing characters, a solid-gold Yorkshire setting and a slam-bang plot that keeps moving right up to the final chapter."
- Margaret Cannon, The Globe and Mail

It looks like a tranquil Christmas scene in a cosy living-room—log fire, brightly lit tree, sheepskin rug, Vivaldi on the record player—but the appearance is deceptive. Caroline Hartley, the woman lying on the couch, has been brutally murdered.

In *Past Reason Hated*, Detective Chief Inspector Alan Banks uncovers the unusual and disturbing past of a victim for whom secrecy was a way of life. He finds a multitude of suspects: Caroline's lover, Veronica Shildon; Veronica's ex-husband, a famous composer; a feminist poet; the cast of a play Caroline was rehearsing; and her reclusive, haunted brother, Gary.

Chief Inspector Banks's fifth case is a suspenseful, shocking and ultimately satisfying tale of family secrets, hidden passions and desperate violence.

"*Past Reason Hated* is a superior piece of work and [Robinson's] best to date."
- The Toronto Star

 ISBN 0-14-014842-6

Caedmon's Song
by **Peter Robinson**

"This is a powerful and haunting novel, ingenious in construction and both intelligent and compassionate. It is also horrifying. Robinson is a fine novelist."
- The Toronto Star

On a balmy June night, Kirsten, a young university student, strolls home through a silent, moon-lit park. Suddenly her tranquil mood is shattered by a swift and brutal act of violence. When she comes to herself she has lost all memory of that bloody night. But then, slowly and painfully, details reveal themselves to Kirsten—dreams of two figures, one white and one black, hovering over her; wisps of a strange and haunting song; the unfamiliar texture of a rough and deadly hand...

In another part of England, Martha Browne arrives in Whitby, posing as an author doing research for a book. But her research is of a particularly macabre variety. Who is she hunting with such deadly determination? And why?

"Peter Robinson enters the realm of psychological thriller with a satisfying bang....Truly a masterpiece of psychological suspense.
- The Whig Standard (Kingston)

"Robinson has all the elements in this novel well in hand— pacing, place, character, dialogue—and he keeps the suspense moving right down to the twist ending."
- The Globe and Mail

 ISBN 0-14-013290-2